C0-ARW-074

SEVENOAKS

A

STORY OF TO-DAY

BY

JOSIAH G. HOLLAND

THE GREGG PRESS
UPPER SADDLE RIVER, N.J.

First published in 1875 by Scribner, Armstrong & Co.
Republished in 1968 by
The Gregg Press
121 Pleasant Avenue
Upper Saddle River, New Jersey, U. S. A.

Library of Congress Catalog Card Number: 68 - 57531

Printed in United States of America

AMERICAN NOVELS OF MUCKRAKING, PROPAGANDA, AND SOCIAL PROTEST

The United States has suffered quite a few spells of sickness, if one may judge by the long and varied procession of novels dealing with the ills of its society. As each generation has sought assurances for the social hope that springs eternal in a democracy, muckraking, propagandizing, and advocating reforms have been not only implicit in partisan politics but also germane to literary production. While it has been said that Americans are readier to believe in charlatans than in utopias, there remains a sneaking feeling that maybe Oscar Wilde was right when he remarked: "Progress is the realization of utopias." Some such moral–if indeed moral it be–may be derived from the Gregg series of "American Novels of Muckraking, Propaganda, and Social Protest."

One purpose underlying the selection of the titles in the series is to provide examples of socio-economic novels which are presently out of print but which are nevertheless important in showing the history of the genre, a topic so far treated by historians only sporadically. Most of these works can rarely be found in the original editions; and many were printed on paper which is beginning to shatter. The series should prove a boon to librarians and to scholars who work in the fields of literary history and the social sciences. Its usefulness as supplementary reading for college courses in American studies and social history speaks for itself.

In turning the pages of the novels we begin with the groping 1830's and the fabulous 40's–when, as Emerson put it, every man in New England was running around with a plan for reorganizing society in his vestpocket. And we end with the "Era of the Muckrakers"–when the long-existent fervor to remake the world nearer to the mind's desire became a contagious fever, and phrases were bandied about like "frenzied finance," "conspicuous consumption," "malefactors of great wealth," "how the other half lives" and "the shame of the cities." In this series we find artifacts from the days following the panic of 1837, when Horace Greeley devoted a regular column in his *Tribune* to the kind of "associationism" that overtook Brook Farm; and we come along to the period early in the present century when the "yellow" journalism of Hearst and Pulitzer reached full flower and young Sinclair

Lewis swept the floors of Helicon Hall, the socialist community supported by Upton Sinclair with the profits of *The Jungle.* That was the epoch when the young intellectuals stormed college halls to hear Jack London expound the principles of socialism. In between, we find specimens emanating from the Gilded Age, with the ensuing clamor against business combinations eventuating in the Sherman Anti-Trust Act of 1890, and the agricultural depression that aroused Midwestern farmers to "raise less corn and more hell" or to align themselves with the People's Party. Business panics in 1873 and 1893 stirred up the coals, young preachers discovered the social gospel, bewhiskered anarchists were the chief "reds," strikes became for the first time a matter of wide public concern, and the play based on *Uncle Tom's Cabin* was the best money-maker on the stage.

One of the features of the list is a careful selection of works concerned with the Negro. The earliest is *The Slave,* by the historian Richard Hildreth. It was not only the first fully developed antislavery novel, but a pattern-maker for the many subsequent tales presenting the chief character as a light-skinned mulatto. The Russians translated it in the 1950's. Another is Harriet Beecher Stowe's *Dred,* a sequel to *Uncle Tom's Cabin* and perhaps more cogent propaganda. The idea that the Negro is constitutionally unable to cope with American society is curiously set forth in *Liberia,* by Sarah J. Hale, a staunch Yankee best known for her verses about Mary and her little lamb. Mrs. Hale was propagandizing for solving the slavery problem by returning the Negroes to Africa. Presenting the Southern side, *Aunt Phillis's Cabin,* by Mary H. Eastman, has been chosen from the batch of novels which sought in vain to counter the effect of Mrs. Stowe's world-famed classic of protest. The blasting of Northern prejudice against the Negro after the Civil War is well illustrated in two works: Rebecca Harding Davis's *Waiting for the Verdict,* a title still apt a century after it first appeared, and Albion W. Tourgée's tract for the times *Pactolus Prime,* which vitriolically scores the essential prejudice of white against black and is, apparently, the first American novel dealing with the Negro problem with a setting in Washington, D. C.

Joaquin Miller's *Life Amongst the Modocs* deals with the mistreatment of Indians. Few in number but judiciously chosen for illustrative purposes are stories exposing the white slave traffic—

from the days when the Mann Act was legislated and city slums were being muckraked both in and out of fiction to a degree probably more thorough than is the case even today. Among the other problems considered in these stories are divorce, prisons, and the criminal code, political corruption, pacificism, states rights, the social responsibilities of the churches, the plight of the Jew and the Immigrant, and even medical frauds.

But the theme governing the largest single element in this collection is the business tycoon and the battle between the capitalist power elite and the working class. The range in the picturization of "the typical American figure," as Henry James declared the captain of industry to be, runs quite a gamut in the series, from the romantic treatment in *Sevenoaks,* by the first editor of *Scribner's Magazine,* to the excoriation of corporation machinations by avowed socialists not unacquainted with Karl Marx. The tycoons pilloried range from bankers, real estate promoters, mill owners, and railroad magnates to lumber barons. One might view the development of this theme in the amazing profusion of fictional examples as a symbol of the growing unrest precipitated in a traditionally agrarian society bewildered by its confrontation with huge industrial corporations and big cities. But possibly it proves no more than the homely wisdom distilled into the humorist's wisecrack: "We have met the enemy–and the enemy is us!"

PROFESSOR CLARENCE GOHDES
Duke University
Durham, North Carolina

September, 1968

JOSIAH G. HOLLAND

Josiah G. Holland was born in Belchertown, Massachusetts, in 1819, and died in 1881. His family was extremely poor, and drifted from one town to another, finally settling in Northampton, where Josiah worked nights in a factory to pay his way through high school. He was forced to leave school because of ill health brought on by the strain of working and studying. He then labored at odd jobs, was a teacher, and in 1840 was "apprenticed" to a doctor in order to learn that profession. In 1843 he received his M. D. at the Berkshire Medical College, and attempted to set up practice in Springfield, but failed. He married Elizabeth Chapman two years later, again trying to earn a living as a physician, again with scant success. His meager income was supplemented by articles submitted to the *Knickerbocker Magazine*, and, for a short time, by his *Bay State Weekly Courier.* This paper went bankrupt, and Holland went to Richmond, Virginia, where he taught school. In 1848 he was Superintendent of Schools in Vicksburg, Mississippi, and instituted important reforms in the Mississippi school administration. Two years later, Samuel Bowles asked him to become co-editor of the Springfield *Republican*, a crusading newspaper which opposed slavery and the Mexican War. Holland wrote many "human interest" stories for the *Republican*, and later collected these for publication in book form. During this period he also gave lectures, which were evidently extremely popular. Holland acquired a considerable financial interest in the *Republican*, but sold his holdings in 1857. The next two years he traveled in Europe, returning to become the co-founder and co-editor of *Scribner's Monthly*, which serialized *Sevenoaks.*

Holland's early works were published under the droll pseudonym "Timothy Titcomb," and it was on the basis of innumerable works of awful sentimentality and revolting didacticism that Holland gained an immense reading public among our Victorian forebears. He was the Edgar Guest of the nineteenth century. One of his most popular lyrics reads:

> Heaven is not gained at a single bound,
> But we build the ladder by which we rise

From the lowly earth to the vaulted skies,
And we mount to its summit round by round.

And the titles *Timothy Titcomb's Letters to Young People: Single and Married* and *Gold Foil Hammered from Popular Proverbs* speak for themselves.

Apparently Holland, like Dickens, was capable of writing a book or a chapter like a sentimental schoolmarm, and then, purged of pious cant and mawkishness, creating devastating and embittered denunciations of middle-class society; of cruelty, filth, and exploitation. This may explain why *Sevenoaks* seems to have been written by another man.

Sevenoaks is the story of the classical sort of nineteenth-century Capitalist villain who exists today only in Marxist mythology. Belcher, the virtual owner of the village of Sevenoaks, is a coarse, ignorant, brutal scoundrel whose wealth is based upon stolen patents; a man "who had spent his life in schemes for absorbing the products of the labor of others." Holland paints a vivid portrait of this aspiring "robber baron": we see him aping the manners of a gentleman, surrounding himself with luxuries, pursuing culture, endowing foundations, and always piling up more money. There are three "institutions" in Sevenoaks–the mill (owned by Belcher), the mansion (also Belcher's), and the poorhouse. As Belcher's property increases, so does the number of unfortunates consigned to the poorhouse. There is only one place to work, one man holds all of the mortgages, and wages are kept so low that there is no opportunity to escape to another city or to save for one's old age or pay for medical expenses. Besides, flight would be senseless, for society in 1875, according to Holland, consisted of towns and cities just like Sevenoaks. (The Western frontier, with its opportunities for the disinherited, is never mentioned.)

The plot of this somber work centers about the ever increasing number of spectacular frauds dreamed up by Belcher. Having gained a foothold in business by forging documents to a valuable patent, and robbing and ruining the inventor, he graduates to selling bogus oil stocks, creating phony holding companies, perpetrating railroad swindles, and promoting questionable real estate operations. As his fortunes grow, so do his vanity and his barely concealed contempt for the people who allow themselves to be cheated so easily. His greatest asset is the reverence with which people regard the captain of industry, for even while being exploited and bilked, the citizens of Sevenoaks look up to Belcher as the epitome of the man who succeeded in the struggle for the "survival of the fittest." Holland is quite skillful in pointing out this strange submissiveness on the part of the ordinary citizens.

The author's descriptions of the factory and the poorhouse are excellent, and were undoubtedly drawn from his own experiences—one thinks of Dickens in the blacking factory. He cannot be accused of exaggeration or caricature in his portrait of Belcher, for the character and nefarious exploits of such neolithic monsters have been carefully chronicled by contemporary historians.

F. C. S.

Upper Saddle River, N. J.
September, 1968

CONTENTS.

CHAPTER XVI.

CHAPTER XVII.

CHAPTER XVIII.

CHAPTER XIX.

CHAPTER XX.

CHAPTER XXI.

CHAPTER XXII.

CHAPTER XXIII.

CHAPTER XXIV.

SEVENOAKS.

CHAPTER I.

WHICH TELLS ABOUT SEVENOAKS, AND HOW MISS BUTTERWORTH PASSED ONE OF HER EVENINGS.

EVERYBODY has seen Sevenoaks, or a hundred towns so much like it, in most particulars, that a description of any one of them would present it to the imagination—a town strung upon a stream, like beads upon a thread, or charms upon a chain. Sevenoaks was richer in chain than charms, for its abundant water-power was only partially used. It plunged, and roared, and played, and sparkled, because it had not half enough to do. It leaped down three or four cataracts in passing through the village; and, as it started from living springs far northward among the woods and mountains, it never failed in its supplies.

Few of the people of Sevenoaks—thoughtless workers, mainly—either knew or cared whence it came, or whither it went. They knew it as "The Branch;" but Sevenoaks was so far from the trunk, down to which it sent its sap, and from which it received no direct return, that no significance was attached to its name. But it roared all day, and roared all night, summer and winter alike, and the sound became a part of the atmosphere.

Resonance was one of the qualities of the oxygen which the people breathed, so that if, at any midnight moment, the roar had been suddenly hushed, they would have waked with a start and a sense of suffocation, and leaped from their beds.

Among the charms that dangled from this liquid chain —depending from the vest of a landscape which ended in a ruffle of woods toward the north, overtopped by the head of a mountain—was a huge factory that had been added to from time to time, as necessity demanded, until it had become an imposing and not uncomely pile. Below this were two or three dilapidated saw-mills, a grist-mill in daily use, and a fulling-mill—a remnant of the old times when homespun went its pilgrimage to town—to be fulled, colored, and dressed—from all the sparsely-settled country around.

On a little plateau by the side of The Branch was a row of stores and dram shops and butchers' establishments. Each had a sort of square, false front, pierced by two staring windows and a door, that reminded one of a lion *couchant*—very large in the face and very thin in the flank. Then there were crowded in, near the mill, little rows of one-story houses, occupied entirely by operatives, and owned by the owner of the mill. All the inhabitants, not directly connected with the mill, were as far away from it as they could go. Their houses were set back upon either acclivity which rose from the gorge that the stream had worn, dotting the hill-sides in every direction. There was a clumsy town-hall, there were three or four churches, there was a high school and a low tavern. It was, on the whole, a village of importance, but the great mill was somehow its soul and centre. A fair farming and grazing country stretched back from it eastward and westward, and Sevenoaks was its only home market.

It is not proposed, in this history, to tell where Sevenoaks was, and is to-day. It may have been, or may be, in Maine, or New Hampshire, or Vermont, or New York. It was in the northern part of one of these States, and not far from the border of a wilderness almost as deep and silent as any that can be found beyond the western limit of settlement and civilization. The red man had left it forever, but the bear, the deer, and the moose remained. The streams and lakes were full of trout ; otter and sable still attracted the trapper, and here and there a lumberman lingered alone in his cabin, enamored of the solitude and the wild pursuits to which a hardly gentler industry had introduced him. Such lumber as could be drifted down the streams had long been cut and driven out, and the woods were left to the hunter and his prey, and to the incursions of sportsmen and seekers for health, to whom the rude residents became guides, cooks, and servants of all work, for the sake of occasional society, and that ever-serviceable consideration—money.

There were two establishments in Sevenoaks which stood so far away from the stream that they could hardly be described as attached to it. Northward, on the top of the bleakest hill in the region, stood the Sevenoaks poor-house. In dimensions and population it was utterly out of proportion to the size of the town, for the people of Sevenoaks seemed to degenerate into paupers with wonderful facility. There was one man in the town who was known to be getting rich, while all the rest grew poor. Even the keepers of the dram-shops, though they seemed to do a thriving business, did not thrive. A great deal of work was done, but people were paid very little for it. If a man tried to leave the town for the purpose of improving his condition, there was always some mortgage on his property, or some impossibility of selling what he had for money, or his absolute dependence on each day's labor for each day's bread, that stood in the way. One by one—sick, disabled, dis couraged, dead-beaten—they drifted into the poor-house, which, as the years went on, grew into a shabby, double pile of buildings, between which ran a county road.

This establishment was a county as well as a town institution, and, theoretically, one group of its buildings was devoted to the reception of county paupers, while the other was assigned to the poor of Sevenoaks. Practically, the keeper of both mingled his boarders indiscriminately, to suit his personal convenience.

The hill, as it climbed somewhat abruptly from the western bank of the stream—it did this in the grand leisure of the old geologic centuries—apparently got out of breath and sat down when its task was half done. Where it sat it left a beautiful plateau of five or six acres, and from this it rose, and went on climbing, until it reached the summit of its effort, and descended the other side. On the brow of this plateau stood seven huge oaks which the chopper's axe, for some reason or another, had spared ; and the locality, in all the early years of settlement, was known by the name of "The Seven Oaks." They formed a notable landmark, and, at last, the old designation having been worn by usage, the town was incorporated with the name of Sevenoaks, in a single word.

On this plateau the owner of the mill, Mr. Robert Belcher—himself an exceptional product of the village—had built his residence—a large, white, pretentious dwelling, surrounded and embellished by all the appointments of wealth. The house was a huge cube, ornamented at its corners and cornices with all possible flowers of a rude architecture, reminding one of an elephant that, in a fit of incontinent playfulness, had indulged in antics characteristic of its clumsy bulk and brawn. Outside were ample stables, a green-house, a Chinese pagoda that was called "the summer-house."

an exquisite garden and trees, among which latter were carefully cherished the seven ancient oaks that had given the town its name.

Robert Belcher was not a gentleman. He supposed himself to be one, but he was mistaken. Gentlemen of wealth usually built a fine house; so Mr. Belcher built one. Gentlemen kept horses, a groom and a coachman; Mr. Belcher did the same. Gentlemen of wealth built green-houses for themselves and kept a gardener; Mr. Belcher could do no less. He had no gentlemanly tastes, to be sure, but he could buy or hire these for money; so he bought and hired them; and when Robert Belcher walked through his stables and jested with his men, or sauntered into his green-house and about his grounds, he rubbed his heavy hands together, and fancied that the costly things by which he had surrounded himself were the insignia of a gentleman.

From his windows he could look down upon the village, all of which he either owned or controlled. He owned the great mill; he owned the water-privilege; he owned many of the dwellings, and held mortgages on many others; he owned the churches, for all purposes practical to himself; he owned the ministers—if not, then this was another mistake that he had made. So long as it was true that they could not live without him, he was content with his title. He patronized the church, and the church was too weak to decline his ostentatious courtesy. He humiliated every man who came into his presence, seeking a subscription for a religious or charitable purpose, but his subscription was always sought, and as regularly obtained. Humbly to seek his assistance for any high purpose was a concession to his power, and to grant the assistance sought was to establish an obligation. He was willing to pay for personal influence and personal glory, and he often paid right royally.

Of course Mr. Belcher's residence had a library ; all gentlemen have libraries. Mr. Belcher's did not contain many books, but it contained a great deal of room for them. Here he spent his evenings, kept his papers in a huge safe built into the wall, smoked, looked down on the twinkling village and his huge mill, counted his gains, and constructed his schemes. Of Mrs. Belcher and the little Belchers, he saw but little. He fed and dressed them well, as he did his horses. All gentlemen feed and dress their dependents well. He was proud of his family as he saw them riding in their carriage. They looked gay and comfortable, and were, as he thought, objects of envy among the humbler folk of the town, all of which reflected pleasantly upon himself.

On a late April evening, of a late spring in 18—, he was sitting in his library, buried in a huge easy-chair, thinking, smoking, scheming. The shutters were closed, the lamps were lighted, and a hickory fire was blazing upon the hearth. Around the rich man were spread the luxuries which his wealth had bought—the velvet carpet, the elegant chairs, the heavy library table, covered with costly appointments, pictures in broad gold frames, and one article of furniture that he had not been accustomed to see in a gentleman's library—an article that sprang out of his own personal wants. This was an elegant pier-glass, into whose depths he was accustomed to gaze in self-admiration. He was flashily dressed in a heavy coat, buff waistcoat, and drab trousers. A gold chain of fabulous weight hung around his neck and held his Jurgensen repeater.

He rose and walked his room, and rubbed his hands, as was his habit ; then paused before his mirror, admired his robust figure and large face, brushed his hair back from his big brow, and walked on again. Finally he paused before his glass, and indulged in another habit peculiar to himself.

"Robert Belcher," said he, addressing the image in the mirror, "you are a brick! Yes, sir, you are a brick! You, Robert Belcher, sir, are an almighty smart man. You've outwitted the whole of 'em. Look at me, sir! Dare you tell me, sir, that I am not master of the situation? Ah! you hesitate; it is well! They all come to me, every man of 'em. It is 'Mr. Belcher, will you be so good?' and 'Mr. Belcher, I hope you are very well,' and 'Mr. Belcher, I want you to do better by me.' Ha! ha! ha! ha! My name is Norval. It isn't? Say that again and I'll throttle you! Yes, sir, I'll shake your rascally head off your shoulders! Down, down in the dust, and beg my pardon! It is well; go! Get you gone, sir, and remember not to beard the lion in his den!"

Exactly what this performance meant, it would be difficult to say. Mr. Belcher, in his visits to the city, had frequented theatres and admired the villains of the plays he had seen represented. He had noticed figures upon the boards that reminded him of his own. His addresses to his mirror afforded him an opportunity to exercise his gifts of speech and action, and, at the same time, to give form to his self-gratulations. They amused him; they ministered to his preposterous vanity. He had no companions in the town, and the habit gave him a sense of society, and helped to pass away his evenings. At the close of his effort he sat down and lighted another cigar. Growing drowsy, he laid it down on a little stand at his side, and settled back in his chair for a nap. He had hardly shut his eyes when there came a rap upon his door.

"Come in!"

"Please, sir," said a scared-looking maid, opening the door just wide enough to make room for her face.

"Well?" in a voice so sharp and harsh that the girl cringed.

"Please, sir, Miss Butterworth is at the door, and would like to see you."

Now, Miss Butterworth was the one person in all Sevenoaks who was not afraid of Robert Belcher. She had been at the public school with him when they were children; she had known every circumstance of his history; she was not dependent on him in any way, and she carried in her head an honest and fearless tongue. She was an itinerant tailoress, and having worked, first and last, in nearly every family in the town, she knew the circumstances of them all, and knew too well the connection of Robert Belcher with their troubles and reverses. In Mr. Belcher's present condition of self-complacency and somnolency, she was not a welcome visitor. Belligerent as he had been toward his own image in the mirror, he shrank from meeting Keziah Butterworth, for he knew instinctively that she had come with some burden of complaint.

"Come in," said Mr. Belcher to his servant, "and shut the door behind you."

The girl came in, shut the door, and waited, leaning against it.

"Go," said her master in a low tone, "and tell Mrs. Belcher that I am busy, and that she must choke her off. I can't see her to-night. I can't see her."

The girl retired, and soon afterward Mrs. Belcher came, and reported that she could do nothing with Miss Butterworth—that Miss Butterworth was determined to see him before she left the house.

"Bring her in; I'll make short work with her."

As soon as Mrs. Belcher retired, her husband hurried to the mirror, brushed his hair back fiercely, and then sat down to a pile of papers that he always kept conveniently upon his library table.

"Come in," said Mr. Belcher, in his blandest tone, when Miss Butterworth was conducted to his room.

"Ah! Keziah?" said Mr. Belcher, looking up with a smile, as if an unexpected old friend had come to him.

"My name is Butterworth, and it's got a handle to it," said that bumptious lady, quickly.

"Well, but, Keziah, you know we used to——"

"My name is Butterworth, I tell you, and it's got a handle to it."

"Well, Miss Butterworth—happy to see you—hope you are well—take a chair."

"Humph," exclaimed Miss Butterworth, dropping down upon the edge of a large chair whose back felt no pressure from her own during the interview. The expression of Mr. Belcher's happiness in seeing her, and his kind suggestion concerning her health, had overspread Miss Butterworth's countenance with a derisive smile, and though she was evidently moved to tell him that he lied, she had reasons for restraining her tongue.

They formed a curious study, as they sat there together, during the first embarrassing moments. The man had spent his life in schemes for absorbing the products of the labor of others. He was cunning, brutal, vain, showy, and essentially vulgar, from his head to his feet, in every fibre of body and soul. The woman had earned with her own busy hands every dollar of money she had ever possessed. She would not have wronged a dog for her own personal advantage. Her black eyes, lean and spirited face, her prematurely whitening locks, as they were exposed by the backward fall of her old fashioned, quilted hood, presented a physiognomy at once piquant and prepossessing.

Robert Belcher knew that the woman before him was fearless and incorruptible. He knew that she despised him—that bullying and brow-beating would have no influence with her, that this ready badinage would not avail, and that coaxing and soft words would be equally useless. In her presence he was shorn of all his weapons, and he never felt so defenceless and ill at ease in his life.

As Miss Butterworth did not seem inclined to begin conversation, Mr. Belcher hem'd and haw'd with affected nonchalance, and said :

"Ah!—to—what am I indebted for this visit, Miss—ah—Butterworth ?"

"I'm thinking!" she replied sharply, looking into the fire, and pressing her lips together.

There was nothing to be said to this, so Mr. Belcher looked doggedly at her, and waited.

"I'm thinking of a man, and-he-was-a-man-every-inch-of-him, if there ever was one, and a gentleman too, if-I-know-what-a-gentleman-is, who came to this town ten years ago, from-nobody-knows-where, with a wife that was an angel, if-there-is-any-such-thing-as-an-angel."

Here Miss Butterworth paused. She had laid her foundation, and proceeded at her leisure.

"He knew more than any man in Sevenoaks, but he didn't know how to take care of himself," she went on. "He was the most ingenious creature God ever made, I do think, and his name was Paul Benedict."

Mr. Belcher grew pale and fidgeted in his chair.

"And his name was Paul Benedict. He invented something, and then he took it to Robert Belcher, and he put it into his mill, and-paid-him-just-as-little-for-it-as-he-could. And then he invented something more, and-that-went-into-the-mill ; and then something more. and the patent was used by Mr. Belcher for a song, and the man grew poorer and poorer, while-Mr.-Belcher-grew-richer-and-richer-all-the-time. And then he invented a gun, and then his little wife died, and what with the expenses of doctors and funerals and such things, and the money it took to get his patent, which-I-begged-him-for-conscience'-sake-to-keep-out-of-Robert-Belcher's-hands, he almost starved with his little boy, and had to go to Robert Belcher for money."

"And got it," said Mr. Belcher.

"How much, now? A hundred little dollars for what was worth a hundred thousand, unless-everybody-lies. The whole went in a day, and then he went crazy."

"Well, you know I sent him to the asylum," responded Mr. Belcher.

"I know you did—yes, I know you did; and you tried to get him well enough to sign a paper, which the doctor never would let him sign, and which wouldn't have been worth a straw if he had signed it. The-idea-of-getting-a-crazy-man-to-sign-a-paper!"

"Well, but I wanted some security for the money I had advanced," said Mr. Belcher.

"No; you wanted legal possession of a property which would have made him rich; that's what it was, and you didn't get it, and you never will get it. He can't be cured, and he's been sent back, and is up at Tom Buffum's now, and I've seen him to-day."

Miss Butterworth expected that this intelligence would stun Mr. Belcher, but it did not.

The gratification of the man with the news was unmistakable. Paul Benedict had no relatives or friends that he knew of. All his dealings with him had been without witnesses. The only person living, besides Robert Belcher, who knew exactly what had passed between his victim and himself, was hopelessly insane. The difference, to him, between obtaining possession of a valuable invention of a sane or an insane man, was the difference between paying money and paying none. In what way, and with what profit, Mr. Belcher was availing himself of Paul Benedict's last invention, no one in Sevenoaks knew; but all the town knew that he was getting rich, apparently much faster than he ever was before, and that, in a distant town, there was a manufactory of what was known as "The Belcher Rifle."

Mr. Belcher concluded that he was still "master of the situation." Benedict's testimony could not be taken in a court of justice. The town itself was in his hands, so that it would institute no suit on Benedict's behalf, now that he had come upon it for support; for the Tom Buffum, to whom Miss Butterworth had alluded, was the keeper of the poor-house, and was one of his own creatures.

Miss Butterworth had sufficient sagacity to comprehend the reasons for Mr. Belcher's change of look and manner, and saw that her evening's mission would prove fruitless; but her true woman's heart would not permit her to relinquish her project.

"Is poor Benedict comfortable?" he inquired, in his old, off-hand way.

"Comfortable—yes, in the way that pigs are."

"Pigs are very comfortable, I believe, as a general thing," said Mr. Belcher.

"Bob Belcher," said Miss Butterworth, the tears springing to her eyes in spite of herself, and forgetting all the proprieties she had determined to observe, "you are a brute. You know you are a brute. He is in a little cell, no larger than—than—a pig-pen. There isn't a bit of furniture in it. He sleeps on the straw, and in the straw, and under the straw, and his victuals are poked at him as if he were a beast. He is a poor, patient, emaciated wretch, and he sits on the floor all day, and weaves the most beautiful things out of the straw he sits on, and Tom Buffum's girls have got them in the house for ornaments. And he talks about his rifle, and explains it, and explains it, and explains it, when anybody will listen to him, and his clothes are all in rags, and that little boy of his that they have in the house, and treat no better than if he were a dog, knows he is there, and goes and looks at him, and calls to him, and cries about him whenever he dares. And you sit here, in your great house, with your carpets and chairs, that half smother you, and your looking-glasses and your fine clothes, and don't start to your feet when I tell you this. I tell you if God doesn't damn everybody who is responsible for this wickedness, then there is no such thing as a God."

Miss Butterworth was angry, and had grown more and more angry with every word. She had brooded over the matter all the afternoon, and her pent-up indignation had overflowed beyond control. She felt that she had spoken truth which Robert Belcher ought to hear and to heed, yet she knew that she had lost her hold upon him. Mr. Belcher listened with the greatest coolness, while a half smile overspread his face.

"Don't you think I'm a pretty good-natured man to sit here," said he, "and hear myself abused in this way, without getting angry?"

"No, I think you are a bad-natured man. I think you are the hardest-hearted and worst man I ever saw. What in God's name has Paul Benedict done, that he should be treated in this way? There are a dozen there just like him, or worse. Is it a crime to lose one's reason? I wish you could spend one night in Paul Benedict's room."

"Thank you. I prefer my present quarters."

"Yes, you look around on your present quarters, as you call 'em, and think you'll always have 'em. You won't. Mark my words; you won't. Some time you'll overreach yourself, and cheat yourself out of 'em. See if you don't."

"It takes a smart man to cheat himself, Miss Butterworth," responded Mr. Belcher, rubbing his hands.

"There is just where you're mistaken. It takes a fool."

Mr. Belcher laughed outright. Then, in a patronizing

way, he said: "Miss Butterworth, I have given you considerable time, and perhaps you'll be kind enough to state your business. I'm a practical man, and I really don't see anything that particularly concerns me in all this talk. Of course I'm sorry for Benedict and the rest of 'em, but Sevenoaks isn't a very rich town, and it cannot afford to board its paupers at the hotel, or to give them many luxuries."

Miss Butterworth was calm again. She knew that she had done her cause no good, but was determined to finish her errand.

"Mr. Belcher, I'm a woman."

"I know it, Keziah."

"And my name is Butterworth."

"I know it."

"You do? Well, then, here is what I came to say to you. The town-meeting comes to-morrow, and the town's poor are to be sold at auction, and to pass into Tom Buffum's hands again, unless you prevent it. I can't make a speech, and I can't vote. I never wanted to until now. You can do both, and if you don't reform this business, and set Tom Buffum at doing something else, and treat God's poor more like human beings, I shall get out of Sevenoaks before it sinks; for sink it will if there is any hole big enough to hold it."

"Well, I'll think of it," said Mr. Belcher, deliberately.

"Tell me you'll do it."

"I'm not used to doing things in a hurry. Mr. Buffum is a friend of mine, and I've always regarded him as a very good man for the place. Of course, if there's anything wrong it ought to be righted, but I think you've exaggerated."

"No, you don't mean to do anything. I see it. Good-night," and she had swept out of the door before he could say another word, or rise from his chair.

She went down the hill into the village. The earth

was stiffening with the frost that lingered late in that latitude, and there were patches of ice, across which she picked her way. There was a great moon overhead, but just then all beautiful things, and all things that tended to lift her thoughts upward, seemed a mockery. She reached the quiet home of Rev. Solomon Snow.

"Who knows but he can be spurred up to do something?" she said to herself.

There was only one way to ascertain—so she knocked at the door, and was received so kindly by Mr. Snow and Mrs. Snow and the three Misses Snow, that she sat down and unburdened herself—first, of course, as regarded Mr. Robert Belcher, and second, as concerned the Benedicts, father and son.

The position of Mr. Belcher was one which inspired the minister with caution, but the atmosphere was freer in his house than in that of the proprietor. The vocal engine whose wheels had slipped upon the track with many a whirr, as she started her train in the great house on the hill, found a down grade, and went off easily. Mr. Snow sat in his arm-chair, his elbows resting on either support, the thumb and every finger of each hand touching its twin at the point, and forming a kind of gateway in front of his heart, which seemed to shut out or let in conviction at his will. Mrs. Snow and the girls, whose admiration of Miss Butterworth for having dared to invade Mr. Belcher's library was unbounded, dropped their work, and listened with eager attention. Mr. Snow opened the gate occasionally to let in a statement, but for the most part kept it closed. The judicial attitude, the imperturbable spectacles, the long, pale face and white cravat did not prevent Miss Butterworth from "freeing her mind;" and when she finished the task, a good deal had been made of the case of the insane paupers of Sevenoaks, and there was very little left of Mr Robert Belcher and Mr. Thomas Buffum.

At the close of her account of what she had seen at the poor-house, and what had passed between her and the great proprietor, Mr. Snow cast his eyes up to the ceiling, pursed his lips, and somewhere in the profundities of his nature, or in some celestial laboratory, unseen by any eyes but his own, prepared his judgments.

"Cases of this kind," said he, at last, to his excited visitor, whose eyes glowed like coals as she looked into his impassive face, "are to be treated with great prudence. We are obliged to take things as they air. Personally (with a rising inflection and a benevolent smile), I should rejoice to see the insane poor clothed and in their right mind."

"Let us clothe 'em, then, anyway," interjected Miss Butterworth, impatiently. "And, as for being in their right mind, that's more than can be said of those that have the care of 'em."

"Personally—Miss Butterworth, excuse me—I should rejoice to see them clothed and in their right mind, but the age of miracles is past. We have to deal with the facts of to-day—with things as they air. It is possible, nay, for aught I know, it may be highly probable, that in other towns pauperism may fare better than it does with us. It is to be remembered that Sevenoaks is itself poor, and its poverty becomes one of the factors of the problem which you have propounded to us. The town of Buxton, our neighbor over here, pays taxes, let us say, of seven mills on the dollar; we pay seven mills on the dollar. Buxton is rich; we are poor. Buxton has few paupers; we have many. Consequently, Buxton may maintain its paupers in what may almost be regarded as a state of affluence. It may go as far as featherbeds and winter fires for the aged; nay, it may advance to some economical form of teeth-brushes, and still demand no more sacrifice from its people than is constantly demanded of us to maintain our poor in a humbler way. Then there are certain prudential considerations—certain, I might almost say, moral considerations—which are to be taken into account. It will never do, in a town like ours, to make pauperism attractive—to make our pauper establishments comfortable asylums for idleness. It must, in some way, be made to seem a hardship to go to the poor-house."

"Well, Sevenoaks has taken care of that with a vengeance," burst out Miss Butterworth.

"Excuse me, Miss Butterworth; let me repeat, that it must be made to seem a hardship to go to the poor-house. Let us say that we have accomplished this very desirable result. So far, so good. Give our system whatever credit may belong to it, and still let us frankly acknowledge that we have suffering left that ought to be alleviated. How much? In what way? Here we come into contact with another class of facts. Paupers have less of sickness and death among them than any other class in the community. There are paupers in our establishment that have been there for twenty-five years—a fact which, if it proves anything, proves that a large proportion of the wants of our present civilization are not only artificial in their origin, but harmful in their gratifications. Our poor are compelled to go back nearer to nature—to old mother nature—and they certainly get a degree of compensation for it. It increases the expenses of the town, to be sure."

"Suppose we inquire of them," struck in Miss Butterworth again, "and find out whether they would not rather be treated better and die earlier."

"Paupers are hardly in a position to be consulted in that way," responded Mr. Snow, "and the alternative is one which, considering their moral condition, they would have no right to entertain."

Miss Butterworth had sat through this rather desultory disquisition with what patience she could command, breaking in upon it impulsively at various points, and seen that it was drifting nowhere—at least, that it was not drifting toward the object of her wishes. Then she took up the burden of talk, and carried it on in her very direct way.

"All you say is well enough, I suppose," she began, "but I don't stop to reason about it, and I don't wish to. Here is a lot of human beings that are treated like brutes —sold every year to the lowest bidder, to be kept. They go hungry, and naked, and cold. They are in the hands of a man who has no more blood in his heart than there is in a turnip, and we pretend to be Christians, and go to church, and coddle ourselves with comforts, and pay no more attention to them than we should if their souls had gone where their money went. I tell you it's a sin and a shame, and I know it. I feel it. And there's a gentleman among 'em, and his little boy, and they must be taken out of that place, or treated better in it. I've made up my mind to that, and if the men of Sevenoaks don't straighten matters on that horrible old hill, then they're just no men at all."

Mr. Snow smiled a calm, self-respectful smile, that said, as plainly as words could say: "Oh! I know women: they are amiably impulsive, but impracticable."

"Have you ever been there?" inquired Miss Butterworth, sharply.

"Yes, I've been there."

"And conscience forbid!" broke in Mrs. Snow, "that he should go again, and bring home what he brought home that time. It took me the longest time to get them out of the house!"

"Mrs. Snow! my dear! You forget that we have a stranger present."

"Well, I don't forget those strangers, anyway!"

The three Misses Snow tittered, and looked at one

another, but were immediately solemnized by a glance from their father.

Mrs. Snow, having found her tongue—a characteristically lively and emphatic one—went on to say:

"I think Miss Butterworth is right. It's a burning shame, and you ought to go to the meeting to-morrow, and put it down."

"Easily said, my dear," responded Mr. Snow, "but you forget that Mr. Belcher is Buffum's friend, and that it is impossible to carry any measure against him in Sevenoaks. I grant that it ought not to be so. I wish it were otherwise; but we must take things as they air."

"To take things as they air," was a cardinal aphorism in Mr. Snow's budget of wisdom. It was a good starting-point for any range of reasoning, and exceedingly useful to a man of limited intellect and little moral courage. The real truth of the case had dawned upon Miss Butterworth, and it had rankled in the breast of Mrs. Snow from the beginning of his pointless talk. He was afraid of offending Robert Belcher, for not only did his church need repairing, but his salary was in arrears, and the wolf that had chased so many up the long hill to what was popularly known as Tom Buffum's Boarding House he had heard many a night, while his family was sleeping, howling with menace in the distance.

Mrs. Snow rebelled, in every part of her nature, against the power which had cowed her reverend companion. There is nothing that so goads a spirited woman to madness as the realization that any man controls her husband. He may be subservient to her—a cuckold even—but to be mated with a man whose soul is neither his own nor wholly hers, is to her the torment of torments.

"I wish Robert Belcher was hanged," said Mrs. Snow, spitefully.

"Amen! and my name is Butterworth," responded that lady, making sure that there should be no mistake as to the responsibility for the utterance.

"Why, mother!" exclaimed the three Misses Snow, in wonder.

"And drawn and quartered!" added Mrs. Snow, emphatically.

"Amen, again!" responded Miss Butterworth.

"Mrs. Snow! my dear! You forget that you are a Christian pastor's wife, and that there is a stranger present."

"No, that is just what I don't forget," said Mrs. Snow. "I see a Christian pastor afraid of a man of the world, who cares no more about Christianity than he does about a pair of old shoes, and who patronizes it for the sake of shutting its mouth against him. It makes me angry, and makes me wish I were a man; and you ought to go to that meeting to-morrow, as a Christian pastor, and put down this shame and wickedness. You have influence, if you will use it. All the people want is a leader, and some one to tell them the truth."

"Yes, father, I'm sure you have a *great* deal of influence," said the elder Miss Snow.

"A great *deal* of influence," responded the next in years.

"Yes, indeed," echoed the youngest.

Mr. Snow established the bridge again, by bringing his fingers together—whether to keep out the flattery that thus came like a subtle balm to his heart, or to keep in the self-complacency which had been engendered, was not apparent.

He smiled, looking benevolently out upon the group, and said: "Oh, you women are so hasty, so hasty, so hasty! I had not said that I would not interfere. Indeed, I had pretty much made up my mind to do so. But I wanted you in advance to see things as they air. It may be that something can be done, and it certainly will be a great satisfaction to me if I can be the humble instrument for the accomplishment of a reform."

"And you will go to the meeting? and you will speak?" said Miss Butterworth, eagerly.

"Yes!" and Mr. Snow looked straight into Miss Butterworth's tearful eyes, and smiled.

"The Lord add his blessing, and to his name be all the praise! Good-night!" said Miss Butterworth, rising and making for the door.

"Dear," said Mrs. Snow, springing and catching her by the arm, "don't you think you ought to put on something more? It's very chilly to-night."

"Not a rag. I'm hot. I believe I should roast if I had on a feather more."

"Wouldn't you like Mr. Snow to go home with you? He can go just as well as not," insisted Mrs. Snow.

"Certainly, just as well as not," repeated the elder Miss Snow, followed by the second with: "as well as not," and by the third with: "and be glad to do it."

"No—no—no—no"—to each. "I can get along better without him, and I don't mean to give him a chance to take back what he has said."

Miss Butterworth ran down the steps, the whole family standing in the open door, with Mr. Snow, in his glasses, behind his good-natured, cackling flock, thoroughly glad that his protective services were deemed of so small value by the brave little tailoress.

Then Miss Butterworth could see the moon and the stars. Then she could see how beautiful the night was. Then she became conscious of the everlasting roar of the cataracts, and of the wreaths of mist that they sent up into the crisp evening air. To the fear of anything in Sevenoaks, in the day or in the night, she was a stranger; so, with a light heart, talking and humming to herself, she went by the silent mill, the noisy dram-shops, and, with her benevolent spirit full of hope and purpose, reached the house where, in a humble hired room, she had garnered all her treasures, including the bed and the linen which she had prepared years before for an event that never took place.

"The Lord add his blessing, and to his name be all the praise," she said, as she extinguished the candle, laughing in spite of herself, to think how she had blurted out the prayer and the ascription in the face of Solomon Snow. "Well, he's a broken reed—a broken reed—but I hope Mrs. Snow will tie something to him—or starch him —or—something—to make him stand straight for once," and then she went to sleep, and dreamed of fighting with Robert Belcher all night.

CHAPTER II.

MR. BELCHER CARRIES HIS POINT AT THE TOWN-MEETING, AND THE POOR ARE KNOCKED DOWN TO THOMAS BUFFUM.

THE abrupt departure of Miss Butterworth left Mr. Belcher piqued and surprised. Although he regarded himself as still "master of the situation"—to use his own pet phrase—the visit of that spirited woman had in various ways humiliated him. To sit in his own library, with an intruding woman who not only was not afraid of him but despised him—to sit before her patiently and be called "Bob Belcher," and a brute, and not to have the privilege of kicking her out-of-doors, was the severest possible trial of his equanimity. She left him so suddenly that he had not had the opportunity to insult her, for he had fully intended to do this before she retired. He had determined, also, as a matter of course, that in regard to the public poor of Sevenoaks he would give all his influence toward maintaining the existing state of things. The idea of being influenced by a woman, particularly by a woman over whom he had no influence, to change his policy with regard to anything, public or private, was one against which all the brute within him rebelled.

In this state of mind, angry with himself for having tolerated one who had so boldly and ruthlessly wounded his self-love, he had but one resort. He could not confess his humiliation to his wife; and there was no one in the world with whom he could hold conversation on the subject, except his old confidant who came into the mirror when wanted, and conveniently retired when the interview closed.

Rising from his chair, and approaching his mirror as if he had been whipped, he stood a full minute regarding his disgraced and speechless image. "Are you Robert Belcher, Esquire, of Sevenoaks?" he inquired, at length. "Are you the person who has been insulted by a woman? Look at me, sir! Turn not away! Have you any constitutional objections to telling me how you feel? Are you, sir, the proprietor of this house? Are you the owner of yonder mill? Are you the distinguished person who carries Sevenoaks in his pocket? How are the mighty fallen! And you, sir, who have been insulted by a tailoress, can stand here, and look me in the face, and still pretend to be a man! You are a scoundrel, sir—a low, mean-spirited scoundrel, sir. You are nicely dressed, but you are a puppy. Dare to tell me you are not, and I will grind you under my foot, as I would grind a worm. Don't give me a word—not a word! I am not in a mood to bear it!"

Having vented his indignation and disgust, with the fiercest facial expression and the most menacing gesticulations, he became calm, and proceeded:

"Benedict at the poor-house, hopelessly insane! Tell me now, and, mark you, no lies here! Who developed his inventions? Whose money was risked? What did it cost Benedict? Nothing. What did it cost Robert Belcher? More thousands than Benedict ever dreamed of. Have you done your duty, Robert Belcher? Ay, ay, sir! I believe you. Did you turn his head? No, sir. I believe you; it is well! I have spent money for him—first and last, a great deal of money for him; and any man or woman who disputes me is a liar—a base, malignant liar! Who is still master of the situation? Whose name is Norval? Whose are these Grampian Hills? Who intends to go to the town-meeting to-morrow, and have things fixed about as he wants them? Who will make Keziah Butterworth weep and howl with anguish? Let Robert Belcher alone! Alone! Far in azure depths of space (here Mr. Belcher extended both arms heavenward, and regarded his image admiringly), far—far away! Well, you're a pretty good-looking man, after all, and I'll let you off this time; but don't let me catch you playing baby to another woman! I think you'll be able to take care of yourself [nodding slowly]. By-by! Good-night!"

Mr. Belcher retired from the glass with two or three profound bows, his face beaming with restored self-complacency, and, taking his chair, he resumed his cigar. At this moment, there arose in his memory a single sentence he had read in the warrant for the meeting of the morrow: "To see if the town will take any steps for the improvement of the condition of the poor, now supported at the public charge."

When he read this article of the warrant, posted in the public places of the village, it had not impressed him particularly. Now he saw Miss Butterworth's hand in it. Evidently Mr. Belcher was not the only man who had been honored by a call from that philanthropic woman. As he thought the matter over, he regretted that, for the sake of giving form and force to his spite against her, he should be obliged to relinquish the popularity he might have won by favoring a reformative measure. He saw something in it, also, that might be made to add to Tom Buffum's profits, but even this consideration weighed nothing against his desire for personal revenge, to be exhibited in the form of triumphant personal power.

He rose from his chair, walked his room, swinging his hands backward and forward, casting furtive glances into his mirror, and then rang his bell. He had arrived at a conclusion. He had fixed upon his scheme, and was ready for work.

"Tell Phipps to come here," he said to the maid who responded to the summons.

Phipps was his coachman, body-servant, table-waiter, pet, butt for his jests, tool, man of all occasions. He considered himself a part of Mr. Belcher's personal property. To be the object of his clumsy badinage, when visitors were present and his master was particularly amiable, was equivalent to an honorable public notice. He took Mr. Belcher's cast-off clothes, and had them reduced in their dimensions for his own wearing, and was thus always able to be nearly as well dressed and foppish as the man for whom they were originally made. He was as insolent to others as he was obsequious to his master—a flunky by nature and long education.

Phipps appeared.

"Well, Phipps, what are you here for?" inquired Mr. Belcher.

"I was told you wanted me, sir," looking doubtfully with his cunning eyes into Mr. Belcher's face, as if questioning his mood.

"How is your health? You look feeble. Overwhelmed by your tremendous duties? Been sitting up late along back? Eh? You rascal! Who's the happy woman?"

Phipps laughed, and twiddled his fingers.

"You're a precious fellow, and I've got to get rid of you. You are altogether too many for me. Where did you get that coat? It seems to me I've seen something like that before. Just tell me how you do it, man. I can't dress the way you do. Yes, Phipps, you're too many for me!"

Phipps smiled, aware that he was expected to make no reply.

"Phipps, do you expect to get up to-morrow morning?"

"Yes, sir."

"Oh, you do! Very well! See that you do."

"Yes, sir."

"And Phipps——"

"Yes, sir."

"Bring the grays and the light wagon to the door to-morrow morning at seven o'clock."

"Yes, sir."

"And Phipps, gather all the old clothes about the house that you can't use yourself, and tie 'em up in a bundle, and put 'em into the back of the wagon. Mum is the word, and if Mrs. Belcher asks you any questions, tell her I think of turning Sister of Charity."

Phipps snickered.

"And Phipps, make a basket of cold meat and goodies, and put in with the clothes."

"Yes, sir."

"And Phipps, remember: seven o'clock, sharp, and no soldiering."

"Yes, sir."

"And Phipps, here is a cigar that cost twenty-five cents. Do it up in a paper, and lay it away. Keep it to remember me by."

This joke was too good to be passed over lightly, and so Phipps giggled, took the cigar, put it caressingly to his nose, and then slipped it into his pocket.

"Now make yourself scarce," said his master, and the man retired, entirely conscious that the person he served had some rascally scheme on foot, and heartily sympathetic with him in the project of its execution.

Promptly at seven the next morning, the rakish pair of trotters stood before the door, with a basket and a large bundle in the back of the rakish little wagon. Almost at the same moment, the proprietor came out, buttoning his overcoat. Phipps leaped out, then followed his master into the wagon, who, taking the reins, drove off at a rattling pace up the long hill toward Tom Buffum's boarding-house. The road lay entirely outside of the village, so that the unusual drive was not observed.

Arriving at the poor-house, Mr. Belcher gave the reins to his servant, and, with a sharp rap upon the door with the butt of his whip, summoned to the latch the red-faced and stuffy keeper. What passed between them, Phipps did not hear, although he tried very hard to do so. At the close of a half hour's buzzing conversation, Tom Buffum took the bundle from the wagon, and pitched it into his doorway. Then, with the basket on his arm, he and Mr. Belcher made their way across the street to the dormitories and cells occupied by the paupers of both sexes and all ages and conditions. Even the hard-hearted proprietor saw that which wounded his blunted sensibilities; but he looked on with a bland face, and witnessed the greedy consumption of the stale dainties of his own table.

It was by accident that he was led out by a side passage, and there he caught glimpses of the cells to which Miss Butterworth had alluded, and inhaled an atmosphere which sickened him to paleness, and brought to his lips the exclamation : "For God's sake let's get out of this."

"Ay! ay!" came tremblingly from behind the bars of a cell, "let's get out of this"

Mr. Belcher pushed toward the light, but not so quickly that a pair of eyes, glaring from the straw, failed to recognize him.

"Robert Belcher! Oh, for God's sake! Robert Belcher!"

It was a call of wild distress—a whine, a howl, an objurgation, all combined. It was repeated as long as he could hear it. It sounded in his ears as he descended the hill. It came again and again to him as he was seated at his comfortable breakfast. It rang in the chambers of his consciousness for hours, and only a firm and despotic will expelled it at last. He knew the voice, and he never wished to hear it again.

What he had seen that morning, and what he had done, where he had been, and why he had gone, were secrets to which his wife and children were not admitted. The relations between himself and his wife were not new in the world. He wished to retain her respect, so he never revealed to her his iniquities. She wished as far as possible to respect him, so she never made uncomfortable inquiries. He was bountiful to her. He had been bountiful to many others. She clothed and informed all his acts of beneficence with the motives which became them. If she was ever shocked by his vulgarity, he never knew it by any word of hers, in disapproval. If she had suspicions, she did not betray them. Her children were trained to respect their father, and among them she found the satisfactions of her life. He had long ceased to be her companion. As an associate, friend, lover, she had given him up, and, burying in her heart all her griefs and all her loneliness, had determined to make the best of her life, and to bring her children to believe that their father was a man of honor, of whom they had no reason to be ashamed. If she was proud, hers was an amiable pride, and to Mr. Belcher's credit let it be said that he respected her as much as he wished her to honor him.

For an hour after breakfast Mr. Belcher was occupied in his library, with his agent, in the transaction of his daily business. Then, just as the church-bell rang its preliminary summons for the assembling of the town-meeting, Phipps came to the door again with the rakish grays and the rakish wagon, and Mr. Belcher drove down the steep hill into the village, exchanging pleasant words with the farmers whom he encountered on the way, and stopping at various shops, to speak with those upon whom he depended for voting through whatever public schemes he found it desirable to favor.

The old town-hall was thronged for half an hour before the time designated in the warrant. Finally, the bell ceased to ring, at the exact moment when Mr. Belcher drove to the door and ascended the steps. There was a buzz all over the house when he entered, and he was surrounded at once.

"Have it just as you want it," shaking his head ostentatiously and motioning them away, "don't mind anything about me. I'm a passenger," he said aloud, and with a laugh, as the meeting was called to order and the warrant read, and a nomination for moderator demanded.

"Peter Vernol," shouted a dozen voices in unison.

Peter Vernol had represented the district in the Legislature, and was supposed to be familiar with parliamentary usage. He was one of Mr. Belcher's men, of course—as truly owned and controlled by him as Phipps himself.

Peter Vernol became moderator by acclamation. He was a young man, and, ascending the platform very red in the face, and looking out upon the assembled voters of Sevenoaks, he asked with a trembling voice :

" What is the further pleasure of the meeting ?"

" I move you," said Mr. Belcher, rising, and throwing open his overcoat, " that the Rev. Solomon Snow, whom I am exceedingly glad to see present, open our deliberations with prayer."

The moderator, forgetting apparently that the motion had not been put, thereupon invited the reverend gentleman to the platform, from which, when his service had been completed, he with dignity retired—but with the painful consciousness that in some way Mr. Belcher had become aware of the philanthropic task he had undertaken. He knew he was beaten, at the very threshold of his enterprise—that his conversations of the morning among his neighbors had been reported, and that Paul Benedict and his fellow-sufferers would be none the better for him.

The business connected with the various articles of the warrant was transacted without notable discussion or difference. Mr. Belcher's ticket for town officers, which he took pains to show to those around him, was unanimously adopted. When it came to the question of schools, Mr. Belcher indulged in a few flights of oratory. He thought it impossible for a town like Sevenoaks to spend too much money for schools. He felt himself indebted to the public school for all that he was, and all that he had won. The glory of America, in his view—its pre-eminence above all the exhausted and decayed civilizations of the Old World—was to be found in popular education. It was the distinguishing feature of our new and abounding national life. Drop it, falter, recede, and the darkness that now hangs over England, and the thick darkness that envelops the degenerating hordes of the Continent, would settle down upon fair America, and blot her out forever from the list of the earth's teeming nations. He would pay good wages to teachers. He would improve school-houses, and he would do it as a matter of economy. It was, in his view, the only safeguard against the encroachments of a destructive pauperism. "We are soon," said Mr. Belcher, to consider whether we will take any steps for the improvement of the condition of the poor, now supported at the public charge. Here is our first step. Let us endow our children with such a degree of intelligence that pauperism shall be impossible. In this thing I go hand-in-hand with the clergy. On many points I do not agree with them, but on this matter of popular education I will do them the honor to say that they have uniformly been in advance of the rest of us. I join hands with them here to-day, and, as any advance in our rate of taxation for schools will bear more heavily upon me than upon any other citizen—I do not say it boastingly, gentlemen—I pledge myself to support and stand by it."

Mr. Belcher's speech, delivered with majestic swellings of his broad chest, the ostentatious removal of his overcoat, and brilliant passages of oratorical action, but most imperfectly summarized in this report, was received with cheers. Mr. Snow himself feebly joined in the approval, although he knew it was intended to disarm him. His strength, his resolution, his courage, ebbed away with sickening rapidity; and he was not reassured by a glance toward the door, where he saw, sitting quite alone, Miss Butterworth herself, who had come in for the purpose partly of strengthening him, and partly of informing herself concerning the progress of a reform which had taken such strong hold upon her sympathies.

At length the article in the warrant which most interested that good lady was taken up, and Mr. Snow rose to speak upon it. He spoke of the reports he had heard concerning the bad treatment that the paupers, and especially those who were hopelessly insane, had received in the almshouse, enlarged upon the duties of humanity and Christianity, and expressed the conviction that the enlightened people of Sevenoaks should spend more money for the comfort of the unfortunate whom Heaven had thrown upon their charge, and particularly that they should institute a more searching and competent inspection of their pauper establishment.

As he took his seat, all eyes were turned upon Mr. Belcher, and that gentleman rose for a second exhibition of his characteristic eloquence.

"I do not forget," said Mr. Belcher, "that we have present here to-day an old and well-tried public servant. I see before me Mr. Thomas Buffum, who, for years, has had in charge the poor, not only of this town, but of this county. I do not forget that his task has been one of great delicacy, with the problem constantly before him how to maintain in comfort our most unfortunate class of population, and at the same time to reduce to its minimum the burden of our tax-payers. That he has solved this problem and served the public well, I most firmly believe. He has been for many years my trusted personal friend, and I cannot sit here and hear his administration questioned, and his integrity and humanity doubted, without entering my protest. [Cheers, during which Mr. Buffum grew very red in the face.] He has had a task to perform before which the bravest of us would shrink. We, who sit in our peaceful homes, know little of the hardships to which this faithful public servant has been subjected. Pauperism is ungrateful. Pauperism is naturally filthy. Pauperism is noisy. It consists of humanity in its most repulsive forms, and if we have among us a man who can—who can—stand it, let us stand by him." [Tremendous cheers.]

Mr. Belcher paused until the wave of applause had subsided, and then went on:

"An open-hand, free competition: this has been my

policy, in a business of whose prosperity you are the best judges. I say an open-hand and free competition in everything. How shall we dispose of our poor? Shall they be disposed of by private arrangement—sold out to favorites, of whose responsibility we know nothing? [Cries of no, no, no!] If anybody who is responsible—and now he is attacked, mark you, I propose to stand behind and be responsible for Mr. Buffum myself—can do the work cheaper and better than Mr. Buffum, let him enter at once upon the task. But let the competition be free, nothing covered up. Let us have clean hands in this business, if nowhere else. If we cannot have impartial dealing, where the interests of humanity are concerned, we are unworthy of the trust we have assumed. I give the Rev. Mr. Snow credit for motives that are unimpeachable—unimpeachable, sir. I do not think him capable of intentional wrong, and I wish to ask him, here and now, whether, within a recent period, he has visited the pauper establishment of Sevenoaks."

Mr. Snow rose and acknowledged that it was a long time since he had entered Mr. Buffum's establishment.

"I thought so. He has listened to the voice of rumor. Very well. I have to say that I have been there recently, and have walked through the establishment. I should do injustice to myself, and fail to hint to the reverend gentleman, and all those who sympathize with him, what I regard as one of their neglected duties, if I should omit to mention that I did not go empty-handed. [Loud cheers.] It is easy for those who neglect their own duties to suspect that others do the same. I know our paupers are not supported in luxury. We cannot afford to support them in luxury; but I wash my hands of all responsibility for inhumanity and inattention to their reasonable wants. The reverend gentleman himself knows, I think, whether any man ever came to me for assistance on behalf of any humane or religious object, and went away without aid. I cannot consent to be placed in a position that reflects upon my benevolence, and, least of all, by the reverend gentleman who has reflected upon that administration of public charity which has had, and still retains, my approval. I therefore move that the usual sum be appropriated for the support of the poor, and that at the close of this meeting the care of the poor for the ensuing year be disposed of at public auction to the lowest bidder."

Mr. Snow was silent, for he knew that he was impotent.

Then there jumped up a little man with tumbled hair, weazened face, and the general look of a broken-down gentleman, who was recognized by the moderator as "Dr. Radcliffe."

"Mr. Moderator," said he, in a screaming voice, "as I am the medical attendant and inspector of our pauper establishment, it becomes proper for me, in seconding the motion of Mr. Belcher, as I heartily do, to say a few words, and submit my report for the past year."

Dr. Radcliffe was armed with a large document, and the assembled voters of Sevenoaks were getting tired.

"I move," said Mr. Belcher, "that, as the hour is late, the reading of the report be dispensed with." The motion was seconded, and carried *nem. con.*

The Doctor was wounded in a sensitive spot, and was determined not to be put down.

"I may at least say," he went on, "that I have made some discoveries during the past year that ought to be in the possession of the scientific world. It takes less food to support a pauper than it does any other man, and I believe the reason is that he hasn't any mind. If I take two potatoes, one goes to the elaboration of mental processes, the other to the support of the physical economy. The pauper has only a physical economy, and he needs but one potato. Anæmia is the normal condition of the pauper. He breathes comfortably an atmosphere which would give a healthy man asphyxia. Hearty food produces inflammatory diseases and a general condition of hypertrophy. The character of the diseases at the poor-house, during the past year, has been typhoid. I have suggested to Mr. Buffum better ventilation, a change from farinaceous to nitrogenous food as conducive to a better condition of the mucous surfaces and a more perfect oxidation of the vital fluids. Mr. Buffum——"

"Oh, git out!" shouted a voice at the rear.

"Question! question!" called a dozen voices.

The moderator caught a wink and a nod from Mr. Belcher, and put the question, amid the protests of Dr. Radcliffe; and it was triumphantly carried.

And now, as the town-meeting drops out of this story, let us leave it, and leave Mr. Thomas Buffum at its close to underbid all contestants for the privilege of feeding the paupers of Sevenoaks for another year.

CHAPTER III.

IN WHICH JIM FENTON IS INTRODUCED TO THE READER AND INTRODUCES HIMSELF TO MISS BUTTERWORTH.

MISS BUTTERWORTH, while painfully witnessing the defeat of her hopes from the last seat in the hall, was conscious of the presence at her side of a very singular-looking personage, who evidently did not belong in Sevenoaks. He was a woodsman, who had been attracted to the hall by his desire to witness the proceedings. His clothes, originally of strong material, were patched; he held in his hand a fur cap without a visor;

and a rifle leaned on the bench at his side. She had been attracted to him by his thoroughly good-natured face, his noble, muscular figure, and certain exclamations that escaped from his lips during the speeches. Finally, he turned to her, and with a smile so broad and full that it brought an answer to her own face, he said: "This 'ere breathin' is worse nor an old swamp. I'm goin', and good-by to ye!"

Why this remark, personally addressed to her, did not offend her, coming as it did from a stranger, she did not know; but it certainly did not seem impudent. There was something so simple and strong and manly about him, as he had sat there by her side, contrasted with the baser and better dressed men before her, that she took his address as an honorable courtesy.

When the woodsman went out upon the steps of the town-hall, to get a breath, he found there such an assembly of boys as usually gathers in villages on the smallest public occasion. Squarely before the door stood Mr. Belcher's grays, and in Mr. Belcher's wagon sat Mr. Belcher's man, Phipps. Phipps was making the most of his position. He was proud of his horses, proud of his clothes, proud of the whip he was carelessly snapping, proud of belonging to Mr. Belcher. The boys were laughing at his funny remarks, envying him his proud eminence, and discussing the merits of the horses and the various points of the attractive establishment.

As the stranger appeared, he looked down upon the boys with a broad smile, which attracted them at once, and quite diverted them from their flattering attentions to Phipps—a fact quickly perceived by the latter, and as quickly revenged in a way peculiar to himself and the man from whom he had learned it.

"This is the hippopotamus, gentlemen," said Phipps, "fresh from his native woods. He sleeps underneath the banyan-tree, and lives on the nuts of the hick-o-ree, and pursues his prey with his tail extended upward and one eye open, and has been known when excited by hunger to eat small boys, spitting out their boots with great violence. Keep out of his way, gentlemen! Keep out of his way, and observe his wickedness at a distance."

Phipps' saucy speech was received with a great roar by the boys, who were surprised to notice that the animal himself was not only not disturbed, but very much amused by being shown up as a curiosity.

"Well, you're a new sort of a monkey, any way," said the woodman, after the laugh had subsided. "I never hearn one talk afore."

"You never will again," retorted Phipps, "if you give me any more of your lip."

The woodman walked quickly toward Phipps, as if he were about to pull him from his seat.

Phipps saw the motion, started the horses, and was out of his way in an instant.

The boys shouted in derision, but Phipps did not come back, and the stranger was the hero. They gathered around him, asking questions, all of which he good-naturedly answered. He seemed to be pleased with their society, as if he were only a big boy himself, and wanted to make the most of the limited time which his visit to the town afforded him.

While he was thus standing as the centre of an inquisitive and admiring group, Miss Butterworth came out of the town-hall. Her eyes were full of tears, and her eloquent face expressed vexation and distress. The stranger saw the look and the tears, and, leaving the boys, he approached her without the slightest awkwardness, and said:

"Has anybody teched ye, mum?"

"Oh, no, sir," Miss Butterworth answered.

"Has anybody spoke ha'sh to ye?"

"Oh, no, sir;" and Miss Butterworth pressed on, conscious that in that kind inquiry there breathed as genuine respect and sympathy as ever had reached her ears in the voice of a man.

"Because," said the man, still walking along at her side, "I'm spilin' to do somethin' for somebody, and I wouldn't mind thrashin' anybody you'd p'int out."

"No, you can do nothing for me. Nobody can do anything in this town for anybody until Robert Belcher is dead," said Miss Butterworth.

"Well, I shouldn't like to kill 'im," responded the man, "unless it was an accident in the woods—a great ways off—for a turkey or a hedgehog—and the gun half-cocked."

The little tailoress smiled through her tears, though she felt very uneasy at being observed in company and conversation with the rough-looking stranger. He evidently divined the thoughts which possessed her, and said, as if only the mention of his name would make him an acquaintance:

"I'm Jim Fenton. I trap for a livin' up in Number Nine, and have jest brung in my skins."

"My name is Butterworth," she responded mechanically.

"I know'd it," he replied. "I axed the boys."

"Good-by," he said. "Here's the store, and I must shoulder my sack and be off. I don't see women much, but I'm fond of 'em, and they're pretty apt to like me."

"Good-by," said the woman. "I think you're the best man I've seen to-day;" and then, as if she had said more than became a modest woman, she added, "and that isn't saying very much."

They parted, and Jim Fenton stood perfectly still in the street and looked at her, until she disappeared around a corner. "That's what I call a genuine creetur'," he muttered to himself at last, "a genuine creetur'."

Then Jim Fenton went into the store, where he had sold his skins and bought his supplies, and, after exchanging a few jokes with those who had observed his interview with Miss Butterworth, he shouldered his sack as he called it, and started for Number Nine. The sack was a contrivance of his own, with two pouches which depended, one before and one behind, from his broad shoulders. Taking his rifle in his hand, he bade the group that had gathered around him a hearty good-by, and started on his way.

The afternoon was not a pleasant one. The air was raw, and, as the sun went toward its setting, the wind came on to blow from the northwest. This was just as he would have it. It gave him breath, and stimulated the vitality that was necessary to him in the performance of his long task. A tramp of forty miles was not play, even to him, and this long distance was to be accomplished before he could reach the boat that would bear him and his burden into the woods.

He crossed the Branch at its principal bridge, and took the same path up the hill that Robert Belcher had travelled in the morning. About half-way up the hill, as he was going on with the stride of a giant, he saw a little boy at the side of the road, who had evidently been weeping. He was thinly and very shabbily clad, and was shivering with cold. The great, healthy heart within Jim Fenton was touched in an instant.

"Well, bub," said he, tenderly, "how fare ye? How fare ye? Eh?"

"I'm pretty well, I thank you, sir," replied the lad.

"I guess not. You're as blue as a whetstone. You haven't got as much on you as a picked goose."

"I can't help it, sir," and the boy burst into tears.

"Well, well, I didn't mean to trouble you, boy. Here, take this money, and buy somethin' to make you happy. Don't tell your dad you've got it. It's yourn."

The boy made a gesture of rejection, and said: "I don't wish to take it, sir."

"Now, that's good! Don't wish to take it! Why, what's your name? You're a new sort o' boy."

"My name is Harry Benedict."

"Harry Benedict? And what's your pa's name?"

"His name is Paul Benedict."

"Where is he now?"

"He is in the poor-house."

"And you too?"

"Yes, sir," and the lad found expression for his distress in another flow of tears.

"Well, well, well, well! If that ain't the strangest thing I ever hearn on! Paul Benedict, of Sevenoaks, in Tom Buffum's boardin'-house!"

"Yes, sir, and he's very crazy, too."

Jim Fenton set his rifle against a rock at the roadside, slowly lifted off his pack and placed it near the rifle, and then sat down on a stone and called the boy to him, folding him in his great warm arms to his warm breast.

"Harry, my boy," said Jim, "your pa and me was old friends. We have hunted together, fished together, eat together, and slept together many's the day and night. He was the best shot that ever come into the woods. I've seed him hit a deer at fifty rod many's the time, and he used to bring up the nicest tackle for fishin', every bit of it made with his own hands. He was the curisist creetur' I ever seed in my life, and the best; and I'd do more fur 'im nor fur any livin' live man. Oh, I tell ye, we used to have high old times. It was wuth livin' a year in the woods jest to have 'im with me for a fortnight. I never charged 'im a red cent fur nothin', and I've got some of his old tackle now that he give me. Him an' me was like brothers, and he used to talk about religion, and tell me I ought to shift over, but I never could see 'zactly what I ought to shift over from, or shift over to; but I let 'im talk, 'cause he liked to. He used to go out behind the trees nights, and I hearn him sayin' somethin'—somethin' very low, as I am talkin' to ye now. Well, he was prayin'; that's the fact about it, I s'pose; and ye know I felt jest as safe when that man was round! I don't believe I could 'a' been drownded when he was in the woods any more'n if I'd 'a' been a mink. An' Paul Benedict is in the poor-house! I vow I don't 'zactly see why the Lord let that man go up the spout; but perhaps it'll all come out right. Where's your ma, boy?"

Harry gave a great, shuddering gasp, and, answering him that she was dead, gave himself up to another fit of crying.

"Oh, now don't! now don't!" said Jim tenderly, pressing the distressed lad still closer to his heart. "Don't ye do it; it don't do no good. It jest takes the spunk all out o' ye. Ma's have to die like other folks, or go to the poor-house. You wouldn't like to have yer ma in the poor-house. She's all right. God Almighty's bound to take care o' her. Now, ye jest stop that sort o' thing. She's better off with him nor she would be with Tom Buffum—any amount better off. Doesn't Tom Buffum treat your pa well?"

"Oh, no, sir; he doesn't give him enough to eat, and he doesn't let him have things in his room, because he says he'll hurt himself, or break them all to pieces, and he doesn't give him good clothes, nor anything to cover himself up with when it's cold."

"Well, boy," said Jim, his great frame shaking with indignation, "do ye want to know what I think of Tom Buffum?"

"Yes, sir."

"It won't do fur me to tell ye, 'cause I'm rough, but if there's anything awful bad—oh, bad as anything can be—

in Skeezacks, I should say that Tom Buffum was an old Skeezacks."

Jim Fenton was feeling his way.

"I should say he was an infernal old Skeezacks. That isn't very bad, is it?"

"I don't know, sir," replied the boy.

"Well, a d—d rascal; how's that?"

"My father never used such words," replied the boy.

"That's right, and I take it back. I oughtn't to have said it, but unless a feller has got some sort o' religion he has a mighty hard time namin' people in this world. What's that?"

Jim started with the sound in his ear of what seemed to be a cry of distress.

"That's one of the crazy people. They do it all the time."

Then Jim thought of the speeches he had heard in the town-meeting, and recalled the distress of Miss Butterworth, and the significance of all the scenes he had so recently witnessed.

"Look 'ere, boy; can ye keep right 'ere," tapping him on his breast, "whatsomever I tell ye? Can you keep yer tongue still?—hope you'll die if ye don't?"

There was something in these questions through which the intuitions of the lad saw help, both for his father and himself. Hope strung his little muscles in an instant, his attitude became alert, and he replied:

"I'll never say anything if they kill me."

"Well, I'll tell ye what I'm goin' to do. I'm goin' to stay to the poor-house to-night, if they'll keep me, an' I guess they will; and I'm goin' to see yer pa too, and somehow you and he must be got out of this place."

The boy threw his arms around Jim's neck, and kissed him passionately, again and again, without the power, apparently, to give any other expression to his emotions.

"Oh, God! don't, boy! That's a sort o' thing I can't stand. I ain't used to it."

Jim paused, as if to realize how sweet it was to hold the trusting child in his arms, and to be thus caressed, and then said: "Ye must be mighty keerful, and do just as I bid ye. If I stay to the poor-house to-night, I shall want to see ye in the mornin', and I shall want to see ye alone. Now ye know there's a big stump by the side of the road, half-way up to the old school-house."

Harry gave his assent.

"Well, I want ye to be thar, ahead o' me, and then I'll tell ye jest what I'm a goin' to do, and jest what I want to have ye do."

"Yes, sir."

"Now mind, ye mustn't know me when I'm about the house, and mustn't tell anybody you've seed me, and I must n't know you. Now ye leave all the rest to Jim Fenton, yer pa's old friend. Don't ye begin to feel a little better now?"

"Yes, sir."

"You can kiss me again, if ye want to. I didn't mean to choke ye off. That was all in fun, ye know."

Harry kissed him, and then Jim said: "Now make tracks for yer old boardin'-house. I'll be along bimeby."

The boy started upon a brisk run, and Jim still sat upon the stone watching him until he disappeared somewhere among the angles of the tumble-down buildings that constituted the establishment.

"Well, Jim Fenton," he said to himself, "ye've been spilin' fur somethin' to do fur somebody. I guess ye've got it, and not a very small job neither."

Then he shouldered his pack, took up his rifle, looked up at the cloudy and blustering sky, and pushed up the hill, still talking to himself, and saying: "A little boy of about his haighth and bigness ain't a bad thing to take."

CHAPTER IV.

IN WHICH JIM FENTON APPLIES FOR LODGINGS AT TOM BUFFUM'S BOARDING-HOUSE, AND FINDS HIS OLD FRIEND.

As Jim walked up to the door of the building occupied by Tom Buffum's family, he met the head of the family coming out; and as hitherto that personage has escaped description, it will be well for the reader to make his acquaintance. The first suggestion conveyed by his rotund figure was, that however scantily he furnished his boarders, he never stinted himself in the matter of food. He had the sluggish, clumsy look of a heavy eater. His face was large, his almost colorless eyes were small, and, if one might judge by the general expression of his features, his favorite viand was pork. Indeed, if the swine into which the devils once entered had left any descendants, it would be legitimate to suppose that the breed still thrived in the most respectable sty connected with his establishment. He was always hoarse, and spoke either in a whisper or a wheeze. For this or for some other reason not apparent, he was a silent man, rarely speaking except when addressed by a question, and never making conversation with anybody. From the time he first started independently in the world, he had been in some public office. Men with dirty work to do had found him wonderfully serviceable, and, by ways which it would be hard to define to the ordinary mind, he had so managed that every town and county office, in which there was any money, had been by turns in his hands.

"Well, Mr. Buffum, how fare ye?" said Jim, walking heartily up to him, and shaking his hand, his face glowing with good-nature.

Mr. Buffum's attempt to respond to this address ended in a wheeze and a cough.

"Have ye got room for another boarder to-night? Faith, I never expected to come to the poor-house, but here I am. I'll take entertainment for man or beast. Which is the best, and which do you charge the most for? Somebody's got to keep me to-night, and ye're the man to bid low."

Buffum made no reply, but stooped down, took a sliver from a log, and began to pick his teeth. Jim watched him with quiet amusement. The more Mr. Buffum thought, the more furious he grew with his toothpick.

"Pretty tough old beef, wasn't it?" said Jim, with a hearty laugh.

"You go in and see the women," said Mr. Buffum, in a wheezy whisper.

This, to Jim, was equivalent to an honorable reception. He had no doubt of his ability to make his way with "the women," who, he was fully aware, had been watching him all the time from the window.

To the women of Tom Buffum's household a visitor was a godsend. Socially, they had lived all their lives in a state of starvation. They knew all about Jim Fenton, and had exchanged many a saucy word with him, as he had passed their house on his journeys to and from Sevenoaks.

"If you can take up with what we've got," said Mrs. Buffum, suggestively.

"In course," responded Jim, "an' I can take up with what ye haven't got."

"Our accommodations is very crowded," said Mrs. Buffum.

"So is mine to home," responded Jim. "I allers sleep hangin' on a gambrel, between two slabs."

While Mr. Tom Buffum's "women" were laughing, Jim lifted off his pack, placed his rifle in the corner of the room, and sat down in front of the fire, running on with his easy-going tongue through preposterous stories, and sundry flattering allusions to the beauty and attractiveness of the women to whose hospitalities he had committed himself.

After supper, to which he did full justice, the family drew around the evening fire, and while Mr. Buffum went, or seemed to go, to sleep, in his chair, his guest did his best to entertain the minor members of the group.

"This hollerin' ye have here reminds me," said Jim, "of Number Nine. Ther's some pretty tall hollerin' thar nights. Do you see how my ha'r sticks up? I can't keep it down. It riz one night jest about where you see it now, and it's mostly been thar ever sence. Combin' don't do no good. Taller don't do no good. Nothin' don't do no good. I s'pose if Mr. Buffum, a-snorin' jest as hard as he does now, should set on it for a fortnight, it would spring right up like a staddle, with a b'ar ketched at the eend of it, jest as quick as he let up on me." At this there was a slight rumble in Mr. Buffum's throat.

"Why, what made it rise so?" inquired the most interested and eldest Miss Buffum.

"Now, ain't your purty eyes wide open?" said Jim.

"You're jest fooling; you know you are," responded Miss Buffum, blushing.

"Do ye see the ha'r on the back of my hand?" said Jim, patting one of those ample instruments with the other. "That stands up jest as it does on my head. I'm a regular hedgehog. It all happened then."

"Now, Jim Fenton, you shall go along and tell your story, and not keep us on tenter-hooks all night," said Miss Buffum sharply.

"I don't want to scare the dear little heart out o' ye," said Jim, with a killing look of his eyes, "but if ye will hear it, I s'pose I must tell ye. Ye see I'm alone purty much all the time up thar. I don't have no such times as I'm havin' here to-night, with purty gals 'round me. Well, one night I hearn a loon, or thought I hearn one. It sounded 'way off on the lake, and bimeby it come nigher, and then I thought it was a painter, but it didn't sound 'zactly like a painter. My dog Turk he don't mind such things, but he knowed it warn't a loon and warn't a painter. So he got up and went to the door, and then the yell come agin, and he set up the most un-'arthly howl I ever hearn. I flung one o' my boots at 'im, but he didn't mind anything more about it than if it had been a feather. Well, ye see, I couldn't sleep, and the skeeters was purty busy, and I thought I'd get up. So I went to my cabin door and flung it open. The moon was shinin', and the woods was still, but Turk, he rushed out, and growled and barked like mad. Bimeby he got tired, and come back lookin' kind o' skeered, and says I: 'Ye're a purty dog, ain't ye?' Jest then I hearn the thing nigher, and I begun to hear the brush crack. I knowed I'd got to meet some new sort of a creetur', and I jest stepped back and took my rifle. When I stood in the door agin, I seen somethin' comin'. It was a walkin' on two legs like a man, and it was a man, or somethin' that looked like one. He come toward the cabin, and stopped about three rod off. He had long white hair that looked jest like silk under the moon, and his robes was white, and he had somethin' in his hand that shined like silver. I jest drew up my rifle, and says I: 'Who-somever you be, stop, or I'll plug ye.' What do ye s'pose he did? He jest took that shinin' thing and swung it round and round his head, and I begun to feel the ha'r start, and up it come all over me. Then he put suthin' to his mouth, and then I knowed it was a trumpet, and he jest blowed till all the woods rung, and rung, and rung agin, and I hearn it comin' back from the mountain, louder nor it was itself. And then says I to my-self: 'There's another one, and Jim Fenton's a goner;'

but I didn't let on that I was skeered, and says I to him: 'That's a good deal of a toot; who be ye callin' to dinner?' And says he: 'It's the last day! Come to jedgment! I'm the Angel Gabr'el!' 'Well,' says I, 'if ye're the Angel Gabr'el, cold lead won't hurt ye, so mind yer eyes!' At that I drew a bead on 'im, and if ye'll b'lieve it, I knocked a tin horn out of his hands and picked it up the next mornin', and he went off into the woods like a streak o' lightnin'. But my ha'r hain't never come down."

Jim stroked the refractory locks toward his forehead with his huge hand, and they rose behind it like a wheat-field behind a summer wind. As he finished the manipulation, Mr. Buffum gave symptoms of life. Like a volcano under premonitory signs of an eruption, a wheezy chuckle seemed to begin somewhere in the region of his boots, and rise, growing more and more audible, until it burst into a full demonstration, that was half laugh and half cough.

"Why, what are you laughing at, father?" exclaimed Miss Buffum.

The truth was that Mr. Buffum had not slept at all. The simulation of sleep had been indulged in simply to escape the necessity of talking.

"It was old Tilden," said Mr. Buffum, and then went off into another fit of coughing and laughing that nearly strangled him.

"I wonder if it was!" seemed to come simultaneously from the lips of the mother and her daughters.

"Did you ever see him again?" inquired Mr. Buffum.

"I seen 'im oncet, in the spring, I s'pose," said Jim, "what there was left of 'im. There wasn't much left but an old shirt and some bones, an' I guess he wa'n't no great shakes of an angel. I buried 'im where I found 'im, and said nothin' to nobody."

"That's right," wheezed Mr. Buffum. "It's just as well."

"The truth is," said Mrs. Buffum, "that folks made a great fuss about his gettin' away from here and never bein' found. I thought 'twas a good riddance myself, but people seem to think that these crazy critturs are just as much consequence as anybody, when they don't know a thing. He was always arter our dinner-horn, and blowin', and thinkin' he was the Angel Gabriel. Well, it's a comfort to know he's buried, and isn't no more expense."

"I sh'd like to see some of these crazy people," said Jim. "They must be a jolly set. My ha'r can't stand any straighter nor it does now, and when you feed the animals in the mornin', I'd kind o' like to go round with ye."

The women insisted that he ought not to do it. Only those who understood them, and were used to them, ought to see them.

"You see, we can't give 'em much furnitur'," said Mrs. Buffum. "They break it, and they tear their beds to pieces, and all we can do is to jest keep them alive. As for keepin' their bodies and souls together, I don't s'pose they've got any souls. They are nothin' but animils, as you say, and I don't see why anybody should treat an animil like a human bein'. They hav'n't no sense of what you do for 'em."

"Oh, ye needn't be afraid o' my blowin'. I never blowed about old Tilden, as you call 'im, an' I never expect to," said Jim.

"That's right," wheezed Mr. Buffum. "It's just as well."

"Well, I s'pose the Doctor'll be up in the mornin'," said Mrs. Buffum, "and we shall clean up a little, and put in new straw, and p'r'aps you can go round with him?"

Mr. Buffum nodded his assent, and after an evening spent in story-telling and chaffing, Jim went to bed upon the shake-down in an upper room to which he was conducted.

Long before he was on his feet in the morning, the paupers of the establishment had been fed, and things had been put in order for the medical inspector. Soon after breakfast, the Doctor's crazy little gig was seen ascending the hill, and Mr. Buffum and Jim were at the door when he drove up. Buffum took the Doctor aside, and told him of Jim's desire to make the rounds with him. Nothing could have delighted the little man more than a proposition of this kind, because it gave him an opportunity to talk. Jim had measured his man when he heard him speak the previous day, and as they crossed the road together, he said: "Doctor, they didn't treat ye very well down there yesterday. I said to myself: 'Jim Fenton, what would ye done if ye had knowed as much as that doctor, an' had worked as hard as he had, and then be'n jest as good as stomped on by a set o' fellows that didn't know a hole in the ground when they seen it?' and, says I, answerin' myself, 'Ye'd 'a' made the fur fly, and spilt blood.'"

"Ah," responded the Doctor, "violence resteth in the bosom of fools."

"Well, it wouldn't 'a' rested in my bosom long. I'd 'a' made a young 'arthquake there in two minutes."

The Doctor smiled, and said with a sigh:

"The vulgar mind does not comprehend science."

"Now, jest tell me what science is," said Jim. "I hearn a great deal about science, but I live up in the woods, and I can't read very much, and ye see I ain't edicated, and I made up my mind if I ever found a man as knowed what science was, I'd ask him."

"Science, sir, is the sum of organized and systematized knowledge," replied the Doctor.

"Now, that seems reasomble," said Jim, "but what is it like? What do they do with it? Can a feller get a livin' by it?"

“Not in Sevenoaks,” replied the Doctor, with a bitter smile.

“Then, what's the use of it?”

“Pardon me, Mr. Fenton,” replied the Doctor. “You'll excuse me, when I tell you that you have not arrived at that mental altitude—that intellectual plane—”

“No,” said Jim, “I live on a sort of a medder.”

The case being hopeless, the Doctor went on and opened the door into what he was pleased to call the “insane ward.” As Jim put his head into the door, he uttered a “Phew!” and then said:

“This is worser nor the town-meetin'.”

The moment Jim's eyes beheld the misery that groaned out its days and nights within the stingy cells, his great heart melted with pity. For the first moments, his disposition to jest passed away, and all his soul rose up in indignation. If profane words came to his lips, they came from genuine commiseration, and a sense of the outrage that had been committed upon those who had been stamped with the image of the Almighty.

“This is a case of Shakespearean madness,” said Dr. Radcliffe, pausing before the barred and grated cell that held a half-nude woman. It was a little box of a place, with a rude bedstead in one corner, filthy beyond the power of water to cleanse. The occupant sat on a little bench in another corner, with her eyes rolled up to Jim's in a tragic expression which would make the fortune of an actress. He felt of his hair, impulsively.

“How are ye now? How do ye feel?” inquired Jim, tenderly.

She gave him no answer, but glared at him as if she would search the very depths of his heart.

“If ye'll look t'other way, ye'll obleege me,” said Jim.

But the woman gazed on, speechless, as if all the soul that had left her brain had taken up its residence in her large, black eyes.

"Is she tryin' to look me out o' countenance, Doctor?" inquired Jim; "'cause if she is, I'll stand here and let 'er try it on; but if she ain't I'll take the next one."

"Oh, she doesn't know what she's about, but it's a very curious form of insanity, and has almost a romantic interest attached to it from the fact that it did not escape the notice of the great bard."

"I notice, myself," said Jim, "that she's grated and barred."

The Doctor looked at his visitor inquisitively, but the woodman's face was as innocent as that of a child. Then they passed on to the next cell, and there they found another woman sitting quietly in the corner, among the straw.

"How fare ye, this mornin'?" inquired Jim, with a voice full of kindness.

"I'm just on the verge of eternity," replied the woman.

"Don't ye be so sure o' that, now," responded Jim. "Ye're good for ten year yit."

"No," said the woman, "I shall die in a minute."

"Does she mean that?" inquired Jim, turning to the Doctor.

"Yes, and she has been just on the verge of eternity for fifteen years," replied the Doctor, coolly. "That's rather an interesting case, too. I've given it a good deal of study. It's hopeless, of course, but it's a marked case, and full of suggestion to a scientific man."

"Isn't it a pity," responded Jim, "that she isn't a scientific man herself? It might amuse her, you know."

The Doctor laughed, and led him on to the next cell, and here he found the most wretched creature he had ever seen. He greeted her as he had greeted the others, and she looked up to him with surprise, raised herself from the straw, and said:

"You speak like a Christian."

The tears came into Jim's eyes, for he saw in that little sentence the cruelty of the treatment she had received.

"Well, I ain't no Christian, as I knows on," he responded, "an' I don't think they're very plenty in these parts; but I'm right sorry for ye. You look as if you might be a good sort of a woman."

"I should have been if it hadn't been forthe pigeons," said the woman. "They flew over a whole day, in flocks, and flocks, and cursed the world. All the people have got the plague, and they don't know it. My children all died of it, and went to hell. Everybody is going to hell, and nothing can save them. Old Buffum'll go first. Robert Belcher'll go next. Dr. Radcliffe will go next."

"Look here, old woman, ye jest leave me out of that calkerlation," said Jim.

"Will you have the kindness to kill me, sir?" said the woman.

"I really can't, this mornin'," he replied, "for I've got a good ways to tramp to-day; but if I ever want to kill anybody I'll come round, p'r'aps, and 'commodate ye."

"Thank you," she responded heartily.

The Doctor turned to Jim, and said:

"Do you see that hole in the wall, beyond her head? Well, that hole was made by Mr. Buffum. She had begged him to kill her so often that he thought he would put her to the test, and he agreed he would do so. So he set her up by that wall, and took a heavy stick from the wood-pile, raised it as high as the room would permit, and then brought it down with great violence, burying the end of the bludgeon in the plastering. I suppose he came within three inches of her head, and she never winked. It was a very interesting experiment, as it illustrated the genuineness of her desire for death. Otherwise the case is much like many others."

"Very interestin'," responded Jim, "very! Didn't you never think of makin' her so easy and comfortable that she wouldn't want anybody to kill her? I sh'd think that would be an interestin' experiment."

Now the Doctor had one resort, which, among the people of Sevenoaks, was infallible, whenever he wished to check argumentation on any subject relating to his profession. Any man who undertook to argue a medical question with him, or make a suggestion relating to medical treatment, he was in the habit of flooring at once, by wisely and almost pityingly shaking his head, and saying: "It's very evident to me, sir, that you've not received a medical education." So, when Jim suggested, in his peculiar way, that the woman ought to be treated better, the Doctor saw the point, and made his usual response.

"Mr. Fenton," said he, "excuse me, sir, but it's very evident that you've not had a medical education."

"There's where you're weak," Jim responded. "I'm a reg'lar M.D., three C's, double X., two I's. That's the year I was born, and that's my perfession. I studied with an Injun, and I know more 'arbs, and roots, and drawin' leaves than any doctor in a hundred mile; and if I can be of any use to ye, Doctor, there's my hand."

And Jim seized the Doctor's hand, and gave it a pressure which raised the little man off the floor.

The Doctor looked at him with eyes equally charged with amusement and amazement. He never had been met in that way before, and was not inclined to leave the field without in some way convincing Jim of his own superiority.

"Mr. Fenton," said he, "did you ever see a medulla oblongata?"

"Well, I seen a good many garters," replied the woodsman, "in the stores, an' I guess they was mostly oblong."

"Did you ever see a solar plexus?" inquired the Doctor, severely.

"Dozens of 'em. I allers pick a few in the fall, but I don't make much use of 'em."

"Perhaps you've seen a pineal gland," suggested the disgusted Doctor.

"I make 'em," responded Jim. "I whittle 'em out evenin's, ye know."

"If you were in one of these cells," said the Doctor, "I should think you were as mad as a March hare."

At this moment the Doctor's attention was called to a few harmless patients who thronged toward him as soon as they learned that he was in the building, begging for medicine; for if there is anything that a pauper takes supreme delight in, it is drugs. Passing along with them to a little lobby, where he could inspect them more conveniently, he left Jim behind, as that personage did not prove to be so interesting and impressible as he had hoped. Jim watched him, as he moved away, with a quiet chuckle, and then turned to pursue his investigations. The next cell he encountered held the man he was looking for. Sitting in the straw, talking to himself or some imaginary companion, he saw his old friend. It took him a full minute to realize that the gentle sportsman, the true Christian, the delicate man, the delightful companion, was there before him, a wreck—cast out from among his fellows, confined in a noisome cell, and hopelessly given over to his vagrant fancies and the tender mercies of Thomas Buffum. When the memory of what Paul Benedict had been to him, at one period of his life, came to Jim, with the full realization of his present misery and degradation, the strong man wept like a child. He drew an old silk handkerchief from his pocket, blew his nose as if it had been a trumpet, and then slipped up to the cell and said, softly: "Paul Benedict, give us your benediction."

" Jim ! " said the man, looking up quickly

" Good God ! he knows me," said Jim, whimpering " Yes, Mr. Benedict, I'm the same rough old fellow. How fare ye ? "

" I'm miserable," replied the man.

" Well, ye don't look as ef ye felt fust-rate. How did ye git in here ? "

" Oh, I was damned when I died. It's all right, I know ; but it's terrible."

" Why, ye don't think ye're in hell, do ye ? " inquired Jim.

" Don't you see ? " inquired the wretch, looking around him.

" Oh, yes ; I see ! I guess you're right," said Jim, falling in with his fancy.

" But where did you come from, Jim ? I never heard that you were dead."

" Yes ; I'm jest as dead as you be."

" Well, what did you come here for ? "

" Oh, I thought I'd call round," replied Jim carelessly.

" Did you come from Abraham's bosom ? " inquired Mr. Benedict eagerly.

" Straight."

" I can't think why you should come to see me, into such a place as this ! " said Benedict, wonderingly.

" Oh, I got kind o' oneasy. Don't have much to do over there, ye know."

" How did you get across the gulf ? "

" I jest shoved over in a birch, an' ye must be perlite enough to return the call," replied Jim, in the most matter-of-course manner possible.

Benedict looked down upon his torn and wretched clothing, and then turned his pitiful eyes up to Jim, who saw the thoughts that were passing in the poor man's mind.

" Never mind your clo'es," he said. " I dress jes'

the same there as I did in Number Nine, and nobody says a word. The fact is, they don't mind very much about clo'es there, any way. I'll come over and git ye, ye know, an' interjuce ye, and ye shall have jest as good a time as Jim Fenton can give ye."

"Shall I take my rifle along?" inquired Benedict.

"Yes, an' plenty of amanition. There ain't no game to speak on—only a few pa'tridge; but we can shoot at a mark all day, ef we want to."

Benedict tottered to his feet and came to the grated door, with his eyes all alight with hope and expectation. "Jim, you always were a good fellow," said he, dropping his voice to a whisper. "I'll show you my improvements. Belcher mustn't get hold of them. He's after them. I hear him round nights, but he shan't have them. I've got a new tumbler, and——"

"Well, never mind now," replied Jim. "It'll be jest as well when ye come over to spend the day with me. Now ye look a here! Don't you say nothin' about this to nobody. They'll all want to go, and we can't have 'em. You an' I want to git red of the crowd, ye know. We allers did. So when I come arter ye, jest keep mum, and we'll have a high old time."

All the intellect that Benedict could exercise was summoned to comprehend this injunction. He nodded his head; he laid it up in his memory. Hope had touched him, and he had won at least a degree of momentary strength and steadiness from her gracious finger.

"Now jest lay down an' rest, an' keep your thoughts to yerself till I come agin. Don't tell nobody I've be'n here, and don't ask leave of nobody. I'll settle with the old boss if he makes any sort of a row; and ye know when Jim Fenton says he'll stand between ye and all harm he means it, an' nothin' else."

"Yes, Jim."

"An' when I come here—most likely in the night—I'll bring a robe to put on ye, and we'll go out still."

"Yes, Jim."

"Sure you understand?"

"Yes, Jim."

"Well, good-by. Give us your hand. Here's hop in'."

Benedict held himself up by the slats of the door, while Jim went along to rejoin the Doctor. Outside of this door was still a solid one, which had been thrown wide open in the morning for the purpose of admitting the air. In this door Jim discovered a key, which he quietly placed in his pocket, and which he judged, by its size, was fitted to the lock of the inner as well as the outer door. He had already discovered that the door by which he entered the building was bolted upon the outside, the keeper doubtless supposing that no one would wish to enter so foul a place, and trusting thus to keep the inmates in durance.

"Well, Doctor," said Jim, "this sort o' thing is too many for me. I gi'en it up. It's very interestin', I s'pose, but my head begins to spin, an' it seems to me it's gettin' out of order. Do ye see my har, Doctor?" said he, exposing the heavy shock that crowned his head.

"Yes, I see it," replied the Doctor tartly. He thought he had shaken off his unpleasant visitor, and his return disturbed him.

"Well, Doctor, that has all riz sence I come in here."

"Are you sure?" inquired the Doctor, mollified in the presence of a fact that might prove to be of scientific interest.

"I'd jest combed it when you come this mornin'. D'ye ever see anythin' like that? How am I goin' to git it down?"

"Very singular," said the Doctor.

"Yes, an' look here! D'ye see the har on the back o'

my hand? That stands up jest the same. Why, Doctor, I feel like a hedgehog! What am I goin' to do?"

"Why, this is really very interesting!" said the Doctor, taking out his note-book. "What is your name?"

"Jim Fenton."

"Age?"

"Thirty or forty—somewhere along there."

"H'm!" exclaimed the Doctor, writing out the whole reply. "Occupation?"

"M.D., three C's, double X., two I's."

"H'm! What do you do?"

"Trap, mostly."

"Religious?"

"When I'm skeered."

"Nativity?"

"Which?"

"What is your parentage? Where were you born?"

"Well, my father was an Englishman, my mother was a Scotchman, I was born in Ireland, raised in Canady, and have lived for ten year in Number Nine."

"How does your head feel now?"

"It feels as if every har was a pin. Do you s'pose it'll strike in?"

The Doctor looked him over as if he were a bullock, and went on with his statistics: "Weight, about two hundred pounds; height, six feet two; temperament, sanguine-bilious."

"Some time when you are in Sevenoaks," said the Doctor, slipping his pencil into its sheath in his note-book, and putting his book in his pocket, "come and see me."

"And stay all night?" inquired Jim, innocently.

"I'd like to see the case again," said Dr. Radcliffe, nodding. "I shall not detain you long. The matter has a certain scientific interest."

"Well, good-by, Doctor," said Jim, holding down his

hair. "I'm off for Number Nine. I'm much obleeged for lettin' me go round with ye; an' I never want to go agin."

Jim went out into the pleasant morning air. The sun had dispelled the light frost of the night, the sky was blue overhead, and the bluebirds, whose first spring notes were as sweet and fresh as the blossoms of the arbutus, were carolling among the maples. Far away to the north he could see the mountain at whose foot his cabin stood, red in the sunshine, save where in the deeper gorges the snow still lingered. Sevenoaks lay at the foot of the hill, on the other hand, and he could see the people passing to and fro along its streets, and, perched upon the hill-side among its trees and gardens, the paradise that wealth had built for Robert Belcher. The first emotion that thrilled him as he emerged from the shadows of misery and mental alienation was that of gratitude. He filled his lungs with the vitalizing air, but expired his long breath with a sigh.

"What bothers me," said Jim to himself, "is, that the Lord lets one set of people that is happy make it so thunderin' rough for another set of people that is onhappy. An' there's another thing that bothers me," he said, continuing his audible cogitations. "How do they 'xpect a feller is goin' to git well, when they put 'im where a well feller'd git sick? I vow I think that poor old creetur that wanted me to kill her is straighter in her brains than anybody I seen on the lot. I couldn't live there a week, an' if I was a hopeless case, an' know'd it, I'd hang myself on a nail."

Jim saw his host across the road, and went over to him. Mr. Buffum had had a hard time with his pipes that morning, and was hoarse and very red in the face.

"Jolly lot you've got over there," said Jim. "If I had sech a family as them, I'd take 'em 'round for a show, and hire Belcher's man to do the talkin'. 'Walk up, gentlemen, walk up, and see how a Christian can treat a feller bein'. Here's a feller that's got sense enough left to think he's in hell. Observe his wickedness, gentlemen, and don't be afraid to use your handkerchers.' "

As Jim talked, he found he was getting angry, and that the refractory hair that covered his poll began to feel hot. It would not do to betray his feelings, so he ended his sally with a huge laugh that had about as much music and heartiness in it as the caw of a crow. Buffum joined him with his wheezy chuckle, but having sense enough to see that Jim had really been pained, he explained that he kept his paupers as well as he could afford to.

"Oh, I know it," said Jim. "If there's anything wrong about it, it don't begin with you, Buffum, nor it don't end with you; but it seems a little rough to a feller like me to see people shut up, an' in the dark, when there's good breathin' an' any amount o' sunshine to be had, free gratis for nothin'."

"Well, they don't know the difference," said Buffum.

"Arter a while, I guess they don't," Jim responded "an', now, what's the damage? for I've got to go 'long."

"I shan't charge you anything," whispered Mr. Buffum. "You haven't said anything about old Tilden, and it's just as well."

Jim winked, nodded, and indicated that he not only understood Mr. Buffum, but would act upon his hint. Then he went into the house, bade good-by to Mr. Buffum's "women," kissed his hand gallantly to the elder Miss Buffum—who declared, in revenge, that she would not help him on with his pack, although she had intended to do so—and, after having gathered his burdens, trudged off northward.

From the time he entered the establishment on the previous evening, he had not caught a glimpse of Harry Benedict. "He's cute," said Jim, "an' jest the little chap for this business." As he came near the stump over the brow of the hill, behind which the poor-house buildings disappeared, he saw first the brim of an old hat, then one eye, then an eager, laughing face, and then the whole trim little figure. The lad was transformed. Jim thought when he saw him first that he was a pretty boy, but there was something about him now that thrilled the woodsman with admiration.

Jim came up to him with, "Mornin,' Harry!" and the mountain that shone so gloriously in the light before him was not more sunny than Jim's face. He sat down behind the stump without removing his pack, and once more had the little fellow in his arms.

"Harry," said Jim, "I've had ye in my arms all night—a little live thing—an' I've be'n a longin' to git at ye agin. If ye want to, very much, you can put yer arms round my neck, an' hug me like a little bar. Thar, that's right, that's right. I shall feel it till I see ye agin. Ye've been thinkin' 'bout what I telled ye last night?"

"Oh yes!" responded the boy eagerly, "all the time."

"Well, now, do you know the days—Sunday, Monday, Tuesday, and the rest of 'em?"

"Yes, sir, all of them."

"Now, remember, to-day is Wednesday. It will be seven days to next Wednesday, then Thursday will be eight, Friday nine, Saturday ten. You always know when Saturday comes, don't ye?"

"Yes, because it's our school holiday," replied Harry.

"Well, then, in ten days—that is, a week from next Saturday—I shall come agin. Saturday night, don't ye go to bed. Leastways, ef ye do, ye must git out of the house afore ten o'clock, and come straight to this old stump. Can ye git away, an' nobody seen ye?"

"Yes, I hope so," replied the boy. "They don't mind anything about us. I could stay out all night, and they wouldn't know where I was."

"Well, that's all right, now. Remember—be jest here with all the clo'es ye've got, at ten o'clock Saturday night—ten days off—cut 'em in a stick every day—the next Saturday after the next one, an' don't git mixed."

The boy assured him that he should make no mistake.

"When I come, I sh'll bring a hoss and wagin. It'll be a stiddy hoss, and I sh'll come here to this stump, an' stop till I seen ye. Then ye'll hold the hoss till I go an' git yer pa, and then we'll wopse 'im up in some blank-its, an' make a clean streak for the woods. It'll be late Sunday mornin' afore anybody knows he's gone, and there won't be no people on the road where we are goin', and ef we're druv into cover, I know where the cover is. Jim Fenton's got friends on the road, and they'll be mum as beetles. Did ye ever seen a beetle, Harry?"

"Yes, sir."

"Well, they work right along and don't say nothin' to nobody, but they keep workin'; an' you an' me has got to be jest like beetles. Remember! an' now git back to Tom Buffum's the best way ye can."

The boy reassured Jim, gave him a kiss, jumped over the fence, and crept along through the bushes toward the house. Jim watched him, wrapped in admiration.

"He's got the ra-al hunter in 'im, jest like his father, but there's more in 'im nor there ever was in his father. I sh'd kinder liked to 'a' knowed his ma," said Jim, as he took up his rifle and started in earnest for his home.

As he plodded along his way, he thought over all the experiences of the morning.

"Any man," said he to himself, "who can string things together in the way Benedict did this mornin' can be cured. Startin' in hell, he was all right, an' every-thing reasomble. The startin' is the principal p'int, an' if I can git 'im to start from Number Nine, I'll fetch 'im round. He never was so much to home as he was in the woods, an' when I git 'im thar, and git 'im fishin' and huntin', and sleepin' on hemlock, an' eatin' venison and corn-dodgers, it'll come to 'im that he's been there afore, and he'll look round to find Abram, an' he won't see 'im, and his craze'll kind o' leak out of 'im afore he knows it."

Jim's theory was his own, but it would be difficult for Dr. Radcliffe, and all his fellow-devotees of science, to controvert it. It contented him, at least; and full of plans and hopes, stimulated by the thought that he had a job on hand that would not only occupy his thoughts, but give exercise to the benevolent impulses of his heart, he pressed on, the miles disappearing behind him and shortening before, as if the ground had been charmed.

He stopped at noon at a settler's lonely house, occupied by Mike Conlin, a friendly Irishman. Jim took the man aside and related his plans. Mike entered at once upon the project with interest and sympathy, and Jim knew that he could trust him wholly. It was arranged that Jim should return to Mike the evening before the proposed descent upon Tom Buffum's establishment, and sleep. The following evening Mike's horse would be placed at Jim's disposal, and he and the Benedicts were to drive through during the night to the point on the river where he would leave his boat. Mike was to find his horse there and take him home.

Having accomplished his business, Jim went on, and before the twilight had deepened into night he found himself briskly paddling up the stream, and at ten o'clock he had drawn his little boat up the beach, and embraced Turk, his faithful dog, whom he had left, not only to take care of his cabin, but to provide for himself. He had already eaten his supper, and five minutes after he entered his cabin he and his dog were snoring side by side in a sleep too profound to be disturbed, even by the trumpet of old Tilden.

CHAPTER V.

IN WHICH JIM ENLARGES HIS ACCOMMODATIONS AND ADOPTS A VIOLENT METHOD OF SECURING BOARDERS.

WHEN Jim Fenton waked from his long and refreshing sleep, after his weary tramp and his row upon the river, the sun was shining brightly, the bluebirds were singing, the partridges were drumming, and a red squirrel, which even Turk would not disturb, was looking for provisions in his cabin, or eyeing him saucily from one of the beams over his head. He lay for a moment, stretching his huge limbs and rubbing his eyes, thinking over what he had undertaken, and exclaiming at last, "Well, Jim, ye've got a big contrack," he jumped up, and, striking a fire, cooked his breakfast.

His first work was to make an addition to his accommodations for lodgers, and he set about it in thorough earnest. Before noon he had stripped bark enough from the trees in his vicinity to cover a building as large as his own. The question with him was whether he should put up an addition to his cabin, or hide a new building somewhere behind the trees in his vicinity. In case of pursuit, his lodgers would need a cover, and this he knew he could not give them in his cabin; for all who were in the habit of visiting the woods were familiar with that structure, and would certainly notice any addition to it, and be curious about it. Twenty rods away there was a thicket of hemlock, and, by removing two or three trees in its centre, he could successfully hide from any but the most inquisitive observation the cabin he proposed to erect. His conclusion was quickly arrived at, and before he slept that night the trees were down, the frame was up, and the bark was gathered. The next day sufficed to make the cabin habitable; but he lingered about the work for several days, putting up various appointments of convenience, building a broad bed of hemlock boughs, so deep and fragrant and inviting, that he wondered he had never undertaken to do as much for himself as he had thus gladly done for others, and making sure that there was no crevice at which the storms of spring and summer could force an entrance.

When he could do no more, he looked it over with approval and said: "Thar! If I'd a done that for Miss Butterworth, I couldn't 'a' done better nor that." Then he went back to his cabin muttering: "I wonder what she'd 'a' said if she'd hearn that little speech o' mine!"

What remained for Jim to do was to make provision to feed his boarders. His trusty rifle stood in the corner of his cabin, and Jim had but to take it in his hand to excite the expectations of his dog, and to receive from him, in language as plain as an eager whine and a wagging tail could express, an offer of assistance. Before night there hung in front of his cabin a buck, dragged with difficulty through the woods from the place where he had shot him. A good part of the following day was spent in cutting from the carcass every ounce of flesh, and packing it into pails, to be stowed in a spring whose water, summer and winter alike, was almost at the freezing-point.

"He'll need a good deal o' lookin' arter, and I shan't hunt much the fust few days," said Jim to himself; "an' as for flour, there's a sack on't, an' as for pertaters, we shan't want many on 'em till they come agin, an' as for salt pork, there's a whole bar'l buried, an' as for the rest, let me alone!"

Jim had put off the removal for ten days, partly to get time for all his preparations, and partly that the rapidly advancing spring might give him warmer weather for the removal of a delicate patient. He found, however, at the conclusion of his labors, that he had two or three spare days on his hands. His mind was too busy and too much excited by his enterprise to permit him to engage in any regular employment, and he roamed around the woods, or sat whittling in the sun, or smoked, or thought of Miss Butterworth. It was strange how, when the business upon his hands was suspended, he went back again and again to his brief interview with that little woman. He thought of her eyes full of tears, of her sympathy with the poor, of her smart and saucy speech when he parted with her, and he said again and again to himself, what he said on that occasion : "She's a genuine creetur'!" and the last time he said it, on the day before his projected expedition, he added: "an' who knows!"

Then a bright idea seized him, and, taking out a huge jack-knife, he went through the hemlocks to his new cabin, and there carved into the slabs of bark that constituted its door the words "Number Ten." This was the crowning grace of that interesting structure. He looked at it close, and then from a distance, and then he went back chuckling to his cabin, to pass his night in dreams of fast driving before the fury of all Sevenoaks, with Phipps and his gray trotters in advance.

Early on Friday morning preceding his proposed descent upon the poor-house, he gave his orders to Turk.

"I'm goin' away, Turk," said he. "I'm goin' away agin. Ye was a good dog when I went away afore, and ye behaved a good deal more like a Christian nor a Turk. Look out for this 'ere cabin, and look out for yerself. I'm a goin' to bring back a sick man, an' a little feller to play with ye. Now, ole feller, won't that be jolly? Ye mustn't make no noise when I come—understand?"

Turk wagged his tail in assent, and Jim departed, believing that his dog had understood every word as completely as if he were a man. "Good-by—here's hopin'," said Jim, waving his hand to Turk as he pushed his boat from the bank, and disappeared down the river. The dog watched him until he passed from sight, and then went back to the cabin to mope away the period of his master's absence.

Jim sat in the stern of his little boat, guiding and propelling it with his paddle. Flocks of ducks rose before him, and swashed down with a fluttering ricochet into the water again, beyond the shot of his rifle. A fish-hawk, perched above his last year's nest, sat on a dead limb and watched him as he glided by. A blue heron rose among the reeds, looked at him quietly, and then hid behind a tree. A muskrat swam shoreward from his track, with only his nose above water. A deer, feeding among the lily-pads, looked up, snorted, and then wheeled and plunged into the woods. All these things he saw, but they made no more impression upon his memory than is left upon the canvas by the projected images of a magic-lantern. His mind was occupied by his scheme, which had never seemed so serious a matter as when he had started upon its fulfilment. All the possibilities of immediate detection and efficient pursuit presented themselves to him. He had no respect for Thomas Buffum, yet there was the thought that he was taking away from him one of the sources of his income. He would not like to have Buffum suppose that he could be guilty of a mean act, or capable of making an ungrateful return for hospitality. Still he did not doubt his own motives, or his ability to do good to Paul Benedict and his boy.

It was nearly ten miles from Jim's cabin, down the winding river, to the point where he was to hide his boat, and take to the road which would lead him to the house of Mike Conlin, half way to Sevenoaks. Remembering before he started that the blind cart-road over which he must bring his patient was obstructed at various points by fallen trees, he brought along his axe, and found himself obliged to spend the whole day on his walk, and in clearing the road for the passage of a wagon. It was six o'clock before he reached Mike's house, the outermost post of the "settlement," which embraced in its definition the presence of women and children.

"Be gorry," said Mike, who had long been looking for him, "I was afeared ye'd gi'en it up. The old horse is ready this two hours. I've took more nor three quarts o' dander out iv 'is hide, and gi'en 'im four quarts o' water and a pail iv oats, an' he'll go."

Mike nodded his head as if he were profoundly sure of it. Jim had used horses in his life, in the old days of lumbering and logging, and was quite at home with them. He had had many a drive with Mike, and knew the animal he would be required to handle—a large, hardy, raw-boned creature, that had endured much in Mike's hands, and was quite equal to the present emergency.

As soon as Jim had eaten his supper, and Mike's wife had put up for him food enough to last him and such accessions to his party as he expected to secure during the night, and supplied him abundantly with wrappings, he went to the stable, mounted the low, strong wagon before which Mike had placed the horse, and with a hearty "Good luck to ye!" from the Irishman ringing in his ears, started on the road to Sevenoaks. This portion of the way was easy. The road was worn somewhat, and moderately well kept; and there was nothing to interfere with the steady jog which measured the distance at the rate of six miles an hour. For three steady hours he went on, the horse no more worried than if he had been standing in the stable. At nine o'clock the lights in the farmers' cottages by the wayside were extinguished, and the families they held were in bed. Then the road began to grow dim, and the sky to become dark. The fickle spring weather gave promise of rain. Jim shuddered at the thought of the exposure to which, in a shower, his delicate friend would be subjected, but thought that if he could but get him to the wagon, and cover him well before its onset, he could shield him from harm.

The town clock was striking ten as he drove up to the stump where he was to meet Benedict's boy. He stopped and whistled. A whistle came back in reply, and a dark little object crept out from behind the stump, and came up to the wagon.

"Harry, how's your pa?" said Jim.

"He's been very bad to-day," said Harry. "He says he's going to Abraham's bosom on a visit, and he's been walking around in his room, and wondering why you don't come for him."

"Who did he say that to?" inquired Jim.

"To me," replied the boy. "And he told me not to speak to Mr. Buffum about it."

Jim breathed a sigh of relief, and saying "All right!" he leaped from the wagon. Then taking out a heavy blanket, he said:

"Now, Harry, you jest stand by the old feller's head till I git back to ye. He's out o' the road, and ye needn't stir if anybody comes along."

Harry went up to the old horse, patted his nose and his breast, and told him he was good. The creature seemed to understand it, and gave him no trouble. Jim then stalked off noiselessly into the darkness, and the boy waited with a trembling and expectant heart.

Jim reached the poor-house, and stood still in the middle of the road between the two establishments. The lights in both had been extinguished, and stillness reigned in that portion occupied by Thomas Buffum and his family. The darkness was so great that Jim could almost feel it. No lights were visible except in the village at the foot of the hill, and these were distant and feeble. Through an open window—left open that the asthmatic keeper of the establishment might be supplied with breath—he heard a stertorous snore. On the other side matters were not so silent. There were groans, and yells, and gabble from the reeking and sleepless patients, who had been penned up for the long and terrible night. Concluding that everything was as safe for his operations as it would become at any time, he slowly felt his way to the door of the ward which held Paul Benedict, and found it fastened on the outside, as he had anticipated. Lifting the bar from the iron arms that held it, and pushing back the bolt, he silently opened the door. Whether the darkness within was greater than that without, or whether the preternaturally quickened ears of the patients detected the manipulations of the fastenings, he did not know, but he was conscious at once that the tumult within was hushed. It was apparent that they had been visited in the night before, and that the accustomed intruder had come on no gentle errand. There was not a sound as Jim felt his way along from stall to stall, sickened almost to retching by the insufferable stench that reached his nostrils and poisoned every inspiration.

On the morning of his previous visit he had taken all the bearings with reference to an expedition in the darkness, and so, feeling his way along the hall, he had little difficulty in finding the cell in which he had left his old friend.

Jim tried the door, but found it locked. His great fear was that the lock would be changed, but it had not been meddled with, and had either been furnished with a new key, or had been locked with a skeleton. He slipped the stolen key in, and the bolt slid back. Opening the outer door, he tried the inner, but the key did not fit the lock. Here was a difficulty not entirely unexpected, but seeming to be insurmountable. He quietly went back to the door of entrance, and as quietly closed it, that no sound of violence might reach and wake the inmates of the house across the road. Then he returned, and whispered in a low voice to the inmate :

"Paul Benedict, give us your benediction."

"Jim," responded the man in a whisper, so light that it could reach no ear but his own.

"Don't make no noise, not even if I sh'd make considable," said Jim.

Then, grasping the bars with both hands, he gave the door a sudden pull, into which he put all the might of his huge frame. A thousand pounds would not have measured it, and the door yielded, not at the bolt, but at the hinges. Screws deeply imbedded were pulled out bodily. A second lighter wrench completed the task, and the door was noiselessly set aside, though Jim was trembling in every muscle.

Benedict stood at the door.

"Here's the robe that Abram sent ye," said Jim, throwing over the poor man's shoulders an ample blanket; and putting one of his large arms around him, he led him shuffling out of the hall, and shut and bolted the door.

He had no sooner done this, than the bedlam inside broke loose. There were yells, and howls, and curses, but Jim did not stop for these. Dizzied with his effort, enveloped in thick darkness, and the wind which preceded the approaching shower blowing a fierce gale, he was obliged to stop a moment to make sure that he was walking in the right direction. He saw the lights of the village, and, finding the road, managed to keep on it until he reached the horse, that had become uneasy under the premonitory tumult of the storm. Lifting Benedict into the wagon as if he had been a child, he wrapped him warmly, and put the boy in behind him, to kneel and see that his father did not fall out. Then he turned the horse around, and started toward Number

Nine. The horse knew the road, and was furnished with keener vision than the man who drove him. Jim was aware of this, and letting the reins lie loose upon his back, the animal struck into a long, swinging trot, in prospect of home and another "pail iv oats."

They had not gone a mile when the gathering tempest came down upon them. It rained in torrents, the lightning illuminated the whole region again and again, and the thunder cracked, and boomed, and rolled off among the woods and hills, as if the day of doom had come.

The war of the elements harmonized strangely with the weird fancies of the weak man who sat at Jim's side. He rode in perfect silence for miles. At last the wind went down, and the rain settled to a steady fall.

"They were pretty angry about my going," said he, feebly.

"Yes," said Jim, "they behaved purty car'less, but I'm too many for 'em."

"Does Father Abraham know I'm coming?" inquired Benedict. "Does he expect me to-night?"

"Yes," responded Jim, "an' he'd 'a' sent afore, but he's jest wore out with company. He's a mighty good-natered man, an' I tell 'im they take the advantage of 'im. But I've posted 'im 'bout ye, and ye're all right."

"Is it very far to the gulf?" inquired Benedict.

"Yes, it's a good deal of a drive, but when ye git there, ye can jest lay right down in the boat, an' go to sleep. I'll wake ye up, ye know, when we run in."

The miles slid behind into the darkness, and, at last, the rain subsiding somewhat, Jim stopped, partly to rest his smoking horse, and partly to feed his half-famished companions. Benedict ate mechanically the food that Jim fished out of the basket with a careful hand, and the boy ate as only boys can eat. Jim himself was hungry, and nearly finished what they left.

At two o'clock in the morning, they descried Mike

Conlin's light, and in ten minutes the reeking horse and the drenched inmates of the wagon drove up to the door Mike was waiting to receive them.

"Mike, this is my particular friend, Benedict. Take 'im in, an' dry 'im. An' this is 'is boy. Toast 'im both sides—brown."

A large, pleasant fire was blazing on Mike's humble hearth, and with sundry cheerful remarks he placed his guests before it, relieving them of their soaked wrappings. Then he went to the stable, and fed and groomed his horse, and returned eagerly, to chat with Jim, who sat steaming before the fire, as if he had just been lifted from a hot bath.

"What place is this, Jim?" said Mr. Benedict.

"This is the half-way house," responded that personage, without looking up.

"Why, this is purgatory, isn't it?" inquired Benedict.

"Yes, Mike is a Catholic, an' all his folks; an' he's got to stay here a good while, an' he's jest settled down an' gone to housekeepin'."

"Is it far to the gulf, now?"

"Twenty mile, and the road is rougher nor a——"

"Ah, it's no twenty mile," responded Mike, "an' the road is jist lovely—jist lovely; an' afore ye start I'm goin' to give ye a drap that'll make ye think so."

They sat a whole hour before the fire, and then Mike mixed the draught he had promised to the poor patient. It was not a heavy one, but, for the time, it lifted the man so far out of his weakness that he could sleep, and the moment his brain felt the stimulus, he dropped into a slumber so profound that when the time of departure came he could not be awakened. As there was no time to be lost, a bed was procured from a spare chamber, with pillows; the wagon was brought to the door, and the man was carried out as unconscious as if he were in his last slumber, and tenderly put to bed in the wagon.

Jim declined the dram that Mike urged upon him, for he had need of all his wits, and slowly walked the horse away on the road to his boat. If Benedict had been wide awake and well, he could not have travelled the road safely faster than a walk; and the sleep, and the bed which it rendered necessary, became the happiest accidents of the journey.

For two long hours the horse plodded along the stony and uneven road, and then the light began to redden in the east, and Jim could see the road sufficiently to increase his speed with safety. It was not until long after the sun had risen that Benedict awoke, and found himself too weak to rise. Jim gave him more food, answered his anxious inquiries in his own way, and managed to keep him upon his bed, from which he constantly tried to rise in response to his wandering impulses. It was nearly noon when they found themselves at the river; and the preparations for embarkation were quickly made. The horse was tied and fed, the wagon unfastened, and the whole establishment was left for Mike to reclaim, according to the arrangement that Jim had made with him.

The woodsman saw that his patient would not be able to sit, and so felt himself compelled to take along the bed. Arranging this with the pillows in the bow of his boat, and placing Benedict upon it, with his boy at his feet, he shoved off, and started up the stream.

After running along against the current for a mile, Benedict, having quietly rested meantime, looked up and said weakly:

"Jim, is this the gulf?"

"Yes," responded Jim, cheerfully. "This is the gulf, and a purty place 'tis too. I've seed a sight o' worser places nor this."

"It's very beautiful," responded Benedict. "We must be getting pretty near."

"It's not very fur now," said Jim.

The poor, wandering mind was trying to realize the heavenly scenes that it believed were about to burst upon its vision. The quiet, sunlit water, the trees still bare but bourgooning, the songs of birds, the blue sky across which fleecy clouds were peacefully floating, the breezes that kissed his fevered cheek, the fragrance of the bordering evergreens, and the electric air that entered his lungs so long accustomed to the poisonous fetor of his cell, were well calculated to foster his delusion, and to fill his soul with a peace to which it had long been a stranger. An exquisite languor stole upon him, and, under the pressure of his long fatigue, his eyelids fell, and he dropped into a quiet slumber.

When the boy saw that his father was asleep, he crept back to Jim and said:

"Mr. Fenton, I don't think it's right for you to tell papa such lies."

"Call me Jim. The Doctor called me 'Mr. Fenton,' and it 'most killed me."

"Well, Jim."

"Now, that sounds like it. You jest look a-here, my boy. Your pa ain't livin' in this world now, an' what's true to him is a lie to us, and what's true to us is a lie to him. I jest go into his world and say what's true whar he lives. Isn't that right?"

This vein of casuistry was new to the boy, and he was staggered.

"When your pa gits well agin, an' here's hopin', Jim Fenton an' he will be together in their brains, ye know, and then they won't be talkin' like a couple of jay-birds, and I won't lie to him no more nor I would to you."

The lad's troubled mind was satisfied, and he crept back to his father's feet, where he lay until he discovered Turk, whining and wagging his tail in front of the little hillock that was crowned by Jim's cabin.

The long, hard, weird journey was at an end. The boat came up broadside to the shore, and Jim leaped out, and showered as many caresses upon his dog as he received from the faithful brute.

CHAPTER VI.

IN WHICH SEVENOAKS EXPERIENCES A GREAT COMMOTION, AND COMES TO THE CONCLUSION THAT BENEDICT HAS MET WITH FOUL PLAY.

THOMAS BUFFUM and his family slept late on Sunday morning, and the operating forces of the establishment lingered in their beds. When, at last, the latter rose and opened the doors of the dormitories, the escape of Benedict was detected. Mr. Buffum was summoned at once, and hastened across the street in his shirt-sleeves, which, by the way, was about as far toward full dress as he ever went when the weather did not compel him to wear a coat. Buffum examined the inner door and saw that it had been forced by a tremendous exercise of muscular power. He remembered the loss of the key, and knew that some one had assisted in the operation.

"Where's that boy?" wheezed the keeper.

An attendant rushed to the room where the boy usually slept, and came back with the report that the bed had not been occupied. Then there was a search outside for tracks, but the rain had obliterated them all. The keeper was in despair. He did not believe that Benedict could have survived the storm of the night, and he did not doubt that the boy had undertaken to hide his father somewhere.

"Go out, all of you, all round, and find 'em,"

hoarsely whispered Mr. Buffum, "and bring 'em back, and say nothing about it."

The men, including several of the more reliable paupers, divided themselves into little squads, and departed without breakfast, in order to get back before the farmers should drive by on their way to church. The orchards, the woods, the thickets—all possible covers—were searched, and searched, of course, in vain. One by one the parties returned to report that they could not find the slightest sign of the fugitives.

Mr. Buffum, who had not a question that the little boy had planned and executed the escape, assisted by the paroxysmal strength of his insane father, felt that he was seriously compromised. The flight and undoubted death of old Tilden were too fresh in the public mind to permit this new reflection upon his faithfulness and efficiency as a public guardian to pass without a popular tumult. He had but just assumed the charge of the establishment for another year, and he knew that Robert Belcher would be seriously offended, for more reasons than the public knew, or than that person would be willing to confess. He had never in his life been in more serious trouble. He hardly tasted his breakfast, and was too crusty and cross to be safely addressed by any member of his family. Personally he was not in a condition to range the fields, and when he had received the reports of the parties who had made the search, he felt that he had a job to undertake too serious for his single handling.

In the meantime, Mr. Belcher had risen at his leisure, in blissful unconsciousness of the calamities that had befallen his *protégé*. He owned a pew in every church in Sevenoaks, and boasted that he had no preferences. Once every Sunday he went to one of these churches; and there was a fine flutter throughout the building whenever he and his family appeared. He felt that the building had received a special honor from his visit; but if he was not guided by his preferences, he certainly was by his animosities. If for three or four Sabbaths in succession he honored a single church by his presence, it was usually to pay off a grudge against some minister or member of another flock. He delighted to excite the suspicion that he had at last become attached to one clergyman, and that the other churches were in danger of being forsaken by him. It would be painful to paint the popular weakness and the ministerial jealousy—painful to describe the lack of Christian dignity—with which these demonstrations of worldly caprice and arrogance were watched by pastor and flock.

After the town-meeting and the demonstration of the Rev. Solomon Snow, it was not expected that Mr. Belcher would visit the church of the latter for some months. During the first Sabbath after this event, there was gloom in that clergyman's congregation; for Mr. Belcher, in his routine, should have illuminated their public services by his presence, but he did not appear.

"This comes," bitterly complained one of the deacons, "of a minister's meddling with public affairs."

But during the week following, Mr. Belcher had had a satisfactory interview with Mr. Snow, and on the morning of the flight of Benedict he drove in the carriage with his family up to the door of that gentleman's church, and gratified the congregation and its reverend head by walking up the broad aisle, and, with his richly dressed flock, taking his old seat.

As he looked around upon the humbler parishioners, he seemed to say, by his patronizing smile: "Mr. Snow and the great proprietor are at peace. Make yourselves easy, and enjoy your sunshine while it lasts."

Mr. Buffum never went to church. He had a theory that it was necessary for him to remain in charge of his establishment, and that he was doing a good thing by sending his servants and dependents. When, therefore, he entered Mr. Snow's church on the Sunday morning which found Mr. Belcher comfortably seated there, and stumped up the broad aisle in his shirt-sleeves, the amazement of the minister and the congregation may be imagined. If he had been one of his own insane paupers *en deshabille* he could not have excited more astonishment or more consternation.

Mr. Snow stopped in the middle of a stanza of the first hymn, as if the words had dried upon his tongue. Everything seemed to stop. Of this, however, Mr. Buffum was ignorant. He had no sense of the proprieties of the house, and was intent only on reaching Mr. Belcher's pew.

Bending to his patron's ear, he whispered a few words, received a few words in return, and then retired. The proprietor's face was red with rage and mortification, but he tried to appear unconcerned, and the services went on to their conclusion. Boys who sat near the windows stretched their necks to see whether smoke was issuing from the poor-house; and it is to be feared that the ministrations of the morning were not particularly edifying to the congregation at large. Even Mr. Snow lost his place in his sermon more frequently than usual. When the meeting was dismissed, a hundred heads came together in chattering surmise, and when they walked into the streets, the report of Benedict's escape with his little boy met them. They understood too, why Buffum had come to Mr. Belcher with his trouble. He was Mr. Belcher's man, and Mr. Belcher had publicly assumed responsibility for him.

No more meetings were held in any of the churches of Sevenoaks that day. The ministers came to perform the services of the afternoon, and, finding their pews empty, went home. A reward of one hundred dollars.

offered by Mr. Belcher to any one who would find Benedict and his boy, "and return them in safety to the home provided for them by the town," was a sufficient apology, without the motives of curiosity and humanity and the excitement of a search in the fields and woods, for a universal relinquishment of Sunday habits, and the pouring out of the whole population on an expedition of discovery.

Sevenoaks and its whole vicinity presented a strange aspect that afternoon. There had slept in the hearts of the people a pleasant and sympathetic memory of Mr. Benedict. They had seen him struggling, dreaming, hopeful, yet always disappointed, dropping lower and lower into poverty, and, at last, under accumulated trials, deprived of his reason. They knew but little of his relations to Mr. Belcher, but they had a strong suspicion that he had been badly treated by the proprietor, and that it had been in the power of the latter to save him from wreck. So, when it became known that he had escaped with his boy from the poor-house, and that both had been exposed to the storm of the previous night, they all—men and boys—covered the fields, and filled the woods for miles around, in a search so minute that hardly a rod of cover was left unexplored.

It was a strange excitement which stirred the women at home, as well as the men afield. Nothing was thought of but the fugitives and the pursuit.

Robert Belcher, in the character of principal citizen, was riding back and forth behind his gray trotters, and stimulating the search in every quarter. Poor Miss Butterworth sat at her window, making indiscriminate inquiries of every passenger, or going about from house to house, working off her nervous anxiety in meaningless activities.

As the various squads became tired by their long and unsuccessful search, they went to the poor-house to report, and, before sunset, the hill was covered by hundreds of weary and excited men. Some were sure they had discovered traces of the fugitives. Others expressed the conviction that they had thrown themselves into a well. One man, who did not love Mr. Belcher, and had heard the stories of his ill-treatment of Benedict, breathed the suspicion that both he and his boy had been foully dealt with by one who had an interest in getting them out of the way.

It was a marvel to see how quickly this suspicion took wing. It seemed to be the most rational theory of the event. It went from mouth to mouth and ear to ear, as the wind breathes among the leaves of a forest; but there were reasons in every man's mind, or instincts in his nature, that withheld the word "murder" from the ear of Mr. Belcher. As soon as the suspicion became general, the aspect of every incident of the flight changed. Then they saw, apparently for the first time, that a man weakened by disease and long confinement, and never muscular at his best, could not have forced the inner door of Benedict's cell. Then they connected Mr. Belcher's behavior during the day with the affair, and, though they said nothing at the time, they thought of his ostentatious anxiety, his evident perturbation when Mr. Buffum announced to him the escape, his offer of the reward for Benedict's discovery, and his excited personal appearance among them. He acted like a guilty man—a man who was trying to blind them, and divert suspicion from himself.

To the great horror of Mr. Buffum, his establishment was thoroughly inspected and ransacked, and, as one after another left the hill for his home, he went with indignation and shame in his heart, and curses on his lips. Even if Benedict and his innocent boy had been murdered, murder was not the only foul deed that had been committed on the hill. The poor-house itself was an embodied crime against humanity and against Christianity, for which the town of Sevenoaks at large was responsible, though it had been covered from their sight by Mr. Belcher and the keeper. It would have taken but a spark to kindle a conflagration. Such was the excitement that only a leader was needed to bring the tumult of a violent mob around the heads of the proprietor and his *protégé*.

Mr. Belcher was not a fool, and he detected, as he sat in his wagon talking with Buffum in a low tone, the change that had come over the excited groups around him. They looked at him as they talked, with a serious scrutiny to which he was unused. They no more addressed him with suggestions and inquiries. They shunned his neighborhood, and silently went off down the hill. He knew, as well as if they had been spoken, that there were not only suspicions against him, but indignation over the state of things that had been discovered in the establishment, for whose keeper he had voluntarily become responsible. Notwithstanding all his efforts to assist them in their search, he knew that in their hearts they charged him with Benedict's disappearance. At last he bade Buffum good-night, and went down the hill to his home.

He had no badinage for Phipps during that drive, and no pleasant reveries in his library during that evening, for all the possibilities of the future passed through his mind in dark review. If Benedict had been murdered, who could have any interest in his death but himself? If he had died from exposure, his secrets would be safe, but the charge of his death would be brought to his door, as Miss Butterworth had already brought the responsibility for his insanity there. If he had got away alive, and should recover, or if his boy should get into hands that would ultimately claim for him his rights, then his prosperity would be interfered with. He did not wish to acknowledge to himself that he desired the poor man's death, but he was aware that in his death he found the most hopeful vision of the night. Angry with the public feeling that accused him of a crime of which he was not guilty, and guilty of a crime of which definitely the public knew little or nothing, there was no man in Sevenoaks so unhappy as he. He loved power and popularity. He had been happy in the thought that he controlled the town, and for the moment, at least, he knew the town had slipped disloyally out of his hands.

An impromptu meeting of citizens was held that evening, at which Mr. Belcher did not assist. The clergymen were all present, and there seemed to be a general understanding that they had been ruled long enough in the interest and by the will of a single man. A subscription was raised for a large amount, and the sum offered to any one who would discover the fugitives.

The next morning Mr. Belcher found the village quiet and very reticent, and having learned that a subscription had been raised without calling upon him, he laughingly expressed his determination to win the reward for himself.

Then he turned his grays up the hill, had a long consultation with Mr. Buffum, who informed him of the fate of old Tilden, and started at a rapid pace toward Number Nine.

CHAPTER VII.

IN WHICH JIM AND MIKE CONLIN PASS THROUGH A GREAT TRIAL AND COME OUT VICTORIOUS.

"THERE, Turk, there they be!" said Jim to his dog, pointing to his passengers, as he stood caressing him, with one foot on the land and the other holding the boat to the shore. "There's the little chap that I've brung to play with ye, an' there's the sick man that we've got to take care on. Now don't ye make no row."

Turk looked up into his master's face, then surveyed the new-comers with a wag of his tail that had all the force of a welcome, and, when Harry leaped on shore, he smelt him over, licked his hand, and accepted him as a satisfactory companion.

Jim towed his boat around a point into a little cove where there was a beach, and then drew it by a long, strong pull entirely out of the water. Lifting Benedict and carrying him to his own cabin, he left him in charge of Harry and the dog, while he went to make his bed in "Number Ten." His arrangements completed, he transferred his patient to the quarters prepared for him, where, upheld and pillowed by the sweetest couch that weary body ever rested upon, he sank into slumber.

Harry and the dog became inseparable companions at once; and as it was necessary for Jim to watch with Benedict during the night, he had no difficulty in inducing the new friends to occupy his cabin together. The dog understood his responsibility and the lad accepted his protector; and when both had been bountifully fed they went to sleep side by side.

It was, however, a troubled night at Number Ten. The patient's imagination had been excited, his frame had undergone a great fatigue, and the fresh air, no less than the rain that had found its way to his person through all his wrappings, on the previous night, had produced a powerful impression upon his nervous system. It was not strange that the morning found Jim unrefreshed, and his patient in a high, delirious fever.

"Now's the time," said Jim to himself, "when a feller wants some sort o' religion or a woman; an' I hain't got nothin' but a big dog an' a little boy, an' no doctor nearer'n forty mile."

Poor Jim! He did not know that the shock to which he had subjected the enfeebled lunatic was precisely what was needed to rouse every effort of nature to effect a cure. He could not measure the influence of the subtle earth-currents that breathed over him. He did not know that there was better medicine in the pure air, in the balsamic bed, in the broad stillness, in the nourishing food and the careful nursing, than in all the drugs of the world. He did not know that, in order to reach the convalescence for which he so ardently longed, his patient must go down to the very basis of his life, and begin and build up anew; that in changing from an old and worn-out existence to a fresh and healthy one, there must come a point between the two conditions where there would seem to be no life, and where death would appear to be the only natural determination. He was burdened with his responsibility; and only the consciousness that his motives were pure and his patient no more hopeless in his hands than in those from which he had rescued him, strengthened his equanimity and sustained his courage.

As the sun rose, Benedict fell into an uneasy slumber, and, while Jim watched his heavy breathing, the door was noiselessly opened, and Harry and the dog looked in. The hungry look of the lad summoned Jim to new duties, and leaving Harry to watch his father, he went off to prepare a breakfast for his family.

All that day and all the following night Jim's time was so occupied in feeding the well and administering to the sick, that his own sleeplessness began to tell upon him. He who had been accustomed to the sleep of a healthy and active man began to look haggard, and to long for the assistance of a trusty hand. It was with a great, irrepressible shout of gratification that, at the close of the second day, he detected the form of Mike Conlin walking up the path by the side of the river, with a snug pack of provisions upon his back.

Jim pushed his boat from the shore, and ferried Mike over to his cabin. The Irishman had reached the land ing ten miles below to learn that the birch canoe in which he had expected to ascend the river had either been stolen or washed away. He was, therefore, obliged to take the old "tote-road" worn in former years by the lumbermen, at the side of the river, and to reach Jim's camp on foot. He was very tired, but the warmth of his welcome brought a merry twinkle to his eyes and the ready blarney to his tongue.

"Och! divil a bit wud ye be glad to see Mike Conlin if ye knowed he'd come to arrist ye. Jim, ye're me prisoner. Ye've been stalin' a pauper—a pair iv' em, faith—an' ye must answer fur it wid yer life to owld Belcher. Come along wid me. None o' yer nonsinse, or I'll put a windy in ye."

Jim eyed him with a smile, but he knew that no ordinary errand had brought Mike to him so quickly.

"Old Belcher sent ye, did he?" said Jim.

"Be gorry he did, an' I've come to git a reward. Now, if ye'll be dacint, ye shall have part of it."

Although Jim saw that Mike was apparently in sport, he knew that the offer of a cash reward for his own betrayal was indeed a sore temptation to him.

"Did ye tell 'im anything, Mike?" inquired Jim, solemnly.

"Divil a bit."

"An' ye knowed I'd lick ye if ye did. Ye knowed that, didn't ye?"

"I knowed ye'd thry it faithful, an' if ye didn't do it there'd be niver a man to blame but Mike Conlin."

Jim said no more, but went to work and got a bountiful supper for Mike. When he had finished, he took him over to Number Ten, where Harry and Turk were watching. Quietly opening the door of the cabin, he entered. Benedict lay on his bed, his rapt eyes looking up to the roof. His clean-cut, deathly face, his long, tangled locks, and the comfortable appointments about him, were all scanned by Mike, and, without saying a word, both turned and retired.

"Mike," said Jim, as they retraced their way, "that man an' me was like brothers. I found 'im in the devil's own hole, an' any man as comes atween me an' him must look out fur 'imself forever arter. Jim Fenton's a good-natered man when he ain't riled, but he'd sooner fight nor eat when he is. Will ye help me, or won't ye?"

Mike made no reply, but opened his pack and brought out a tumbler of jelly. "There, ye bloody blaggard, wouldn't ye be afther lickin' that now?" said he; and then, as he proceeded to unload the pack, his tongue ran on in comment. (A paper of crackers.) "Mash 'em all to smithereens now. Give it to 'em, Jim." (A roasted chicken.) "Pitch intil the rooster, Jim. Crack every bone in 'is body." (A bottle of brandy.) "Knock the head aff his shoolders and suck 'is blood." (A package of tea.) "Down with the tay! It's insulted ye, Jim." (A piece of maple sugar.) "Och! the owld, brown rascal! ye'll be afther doin' Jim Fenton a bad turn, will ye? Ye'll be brakin' 'is teeth fur 'im." Then followed a plate, cup and saucer, and these were supplemented by an old shirt and various knick-knacks that only a woman would remember in trying to provide for an invalid far away from the conveniences and comforts of home.

Jim watched Mike with tearful eyes, which grew more and more loaded and luminous as the disgorgement of the contents of the pack progressed.

"Mike, will ye forgive me?" said Jim, stretching out his hand. "I was afeared the money'd be too many for ye; but barrin' yer big foot an' the ugly nose that's on ye, ye're an angel."

"Niver ye mind me fut," responded Mike. "Me inimies don't like it, an' they can give a good raison fur it ; an' as fur me nose, it'll look worser nor it does now when Jim Fenton gets a crack at it."

"Mike," said Jim, "ye hurt me. Here's my hand, an' honors are easy."

Mike took the hand without more ado, and then sat back and told Jim all about it.

"Ye see, afther ye wint away that night I jist lay down an' got a bit iv a shnooze, an' in the mornin' I shtarted for me owld horse. It was a big thramp to where ye lift him, and comin' back purty slow, I picked up a few shticks and put intil the wagin for me owld woman—pine knots an' the like o' that. I didn't git home much afore darruk, and me owld horse wasn't more nor in the shtable an' I 'atin' me supper, quiet like, afore Belcher druv up to me house wid his purty man on the seat wid 'im. An' says he : 'Mike Conlin ! Mike Conlin ! Come to the dour wid ye !' So I wint to the dour, an' he says, says he : 'Hev ye seen a crazy old feller wid a b'y ?' An' says I : 'There's no crazy owld feller wid a b'y been by me house in the daytime. If they wint by at all at all, it was when me family was aslape.' Then he got out of his wagin and come in, and he looked 'round in all the corners careless like, and thin he said he wanted to go to the barrun. So he wint to the barrun, and he looked all about purty careful, and he says, says he : 'What ye been doin' wid the owld horse on a Sunday, Mike ?' And says I to him, says I : 'Jist a pickin' up a few shticks for the owld woman.' An' when he come out he see the shticks in the wagin, and he says, says he : 'Mike, if ye'll find these fellers in the woods I'll give ye five hundred dollars.' And says I : 'Squire Belcher,' says I (for I knowed he had a wake shpot in 'im), 'ye are richer nor a king, and Mike Conlin's no betther nor a pauper himself. Give me a hundred dollars,' says I, 'an' I'll thry it.' And be gorry I've got it right there' (slapping his pocket).

'Take along somethin' for 'em to ate,' says he, 'and faith I've done that same and found me min; an' now I'll stay wid ye fur a week an' 'arn me hundred dollars."

The week that Mike promised Jim was like a lifetime. To have some one with him to share his vigils and his responsibility lifted a great burden from his shoulders. But the sick man grew weaker and weaker every day. He was assiduously nursed and literally fed with dainties; but the two men went about their duties with solemn faces, and talked almost in a whisper. Occasionally one of them went out for delicate game, and by alternate watches they managed to get sufficient sleep to recruit their exhausted energies.

One morning, after Mike had been there four or five days, both stood by Benedict's bed, and felt that a crisis was upon him. A great uneasiness had possessed him for some hours, and then he had sunk away into a stupor or a sleep, they could not determine which.

The two men watched him for a while, and then went out and sat down on a log in front of the cabin, and held a consultation.

"Mike," said Jim, "somethin' must be did. We've did our best an' nothin' comes on't; an' Benedict is nearer Abram's bosom nor I ever meant he should come in my time. I ain't no doctor; you ain't no doctor. We've nussed 'im the best we knowed, but I guess he's a goner. It's too thunderin' bad, for I'd set my heart on puttin' 'im through."

"Well," said Mike, "I've got me hundred dollars, and you'll git yer pay in the nixt wurruld."

"I don't want no pay," responded Jim. "An' what do ye know about the next world, any way?"

"The praste says there is one," said Mike.

"The priest be hanged! What does he know about it?"

"That's his business," said Mike. "It's not for the like o' me to answer for the praste."

"Well, I wish he was here, in Number Nine, an' we'd see what we could git out of 'im. I 've got to the eend o' my rope."

The truth was that Jim was becoming religious. When his own strong right hand failed in any enterprise, he always came to a point where the possibilities of a superior wisdom and power dawned upon him. He had never offered a prayer in his life, but the wish for some medium or instrument of intercession was strong within him. At last an idea struck him, and he turned to Mike and told him to go down to his old cabin, and stay there while he sent the boy back to him.

When Harry came up, with an anxious face, Jim took him between his knees.

"Little feller," said he, "I need comfortin'. It's a comfort to have ye here in my arms, an' I don't never want to have you go 'way from me. Your pa is awful sick, and perhaps he ain't never goin' to be no better. The rain and the ride, I'm afeared, was too many fur him; but I've did the best I could, and I meant well to both on ye, an' now I can't do no more, and there ain't no doctor here, an' there ain't no minister. Ye've allers been a pretty good boy, hain't ye? And don't ye s'pose ye can go out here a little ways behind a tree and pray? I'll hold on to the dog; an' it seems to me, if I was the Lord, I sh'd pay 'tention to what a little feller like you was sayin'. There ain't nobody here but you to do it now, ye know. I can nuss your pa and fix his vittles, an' set up with 'im nights, but I can't pray. I wasn't brung up to it. Now, if ye'll do this, I won't ax ye to do nothin' else."

The boy was serious. He looked off with his great black eyes into the woods. He had said his prayers many times when he did not know that he wanted anything. Here was a great emergency, the most terrible that he had ever encountered. He, a child, was the only one who could pray for the life of his father; and the thought of the responsibility, though it was only dimly entertained, or imperfectly grasped, overwhelmed him. His eyes, that had been strained so long, filled with tears, and, bursting into a fit of uncontrollable weeping, he threw his arms around Jim's neck, where he sobbed away his sudden and almost hysterical passion. Then he gently disengaged himself and went away.

Jim took off his cap, and holding fast his uneasy and inquiring dog, bowed his head as if he were in a church. Soon, among the songs of birds that were turning the morning into music, and the flash of waves that ran shoreward before the breeze, and the whisper of the wind among the evergreens, there came to his ear the voice of a child, pleading for his father's life. The tears dropped from his eyes and rolled down upon his beard. There was an element of romantic superstition in the man, of which his request was the offspring, and to which the sound of the child's voice appealed with irresistible power.

When the lad reappeared and approached him, Jim said to himself: "Now, if that won't do it, ther' won't nothin'." Reaching out his arms to Harry, as he came up, he embraced him, and said:

"My boy, ye've did the right thing. It's better nor all the nussin', an' ye must do that every mornin'—every mornin'; an' don't ye take no for an answer. Now, jest go in with me an' see your pa."

Jim would not have been greatly surprised to see the rude little room thronged with angels, but he was astonished, almost to fainting, to see Benedict open his eyes, look about him, then turn his questioning gaze upon him, and recognize him by a faint smile, so like the look of other days, so full of intelligence and peace, that the woodsman dropped upon his knees and hid his face in the blankets. He did not say a word, but leaving the boy passionately kissing his father, he ran to his own cabin.

Seizing Mike by the shoulders, he shook him as if he intended to kill him.

"Mike," said he, "by the great horned spoons, the little fellow has fetched 'im! Git yer pa'tridge-broth and yer brandy quicker'n lightnin'. Don't talk to me no more 'bout yer priest; I've got a trick worth two o' that."

Both men made haste back to Number Ten, where they found their patient quite able to take the nourishment and stimulant they brought, but still unable to speak. He soon sank into a refreshing slumber, and gave signs of mending throughout the day. The men who had watched him with such careful anxiety were full of hope, and gave vent to their lightened spirits in the chaffing which, in their careless hours, had become habitual with them. The boy and the dog rejoiced too in sympathy; and if there had been ten days of storm and gloom, ended by a brilliant outshining sun, the aspect of the camp could not have been more suddenly or happily changed.

Two days and nights passed away, and then Mike declared that he must go home. The patient had spoken, and knew where he was. He only remembered the past as a dream. First, it was dark and long, and full of horror, but at length all had become bright; and Jim was made supremely happy to learn that he had had a vision of the glory toward which he had pretended to conduct him. Of the fatherly breast he had slept upon, of the golden streets through which he had walked, of the river of the water of life, of the shining ones with whom he had strolled in companionship, of the marvellous city which hath foundations, and the ineffable beauty of its Maker and Builder, he could not speak in full, until years had passed away; but out of this lovely dream he had emerged into natural life.

"He's jest been down to the bottom, and started new." That was the sum and substance of Jim's philosophy, and it would be hard for science to supplant it.

"Well," said Jim to Mike, "ye've be'n a godsend. Ye've did more good in a week nor ye'll do agin if ye live a thousand year. Ye've 'arned yer hundred dollars, and ye haven't found no pauper, and ye can tell 'em so. Paul Benedict ain't no pauper, an' he ain't no crazy man either."

"Be gorry ye're right!" said Mike, who was greatly relieved at finding his report shaped for him in such a way that he would not be obliged to tell a falsehood.

"An' thank yer old woman for me," said Jim, "an' tell her she's the queen of the huckleberry bushes, an' a jewel to the side o' the road she lives on."

"Divil a bit will I do it," responded Mike. "She'l be so grand I can't live wid her."

"An' tell her when ye've had yer quarrel," said Jim, "that there'll allers be a place for her in Number Ten."

They chaffed one another until Mike passed out of sight among the trees; and Jim, notwithstanding his new society, felt lonelier, as he turned back to his cabin, than he had ever felt when there was no human being within twenty miles of him.

The sun of early May had begun to shine brightly, the willows were growing green by the side of the river, the resinous buds were swelling daily, and making ready to burst into foliage, the birds returned one after another from their winter journeyings, and the thrushes filled the mornings and the evenings alike with their carollings. Spring had come to the woods again, with words of promise and wings of fulfilment, and Jim's heart was full of tender gladness. He had gratified his benevolent impulses, and he found upon his hands that which would tax their abounding energies. Life had never seemed to him so full of significance as it did then. He could see what he had been saving money for, and he felt that out of the service he was rendering to the poor and the distressed was growing a love for them that gave a new and almost divine flavor to his existence.

Benedict mended slowly, but he mended daily, and gave promise of the permanent recovery of a healthy body and a sound mind. It was a happy day for Jim when, with Harry and the dog bounding before him, and Benedict leaning on his arm, he walked over to his old cabin, and all ate together at his own rude table. Jim never encouraged his friend's questions. He endeavored, by every practical way, to restrain his mind from wandering into the past, and encouraged him to associate his future with his present society and surroundings. The stronger the patient grew, the more willing he became to shut out the past, which, as memory sometimes—nay, too often—recalled it, was an unbroken history of trial, disappointment, grief, despair, and dreams of great darkness.

There was one man whom he could never think of without a shudder, and with that man his possible outside life was inseparably associated. Mr. Belcher had always been able, by his command of money and his coarse and despotic will, to compel him into any course or transaction that he desired. His nature was offensive to Benedict to an extreme degree, and when in his presence particularly when he entered it driven by necessity, he felt shorn of his own manhood. He felt him to be without conscience, without principle, without humanity, and was sure that it needed only to be known that the insane pauper had become a sound and healthy man to make him the subject of a series of persecutions or persuasions that would wrest from him the rights and values on which the great proprietor was foully battening. These rights and values he never intended to surrender, and until he was strong and independent enough to secure them to himself, he did not care to expose his gentler will to the machinations of the great scoundrel who had thrived upon his unrewarded genius.

So, by degrees, he came to look upon the woods as his home. He was there at peace. His wife had faded out of the world, his life had been a fatal struggle with the grossest selfishness, he had come out of the shadows into a new life, and in that life's simple conditions, cared for by Jim's strong arms, and upheld by his manly and cheerful companionship, he intended to build safely the structure of his health, and to erect on the foundation of a useful experience a better life.

In June, Jim did his planting, confined almost entirely to vegetables, as there was no mill near enough to grind his wheat and corn should he succeed in growing them. By the time the young plants were ready for dressing, Benedict could assist Jim for an hour every day; and when the autumn came, the invalid of Number Ten had become a heavicr man than he ever was before. Through the disguisc of rags, the sun-browned features, the heavy beard, and the generous and almost stalwart figure, his old and most intimate friends would have failed to recognize the delicate and attenuated man they had once known. Jim regarded him with great pride, and almost with awe. He delighted to hear him talk, for he was full of information and overflowing with suggestion.

"Mr. Benedict," said Jim one day, after they had indulged in one of their long talks, "do ye s'pose ye can make a house?"

"Anything."

"A raal house, all ship-shape for a woman to live in?"

"Anything."

"With a little stoop, an' a bureau, an' some chairs, an' a frame, like, fur posies to run up on?"

"Yes, Jim, and a thousand things you never thought of."

Jim did not pursue the conversation further, but went down very deep into a brown study.

During September, he was in the habit of receiving the visits of sportsmen, one of whom, a New York lawyer, who bore the name of Balfour, had come into the woods every year for several successive years. He became aware that his supplies were running low, and that not only was it necessary to lay in a winter's stock of flour and pork, but that his helpless *protégés* should be supplied with clothing for the coming cold weather. Benedict had become quite able to take care of himself and his boy; so one day Jim, having furnished himself with a supply of money from his long accumulated hoard, went off down the river for a week's absence.

He had a long consultation with Mike Conlin, who agreed to draw his lumber to the river whenever he should see fit to begin his enterprise. He had taken along a list of tools, furnished him by Benedict; and Mike carried him to Sevenoaks with the purpose of taking back whatever, in the way of stores, they should purchase. Jim was full of reminiscences of his night's drive, and pointed out to Mike all the localities of his great enterprise. Things had undergone a transformation about the poor-house, and Jim stopped and inquired tenderly for Tom Buffum, and learned that soon after the escape of Benedict the man had gone off in an apoplectic fit.

"He was a pertickler friend o' mine," said Jim, smiling in the face of the new occupant, "an' I'm glad he went off so quick he didn't know where he was goin' Left some rocks, didn't he?"

The man having replied to Jim's tender solicitude, that he believed the family were sufficiently well provided for, the precious pair of sympathizers went off down the hill.

Jim and Mike had a busy day in Sevenoaks, and at about eight o'clock in the evening, Miss Keziah Butterworth was surprised in her room by the announcement that there was a strange man down-stairs who desired to see her. As she entered the parlor of the little house, she saw a tall man standing upright in the middle of the room, with his fur cap in his hand, and a huge roll of cloth under his arm.

"Miss Butterworth, how fare ye?" said Jim.

"I remember you," said Miss Butterworth, peering up into his face to read his features in the dim light. "You are Jim Fenton, whom I met last spring at the town-meeting."

"I knowed you'd remember me. Women allers does. Be'n purty chirk this summer?"

"Very well, I thank you, sir," and Miss Butterworth dropped a courtesy, and then, sitting down, she pointed him to a chair.

Jim laid his cap on the floor, placed his roll of cloth upright between his knees, and, pulling out his bandanna handkerchief, wiped his perspiring face.

"I've brung a little job fur ye," said Jim.

"Oh, I can't do it," said Miss Butterworth at once. "I'm crowded to death with work. It's a hurrying time of year."

"Yes, I knowed that, but this is a pertickler job."

"Oh, they are all particular jobs," responded Miss Butterworth, shaking her head.

"But this is a job fur pertickler folks."

"Folks are all alike to me," said Miss Butterworth, sharply.

"These clo'es," said Jim, "are fur a good man an' a

little boy. They has nothin' but rags on 'em, an' won't have till ye make these clo'es. The man is a pertickler friend o' mine, an' the boy is a cute little chap, an' he can pray better nor any minister in Sevenoaks. If you knowed what I know, Miss Butterworth, I don't know but you'd do somethin' that you'd be ashamed of, an' I don't know but you'd do something that I sh'd be ashamed of. Strange things has happened, an' if ye want to know what they be, you must make these clo'es."

Jim had aimed straight at one of the most powerful motives in human nature, and the woman began to relent, and to talk more as if it were possible for her to undertake the job.

"It may be," said the tailoress, thinking, and scratching the top of her head with a hair-pin, "that I *can* work it in; but I haven't the measure."

"Well, now, let's see," said Jim, pondering. "Whar is they about such a man? Don't ye remember a man that used to be here by the name of—of—Benedict, wasn't it?—a feller about up to my ear—only fleshier nor he was? An' the little feller—well, he's bigger nor Benedict's boy—bigger, leastways, nor he was then."

Miss Butterworth rose to her feet, went up to Jim, and looked him sharply in the eyes.

"Can you tell me anything about Benedict and his boy?"

"All that any feller knows I know," said Jim, "an' I've never telled nobody in Sevenoaks."

"Jim Fenton, you needn't be afraid of me."

"Oh, I ain't. I like ye better nor any woman I seen."

"But you needn't be afraid to tell me," said Miss Butterworth, blushing.

"An' will ye make the clo'es?"

"Yes, I'll make the clothes, if I make them for nothing, and sit up nights to do it."

"Give us your hand," said Jim, and he had a woman's hand in his own almost before he knew it, and his face grew crimson to the roots of his bushy hair.

Miss Butterworth drew her chair up to his, and in a low tone he told her the whole long story as only he knew it, and only he could tell it.

"I think you are the noblest man I ever saw," said Miss Butterworth, trembling with excitement.

"Well, turn about's fa'r play, they say, an' I think you're the most genuine creetur' I ever seen," responded Jim. "All we want up in the woods now is a woman, an' I'd sooner have ye thar nor any other."

"Poh! what a spoon you are!" said Miss Butterworth, tossing her head.

"Then there's timber enough in me fur the puttiest kind of a buckle."

"But you're a blockhead—a great, good blockhead. That's just what you are," said Miss Butterworth, laughing in spite of herself.

"Well, ye can whittle any sort of a head out of a block," said Jim imperturbably.

"Let's have done with joking," said the tailoress solemnly.

"I hain't been jokin'," said Jim. "I'm in 'arnest. I been thinkin' o' ye ever sence the town-meetin'. I been kinder livin' on yer looks. I've dreamt about ye nights; an' when I've be'n helpin' Benedict, I took some o' my pay, thinkin' I was pleasin' ye. I couldn't help hopin'; an' now, when I come to ye so, an' tell ye jest how the land lays, ye git rampageous, or tell me I'm jokin'. 'Twon't be no joke if Jim Fenton goes away from this house feelin' that the only woman he ever seen as he thought was wuth a row o' pins feels herself better nor he is."

Miss Butterworth cast down her eyes, and trotted her knees nervously. She felt that Jim was really in earnest

—that he thoroughly respected her, and that behind his rough exterior there was as true a man as she had ever seen; but the life to which he would introduce her, the gossip to which she would be subjected by any intimate connection with him, and the uprooting of the active social life into which the routine of her daily labor led her, would be a great hardship. Then there was another consideration which weighed heavily with her. In her room were the memorials of an early affection and the disappointment of a life.

"Mr. Fenton," she said, looking up.

"Jest call me Jim."

"Well, Jim," and Miss Butterworth smiled through tearful eyes, "I must tell you that I was once engaged to be married."

"Sho! You don't say!"

"Yes, and I had everything ready."

"Now, you don't tell me!"

"Yes, and the only man I ever loved died—died a week before the day we had set."

"It must have purty near finished ye off."

"Yes, I should have been glad to die myself."

"Well, now, Miss Butterworth, if ye s'pose that Jim Fenton wouldn't bring that man to life if he could, and go to your weddin' singin' hallelujer, you must think he's meaner nor a rat. But ye know he's dead, an' ye never can see him no more. He's a goner, an' ye're all alone, an' here's a man as'll take care on ye fur him; an' it does seem to me that if he was a reasomble man he'd feel obleeged for what I'm doin'."

Miss Butterworth could not help smiling at Jim's earnestness and ingenuity, but his proposition was so sudden and strange, and she had so long ago given up any thought of marrying, that it was impossible for her to give him an answer then, unless she should give him the answer which he deprecated.

"Jim," she said at last, "I believe you are a good man. I believe you are honorable, and that you mean well toward me; but we have been brought up very differently, and the life into which you wish to bring me would be very strange to me. I doubt whether I could be happy in it."

Jim saw that it would not help him to press his suit further at that time, and recognized the reasonableness of her hesitation. He knew he was rough and unused to every sort of refinement, but he also knew that he was truthful, and honorable, and faithful; and, with trust in his own motives, and trust in Miss Butterworth's good sense and discretion, he withheld any further exhibition of his wish to settle the affair on the spot.

"Well, Miss Butterworth," he said, rising, "ye know yer own business, but there'll be a house, an' a stoop, an' a bureau, an' a little ladder for flowers, an' Mike Conlin will draw the lumber, an' Benedict 'll put it together, an' Jim Fenton 'll be the busiest and happiest man in a hundred mile."

As Jim rose, Miss Butterworth also stood up, and looked up into his face. Jim regarded her with tender admiration.

"Do ye know I take to little things wonderful, if they're only alive?" said he. "There's Benedict's little boy! I feel 'im fur hours arter I've had 'im in my arms, jest because he's alive an' little. An' I don't know—I—I vow, I guess I better go away. Can you git the clo'es made in two days, so I can take 'em home with me? Can't ye put 'em out round? I'll pay ye, ye know."

Miss Butterworth thought she could, and on that promise, Jim remained in Sevenoaks.

How he got out of the house he did not remember, but he went away very much exalted. What he did during those two days it did not matter to him, so long as he could walk over to Miss Butterworth's each night, and watch her light from his cover in the trees.

Before the tailoress closed her eyes in sleep that night, her brisk and ready shears had cut the cloth for the two suits at a venture, and in the morning the work was parcelled among her benevolent friends, as a work of charity whose objects were not to be mentioned.

When Jim called for the clothes, they were done, and there was no money to be paid for the labor. The statement of the fact embarrassed Jim more than anything that had occurred in his interviews with the tailoress.

"I sh'll pay ye some time, even if so be that nothin' happens," said he; "an' if so be that somethin' does happen, it'll be squar' any way. I don't want no man that I do fur to be beholden to workin' women for their clo'es."

Jim took the big bundle under his left arm, and, extending his right hand, he took Miss Butterworth's, and said: "Good-by, little woman; I sh'll see ye agin' an' here's hopin'. Don't hurt yerself, and think as well of me as ye can. I hate to go away an' leave every thing loose like, but I s'pose I must. Yes, I don't like to go away so"—and Jim shook his head tenderly—"an' arter I go ye mustn't kick a stone on the road or scare a bird in the trees, for fear it'll be the heart that Jim Fenton leaves behind him."

Jim departed, and Miss Butterworth went up to her room, her eyes moist with the effect of the unconscious poetry of his closing utterance.

It was still early in the evening when Jim reached the hotel, and he had hardly mounted the steps when the stage drove up, and Mr. Balfour, encumbered with a gun, all sorts of fishing-tackle and a lad of twelve years, leaped out. He was on his annual vacation; and with all the hilarity and heartiness of a boy let loose from school greeted Jim, whose irresistibly broad smile was full of welcome.

It was quickly arranged that Jim and Mike should go on that night with their load of stores; that Mr. Balfour and his boy should follow in the morning with a team to be hired for the occasion, and that Jim, reaching home first, should return and meet his guests with his boat at the landing.

CHAPTER VIII.

IN WHICH MR. BELCHER VISITS NEW YORK, AND BECOMES THE PROPRIETOR OF "PALGRAVE'S FOLLY."

THE shadow of a mystery hung over Sevenoaks for many months. Handbills advertising the fugitives were posted in all directions throughout the country, but nothing came of them but rumors. The newspapers, far and near, told the story, but it resulted in nothing save such an airing of the Sevenoaks poor-house, and the county establishment connected with the same, that Tom Buffum, who had lived for several years on the border-land of apoplexy, passed suddenly over, and went so far that he never returned to meet the official inquiry into his administration. The Augean stables were cleansed by the Hercules of public opinion; and with the satisfied conscience and restored self-complacency procured by this act, the people at last settled down upon the conviction that Benedict and his boy had shared the fate of old Tilden—that they had lost themselves in the distant forest, and met their death alike beyond help and discovery.

Mr. Belcher found himself without influence in the adjustment of the new administration. Sevenoaks turned the cold shoulder to him. Nobody went to him with the reports that connected him with the flight and fate of the crazed inventor, yet he knew, through instincts which men of his nature often possess in a remarkable degree, that he was deeply blamed for the causes of Benedict's misfortunes. It has already been hinted that at first he was suspected of knowing guiltily more about the disappearance of the fugitives than he would be willing to tell, but there were only a few minds in which the suspicion was long permitted to linger. When the first excitement passed away and men began to think, it was impossible for them to imagine motives sufficiently powerful to induce the rich proprietor to pursue a lunatic pauper to his death.

Mr. Belcher never had encouraged the neighborly approaches which, in an emergency like this, might have given him comfort and companionship. Recognizing no equals in Sevenoaks—measuring his own social position by the depth of his purse and the reach of his power—he had been in the habit of dispensing his society as largess to the humble villagers. To recognize a man upon the street, and speak to him in a familiar way, was to him like the opening of his purse and throwing the surprise of a dollar into a beggar's hat. His courtesies were charities; his politeness was a boon; he tossed his jokes into a crowd of dirty employes as he would toss a handful of silver coin. Up to this time he had been sufficient unto himself. By money, by petty revenges, by personal assumption, he had managed to retain his throne for a long decade; and when he found his power partly ignored and partly defied, and learned that his personal courtesies were not accepted at their old value, he not only began to feel lonesome, but he grew angry. He held hot discussions with his image in the mirror night after night, in his lonely library, where a certain measure which had once seemed a distant possibility took shape more and more as a purpose. In some way he would revenge himself upon the people of the town. Even at a personal sacrifice, he would pay them off for their slight upon him ; and he knew there was no way in which he could so effectually do this as by leaving them. He had dreamed many times, as he rapidly accumulated his wealth, of arriving at a point where he could treat his splendid home as a summer resort, and take up his residence in the great city among those of his own kind. He had an uneasy desire for the splendors of city life, yet his interests had always held him to Sevenoaks, and he had contented himself there simply because he had his own way, and was accounted "the principal citizen." His village splendors were without competition. His will was law. His self-complacency, fed and flourishing in his country home, had taken the place of society ; but this had ceased to be all-sufficient, even before the change occurred in the atmosphere around him.

It was six months after the reader's first introduction to him that, showily dressed as he always was, he took his place before his mirror for a conversation with the striking-looking person whom he saw reflected there.

"Robert Belcher, Esquire," said he, "are you played out? Who says played out? Did you address that question to me, sir? Am I the subject of that insulting remark? Do you dare to beard the lion in his den? Withdraw the dagger that you have aimed at my breast, or I will not hold myself responsible for the consequences. Played out, with a million dollars in your pocket? Played out, with wealth pouring in in mighty waves? Whose name is Norval still? Whose are these Grampian Hills? In yonder silent heavens the stars still shine, printing on boundless space the words of golden promise. Will you leave Sevenoaks? Will you go to yonder metropolis, and there reap, in honor and pleasure, the rewards of your enterprise? Will you leave Sevenoaks howling in pain? Will you leave these scurvy ministers to whine for their salaries and whine to empty air? Ye fresh fields and pastures new, I yield, I go, I reside! I spurn the dust of Sevenoaks from my feet. I hail the glories of the distant mart. I make my bow to you, sir. You ask my pardon? It is well! Go!"

The next morning, after a long examination of his affairs, in conference with his confidential agent, and the announcement to Mrs. Belcher that he was about to start for New York on business, Phipps took him and his trunk on a drive of twenty miles, to the northern terminus of a railroad line which, with its connections, would bear him to the city of his hopes.

It is astonishing how much room a richly dressed snob can occupy in a railway car without receiving a request to occupy less, or endangering the welfare of his arrogant eyes. Mr. Belcher occupied always two seats, and usually four. It was pitiful to see feeble women look at his abounding supply, then look at him, and then pass on. It was pitiful to see humbly dressed men do the same. It was pitiful to see gentlemen put themselves to inconvenience rather than dispute with him his right to all the space he could cover with his luggage and his feet. Mr. Belcher watched all these exhibitions with supreme satisfaction. They were a tribute to his commanding personal appearance. Even the conductors recognized the manner of man with whom they had to deal, and shunned him. He not only got the worth of his money in his ride, but the worth of the money of several other people.

Arriving at New York, he went directly to the Astor, then the leading hotel of the city. The clerk not only knew the kind of man who stood before him recording his name, but he knew him; and while he assigned to his betters, men and women, rooms at the top of the house, Mr. Belcher secured, without difficulty, a parlor and bedroom on the second floor. The arrogant snob was not only at a premium on the railway train, but at the hotel. When he swaggered into the dining-room, the head waiter took his measure instinctively, and placed him as a figure-head at the top of the hall, where he easily won to himself the most careful and obsequious service, the choicest viands, and a large degree of quiet observation from the curious guests. In the office, waiters ran for him, hackmen took off their hats to him, his cards were delivered with great promptitude, and even the courtly principal deigned to inquire whether he found everything to his mind. In short, Mr. Belcher seemed to find that his name was as distinctly "Norval" in New York as in Sevenoaks, and that his "Grampian Hills" were movable eminences that stood around and smiled upon him wherever he went.

Retiring to his room to enjoy in quiet his morning cigar and to look over the papers, his eye was attracted, among the "personals," to an item which read as follows:

"Col. Robert Belcher, the rich and well-known manufacturer of Sevenoaks, and the maker of the celebrated Belcher rifle, has arrived in town, and occupies a suite of apartments at the Astor."

His title, he was aware, had been manufactured, in order to give the highest significance to the item, by the enterprising reporter, but it pleased him. The reporter, associating his name with fire-arms, had chosen a military title, in accordance with the custom which makes "commodores" of enterprising landsmen who build and manage lines of marine transportation and travel, and "bosses" of men who control election gangs, employed to dig the dirty channels to political success.

He read it again and again, and smoked, and walked to his glass, and coddled himself with complacent fancies. He felt that all doors opened themselves widely to the man who had money, and the skill to carry it in his own magnificent way. In the midst of pleasant thoughts, there came a rap at the door, and he received from the waiter's little salver the card of his factor, "Mr. Benjamin Talbot." Mr. Talbot had read the "personal" which had so attracted and delighted himself, and had made haste to pay his respects to the principal from whose productions he was coining a fortune.

Mr. Talbot was the man of all others whom Mr. Belcher desired to see; so, with a glance at the card, he told the waiter promptly to show the gentleman up.

No man in the world understood Mr. Belcher better than the quick-witted and obsequious factor. He had been in the habit, during the ten years in which he had handled Mr. Belcher's goods, of devoting his whole time to the proprietor while that person was on his stated visits to the city. He took him to his club to dine; he introduced him to congenial spirits; he went to the theatre with him; he went with him to grosser resorts, which do not need to be named in these pages; he drove with him to the races; he took him to lunch at suburban hotels, frequented by fast men who drove fast horses; he ministered to every coarse taste and vulgar desire possessed by the man whose nature and graceless caprices he so carefully studied. He did all this at his own expense, and at the same time he kept his principal out of the clutches of gamblers and sharpers. It was for his interest to be of actual use to the man whose desires he aimed to gratify, and so to guard and shadow him that no deep harm would come to him. It was for his interest to keep Mr. Belcher to himself, while he gave him the gratifications that a coarse man living in the country so naturally seeks among the opportunities and excitements of the city.

There was one thing, however, that Mr. Talbot had never done. He had never taken Mr. Belcher to his home. Mrs. Talbot did not wish to see him, and Mr.

Talbot did not wish to have her see him. He knew that Mr. Belcher, after his business was completed, wanted something besides a quiet dinner with women and children. His leanings were not toward virtue, but toward safe and half-reputable vice; and exactly what he wanted consistent with his safety as a business man, Mr. Talbot wished to give him. To nurse his good-will, to make himself useful, and, as far as possible, essential to the proprietor, and to keep him sound and make him last, was Mr. Talbot's study and his most determined ambition.

Mr. Belcher was seated in a huge arm-chair, with his back to the door and his feet in another chair, when the second rap came, and Mr. Talbot, with a radiant smile, entered.

"Well, Toll, my boy," said the proprietor, keeping his seat without turning, and extending his left hand. "How are you? Glad to see you. Come round to pay your respects to the Colonel, eh? How's business, and how's your folks?"

Mr. Talbot was accustomed to this style of greeting from his principal, and, responding heartily to it and the inquiries accompanying it, he took a seat. With hat and cane in hand he sat on his little chair, showing his handsome teeth, twirling his light mustache, and looking at the proprietor with his keen gray eyes, his whole attitude and physiognomy expressing the words as plainly as if he had spoken them: "I'm your man; now, what are you up to?"

"Toll," said Mr. Belcher deliberately, "I'm going to surprise you."

"You usually do," responded the factor, laughing.

"I vow, I guess that's true! You fellows, without any blood, are apt to get waked up when the old boys come in from the country. Toll, lock the door."

Mr. Talbot locked the door and resumed his seat.

"Sevenoaks be hanged!" said Mr. Belcher.

"Certainly."

"It's a one-horse town."

"Certainly. Still, I have been under the impression that you owned the horse."

"Yes, I know, but the horse is played out."

"Hasn't he been a pretty good horse, and earned you all he cost you?"

"Well, I'm tired with living where there is so much infernal babble and meddling with other people's business. If I sneeze, the people think there's been an earthquake; and when I whistle, they call it a hurricane."

"But you're the king of the roost," said Talbot.

"Yes; but a man gets tired being king of the roost, and longs for some rooster to fight."

Mr. Talbot saw the point toward which Mr. Belcher was drifting, and prepared himself for it. He had measured his chances for losing his business, and when, at last, his principal came out with the frank statement that he had made up his mind to come to New York to live, he was all ready with his overjoyed "No!" and with his smooth little hand to bestow upon Mr. Belcher's heavy fist the expression of his gladness and his congratulations.

"Good thing, isn't it, Toll?"

"Excellent."

"And you'll stand by me, Toll?"

"Of course I will; but we can't do just the old things, you know. We must be highly respectable citizens, and keep ourselves straight."

"Don't you undertake to teach your grandmother how to suck eggs," responded the proprietor with a huge laugh, in which the factor joined. Then he added, thoughtfully: "I haven't said a word to the woman about it, and she may make a fuss; but she knows me pretty well, and there'll be the biggest kind of a row in the town ; but the fact is, Toll, I'm at the end of my rope there. I'm making money hand over hand, and I've nothing to show for it. I've spent about everything I can up there, and nobody sees it. I might just as well be buried ; and if a fellow can't show what he gets, what's the use of having it ? I haven't but one life to live, and I'm going to spread, and I'm going to do it right here in New York ; and if I don't make some of your nabobs open their eyes, my name isn't Robert Belcher."

Mr. Belcher had exposed motives in this little speech that he had not even alluded to in his addresses to his image in the mirror. Talbot saw that something had gone wrong in the town, that he was playing off a bit of revenge, and, above all, that the vulgar desire for display was more prominent among Mr. Belcher's motives for removal than that person suspected.

"I have a few affairs to attend to," said Mr. Talbot, rising, "but after twelve o'clock I will be at your service while you remain in the city. We shall have no difficulty in finding a house to suit you, I am sure, and you can get everything done in the matter of furniture at the shortest notice. I will hunt houses with you for a week, if you wish."

"Well, by-by, Toll," said Mr. Belcher, giving him his left hand again. "I'll be 'round at twelve."

Mr. Talbot went out, but instead of going to his office, went straight home, and surprised Mrs. Talbot by his sudden reappearance.

"What on earth !"—said she, looking up from a bit of embroidery on which she was dawdling away her morning.

"Kate, who do you suppose is coming to New York to live ?"

"The Great Mogul."

"Yes, the Great Mogul—otherwise, Colonel Robert Belcher."

"Heaven help us!" exclaimed the lady.

"Well, and what's to be done?"

"Oh, my! my! my! my!" exclaimed Mrs. Talbot, her possessive pronoun stumbling and fainting away without reaching its object. "*Must* we have that bear in the house? Does it pay?"

"Yes, Kate, it pays," said Mr. Talbot.

"Well, I suppose that settles it."

The factor and his wife were very quick to comprehend the truth that a principal out of town, and away from his wife and family, was a very different person to deal with from one in the town and in the occupation of a grand establishment, with his dependants. They saw that they must make themselves essential to him in the establishment of his social position, and that they must introduce him and his wife to their friends. Moreover, they had heard good reports of Mrs. Belcher, and had the impression that she would be either an inoffensive or a valuable acquisition to their circle of friends.

There was nothing to do, therefore, but to make a dinner-party in Mr. Belcher's honor. The guests were carefully selected, and Mrs. Talbot laid aside her embroidery and wrote her invitations, while Mr. Talbot made his next errand at the office of the leading real estate broker, with whom he concluded a private arrangement to share in the commission of any sale that might be made to the customer whom he proposed to bring to him in the course of the day. Half an hour before twelve, he was in his own office, and in the thirty minutes that lay between his arrival and the visit of the proprietor, he had arranged his affairs for any absence that would be necessary.

When Mr. Belcher came in, looking from side to side, with the air of a man who owned all he saw, even the clerks who respectfully bowed to him as he passed, he found Mr. Talbot waiting ; also, a bunch of the costliest cigars.

" I remembered your weakness, you see," said Talbot.

" Toll, you're a jewel," said Mr. Belcher, drawing out one of the fragrant rolls and lighting it.

"Now, before we go a step," said Talbot, " you must agree to come to my house to-morrow night to dinner, and meet some of my friends. When you come to New York, you'll want to know somebody."

" Toll, I tell you you're a jewel."

" And you'll come ? "

" Well, you know I'm not rigged exactly for that sort of thing, and, faith, I'm not up to it, but I suppose all a man has to do is to put on a stiff upper lip, and take it as it comes."

" I'll risk you anywhere."

" All right ! I'll be there."

" Six o'clock, sharp ; and now let's go and find a broker. I know the best one in the city, and I'll show you the inside of more fine houses before night than you have ever seen."

Talbot took the proprietor's arm and led him to a carriage in waiting. Then he took him to Pine street, and introduced him, in the most deferential manner, to the broker who held half of New York at his disposal, and knew the city as he knew his alphabet.

The broker took the pair of house-hunters to a private room, and unfolded a map of the city before them. On this he traced, with a well-kept finger-nail, a series of lines,—like those fanciful isothermal definitions that embrace the regions of perennial summer on the range of the Northern Pacific Railroad,—within which social respectability made its home. Within certain avenues and certain streets, he explained that it was a respectable thing to live. Outside of these arbitrary boundaries, nobody who made any pretence to respectability should buy a house. The remainder of the city was for the vulgar—craftsmen, petty shopkeepers, salaried men, and the shabby-genteel. He insisted that a wealthy man, making an entrance upon New York life, should be careful to locate himself somewhere upon the charmed territory which he defined. He felt in duty bound to say this to Mr. Belcher, as he was a stranger ; and Mr. Belcher was, of course, grateful for the information.

Then he armed Mr. Talbot, as Mr. Belcher's city friend and helper, with a bundle of permits, with which they set off upon their quest.

They visited a dozen houses in the course of the afternoon, carefully chosen in their succession by Mr. Talbot, who was as sure of Mr. Belcher's tastes as he was of his own. One street was too quiet, one was too dark ; one house was too small, and one was too tame ; one house had no stable, another had too small a stable. At last, they came out upon Fifth Avenue, and drove up to a double front, with a stable almost as ample and as richly appointed as the house itself. It had been built, and occupied for a year or two, by an exploded millionnaire, and was an elephant upon the hands of his creditors. Robert Belcher was happy at once. The marvellous mirrors, the plate glass, the gilded cornices, the grand staircase, the glittering chandeliers, the evidences of lavish expenditure in every fixture and in all the finish, excited him like wine.

"Now you talk!" said he to the smiling factor ; and as he went to the window, and saw the life of the street, rolling by in costly carriages, or sweeping the sidewalks with shining silks and mellow velvets, he felt that he was at home. Here he could see and be seen. Here his splendors could be advertised. Here he could find an expression for his wealth, by the side of which his establishment at Sevenoaks seemed too mean to be thought of without humiliation and disgust. Here was a house that gratified his sensuous nature through and through, and appealed irresistibly to his egregious vanity. He did not know that the grand and gaudy establishment bore the name of "Palgrave's Folly," and, probably, it would have made no difference with him if he had. It suited him, and would, in his hands, become Belcher's Glory.

The sum demanded for the place, though very large, did not cover its original cost, and in this fact Mr. Belcher took great comfort. To enjoy fifty thousand dollars, which somebody else had made, was a charming consideration with him, and one that did much to reconcile him to an expenditure far beyond his original purpose.

When he had finished his examination of the house, he returned to his hotel, as business hours were past, and he could make no further headway that day in his negotiations. The more he thought of the house, the more uneasy he became. Somebody might have seen him looking at it, and so reached the broker first, and snatched it from his grasp. He did not know that it had been in the market for two years, waiting for just such a man as himself.

Talbot was fully aware of the state of Mr. Belcher's mind, and knew that if he did not reach him early the next morning, the proprietor would arrive at the broker's before him. Accordingly, when Mr. Belcher finished his breakfast that morning, he found his factor waiting for him, with the information that the broker would not be in his office for an hour and a half, and that there was time to look further, if further search were desirable. He hoped that Mr. Belcher would not be in a hurry, or take any step that he would ultimately regret. Mr. Belcher assured him that he knew what he wanted when he saw it, and had no fears about the matter, except that somebody might anticipate him.

"You have determined, then, to buy the house at the price?" said Talbot.

"Yes; I shall just shut my eyes and swallow the whole thing."

"Would you like to get it cheaper?"

"Of course!"

"Then, perhaps, you had better leave the talking to me," said Talbot. "These fellows all have a price that they ask, and a smaller one that they will take."

"That's one of the tricks, eh?"

"Yes."

"Then go ahead."

They had a long talk about business, and then Talbot went out, and, after an extended interview with the broker, sent a messenger for Mr. Belcher. When that gentleman came in, he found that Talbot had bought the house for ten thousand dollars less than the price originally demanded. Mr. Belcher deposited a handsome sum as a guaranty of his good faith, and ordered the papers to be made out at once.

After their return to the hotel, Mr. Talbot sat down to a table, and went through a long calculation.

"It will cost you, Mr. Belcher," said the factor deliberately, "at least twenty-five thousand dollars to furnish that house satisfactorily."

Mr. Belcher gave a long whistle.

"At least twenty-five thousand dollars, and I doubt whether you get off for less than thirty thousand."

"Well, I'm in for it, and I'm going through," said Mr. Belcher.

"Very well," responded Talbot, "now let's go to the best furnisher we can find. I happen to know the man who is at the top of the style, and I suppose the best thing—as you and I don't know much about the matter—

is to let him have his own way, and hold him responsible for the results."

"All right," said Belcher; "show me the man."

They found the arbiter of style in his counting-room. Mr. Talbot approached him first, and held a long private conversation with him. Mr. Belcher, in his self-complacency, waited, fancying that Talbot was representing his own importance and the desirableness of so rare a customer, and endeavoring to secure reasonable prices on a large bill. In reality, he was arranging to get a commission out of the job for himself.

If it be objected to Mr. Talbot's mode of giving assistance to his country friends, that it savored of mercenariness amounting to villany, it is to be said, on his behalf, that he was simply practising the morals that Mr. Belcher had taught him. Mr. Belcher had not failed to debauch or debase the moral standard of every man over whom he had any direct influence. If Talbot had practised his little game upon any other man, Mr. Belcher would have patted his shoulder and told him he was a "jewel." So much of Mr. Belcher's wealth had been won by sharp and more than doubtful practices, that that wealth itself stood before the world as a premium on rascality, and thus became, far and wide, a demoralizing influence upon the feverishly ambitious and the young. Besides, Mr. Talbot quieted what little conscience he had in the matter by the consideration that his commissions were drawn, not from Mr. Belcher, but from the profits which others would make out of him, and the further consideration that it was no more than right for him to get the money back that he had spent, and was spending, for his principal's benefit.

Mr. Belcher was introduced, and the arbiter of style conversed learnedly of Tuscan, Pompeiian, Elizabethan, Louis Quatorze, buhl, *marqueterie*, etc., etc., till the head of the proprietor, to whom all these words were strangers, and all his talk Greek, was thrown into a hopeless muddle.

Mr. Belcher listened to him as long as he could do so with patience, and then brought him to a conclusion by a slap upon his knee.

"Come, now!" said he, "you understand your business, and I understand mine. If you were to take up guns and gutta-percha, I could probably talk your head off, but I don't know anything about these things. What I want is something right. Do the whole thing up brown. Do you understand that?"

The arbiter of style smiled pityingly, and admitted that he comprehended his customer.

It was at last arranged that the latter should make a study of the house, and furnish it according to his best ability, within a specified sum of expenditure and a specified period of time; and then the proprietor took his leave.

Mr. Belcher had accomplished a large amount of business within two days, but he had worked according to his habit. The dinner party remained, and this was the most difficult business that he had ever undertaken, yet he had a strong desire to see how it was done. He learned quickly what he undertook, and he had already "discounted," to use his own word, a certain amount of mortification connected with the affair.

CHAPTER IX.

MRS. TALBOT GIVES HER LITTLE DINNER PARTY, AND MR. BELCHER MAKES AN EXCEEDINGLY PLEASANT ACQUAINTANCE.

MRS. TALBOT had a very dear friend. She had been her dear friend ever since the two had roomed together at boarding-school. Sometimes she had questioned whether in reality Mrs. Helen Dillingham was her dear friend, or whether the particular friendship was all on the other side; but Mrs. Dillingham had somehow so manipulated the relation as always to appear to be the favored party. When, therefore, the dinner was determined upon, Mrs. Dillingham's card of invitation was the first one addressed. She was a widow and alone. She complemented Mr. Belcher, who was also alone.

Exactly the position Mrs. Dillingham occupied in society, it would be hard to define. Everybody invited her, and yet everybody, without any definite reason, considered her a little "off color." She was beautiful, she was accomplished, she talked wonderfully well, she was *au fait* in art, literature, society. She was superficially religious, and she formed the theatre of the struggle of a black angel and a white one, neither of whom ever won a complete victory, or held whatever advantage he gained for any considerable length of time. Nothing could be finer than Mrs. Dillingham in her fine moods; nothing coarser when the black angel was enjoying one of his victories, and the white angel had sat down to breathe. It was the impression given in these latter moments that fixed upon her the suspicion that she was not quite what she ought to be. The flowers bloomed where she walked, but there was dust on them. The cup she handed to her friends was pure to the eye, but it had a muddy taste. She was a whole woman in sympathy, power, beauty, and sensibility, and yet one felt that somewhere within she harbored a devil—a refined devil in its play, a gross one when it had the woman at unresisting advantage.

Next came the Schoonmakers, an elderly gentleman and his wife, who dined out a great deal, and lived on the ancient respectability of their family. They talked much about "the old New Yorkers," and of the inroads and devastations of the parvenu. They were thoroughly posted on old family estates and mansions, the intermarriages of the Dutch aristocracy, and the subject of heraldry. Mr. Schoonmaker made a hobby of old Bibles, and Mrs. Schoonmaker of old lace. The two hobbies combined gave a mingled air of erudition and gentility to the pair that was quite impressive, while their unquestionably good descent was a source of social capital to all of humbler origin who were fortunate enough to draw them to their tables.

Next came the Tunbridges. Mr. Tunbridge was the president of a bank, and Mrs. Tunbridge was the president of Mr. Tunbridge—a large, billowy woman, who "brought him his money," according to the speech of the town. Mr. Tunbridge had managed his trust with great skill, and was glad at any time, and at any social sacrifice, to be brought into contact with men who carried large deposit accounts.

Next in order were Mr. and Mrs. Cavendish. Mr. Cavendish was a lawyer—a hook-nosed, hawk-eyed man, who knew a little more about everything than anybody else did, and was celebrated in the city for successfully managing the most intractable cases, and securing the most princely fees. If a rich criminal were brought into straits before the law, he always sent for Mr. Cavendish. If the unprincipled managers of a great corporation wished to ascertain just how closely before the wind they could sail without being swamped, they consulted Mr. Cavendish. He was everywhere accounted a great lawyer by those who estimated acuteness to be above astuteness, strategy better than an open and fair fight, and success more to be desired than justice.

It would weary the reader to go through with a description of Mrs. Talbot's dinner party in advance. They were such people as Mr. and Mrs. Talbot naturally drew around them. The minister was invited, partly as a matter of course, and partly to occupy Mr. Schoonmaker on the subject of Bibles. The doctor was invited because Mrs. Talbot was fond of him, and because he always took "such an interest in the family."

When Mr. Belcher arrived at Talbot's beautiful but quiet house, the guests had all assembled, and, clothing their faces with that veneer of smile which hungry people who are about to dine at another man's expense feel compelled to wear in the presence of their host, they were chatting over the news of the day.

It is probable that the great city was never the scene of a personal introduction that gave more quiet amusement to an assemblage of guests than that of the presentation of Mr. Belcher. That gentleman's first impression as he entered the room was that Talbot had invited a company of clergymen to meet him. His look of surprise as he took a survey of the assembly was that of a knave who found himself for the first time in good company; but as he looked from the gentlemen to the ladies, in their gay costumes and display of costly jewelry, he concluded that they could not be the wives of clergymen. The quiet self-possession of the group, and the consciousness that he was not *en régle* in the matter of dress, oppressed him; but he was bold, and he knew that they knew that he was worth a million of dollars.

The "stiff upper lip" was placed at its stiffest in the

midst of his florid expanse of face, as, standing still, in the centre of the room, he greeted one after another to whom he was presented, in a way peculiarly his own.

He had never been in the habit of lifting his hat, in courtesy to man or woman. Even the touching its brim with his fingers had degenerated into a motion that began with a flourish toward it, and ended with a suave extension of his palm toward the object of his obeisance. On this occasion he quite forgot that he had left his hat in the hall, and so, assuming that it still crowned his head, he went through with eight or ten hand flourishes that changed the dignified and self-contained assembly into a merry company of men and women, who would not have been willing to tell Mr. Belcher what they were laughing at.

The last person to whom he was introduced was Mrs. Dillingham, the lady who stood nearest to him—so near that the hand flourish seemed absurd even to him, and half died in the impulse to make it. Mrs. Dillingham, in her black and her magnificent diamonds, went down almost upon the floor in the demonstration of her admiring and reverential courtesy, and pronounced the name of Mr. Belcher with a musical distinctness of enunciation that arrested and charmed the ears of all who heard it. It seemed as if every letter were swimming in a vehicle compounded of respect, veneration, and affection. The consonants flowed shining and smooth like gold-fish through a globe of crystal illuminated by the sun. The tone in which she spoke the name seemed to rob it of all vulgar associations, and to inaugurate it as the key-note of a fine social symphony.

Mr. Belcher was charmed, and placed by it at his ease. It wrought upon him and upon the company the effect which she designed. She was determined he should not only show at his best, but that he should be conscious of the favor she had won for him.

Before dinner was announced, Mr. Talbot made a little speech to his guests, ostensibly to give them the good news that Mr. Belcher had purchased the mansion, built and formerly occupied by Mr. Palgrave, but really to explain that he had caught him in town on business, and taken him at the disadvantage of distance from his evening dress, though, of course, he did not say it in such and so many words. The speech was unnecessary, Mrs. Dillingham had told the whole story in her own unapproachable way.

When dinner was announced Mr. Belcher was requested to lead Mrs. Talbot to her seat, and was himself placed between his hostess and Mrs. Dillingham. Mrs. Talbot was a stately, beautiful woman, and bore off her elegant toilet like a queen. In her walk into the dining-room, her shapely arm rested upon the proprietor's, and her brilliant eyes looked into his with an expression that flattered to its utmost all the fool there was in him. There was a little rivalry between the "dear friends;" but the unrestricted widow was more than a match for the circumspect and guarded wife, and Mr. Belcher was delighted to find himself seated side by side with the former.

He had not talked five minutes with Mrs. Dillingham before he knew her. The exquisite varnish that covered her person and her manners not only revealed, but made beautiful, the gnarled and stained wood beneath. Underneath the polish he saw the element that allied her with himself. There was no subject upon which she could not lead or accompany him with brilliant talk, yet he felt that there was a coarse under-current of sympathy by which he could lead her, or she could lead him —where?

The courtly manners of the table, the orderly courses that came and went as if the domestic administration were some automatic machine, and the exquisite appointments of the board, all exercised a powerful moral influence upon him; and though they did not wholly suppress him, they toned him down, so that he really talked well. He had a fund of small wit and drollery that was sufficient, at least, for a single dinner; and, as it was quaint and fresh, the guests were not only amused, but pleased. In the first place, much could be forgiven to the man who owned Palgrave's Folly. No small consideration was due to one who, in a quiet country town, had accumulated a million dollars. A person who had the power to reward attention with grand dinners and splendid receptions was certainly not a person to be treated lightly.

Mr. Tunbridge undertook to talk finance with him, but retired under the laugh raised by Mr. Belcher's statement that he had been so busy making money that he had had no time to consider questions of finance. Mr. Schoonmaker and the minister were deep in Bibles, and on referring some question to Mr. Belcher concerning "The Breeches Bible," received in reply the statement that he had never arrived any nearer a Breeches Bible than a pocket handkerchief with the Lord's Prayer on it. Mr. Cavendish simply sat and criticised the rest. He had never seen anybody yet who knew anything about finance. The Chamber of Commerce was a set of old women, the Secretary of the Treasury was an ass, and the Chairman of the Committee of Ways and Means was a person he should be unwilling to take as an office-boy. As for him, he never could see the fun of old Bibles. If he wanted a Bible he would get a new one.

Each man had his shot, until the conversation fell from the general to the particular, and at last Mr. Belcher found himself engaged in the most delightful conversation of his life with the facile woman at his side. He could make no approach to her from any quarter without being promptly met. She was quite as much at home, and quite as graceful, in bandying badinage as in expa tiating upon the loveliness of country life and the ritual of her church.

Mr. Talbot did not urge wine upon his principal, for he saw that he was excited and off his guard ; and when, at length, the banquet came to its conclusion, the proprietor declined to remain with the gentlemen and the supplementary wine and cigars, but took coffee in the drawing-room with the ladies. Mrs. Dillingham's eye was on Mrs. Talbot, and when she saw her start toward them from her seat, she took Mr. Belcher's arm for a tour among the artistic treasures of the house.

"My dear Kate," said Mrs. Dillingham, "give me the privilege of showing Mr. Belcher some of your beautiful things."

"Oh, certainly," responded Mrs. Talbot, her face flushing, "and don't forget yourself, my child, among the rest."

Mrs. Dillingham pressed Mr. Belcher's arm, an action which said : "Oh, the jealous creature ! "

They went from painting to painting, and sculpture to sculpture, and then, over a cabinet of bric-à-brac, she quietly led the conversation to Mr. Belcher's prospective occupation of the Palgrave mansion. She had nothing in the world to do. She should be so happy to assist poor Mrs. Belcher in the adjustment of her housekeeping. It would be a real pleasure to her to arrange the furniture, and do anything to help that quiet country lady in inaugurating the splendors of city life. She knew all the caterers, all the confectioners, all the modistes, all the city ways, and all the people worth knowing. She was willing to become, for Mrs. Belcher's sake, city-directory, commissionaire, adviser, director, everything. She would take it as a great kindness if she could be permitted to make herself useful.

All this was honey to the proprietor. How Mrs. Dillingham would shine in his splendid mansion! How she would illuminate his landau! How she would save his quiet wife, not to say himself, from the *gaucheries* of which both would be guilty until the ways of the polite world could be learned! How delightful it would be to have a sympathetic friend whose intelligent and considerate advice would be always ready!

When the gentlemen returned to the drawing-room, and disturbed the confidential *tête-à-tête* of these new friends, Mrs. Dillingham declared it was time to go, and Mr. Belcher insisted on seeing her home in his own carriage.

The dinner party broke up with universal hand-shakings. Mr. Belcher was congratulated on his magnificent purchase and prospects. They would all be happy to make Mrs. Belcher's acquaintance, and she really must lose no time in letting them know when she would be ready to receive visitors.

Mr. Belcher saw Mrs. Dillingham home. He held her pretty hands at parting, as if he were an affectionate older brother who was about to sail on a voyage around the world. At last he hurriedly relinquished her to the man-servant who had answered her summons, then ran down the steps and drove to his hotel.

Mounting to his rooms, he lit every burner in his parlor, and then surveyed himself in the mirror.

"Where did she find it, old boy? Eh? Where did she find it? Was it the figure? Was it the face? Hang the swallow tails! Must you, sir, come to such a humiliation? How are the mighty fallen! The lion of Sevenoaks in the skin of an ass! But it must be. Ah! Mrs. Belcher—Mrs. Belcher—Mrs. Belcher! You are good, but you are lumpy. You were pretty once, but you are no Mrs. Dillingham. By the gods! Wouldn't she swim around my house like a queen! Far in azure depths of space, I behold a star! Its light shines for me. It doesn't? It must not? Who says that? Did you address that remark to me, sir? By the way, how do you think you got along? Did you make a fool of yourself, or did you make a fool of somebody? Honors are easy. Let Robert Belcher alone! Is Toll making money a little too fast? What do you think? Perhaps you will settle that question by and by. You will keep him while you can use him. Then Toll, my boy, you can drift. In the meantime, splendor! and in the meantime let Sevenoaks howl, and learn to let Robert Belcher alone."

From these dizzy heights of elation Mr. Belcher descended to his bed and his heavy dreams, and the next morning found him whirling away at the rate of thirty miles an hour, but not northward. Whither was he going?

CHAPTER X.

WHICH TELLS HOW A LAWYER SPENT HIS VACATION IN CAMP, AND TOOK HOME A SPECIMEN OF GAME THAT HE HAD NEVER BEFORE FOUND IN THE WOODS.

IT was a bright moonlight night when Mike Conlin and Jim started off from Sevenoaks for home, leaving Mr. Balfour and his boy to follow. The old horse had a heavy load, and it was not until an hour past midnight that Mike's house was reached. There Jim made the new clothes, comprising a complete outfit for his boarders at Number Ten, into a convenient package, and swinging it over his shoulders, started for his distant cabin on foot. Mike, after resting himself and his horse, was to follow in the morning with the tools and stores, so as to arrive at the river at as early an hour as Mr. Balfour could complete the journey from Sevenoaks, with his lighter load and swifter horses.

Jim Fenton, who had lain still for several days, and was full of his schemes for Mr. Balfour and his *protégés* in camp, and warm with his memories of Miss Butterworth, simply gloried in his moonlight tramp. The accumulated vitality of his days of idleness was quite enough to make all the fatigues before him light and pleasant. At nine o'clock the next morning he stood by the side of his boat again. The great stillness of the woods, responding in vivid color to the first kisses of the frost, half intoxicated him. No world-wide wanderer, returning after many years to the home of his childhood, could have felt more exulting gladness than he, as he shoved his boat from the bank and pushed up the shining stream in the face of the sun.

Benedict and Harry had not been idle during his absence. A deer had been shot and dressed; trout had been caught and saved alive; a cave had been dug for the preservation of vegetables; and when Jim shouted, far down the stream, to announce his approach, there were three happy persons on shore, waiting to welcome him—Turk being the third, and apparently oblivious of the fact that he was not as much a human being as any of the party. Turk added the "tiger" to Harry's three cheers, and Jim was as glad as a boy when his boat touched the shore, and he received the affectionate greetings of the party.

A choice meal was nearly in readiness for him, but not a mouthful would he taste until he had unfolded his treasures, and displayed to the astonished eyes of Mr. Benedict and the lad the comfortable clothing he had brought for them.

"Take 'em to Number Ten and put 'em on," said Jim. "I'm a goin' to eat with big folks to-day, if clo'es can make 'em. Them's yer stockin's and them's yer boots, and them's yer indigoes and them's yer clo'es."

Jim's idea of the word "indigoes" was, that it drew its meaning partly from the color of the articles designated, and partly from their office. They were blue undergoes—in other words, blue flannel shirts.

Jim sat down and waited. He saw that, while Harry was hilarious over his good fortune, Mr. Benedict was very silent and humble. It was twenty minutes before Harry reappeared; and when he came bounding toward Jim, even Turk did not know him. Jim embraced him, and could not help feeling that he had acquired a certain amount of property in the lad.

When Mr. Benedict came forth from the little cabin, and found Jim chaffing and petting his boy, he was much embarrassed. He could not speak, but walked directly past the pair, and went out upon the bank of the river, with his eyes averted.

Jim comprehended it all. Leaving Harry, he went up to his guest, and placed his hand upon his shoulder. "Will ye furgive me, Mr. Benedict? I didn't go fur to make it hard fur ye."

"Jim," said Mr. Benedict, struggling to retain his composure, "I can never repay your overwhelming kindness, and the fact oppresses me."

"Well," said Jim, "I s'pose I don't make 'lowance enough fur the difference in folks. Ye think ye oughter pay fur this sort o' thing, an' I don't want no pay. I git comfort enough outen it, any way."

Benedict turned, took and warmly pressed Jim's hand, and then they went back to their dinner. After they had eaten, and Jim had sat down to his pipe, he told his guests that they were to have visitors that night—a man from the city and his little boy—and that they would spend a fortnight with them. The news alarmed Mr. Benedict, for his nerves were still weak, and it was a long time before he could be reconciled to the thought of intrusion upon his solitude ; but Jim reassured him by his enthusiastic accounts of Mr. Balfour, and Harry was overjoyed with the thought of having a companion in the strange lad.

"I thought I'd come home an' git ye ready," said Jim ; "fur I knowed ye'd feel bad to meet a gentleman in yer old poor-house fixin's. Burn 'em or bury 'em as soon as I'm gone. I don't never want to see them things agin."

Jim went off again down the river, and Mr. Benedict and Harry busied themselves in cleaning the camp, and preparing Number Ten for the reception of Mr. Balfour and his boy, having previously determined to take up their abode with Jim for the winter. The latter had a hard afternoon. He was tired with his night's tramp, and languid with loss of sleep. When he arrived at the landing he found Mr. Balfour waiting. He had passed Mike Conlin on the way, and even while they were talking the Irishman came in sight. After half-an-hour of busy labor, the goods and passengers were bestowed, Mike was paid for the transportation, and the closing journeys of the day were begun.

When Jim had made half of the weary row up the river, he ran into a little cove to rest and wipe the perspiration from his forehead. Then he informed Mr. Balfour that he was not alone in the camp, and, in his own inimitable way, having first enjoined the strictest secrecy, he told the story of Mr. Benedict and his boy.

"Benedict will hunt and fish with ye better nor I can," said he, "an' he's a better man nor I be any way ; but I'm at yer service, and ye shall have the best time in the woods that I can give ye."

Then he enlarged upon the accomplishments of Benedict's boy.

"He favors yer boy a little," said Jim, eyeing the lad

closely. "Dress 'em alike, and they wouldn't be a bad pair o' brothers."

Jim did not recognize the germs of change that existed in his accidental remark, but he noticed that a shade of pain passed over the lawyer's face.

"Where is the other little feller that ye used to brag over, Mr. Balfour?" inquired Jim.

"He's gone, Jim; I lost him. He died a year ago."

Jim had no words with which to meet intelligence of this character, so he did not try to utter any; but, after a minute of silence, he said: "That's what floors me. Them dies that's got everything, and them lives that's got nothin'—lives through thick and thin. It seems sort o' strange to me that the Lord runs everything so kind o' car'less like, when there ain't nobody to bring it to his mind."

Mr. Balfour made no response, and Jim resumed his oars. But for the moon, it would have been quite dark when Number Nine was reached, but, once there, the fatigues of the journey were forgotten. It was Thede Balfour's first visit to the woods, and he was wild with excitement. Mr. Benedict and Harry gave the strangers a cordial greeting. The night was frosty and crisp, and Jim drew his boat out of the water, and permitted his stores to remain in it through the night. A hearty supper prepared them all for sleep, and Jim led his city friends to Number Ten, to enjoy their camp by themselves. A camp-fire, recently lighted, awaited them, and, with its flames illuminating the weird scenes around them, they went to sleep.

The next day was Sunday. To the devoutly disposed, there is no silence that seems so deeply hallowed as that which pervades the forest on that holy day. No steamer ploughs the river; no screaming, rushing train profanes the stillness; the beasts that prowl, and the birds that fly, seem gentler than on other days; and the wilderness, with its pillars and arches, and aisles, becomes a sanctuary. Prayers that no ears can hear but those of the Eternal; psalms that win no responses except from the echoes; worship that rises from hearts unencumbered by care, and undistracted by pageantry and dress—all these are possible in the woods; and the great Being to whom the temples of the world are reared cannot have failed to find, in ten thousand instances, the purest offerings in lonely camps and cabins.

They had a delightful and bountiful breakfast, and, at its close, they divided themselves naturally into a double group. The two boys and Turk went off by themselves to watch the living things around them, while the men remained together by the camp-fire.

Mr. Balfour drew out a little pocket-Testament, and was soon absorbed in reading. Jim watched him, as a hungry dog watches a man at his meal, and at last, having grown more and more uneasy, he said:

"Give us some o' that, Mr. Balfour."

Mr. Balfour looked up and smiled, and then read to him the parable of the talents.

"I don't know nothin' 'bout it," said Jim, at the conclusion, "but it seems to me the man was a little rough on the feller with one talent. 'Twas a mighty small capital to start with, an' he didn't give 'im any chance to try it over; but what bothers me the most is about the man's trav'lin' into a fur country. They hadn't no chance to talk with 'im about it, and git his notions. It stan's to reason that the feller with one talent would think his master was stingy, and be riled over it."

"You must remember, Jim, that all he needed was to ask for wisdom in order to receive it," said Mr. Benedict.

"No; the man that travelled into a fur country stan's for the Almighty, and he'd got out o' the way. He'd jest gi'n these fellers his capital, and quit, and left 'em to go it alone. They couldn't go arter 'im, and he couldn't 'a' hearn a word they said. He did what he thought was all right, and didn't want to be bothered. I never think about prayin' till I git into a tight place. It stan's to reason that the Lord don't want people comin' to him to do things that they can do theirselves. I shouldn't pray for breath; I sh'd jest h'ist the winder. If I wanted a bucket o' water, I sh'd go for it. If a man's got common sense, and a pair o' hands, he hain't no business to be botherin' other folks till he gits into what he can't git out of. When he's squeezed, then in course he'll squeal. It seems to me that it makes a sort of a spooney of a man to be always askin' for what he can git if he tries. If the feller that only had one talent had brushed round, he could 'a' make a spec on it, an' had somethin' to show fur it, but he jest hid it. I don't stan' up for 'im. I think he was meaner nor pusly not to make the best on't, but he didn't need to pray for sense, for the man didn't want 'im to use no more nor his nateral stock, an' he knowed if he used that he'd be all right."

"But we are told to pray, Jim," said Mr. Balfour, "and assured that it is pleasant to the Lord to receive our petitions. We are even told to pray for our daily bread."

"Well, it can't mean jest that, fur the feller that don't work for't don't git it, an' he hadn't oughter git it. If he don't lift his hands, but jest sets with his mouth open, he gits mostly flies. The old birds, with a nest full o' howlin' young ones, might go on, I s'pose, pickin' up grasshoppers till the cows come home, an' feedin' 'em, but they don't. They jest poke 'em out o' the nest, an' larn 'em to fly an' pick up their own livin'; an' that's what makes birds on 'em. They pray mighty hard fur their daily bread, I tell ye, and the way the old birds answer is jest to poke 'em out, and let 'em slide. I don't see many prayin' folks, an' I don't see many folks any way; but I have a consait that a feller can pray so much an' do so little, that he won't be nobody. He'll jest grow weaker an' weaker all the time."

"I don't see," said Mr. Balfour, laughing, and turning to Mr. Benedict, "but we've had the exposition of our Scripture."

The former had always delighted to hear Jim talk, and never lost an opportunity to set him going; but he did not know that Jim's exposition of the parable had a personal motive. Mr. Benedict knew that it had, and was very serious over it. His nature was weak in many respects. His will was weak; he had no combativeness; he had a wish to lean. He had been baffled and buffeted in the world. He had gone down into the darkness, praying all the way; and now that he had come out of it, and had so little society; now that his young life was all behind him, and so few earthly hopes beckoned him on, he turned with a heart morbidly religious to what seemed to him the only source of comfort open to him. Jim had watched him with pain. He had seen him, from day to day, spending his hours alone, and felt that prayer formed almost the staple of his life. He had seen him willing to work, but knew that his heart was not in it. He was not willing to go back into the world, and assert his place among men. The poverty, disease, and disgrace of his former life dwelt in his memory, and he shrank from the conflicts and competitions which would be necessary to enable him to work out better results for himself.

Jim thoroughly believed that Benedict was religiously diseased, and that he never could become a man again until he had ceased to live so exclusively in the spiritual world. He contrived all possible ways to keep him employed. He put responsibility upon him. He stimulated him with considerations of the welfare of Harry. He disturbed him in his retirement. He contrived fatigues that would induce sound sleep. To use his own language, he had tried to cure him of "loppin'," but with very unsatisfactory results.

Benedict comprehended Jim's lesson, and it made an impression upon him; but to break himself of his habit of thought and life was as difficult as the breaking of morbid habits always is. He knew that he was a weak man, and saw that he had never fully developed that which was manliest within him. He saw plainly, too, that his prayers would not develop it, and that nothing but a faithful, bold, manly use of his powers could accomplish the result. He knew that he had a better brain, and a brain better furnished, than that of Robert Belcher, yet he had known to his sorrow, and well-nigh to his destruction, that Robert Belcher could wind him around his finger. Prayer had never saved him from this, and nothing could save him but a development of his own manhood. Was he too old for hope? Could he break away from the delights of his weakness, and grow into something stronger and better? Could he so change the attitude of his soul that it should cease to be exigent and receptive, and become a positive, self-poised, and active force? He sighed when these questions came to him, but he felt that Jim had helped him in many practical ways, and could help him still further.

A stranger, looking upon the group, would have found it a curious and interesting study. Mr. Balfour was a tall, lithe man, with not a redundant ounce of flesh on him. He was as straight as an arrow, bore on his shoulders a fine head that gave evidence in its contour of equal benevolence and force, and was a practical, fearless, straightforward, true man. He enjoyed humor, and though he had a happy way of evoking it from others, possessed or exhibited very little himself. Jim was better than a theatre to him. He spent so much of his time in the conflicts of his profession, that in his vacations he simply opened heart and mind to entertainment. A shrewd, frank, unsophisticated nature was a constant feast to him, and though he was a keen sportsman, the woods would have had few attractions without Jim.

Mr. Benedict regarded him with profound respect, as a man who possessed the precise qualities which had been denied to himself—self-assertion, combativeness, strong will, and "push." Even through Benedict's ample beard, a good reader of the human face would have detected the weak chin, while admiring the splendid brow, silken curls, and handsome eyes above it. He was a thoroughly gentle man, and, curiously enough, attracted the interest of Mr. Balfour in consequence of his gentleness. The instinct of defence and protection to everything weak and dependent was strong within the lawyer; and Benedict affected him like a woman. It was easy for the two to become friends, and as Mr. Balfour grew familiar with the real excellences of his new acquaintance, with his intelligence in certain directions, and his wonderful mechanical ingenuity, he conceived just as high a degree of respect for him as he could entertain for one who was entirely unfurnished with those weapons with which the battles of life are fought.

It was a great delight to Jim to see his two friends get along so well together, particularly as he had pressing employment on his hands, in preparing for the winter. So, after the first day, Benedict became Mr. Balfour's guide during the fortnight which he passed in the woods.

The bright light of Monday morning was the signal for the beginning of their sport, and Thede, who had never thrown a fly, was awake at the first daylight; and before Jim had the breakfast of venison and cakes ready, he had strung his tackle and leaned his rod against the cabin in readiness for his enterprise. They had a day of satisfactory fishing, and brought home half a hundred spotted beauties that would have delighted the eyes of any angler in the world; and when their golden flesh stood open and broiling before the fire, or hissed and sputtered in the frying-pan, watched by the hungry and admiring eyes of the fishermen, they were attractive enough to be the food of the gods. And when, at last, the group gathered around the rude board, with appetites that seemed measureless, and devoured the dainties prepared for them, the pleasures of the day were crowned.

But all this was comparatively tame sport to Mr. Balfour. He had come for larger game, and waited only for the nightfall to deepen into darkness to start upon his hunt for deer. The moon had passed her full, and would not rise until after the ordinary bedtime. The boys were anxious to be witnesses of the sport, and it was finally concluded, that for once, at least, they should be indulged in their desire.

The voice of a hound was never heard in the woods, and even the "still hunting" practised by the Indian was never resorted to until after the streams were frozen.

Jim had been busy during the day in picking up pine knots, and digging out old stumps whose roots were charged with pitch. These he had collected and split up into small pieces, so that everything should be in readiness for the "float." As soon as the supper was finished, he brought a little iron "Jack," mounted upon a standard, and proceeded to fix this upright in the bow of the boat. Behind this he placed a square of sheet-iron, so that a deer, dazzled by the light of the blazing pine, would see nothing behind it, while the occupants of the boat could see everything ahead without being blinded by the light, of which they could see nothing. Then he fixed a knob of tallow upon the forward sight of Mr. Balfour's gun, so that, projecting in front of the sheet-iron screen, it would be plainly visible and render necessary only the raising of the breech to the point of half hiding the tallow, in order to procure as perfect a range as if it were broad daylight.

All these preparations were familiar to Mr. Balfour, and, loading his heavy shot-gun with a powerful charge, he waited impatiently for the darkness.

At nine o'clock, Jim said it was time to start, and, lighting his torch, he took his seat in the stern of the boat, and bade Mr. Balfour take his place in the bow, where a board, placed across the boat, made him a comfortable seat. The boys, warmly wrapped, took their places together in the middle of the boat, and, clasping one another's hands and shivering with excitement, bade good-night to Mr. Benedict, who pushed them from the shore.

The night was still, and Jim's powerful paddle urged the little craft up the stream with a push so steady, strong, and noiseless, that its passengers might well have imagined that the unseen river-spirits had it in tow. The torch cast its long glare into the darkness on either bank, and made shadows so weird and changeful that the boys imagined they saw every form of wild beast and flight of strange bird with which pictures had made them familiar. Owls hooted in the distance. A wild-cat screamed like a frightened child. A partridge, waked from its perch by a flash of the torch, whirred off into the woods.

At length, after paddling up the stream for a mile, they heard the genuine crash of a startled animal. Jim stopped and listened. Then came the spiteful stroke of a deer's forefeet upon the leaves, and a whistle so sharp, strong and vital, that it thrilled every ear that heard it. It was a question, a protest, a defiance all in one; but not a sign of the animal could be seen. He was back in the cover, wary and watching, and was not to be tempted nearer by the light.

Jim knew the buck, and knew that any delay on his account would be useless.

"I knowed 'im when I hearn 'im whistle, an' he knowed me. He's been shot at from this boat more nor twenty times. 'Not any pine-knots on my plate,' says he. 'I seen 'em afore, an' you can pass.' I used to git kind o' mad at 'im, an' promise to foller 'im, but he's so 'cute, I sort o' like 'im. He 'muses me."

While Jim waited and talked in a low tone, the buck was evidently examining the light and the craft, at his leisure and at a distance. Then he gave another lusty whistle that was half snort, and bounded off into the woods by leaps that struck every foot upon the ground at the same instant, and soon passed beyond hearing.

"Well, the old feller's gone," said Jim, "an' now I know a patch o' lily-pads up the river where I guess we can find a beast that hasn't had a public edication."

The tension upon the nerves of the boys was relieved, and they whispered between themselves about what they had seen, or thought they had seen.

All became still, as Jim turned his boat up the stream again. After proceeding for ten or fifteen minutes in perfect silence, Jim whispered:

"Skin yer eyes, now, Mr. Balfour; we're comin' to a lick."

Jim steered his boat around a little bend, and in a moment it was running in shallow water, among grass and rushes. The bottom of the stream was plainly visible, and Mr. Balfour saw that they had left the river, and were pushing up the debouchure of a sluggish little affluent. They brushed along among the grass for twenty or thirty rods, when, at the same instant, every eye detected a figure in the distance. Two blazing, quiet, curious eyes were watching them. Jim had an instinct which assured him that the deer was fascinated by the light, and so he pushed toward him silently, then stopped, and held his boat perfectly still. This was the signal for Mr. Balfour, and in an instant the woods were startled by a discharge that deafened the silence.

There was a violent splash in the water, a scramble up the bank, a bound or two toward the woods, a pitiful bleat, and then all was still.

"We've got 'im," said Jim. "He's took jest one buckshot through his heart. Ye didn't touch his head nor his legs. He jest run till the blood leaked out and he gi'n it up. Now, boys, you set here, and sing hallelujer till we bring 'im in."

The nose of the little craft was run against the bank, and Mr. Balfour, seizing the torch, sprang on shore, and Jim followed him into the woods. They soon found track of the game by the blood that dabbled the bushes, and stumbled upon the beautiful creature stone dead—fallen prone, with his legs doubled under him. Jim swung him across his shoulders, and, tottering behind Mr. Balfour, bore him back to the boat. Placing him in the bottom, the two men resumed their seats, and Jim, after carefully working himself out of the inlet into the river, settled down to a long, swift stroke that bore them back to the camp just as the moon began to show herself above the trees.

It was a night long to be remembered by the boys, a fitting inauguration of the lawyer's vacation, and an introduction to woodcraft from which, in after years, the neophytes won rare stores of refreshment and health.

Mr. Benedict received them with hearty congratulations, and the perfect sleep of the night only sharpened their desire for further depredations upon the game that lived around them, in the water and on the land.

As the days passed on, they caught trout until they were tired of the sport; they floated for deer at night; they took weary tramps in all directions, and at evening, around the camp-fires, rehearsed their experiences.

During all this period, Mr. Balfour was watching

Harry Benedict. The contrast between the lad and his own son was as marked as that between the lad's father and himself, but the positions were reversed. Harry led, contrived, executed. He was positive, facile, amiable, and the boys were as happy together as their parents were. Jim had noticed the remarkable interest that Mr. Balfour took in the boy, and had begun to suspect that he entertained intentions which would deprive the camp of one of its chief sources of pleasure.

One day when the lawyer and his guide were quietly eating their lunch in the forest, Mr. Balfour went to work, in his quiet, lawyer-like way, to ascertain the details of Benedict's history; and he heard them all. When he heard who had benefited by his guide's inventions, and learned just how matters stood with regard to the Belcher rifle, he became, for the first time since he had been in the woods, thoroughly excited. He had a law-case before him as full of the elements of romance as any that he had ever been engaged in. A defrauded inventor, living in the forest in poverty, having escaped from the insane ward of an alms-house, and the real owner of patent rights that were a mine of wealth to the man who believed that death had blotted out all the evidences of his villany—this was quite enough to excite his professional interest, even had he been unacquainted with the man defrauded. But the position of this uncomplaining, dependent man, who could not fight his own battles, made an irresistible appeal to his sense of justice and his manhood.

The moment, however, that the lawyer proposed to assist in righting the wrong, Mr. Benedict became dangerously excited. He could tell his story, but the thought of going out into the world again, and, particularly of engaging in a conflict with Robert Belcher, was one that he could not entertain. He was happier in the woods than he had been for many years. The life was gradually strengthening him. He hoped the time would come when he could get something for his boy, but, for the present, he could engage in no struggle for reclaiming and maintaining his rights. He believed that an attempt to do it would again drive him to distraction, and that, somehow, Mr. Belcher would get the advantage of him. His fear of the great proprietor had become morbidly acute, and Mr. Balfour could make no headway against it. It was prudent to let the matter drop for a while.

Then Mr. Balfour opened his heart in regard to the boy. He told Benedict of the loss with which he had already acquainted Jim, of the loneliness of his remaining son, of the help that Harry could afford him, the need in which the lad stood of careful education, and the accomplishments he could win among better opportunities and higher society. He would take the boy, and treat him, up to the time of his majority, as his own. If Mr. Benedict could ever return the money expended for him, he could have the privilege of doing so, but it would never be regarded as a debt. Once every year the lawyer would bring the lad to the woods, so that he should not forget his father, and if the time should ever come when it seemed practicable to do so, a suit would be instituted that would give him the rights so cruelly withheld from his natural protector.

The proposition was one which taxed to its utmost Mr. Benedict's power of self-control. He loved his boy better than he loved himself. He hoped that, in some way, life would be pleasanter and more successful to the lad than it had been to him. He did not wish him to grow up illiterate and in the woods; but how he was to live without him he could not tell. The plucking out of an eye would have given him less pain than the parting with his boy, though he felt from the first that the lad would go.

Nothing could be determined without consulting Jim, and as the conversation had destroyed the desire for further sport, they packed their fishing-tackle and returned to camp.

"The boy wasn't got up for my 'commodation," said Jim, when the proposition was placed before him. "I seen the thing comin' for a week, an' I've brung my mind to't. We hain't got no right to keep 'im up here, if he can do better. Turk ain't bad company fur them as likes dogs, but he ain't improvin'. I took the boy away from Tom Buffum 'cause I could do better by 'im nor he could, and when a man comes along that can do better by him nor I can, he's welcome to wade in. I hain't no right to spile a little feller's life 'cause I like his company. I don't think much of a fellow that would cheat a man out of a jews-harp 'cause he liked to fool with it. Arter all, this sendin' the boy off is just turnin' 'im out to pastur' to grow, an' takin' 'im in in the fall. He may git his head up so high t' we can't git the halter on 'im again, but he'll be worth more to somebody that can, nor if we kep 'im in the stable. I sh'll hate to say good-bye t' the little feller, but I sh'll vote to have 'im go, unanimous."

Mr. Benedict was not a man who had will enough to withstand the rational and personal considerations that were brought to bear upon him, and then the two boys were brought into the consultation. Thede was overjoyed with the prospect of having for a home companion the boy to whom he had become so greatly attached, and poor Harry was torn by a conflict of inclinations. To leave Jim and his father behind was a great sorrow; and he was half angry with himself to think that he could find any pleasure in the prospect of a removal. But the love of change, natural to a boy, and the desire to see the wonders of the great city, with accounts of which Thede had excited his imagination, overcame his inclination to remain in the camp. The year of separation would be very short, he thought, so that, after all, it was only a temporary matter. The moment the project of going away took possession of him, his regrets died, and the exit from the woods seemed to him like a journey into dreamland, from which he should return in the morning.

How to get the lad through Sevenoaks, where he would be sure to be recognized, and so reveal the hiding-place of his father, became at once a puzzling question. Mr. Balfour had arranged with the man who brought him into the woods to return in a fortnight and take him out, and as he was a man who had known the Benedicts it would not be safe to trust to his silence.

It was finally arranged that Jim should start off at once with Harry, and engage Mike Conlin to go through Sevenoaks with him in the night, and deliver him at the railroad at about the hour when the regular stage would arrive with Mr. Balfour. The people of Sevenoaks were not travellers, and it would be a rare chance that should bring one of them through to that point. The preparations were therefore made at once, and the next evening poor Benedict was called upon to part with his boy. It was a bitter struggle, but it was accomplished, and, excited by the strange life that was opening before him, the boy entered the boat with Jim, and waved his adieus to the group that had gathered upon the bank to see them off.

Poor Turk, who had apparently understood all that had passed in the conversations of the previous day, and become fully aware of the bereavement that he was about to suffer, stood upon the shore and howled and whined as they receded into the distance. Then he went up to Thede, and licked his hand, as if he would say: "Don't leave me as the other boy has done; if you do I shall be inconsolable."

Jim effected his purpose, and returned before light

the next morning, and on the following day he took Mr. Balfour and Thede down the river, and delivered them to the man whom he found waiting for them. The programme was carried out in all its details, and two days afterward the two boys were sitting side by side in the railway-car that was hurrying them toward the great city.

CHAPTER XI.

WHICH RECORDS MR. BELCHER'S CONNECTION WITH A GREAT SPECULATION AND BRINGS TO A CLOSE HIS RESIDENCE IN SEVENOAKS.

WHITHER was he going? He had a little fortune in his pockets—more money than prudent men are in the habit of carrying with them—and a scheme in his mind. After the purchase of Palgrave's Folly, and the inauguration of a scale of family expenditure far surpassing all his previous experience, Mr. Belcher began to feel poor, and to realize the necessity of extending his enterprise. To do him justice, he felt that he had surpassed the proprieties of domestic life in taking so important a step as that of changing his residence without consulting Mrs. Belcher. He did not wish to meet her at once; so it was easy for him, when he left New York, to take a wide diversion on his way home.

For several months the reports of the great oil discoveries of Pennsylvania had been floating through the press. Stories of enormous fortunes acquired in a single week, and even in a single day, were rife; and they had excited his greed with a strange power. He had witnessed, too, the effect of these stories upon the minds of the humble people of Sevenoaks. They were uneasy in their poverty, and were in the habit of reading with avidity all the accounts that emanated from the new centre of speculation. The monsters of the sea had long been chased into the ice, and the whalers had returned with scantier fares year after year; but here was light for the world. The solid ground itself was echoing with the cry: "Here she blows!" and "There she blows!" and the long harpoons went down to its vitals, and were fairly lifted out by the pressure of the treasure that impatiently waited for deliverance.

Mr. Belcher had long desired to have a hand in this new business. To see a great speculation pass by without yielding him any return was very painful to him. During his brief stay in New York he had been approached by speculators from the new field of promise; and had been able by his quick wit and ready business instinct to ascertain just the way in which money was made and was to be made. He dismissed them all, for he had the means in his hands of starting nearer the sources of profit than themselves, and to be not only one of the "bottom ring," but to be the bottom man. No moderate profit and no legitimate income would satisfy him. He would gather the investments of the multitude into his own capacious pockets, or he would have nothing to do with the matter. He would sweep the board, fairly or foully, or he would not play.

As he travelled along westward, he found that the company was made up of men whose tickets took them to his own destination. Most of them were quiet, with ears open to the few talkers who had already been there, and were returning. Mr. Belcher listened to them, laughed at them, scoffed at their schemes, and laid up carefully all that they said. Before he arrived at Corry he had acquired a tolerable knowledge of the oil-fields, and determined upon his scheme of operations.

As he drew nearer the great centre of excitement, he

came more into contact with the masses who had gathered there, crazed with the spirit of speculation. Men were around him whose clothes were shining with bitumen. The air was loaded with the smell of petroleum Derricks were thrown up on every side ; drills were at work piercing the earth ; villages were starting among stumps still fresh at the top, as if their trees were cut but yesterday ; rough men in high boots were ranging the country ; the depots were glutted with portable steam-engines and all sorts of mining machinery, and there was but one subject of conversation. Some new well had begun to flow with hundreds of barrels of petroleum *per diem*. Some new man had made a fortune. Farmers, who had barely been able to get a living from their sterile acres, had become millionnaires. The whole region was alive with fortune-hunters, from every quarter of the country. Millions of dollars were in the pockets of men who were ready to purchase. Seedy, crazy, visionary fellows were working as middle-men, to talk up schemes, and win their bread, with as much more as they could lay their hands on. The very air was charged with the contagion of speculation, and men seemed ready to believe anything and do anything. It appeared, indeed, as if a man had only to buy, to double his money in a day ; and half the insane multitude believed it.

Mr. Belcher kept himself quiet, and defended himself from the influences around him by adopting and holding his scoffing mood. He believed nothing. He was there simply to see what asses men could make of themselves ; but he kept his ears open. The wretched hotel at which he at last found accommodations was thronged with fortune-seekers, among whom he moved self-possessed and quite at home. On the second day his mood began to tell on those around him. There were men there who knew about him and his great wealth—men who had been impressed with his sagacity. He studied them carefully, gave no one his confidence, and quietly laid his plans. On the evening of the third day he returned to the hotel, and announced that he had had the good fortune to purchase a piece of property that he proposed to operate and improve on his own account.

Then he was approached with propositions for forming a company. He had paid fifty thousand dollars for a farm—paid the money—and before morning he had sold half of it for what he gave for the whole, and formed a company with the nominal capital of half a million of dollars, a moiety of the stock being his own at no cost to him whatever. The arrangements were all made for the issue of stock and the commencement of operations, and when, three days afterward, he started from Titus ville on his way home, he had in his satchel blank certificates of stock, all signed by the officers of the Continental Petroleum Company, to be limited in its issue to the sum of two hundred and fifty thousand dollars. He never expected to see the land again. He did not expect that the enterprise would be of the slightest value to those who should invest in it. He expected to do just what others were doing—to sell his stock and pocket the proceeds, while investors pocketed their losses. It was all an acute business operation with him; and he intended to take advantage of the excitement of the time to "clean out" Sevenoaks and all the region round about his country home, while his confrères operated in their own localities. He chuckled over his plans as if he contemplated some great, good deed that would be of incalculable benefit to his neighbors. He suffered no qualm of conscience, no revolt of personal honor, no spasm of sympathy or pity.

As soon as he set out upon his journey homeward he began to think of his New York purchase. He had taken a bold step, and he wished that he had said something to Mrs. Belcher about his plans, but he had been so much in the habit of managing everything in his business without consulting her, that it did not occur to him before he started from home that any matter of his was not exclusively his own. He would just as soon have thought of taking Phipps into his confidence, or of deferring to his wishes in any project, as of extending those courtesies to his wife. There was another consideration which weighed somewhat heavily upon his mind. He was not entirely sure that he would not be ashamed of Mrs. Belcher in the grand home which he had provided for himself. He respected her, and had loved her in his poor, sensual fashion, some changeful years in the past; he had regarded her as a good mother, and, at least, as an inoffensive wife; but she was not Mrs. Dillingham. She would not be at home in the society of which he had caught a glimpse, or among the splendors to which he would be obliged to introduce her. Even Talbot, the man who was getting rich upon the products of his enterprise, had a more impressive wife than he. And thus, with much reflection, this strange, easy-natured brute without a conscience, wrought up his soul into self-pity. In some way he had been defrauded. It never could have been intended that a man capable of winning so many of his heart's desires as he had proved himself to be, should be tied to a woman incapable of illuminating and honoring his position. If he only had a wife of whose person he could be proud! If he only had a wife whose queenly presence and manners would give significance to the splendors of the Palgrave mansion!

There was no way left for him, however, but to make the best of his circumstances, and put a brave face upon the matter. Accordingly, the next morning after his arrival, he told, with such display of enthusiasm as he could assume, the story of his purchase. The children were all attention, and made no hesitation to express their delight with the change that lay before them. Mrs. Belcher grew pale, choked over her breakfast, and was obliged to leave the table. At the close of the meal, Mr. Belcher followed her to her room, and found her with dry eyes and an angry face.

"Robert, you have determined to kill me," she said, almost fiercely.

"Oh, no, Sarah; not quite so bad as that."

"How could you take a step which you knew would give me a life-long pain? Have I not suffered enough? Is it not enough that I have ceased practically to have a husband?—that I have given up all society, and been driven in upon my children? Am I to have no will, no consideration, no part or lot in my own life?"

"Put it through, Sarah; you have the floor, and I'm ready to take it all now."

"And it is all for show," she went on, "and is disgusting. There is not a soul in the city that your wealth can bring to me that will give me society. I shall be a thousand times lonelier there than I have been here; and you compel me to go where I must receive people whom I shall despise, and who, for that reason, will dislike me. You propose to force me into a life that is worse than emptiness. I am more nearly content here than I can ever be anywhere else, and I shall never leave here without a cruel sense of sacrifice."

"Good for you, Sarah!" said Mr. Belcher. "You're more of a trump than I thought you were; and if it will do you any good to know that I think I've been a little rough with you, I don't mind telling you so. But the thing is done, and it can't be undone. You can have your own sort of life there as you do here, and I can have mine. I suppose I could go there and run the house alone; but it isn't exactly the thing for Mrs. Belcher's husband to do. People might talk, you know, and they wouldn't blame me."

"No; they would blame me, and I must go, whether I wish to go or not."

Mrs. Belcher had talked until she could weep, and brushing her eyes she walked to the window. Mr. Belcher sat still, casting furtive glances at her, and drumming with his fingers on his knees. When she could sufficiently command herself, she returned, and said:

"Robert, I have tried to be a good wife to you. I helped you in your first struggles, and then you were a comfort to me. But your wealth has changed you, and you know that for ten years I have had no husband. I have humored your caprices; I have been careful not to cross your will. I have taken your generous provision, and made myself and my children what you desired; but I am no more to you than a part of your establishment. I do not feel that my position is an honorable one. I wish to God that I had one hope that it would ever become so."

"Well, by-by, Sarah. You'll feel better about it."

Then Mr. Belcher stooped and kissed her forehead, and left her.

That little attention—that one shadow of recognition of the old relations, that faint show of feeling—went straight to her starving heart. And then, assuming blame for what seemed, at the moment of reaction, her unreasonable selfishness, she determined to say no more, and to take uncomplainingly whatever life her husband might provide for her.

As for Mr. Belcher, he went off to his library and his cigar with a wound in his heart. The interview with his wife, while it had excited in him a certain amount of pity for her, had deepened his pity for himself. She had ceased to be what she had once been to him; yet his experience in the city had proved that there were still women in the world who could excite in him the old passion, and move him to the old gallantries. It was clearly a case of incipient "incompatibility." It was "the mistake of a lifetime" just discovered, though she had borne his children and held his respect for fifteen years. He still felt the warmth of Mrs. Dillingham's hands within his own, the impression of her confiding clasp upon his arm, and the magnetic influence of her splendid presence. Reason as he would, he felt defrauded of his rights; and he wondered whether any combination of circumstances would ever permit him to achieve them. As this amounted to wondering whether Mrs. Belcher would die, he strove to banish the question from his mind; but it returned and returned again so pertinaciously that he was glad to order his horses and ride to his factory.

Before night it became noised through the village that the great proprietor had been to the oil regions. The fact was talked over among the people in the shops, in the street, in social groups that gathered at evening; and there was great curiosity to know what he had learned, and what opinions he had formed. Mr. Belcher knew how to play his cards, and having set the people talking, he filled out and sent to each of the wives of the five pastors of the village, as a gift, a certificate of five shares of the stock of the Continental Petroleum Company. Of course, they were greatly delighted, and, of course, twenty-four hours had not passed by when every man, woman, and child in Sevenoaks was acquainted with the transaction. People began to revise their judgments of the man whom they had so severely condemned. After all, it was the way in which he had done things in former days, and though they had come to a vivid apprehension of the fact that he had done them for a purpose, which invariably terminated in himself, they could not see what there was to be gained by so munificent a gift. Was he not endeavoring, by self-sacrifice, to win back a portion of the consideration he had formerly enjoyed? Was it not a confession of wrong-doing, or wrong judgment? There were men who shook their heads, and "didn't know about it;" but the preponderance of feeling was on the side of the proprietor, who sat in his library and imagined just what was in progress around him—nay calculated upon it, as a chemist calculates the results of certain combinations in his laboratory. He knew the people a great deal better than they knew him, or even themselves.

Miss Butterworth called at the house of the Rev. Solomon Snow, who, immediately upon her entrance, took his seat in his arm-chair, and adjusted his bridge. The little woman was so combative and incisive that this always seemed a necessary precaution on the part of that gentleman.

"I want to see it!" said Miss Butterworth, without the slightest indication of the object of her curiosity.

Mrs. Snow rose without hesitation, and, going to a trunk in her bedroom, brought out her precious certificate of stock, and placed it in the hands of the tailoress.

It certainly was a certificate of stock, to the amount of five shares, in the Continental Petroleum Company, and Mr. Belcher's name was not among the signatures of the officers.

"Well, that beats me!" exclaimed Miss Butterworth. "What do you suppose the old snake wants now?"

"That's just what I say—just what I say," responded Mrs. Snow. "Goodness knows, if its worth anything, we need it; but what *does* he want?"

"You'll find out some time. Take my word for it, he has a large axe to grind."

"I think," said Mr. Snow judicially, "that it is quite possible that we have been unjust to Mr. Belcher. He is certainly a man of generous instincts, but with great eccentricities. Before condemning him *in toto* (here Mr. Snow opened his bridge to let out the charity that was rising within him, and closed it at once for fear Miss Butterworth would get in a protest), let us be sure that there is a possible selfish motive for this most unexpected munificence. When we ascertain the true state of the case, then we can take things as they air. Until we have arrived at the necessary knowledge, it becomes us to withhold all severe judgments. A generous deed has its reflex influence; and it may be that some good may come to Mr. Belcher from this, and help to mould his character to nobler issues. I sincerely hope it may, and that we shall realize dividends that will add permanently to our somewhat restricted sources of income."

Miss Butterworth sat during the speech, and trotted her knee. She had no faith in the paper, and she frankly said so.

"Don't be fooled," she said to Mrs. Snow. "By and by you will find out that it is all a trick. Don't expect anything. I tell you I know Robert Belcher, and I know he's a knave, if there ever was one. I can feel him—I can feel him now—chuckling over this business, for business it is."

"What would you do if you were in my place?" inquired Mrs. Snow. "Would you send it back to him?"

"Yes, or I'd take it with a pair of tongs and throw it out of the window. I tell you there's a nasty trick done up in that paper; and if you're going to keep it, don't say anything about it."

The family laughed, and even Mr. Snow unbent himself so far as to smile and wipe his spectacles. Then the little tailoress went away, wondering when the mischief would reveal itself, but sure that it would appear in good time. In good time—that is, in Mr. Belcher's good time—it did appear.

To comprehend the excitement that followed, it must

be remembered that the people of Sevenoaks had the most implicit confidence in Mr. Belcher's business sagacity. He had been upon the ground, and knew personally all about the great discoveries. Having investigated for himself, he had invested his funds in this company. If the people could only embark in his boat, they felt that they should be safe. He would defend their interests while defending his own. So the field was all ready for his reaping. Not Sevenoaks alone, but the whole country was open to any scheme which connected them with the profits of these great discoveries, and when the excitement at Sevenoaks passed away at last, and men regained their senses, in the loss of their money, they had the company of a multitude of ruined sympathizers throughout the length and breadth of the land. Not only the simple and the impressible yielded to the wave of speculation that swept the country, but the shrewdest business men formed its crest, and were thrown high and dry beyond all others, in the common wreck, when it reached the shore.

On the evening of the fourth day after his return, Mr. Belcher was waited upon at his house by a self-constituted committee of citizens, who merely called to inquire into the wonders of the region he had explored. Mr. Belcher was quite at his ease, and entered at once upon a narrative of his visit. He had supposed that the excitement was without any good foundation, but the oil was really there; and he did not see why the business was not as legitimate and sound as any in the world. The whole world needed the oil, and this was the one locality which produced it. There was undoubtedly more or less of wild speculation connected with it, and, considering the value of the discoveries, it was not to be wondered at. On the whole, it was the biggest thing that had turned up during his lifetime.

Constantly leading them away from the topic of investment, he regaled their ears with the stories of the enormous fortunes that had been made, until there was not a man before him who was not ready to invest half the fortune he possessed in the speculation. Finally, one of the more frank and impatient of the group informed Mr. Belcher that they had come prepared to invest, if they found his report favorable.

"Gentlemen," said Mr. Belcher, "I really cannot take the responsibility of advising you. I can act for myself, but when it comes to advising my neighbors, it is another matter entirely. You really must excuse me from this. I have gone into the business rather heavily, but I have done it without advice, and you must do the same. It isn't right for any man to lead another into experiments of this sort, and it is hardly the fair thing to ask him to do it. I've looked for myself, but the fact that I am satisfied is no good reason for your being so."

"Very well, tell us how to do it," said the spokesman. "We cannot leave our business to do what you have done, and we shall be obliged to run some risk, if we go into it at all."

"Now, look here," said the wily proprietor, "you are putting me in a hard place. Suppose the matter turns out badly: are you going to come to me, and charge me with leading you into it?"

"Not at all," was responded almost in unison.

"If you want to go into the Continental, I presume there is still some stock to be had. If you wish me to act as your agent, I will serve you with a great deal of pleasure, but, mark you, I take no responsibility. I will receive your money, and you shall have your certificates as soon as the mail will bring them; and, if I can get no stock of the Company, you shall have some of my own."

They protested that they did not wish to put him to inconvenience, but quietly placed their money in his hands. Every sum was carefully counted and recorded, and Mr. Belcher assured them that they should have their certificates within five days.

As they retired, he confidentially told them that they had better keep the matter from any but their particular friends. If there was any man among those friends who would like "a chance in," he might come to him, and he would do what he could for him.

Each of these men went off down the hill, full of dreams of sudden wealth, and, as each of them had three or four particular friends to whom Mr. Belcher's closing message was given, that gentleman was thronged with visitors the next day, each one of whom he saw alone. All of these, too, had particular friends, and within ten days Mr. Belcher had pocketed in his library the munificent sum of one hundred and fifty thousand dollars. After a reasonable period, each investor received a certificate of his stock through the mail.

It was astonishing to learn that there was so much money in the village. It came in sums of one hundred up to five hundred dollars, from the most unexpected sources—little hoards that covered the savings of many years. It came from widows and orphans; it came from clergymen; it came from small tradesmen and farmers; it came from the best business men in the place and region.

The proprietor was in daily communication with his confederates and tools, and the investors were one day electrified by the information that the Continental had declared a monthly dividend of two per cent. This was what was needed to unload Mr. Belcher of nearly all the stock he held, and, within one month of his arrival from the oil-fields, he had realized a sum sufficient to pay for his new purchase in the city, and the costly furniture with which he proposed to illuminate it.

Sevenoaks was happy. The sun of prosperity had

dawned upon the people, and the favored few who supposed that they were the only ones to whom the good fortune had come, were surprised to find themselves a great multitude. The dividend was the talk of the town. Those who had invested a portion of their small means invested more, and those whose good angel had spared them from the sacrifice yielded to the glittering temptation, and joined their lot with their rejoicing neighbors. Mr. Belcher walked or drove among them, and rubbed his hands over their good fortune. He knew very well that if he were going to reside longer among the people, his position would be a hard one ; but he calculated that when the explosion should come, he should be beyond its reach.

It was a good time for him to declare the fact that he was about to leave them ; and this he did. An earthquake would not have filled them with greater surprise and consternation. The industries of the town were in his hands. The principal property of the village was his. He was identified with the new enterprise upon which they had built such high hope, and they had come to believe that he was a kindlier man than they had formerly supposed him to be.

Already, however, there were suspicions in many minds that there were bubbles on their oil, ready to burst, and reveal the shallowness of the material beneath them ; but these very suspicions urged them to treat Mr. Belcher well, and to keep him interested for them. They protested against his leaving them. They assured him of their friendship. They told him that he had grown up among them, and that they could not but feel that he belonged to them. They were proud of the position and prosperity he had won for himself. They fawned upon him, and when, at last, he told them that it was too late —that he had purchased and furnished a home for himself in the city—they called a public meeting, and, after a dozen regretful and complimentary speeches, from clergy and laity, resolved :

"1st. That we have learned with profound regret that our distinguished fellow-citizen, ROBERT BELCHER, Esq., is about to remove his residence from among us, and to become a citizen of the commercial emporium of our country.

"2d. That we recognize in him a gentleman of great business enterprise, of generous instincts, of remarkable public spirit, and a personal illustration of the beneficent influence of freedom and of free democratie institutions.

"3d. That the citizens of Sevenoaks will ever hold in kindly remembrance a gentleman who has been identified with the growth and importance of their beloved village, and that they shall follow him to his new home with heartiest good wishes and prayers for his welfare.

"4th. That whenever in the future his heart and his steps shall turn toward his old home, and the friends of his youth, he shall be greeted with voices of welcome, and hearts and homes of hospitality.

"5th. That these resolutions shall be published in the county papers, and that a copy shall be presented to the gentleman named therein, by a committee to be appointed by the chairman."

As was quite natural, and quite noteworthy, under the circumstances, the committee appointed was composed of those most deeply interested in the affairs of the Continental Petroleum Company.

Mr. Belcher received the committee very graciously, and made them a neat little speech, which he had carefully prepared for the occasion. In concluding, he alluded to the great speculation in which they, with so many of their fellow-citizens, had embarked.

"Gentlemen," said he, "there is no one who holds so large an interest in the Continental as myself. I have parted with many of my shares to gratify the desire of the people of Sevenoaks to possess them, but I still hold more than any of you. If the enterprise prospers, I shall prosper with you. If it goes down, as I sincerely hope it may not—more for your sakes, believe me, than my own—I shall suffer with you. Let us hope for the best. I have already authority for announcing to you that another monthly dividend of two per cent. will be paid you before I am called upon to leave you. That certainly looks like prosperity. Gentlemen, I bid you farewell."

When they had departed, having first heartily shaken the proprietor's hand, that gentleman locked his door, and gazed for a long time into his mirror.

"Robert Belcher," said he, "are you a rascal? Who says rascal? Are you any worse than the crowd? How badly would any of these precious fellow-citizens of yours feel if they knew their income was drawn from other men's pockets? Eh? Wouldn't they prefer to have somebody suffer rather than lose their investments? Verily, verily, I say unto you, they would. Don't talk to me about being a rascal! You're just a little sharper than the rest of them—that's all. They wanted to get money without earning it, and wanted me to help them to do it. I wanted to get money without earning it, and I wanted them to help me to do it. It happens that they will be disappointed and that I am satisfied. Don't say rascal to me, sir. If I ever hear that word again I'll throttle you. Is that question settled? It is? Very well. Let there be peace between us. . . . List! I hear the roar of the mighty city! Who lives in yonder palace? Whose wealth surrounds him thus with luxuries untold? Who walks out of yonder door and gets into that carriage, waiting with impatient steeds? Is that gentleman's name Belcher? Take a good look at him as he rolls away, bowing right and left to the gazing multitude. He is gone. The abyss of heaven swallows up his form, and yet I linger. Why lingerest thou? Farewell! and again I say, farewell!"

Mr. Belcher had very carefully covered all his tracks. He had insisted on having his name omitted from the list of officers of the Continental Petroleum Company. He had carefully forwarded the names of all who had invested in its stock for record, so that, if the books should ever be brought to light, there should be no apparent irregularity in his dealings. His own name was there with the rest, and a small amount of money had been set aside for operating expenses, so that something would appear to have been done.

The day approached for his departure, and his agent, with his family, was installed in his house for its protection; and one fine morning, having first posted on two or three public places the announcement of a second monthly dividend to be paid through his agent to the stockholders in the Continental, he, with his family, rode down the hill in his coach, followed by an enormous baggage-wagon loaded with trunks, and passed through the village. Half of Sevenoaks was out to witness the departure. Cheers rent the air from every group; and if a conqueror had returned from the most sacred patriotic service he could not have received a heartier ovation than that bestowed upon the graceless fugitive. He bowed from side to side in his own lordly way, and flourished and extended his pudgy palm in courtly courtesy.

Mrs. Belcher sat back in her seat, shrinking from all these demonstrations, for she knew that her husband was unworthy of them. The carriages disappeared in the distance, and then—sad, suspicious, uncommunicative—the men went off to draw their last dividend and go about their work. They fought desperately against their own distrust. In the proportion that they doubted the proprietor they were ready to defend him; but there was not a man of them who had not been fairly warned that he was running his own risk, and who had not sought for the privilege of throwing away his money.

CHAPTER XII.

IN WHICH JIM ENLARGES HIS PLANS FOR A HOUSE, AND COMPLETES HIS PLANS FOR A HOUSE-KEEPER.

WHEN, at last, Jim and Mr. Benedict were left alone by the departure of Mr. Balfour and the two lads, they sat as if they had been stranded by a sudden squall after a long and pleasant voyage. Mr. Benedict was plunged into profound dejection, and Jim saw that he must be at once and persistently diverted.

"I telled Mr. Balfour," said he, "afore he went away, about the house. I telled him about the stoop, an' the chairs, an' the ladder for posies to run up on, an' I said somethin' about cubberds and settles, an' other thingembobs that have come into my mind; an' says he: 'Jim, be ye goin' to splice?' An' says I: 'If so be I can find a little stick as'll answer, it wouldn't be strange if I did.' 'Well,' says he, 'now's yer time, if ye're ever goin' to, for the hay-day of your life is a passin' away.' An' says I: 'No, ye don't. My hay-day has jest come, and my grass is dry an' it'll keep. It's good for fodder, an' it wouldn't make a bad bed.'"

"What did he say to that?" inquired Mr. Benedict.

"Says he: 'I shouldn't wonder if ye was right. Have ye found the woman?' 'Yes,' says I. 'I have found a genuine creetur.' An' says he: 'What is her name?' An' says I: 'That's tellin'. It's a name as oughter be changed, an' it won't be my fault if it ain't.' An' then says he : 'Can I be of any 'sistance to ye?' An' says I: 'No. Courtin' is like dyin'; ye can't trust it to another feller. Ye've jest got to go it alone.' An' then he laughed, an says he : 'Jim, I wish ye good luck, an' I hope ye'll live to have a little feller o' yer own.' An' says I: 'Old Jerusalem! If I ever have a little feller o' my own,' says I, 'this world will have to spread to hold me.'"

Then Jim put his head down between his knees, and thought. When it emerged from its hiding his eyes were moist, and he said :

"Ye must 'scuse me, Mr. Benedict, for ye know what the feelin's of a pa is. It never come to me in this way afore."

Benedict could not help smiling at this new exhibition of sympathy; for Jim, in the comprehension of his feelings in the possible event of possessing offspring, had arrived at a more vivid sense of his companion's bereavement.

"Now, I tell ye what it is," said Jim. "You an' me has got to be brushin' round. We can't set here an' think about them that's gone; an' now I want to tell ye 'bout another thing that Mr. Balfour said. Says he: 'Jim, if ye're goin' to build a house, build a big one, an' keep a hotel. I'll fill it all summer for ye,' says he. 'I know lots o' folks,' says he, 'that would be glad to stay with ye, an' pay all ye axed 'em. Build a big house,' says he, 'an' take yer time for't, an' when ye git ready for company, let a feller know.' I tell ye, it made my eyes stick out to think on't. 'Jim Fenton's hotel!' says I. 'I don't b'lieve I can swing it.' 'If ye want any more money'n ye've got,' says he, 'call on me.'"

The idea of a hotel, with all its intrusions upon his privacy and all its diversions, was not pleasant to Mr. Benedict; but he saw at once that no woman worthy of Jim could be expected to be happy in the woods entirely deprived of society. It would establish a quicker and more regular line of communication with Sevenoaks, and thus make a change from its life to that of the woods a smaller hardship. But the building of a large house was a great enterprise for two men to undertake.

The first business was to draw a plan. In this work Mr. Benedict was entirely at home. He could not only make plans of the two floors, but an elevation of the front; and when, after two days of work, with frequent questions and examinations by Jim, his drawings were concluded, they held a long discussion over them. It was all very wonderful to Jim, and all very satisfactory—at least, he said so; and yet he did not seem to be entirely content.

"Tell me, Jim, just what the trouble is," said his architect, "for I see there's something wanting."

"I don't see," said Jim, "jest where ye're goin' to put 'im."

"Who do you mean? Mr. Balfour?"

"No; I don't mean no man."

"Harry? Thede?"

"No; I mean, s'posin'. Can't we put on an ell when we want it?"

"Certainly."

"An' now, can't ye make yer picter look kind o' cozy like, with a little feller playin' on the ground down there afore the stoop?"

Mr. Benedict not only could do this, but he did it; and then Jim took it, and looked at it for a long time.

"Well, little feller, ye can play thar till ye're tired, right on that paper, an' then ye must come into the house, an' let yer ma wash yer face;" and then Jim, realizing the comical side of all this charming dream, laughed till the woods rang again, and Benedict laughed with him. It was a kind of clearing up of the cloud of sentiment that enveloped them both, and they were ready to work. They settled, after a long discussion, upon the site of the new house, which was back from the river, near Number Ten. There were just three things to be done during the remainder of the autumn and the approaching winter. A cellar was to be excavated, the timber for the frame of the new house was to be cut and hewed, and the lumber was to be purchased and drawn to the river. Before the ground should freeze, they determined to complete the cellar, which was to be made small—to be, indeed, little more than a cave beneath the house, that would accommodate such stores as it would be necessary to shield from the frost. A fortnight of steady work, by both the men, not only completed the excavation, but built the wall.

Then came the selection of timber for the frame. It was all found near the spot, and for many days the sound of two axes was heard through the great stillness of the Indian summer; for at this time nature, as well as Jim, was in a dream. Nuts were falling from the hickory trees, and squirrels were leaping along the ground, picking up the stores on which they were to subsist during the long winter that lay before them. The robins had gone away southward, and the voice of the thrushes was still. A soft haze steeped the wilderness in its tender hue—a hue that carried with it the fragrance of burning leaves. At some distant forest shrine, the priestly winds were swinging their censers, and the whole temple was pervaded with the breath of worship. Blue-jays were screaming among leathern-leaved oaks, and the bluer kingfishers made their long diagonal flights from side to side of the river, chattering like magpies. There was one infallible sign that winter was close upon the woods. The wild geese, flying over Number Nine, had called to Jim with news from the Arctic, and he had looked up at the huge harrow scraping the sky, and said: "I seen ye, an' I know what ye mean,"

The timber was cut of appropriate length and rolled

upon low scaffoldings, where it could be conveniently hewed during the winter; then two days were spent in hunting and in setting traps for sable and otter, and then the two men were ready to arrange for the lumber.

This involved the necessity of a calculation of the materials required, and definite specifications of the same. Not only this, but it required that Mr. Benedict should himself accompany Jim on the journey to the mill, three miles beyond Mike Conlin's house. He naturally shrank from this exposure of himself; but so long as he was not in danger of coming in contact with Mr. Belcher, or with any one whom he had previously known, he was persuaded that the trip would not be unpleasant to him. In truth, as he grew stronger personally, and felt that his boy was out of harm's way, he began to feel a certain indefinite longing to see something of the world again, and to look into new faces.

As for Jim, he had no idea of returning to Number Nine again until he had seen Sevenoaks, and that one most interesting person there with whom he had associated his future, although he did not mention his plan to Mr. Benedict.

The ice was already gathering in the stream, and the winter was descending so rapidly that they despaired of taking their boat down to the old landing, and permitting it to await their return, as they would be almost certain to find it frozen in, and be obliged to leave it there until spring. They were compelled, therefore, to make the complete journey on foot, following to the lower landing the "tote-road" that Mike Conlin had taken when he came to them on his journey of discovery.

They started early one morning about the middle of November, and, as the weather was cold, Turk bore them company. Though Mr. Benedict had become quite hardy, the tramp of thirty miles over the frozen ground, that had already received a slight covering of snow, was a cruel one, and taxed to their utmost his powers of endurance.

Jim carried the pack of provisions, and left his companion without a load ; so by steady, quiet, and almost speechless walking, they made the entire distance to Mike Conlin's house before the daylight had entirely faded from the pale, cold sky. Mike was taken by surprise. He could hardly be made to believe that the hearty-looking, comfortably dressed man whom he found in Mr. Benedict was the same whom he had left many months before in the rags of a pauper and the emaciation of a feeble convalescent. The latter expressed to Mike the obligations he felt for the service which Jim informed him had been rendered by the good-natured Irishman, and Mike blushed while protesting that it was "nothing at all, at all," and thinking of the hundred dollars that he earned so easily.

"Did you know, Jim," said Mike, to change the subject, "that owld Belcher has gone to New Yorrk to live ?"

"No."

"Yis, the whole kit an' boodle of 'em is gone, an' the purty man wid 'em."

"Hallelujer!" roared Jim.

"Yis, and be gorry he's got me hundred dollars," said Mike.

"What did ye gi'en it to 'im for, Mike? I didn't take ye for a fool."

"Well, ye see, I wint in for ile, like the rist of 'em. Och! ye shud 'ave seen the owld feller talk! 'Mike,' says he, 'ye can't afford to lose this,' says he. 'I should miss me slape, Mike,' says he, 'if it shouldn't all come back to ye.' 'An' if it don't,' says I, 'there'll be two uv us lyin' awake, an' ye'll have plinty of company; an' what they lose in dhraimin' they'll take out in cussin',' says I. 'Mike,' says he, 'ye hadn't better do it, an' if ye do, I don't take no resk;' an' says I, 'They're all goin' in, an' I'm goin' wid 'em.' 'Very well,' says he, lookin' kind o' sorry, and then, be gorry, he scooped the whole pile, an' barrin' the ile uv his purty spache, divil a bit have I seen more nor four dollars."

"Divil a bit will ye see agin," said Jim, shaking his head. "Mike, ye're a fool."

"That's jist what I tell mesilf," responded Mike; "but there's betther music nor hearin' it repaited; an' I've got betther company in it, barrin' Mr. Benedict's presence, nor I've got here in my own house."

Jim, finding Mike a little sore over his loss, refrained from further allusion to it; and Mr. Benedict declared himself ready for bed. Jim had impatiently waited for this announcement, for he was anxious to have a long talk with Mike about the new house, the plans for which he had brought with him.

"Clear off yer table," said Jim, "an' peel yer eyes, Mike, for I'm goin' to show ye somethin' that'll s'prise ye."

When his order was obeyed, he unrolled the precious plans.

"Now, ye must remember, Mike, that this isn't the house; these is plans, as Mr. Benedict has drawed. That's the kitchen, and that's the settin'-room, and that's the cubberd, and that's the bedroom for us, ye know, and on that other paper is the chambers."

Mike looked at it all earnestly, and with a degree of awe, and then shook his head.

"Jim," said he, "I don't want to bodder ye, but ye've jist been fooled. Don't ye see that divil a place 'ave ye got for the pig?"

"Pig!" exclaimed Jim, with contempt. "D'ye s'pose I build a house for a pig? I ain't no pig, an' she ain't no pig."

"The proof of the puddin' is in the atin', Jim; an' ye don't know the furrst thing about house-kapin'. Ye can no more kape house widout a pig, nor ye can row yer boat widout a paddle. I'm an owld house-kaper, Jim, an' I know ; and a man that don't tend to his pig furrst, is no betther nor a b'y. Ye might put 'im in Number Tin, but he'd go through it quicker nor water through a baskit. Don't talk to me about house-kapin' widout a pig. Ye might give 'im that little shtoop to lie on, an' let 'im run under the house to slape. That wouldn't be bad now, Jim ? "

The last suggestion was given in a tender, judicial tone, for Mike saw that Jim was disappointed, if not disgusted. Jim was looking at his beautiful stoop, and thinking of the pleasant dreams he had associated with it. The idea of Mike's connecting the life of a pig with that stoop was more than he could bear.

" Why, Mike," said he, in an injured tone, " that stoop's the place where she's agoin' to set."

" Oh ! I didn't know, Jim, ye was agoin' to kape hins. Now, ef you're agoin' to kape hins, ye kin do as ye plase, Jim, in coorse ; but ye musn't forgit the pig, Jim. Be gorry, he ates everything that nobody ilse kin ate, and then ye kin ate him."

Mike had had his expression of opinion, and shown to his own satisfaction that his judgments were worth something. Having done this, he became amiable, sympathetic, and even admiring. Jim was obliged to tell him the same things a great many times, and to end at last without the satisfaction of knowing that the Irishman comprehended the precious plans. He would have been glad to make a confidant of Mike, but the Irishman's obtuseness and inability to comprehend his tenderer sentiments, repulsed him, and drove him back upon himself.

Then came up the practical question concerning Mike's ability to draw the lumber for the new house Mike thought he could hire a horse for his keeping, and a sled for a small sum, that would enable him to double his facilities for doing the job ; and then a price for the work was agreed upon.

The next morning, Jim and Mr. Benedict pursued their journey to the lumber-mill, and there spent the day in selecting their materials, and filling out their specifications.

The first person Mr. Benedict saw on entering the mill was a young man from Sevenoaks, whom he had known many years before. He colored as if he had been detected in a crime, but the man gave him no sign that the recognition was mutual. His old acquaintance had no memory of him, apparently ; and then he realized the change that must have passed upon him during his long invalidism and his wonderful recovery.

They remained with the proprietor of the mill during the night.

"I jest call 'im Number Ten," said Jim, in response to the inquiries that were made of him concerning his companion. "He never telled me his name, an' I never axed 'im. I'm 'Number Nine,' an' he's 'Number Ten,' and that's all thar is about it."

Jim's oddities were known, and inquiries were pushed no further, though Jim gratuitously informed his host that the man had come into the woods to get well, and was willing to work to fill up his time.

On the following morning, Jim proposed to Mr. Benedict to go on to Sevenoaks for the purchase of more tools, and the nails and hardware that would be necessary in finishing the house. The experience of the latter during the previous day showed him that he need not fear detection, and, now that Mr. Belcher was out of the way, Jim found him possessed by a strong desire to make the proposed visit. The road was not difficult, and before sunset the two men found themselves housed in the humble lodgings that had for many years been familiar to Jim. Mr. Benedict went into the streets, and among the shops, the next morning, with great reluctance; but this soon wore off as he met man after man whom he knew, who failed to recognize him. In truth, so many things had happened, that the memory of the man who, long ago, had been given up as dead had passed out of mind. The people would have been no more surprised to see a sleeper of the village cemetery among them than they would to have realized that they were talking with the insane pauper who had fled, as they supposed, to find his death in the forest.

They had a great deal to do during the day, and when night came, Jim could no longer be restrained from the visit that gave significance, not only to his journey, but to all his plans. Not a woman had been seen on the street during the day whom Jim had not scanned with an anxious and greedy look, in the hope of seeing the one figure that was the desire of his eyes—but he had not seen it. Was she ill? Had she left Sevenoaks? He would not inquire, but he would know before he slept.

"There's a little business as must be did afore I go," said Jim to Mr. Benedict, in the evening, "an' I sh'd like to have ye go with me, if ye feel up to it." Mr. Benedict felt up to it, and the two went out together. They walked along the silent street, and saw the great mill, ablaze with light. The mist from the falls showed white in the frosty air, and, without saying a word, they crossed the bridge, and climbed a hill dotted with little dwellings.

Jim's heart was in his mouth, for his fears that ill had happened to the little tailoress had made him nervous; and when, at length, he caught sight of the light in her window, he grasped Mr. Benedict by the arm almost fiercely, and exclaimed:

"It's all right. The little woman's in, an' waitin' Can you see my har?"

Having been assured that it was in a presentable condition, Jim walked boldly up to the door and knocked. Having been admitted by the same girl who had received him before, there was no need to announce his name. Both men went into the little parlor of the house, and the girl in great glee ran upstairs to inform Miss Butterworth that there were two men and a dog in waiting, who wished to see her. Miss Butterworth came down from busy work, like one in a hurry, and was met by Jim with extended hand, and the gladdest smile that ever illuminated a human face.

"How fare ye, little woman?" said he. "I'm glad to see ye—gladder nor I can tell ye."

There was something in the greeting so hearty, so warm and tender and full of faith, that Miss Butterworth was touched. Up to that moment he had made no impression upon her heart, and, quite to her surprise, she found that she was glad to see him. She had had a world of trouble since she had met Jim, and the great, wholesome nature, fresh from the woods, and untouched by the trials of those with whom she was in daily association, was like a breeze in the feverish summer, fresh from the mountains. She was, indeed, glad to see him, and surprised by the warmth of the sentiment that sprang within her heart in response to his greeting.

Miss Butterworth looked inquiringly, and with some embarrassment at the stranger.

"That's one o' your old friends, little woman," said Jim. "Don't give 'im the cold shoulder. 'Tain't every day as a feller comes to ye from the other side o' Jordan."

Miss Butterworth naturally suspected the stranger's identity, and was carefully studying his face to assure herself that Mr. Benedict was really in her presence. When some look of his eyes, or motion of his body, brought her the conclusive evidence of his identity, she grasped both his hands, and said :

"Dear, dear, Mr. Benedict! how much you have suffered! I thank God for you, and for the good friend He has raised up to help you. It's like seeing one raised from the dead."

Then she sat down at his side, and, apparently forgetting Jim, talked long and tenderly of the past. She remembered Mrs. Benedict so well! And she had so many times carried flowers and placed them upon her grave! She told him about the troubles in the town, and the numbers of poor poople who had risked their little all and lost it in the great speculation ; of those who were still hoping against hope that they should see their hard-earned money again ; of the execrations that were already beginning to be heaped upon Mr. Belcher ; of the hard winter that lay before the village, and the weariness of sympathy which had begun to tell upon her energies. Life, which had been once so full of the pleasure of action and industry, was settling, more and more, into dull routine, and she could see nothing but trouble ahead, for herself and for all those in whom she was interested.

Mr. Benedict, for the first time since Jim had rescued him from the alms-house, became wholly himself. The sympathy of a woman unlocked his heart, and he talked in his old way. He alluded to his early trials with entire freedom, to his long illness and mental alienation, to his hopes for his boy, and especially to his indebtedness to Jim. On this latter point he poured out his whole heart, and Jim himself was deeply affected by the revelation of his gratitude. He tried in vain to protest, for Mr. Benedict, having found his tongue, would not pause until he had laid his soul bare before his benefactor. The effect that the presence of the sympathetic woman produced upon his *protégé* put a new thought into Jim's mind. He could not resist the conviction that the two were suited to one another, and that the "little woman," as he tenderly called her, would be happier with the inventor than she would be with him. It was not a pleasant thought, but even then he cast aside his selfishness with a great struggle, and determined that he would not stand in the way of an event which would crush his fondest hopes. Jim did not know women as well as he thought he did. He did not see that the two met more like two women than like representatives of opposite sexes. He did not see that the sympathy between the pair was the sympathy of two natures which would be the happiest in dependence, and that Miss Butterworth could no more have chosen Mr. Benedict for a husband than she could have chosen her own sister.

Mr. Benedict had never been informed by Jim of the name of the woman whom he hoped to make his wife, but he saw at once, and with sincere pleasure, that he was in her presence; and when he had finished what he had to say to her, and again heartily expressed his pleasure in renewing her acquaintance, he rose to go.

"Jim, I will not cut your call short, but I must get back to my room and prepare for to-morrow's journey. Let me leave you here, and find my way back to my lodgings alone."

"All right," said Jim, "but we ain't goin' home to-morrer."

Benedict bade Miss Butterworth "good-night," but, as he was passing out of the room, Jim remembered that there was something that he wished to say to him, and so passed out with him, telling Miss Butterworth that he should soon return.

When the door closed behind them, and they stood alone in the darkness, Jim said, with his hand on his companion's shoulder, and an awful lie in his throat:

"I brung ye here hopin' ye'd take a notion to this little woman. She'd do more for ye nor anybody else. She can make yer clo'es, and be good company for ye, an'——"

"And provide for me. No, that won't do, Jim."

"Well, you'd better think on't."

"No, Jim, I shall never marry again."

"Now's yer time. Nobody knows what'll happen afore mornin'."

"I understand you, Jim," said Mr. Benedict, "and I know what all this costs you. You are worthy of her, and I hope you'll get her."

Mr. Benedict tore himself away, but Jim said, "hold on a bit."

Benedict turned, and then Jim inquired :

"Have ye got a piece of Indian rubber?"

"Yes."

"Then jest rub out the picter of the little feller in front of the stoop, an' put in Turk. If so be as somethin' happens to-night, I sh'd want to show her the plans in the mornin' ; an' if she should ax me whose little feller it was, it would be sort o' cumbersome to tell her, an' I sh'd have to lie my way out on't."

Mr. Benedict promised to attend to the matter before he slept, and then Jim went back into the house.

Of the long conversation that took place that night between the woodsman and the little tailoress we shall present no record. That he pleaded his case well and earnestly, and without a great deal of bashfulness, will be readily believed by those who have made his acquaintance. That the woman, in her lonely circumstances, and with her hungry heart, could lightly refuse the offer of his hand and life was an impossibility. From the hour of his last previous visit she had unconsciously gone toward him in her affections, and when she met him she learned, quite to her own surprise, that her heart had found its home. He had no culture, but his nature was manly. He had little education, but his heart was true, and his arm was strong. Compared with Mr. Belcher, with all his wealth, he was nobility personified. Compared with the sordid men around her, with whom he would be an object of supercilious contempt, he seemed like a demigod. His eccentricities, his generosities, his originalities of thought and fancy, were a feast to her. There was more of him than she could find in any of her acquaintances—more that was fresh, piquant, stimulating, and vitally appetizing. Having once come into contact with him, the influence of his presence had remained, and it was with a genuine throb of pleasure that she found herself with him again.

When he left her that night, he left her in tears. Bending over her, with his strong hands holding her cheeks tenderly, as she looked up into his eyes, he kissed her forehead.

"Little woman," said he, "I love ye. I never knowed what love was afore, an' if this is the kind o' thing they have in heaven, I want to go there when you do. Speak a good word for me when ye git a chance."

Jim walked on air all the way back to his lodgings—walked by his lodgings—stood still, and looked up at the stars—went out to the waterfall, and watched the writhing, tumbling, roaring river—wrapped in transcendent happiness. Transformed and transfused by love, the world around him seemed quite divine. He had stumbled upon the secret of his existence. He had found the supreme charm of life. He felt that a new principle had sprung to action within him, which had in it the power to work miracles of transformation. He could never be in the future exactly what he had been in the past. He had taken a step forward and upward—a step irretraceable.

Jim had never prayed, but there was something about

this experience that lifted his heart upward. He looked up to the stars, and said to himself: "He's somewhere up thar, I s'pose. I can't seen 'im, an' I must look purty small to Him if He can seen me; but I hope He knows as I'm obleeged to 'im, more nor I can tell 'im. When He made a good woman, He did the biggest thing out, an' when He started a man to lovin' on her, He set up the best business that was ever did. I hope He likes the 'rangement, and won't put nothin' in the way on't. Amen! I'm goin' to bed."

Jim put his last determination into immediate execution. He found Mr. Benedict in his first nap, from which he felt obliged to rouse him, with the information that it was "all right," and that the quicker the house was finished the better it would be for all concerned.

The next morning, Turk having been substituted for the child in the foreground of the front elevation of the hotel, the two men went up to Miss Butterworth's, and exhibited and talked over the plans. They received many valuable hints from the prospective mistress of the prospective mansion. The stoop was to be made broader for the accommodation of visitors; more room for wardrobes was suggested, with little conveniences for housekeeping, which complicated the plans not a little. Mr. Benedict carefully noted them all, to be wrought out at his leisure.

Jim's love had wrought a miracle in the night. He had said nothing about it to his architect, but it had lifted him above the bare utilities of a house, so that he could see the use of beauty. "Thar's one thing," said he, "as thar hain't none on us thought on; but it come to me last night. There's a place where the two ruffs come together that wants somethin', an' it seems to me it's a cupalo—somethin' to stan' up over the whole thing, and say to them as comes, 'Hallelujer!' We've done a good deal for house-keepin', now let's do somethin' for glory. It's just like a ribbon on a bonnet, or a blow on a potato-vine. It sets it off, an' makes a kind o' Fourth o' July for it. What do ye say, little woman?"

The "little woman" accepted the suggestion, and admitted that it would at least make the building look more like a hotel.

All the details settled, the two men went away, and poor Benedict had a rough time in getting back to camp. Jim could hardly restrain himself from going through in a single day, so anxious was he to get at his traps and resume work upon the house. There was no fatigue too great for him now. The whole world was bright and full of promise; and he could not have been happier or more excited if he had been sure that at the year's end a palace and a princess were to be the reward of his enterprise.

CHAPTER XIII.

WHICH INTRODUCES SEVERAL RESIDENTS OF SEVENOAKS TO THE METROPOLIS AND A NEW CHARACTER TO THE READER.

HARRY BENEDICT was in the great city. When his story was known by Mrs. Balfour—a quiet, motherly woman—and she was fully informed of her husband's plans concerning him, she received him with a cordiality and tenderness which won his heart and made him entirely at home. The wonders of the shops, the wonders of the streets, the wonders of the places of public amusement, the music of the churches, the inspiration of the great tides of life that swept by him on every side, were in such sharp contrast to the mean conditions to which he had been accustomed, that he could hardly sleep. Indeed, the dreams of his unquiet slumbers were formed of less attractive constituents than the visions of his waking hours. He had entered a new world, which stimulated his imagination, and furnished him with marvellous materials for growth. He had been transformed by the clothing of the lad whose place he had taken into a city boy, difficult to be recognized by those who had previously known him. He hardly knew himself, and suspected his own consciousness of cheating him.

For several days he had amused himself in his leisure hours by watching a huge house opposite to that of the Balfours, into which was pouring a stream of furniture. Huge vans were standing in front of it, or coming and departing, from morning until night. Dressing-cases, book-cases, chairs, mirrors, candelabra, beds, tables—everything necessary and elegant in the furniture of a palace, were unloaded and carried in. All day long, too, he could see through the large windows the active figure and beautiful face of a woman who seemed to direct and control the movements of all who were engaged in the work.

The Balfours had noticed the same thing; but, beyond wondering who was rich or foolish enough to purchase and furnish Palgrave's Folly, they had given the matter no attention. They were rich, of good family, of recognized culture and social importance, and it did not seem to them that any one whom they would care to know would be willing to occupy a house so pronounced in vulgar display. They were people whose society no money could buy. If Robert Belcher had been worth a hundred millions instead of one, the fact would not have been taken into consideration in deciding any social question relating to him.

Finally the furnishing was complete; the windows were polished, the steps were furbished, and nothing seemed to wait but the arrival of the family for which the dwelling had been prepared.

Late one afternoon, before the lamps were lighted in the streets, he could see that the house was illuminated; and just as the darkness came on, a carriage drove up and a family alighted. The doors were thrown open, the beautiful woman stood upon the threshold, and all ran up to enter. She kissed the lady of the house, kissed the children, shook hands cordially with the gentleman of the party, and then the doors were swung to, and they were shut from the sight of the street; but just as the man entered, the light from the hall and the light from the street revealed the flushed face and portly figure of Robert Belcher.

Harry knew him, and ran down-stairs to Mrs. Balfour, pale and agitated as if he had seen a ghost. "It is Mr. Belcher," he said, "and I must go back. I know he'll find me; I must go back to-morrow."

It was a long time before the family could pacify him and assure him of their power to protect him; but they did it at last, though they left him haunted with the thought that he might be exposed at any moment to the new companions of his life as a pauper and the son of a pauper. The great humiliation had been burned into his soul. The petty tyrannies of Tom Buffum had cowed him, so that it would be difficult for him ever to emerge from their influence into a perfectly free boyhood and manhood. Had they been continued long enough, they would have ruined him. Once he had been entirely in the power of adverse circumstances and a brutal will, and he was almost incurably wounded.

The opposite side of the street presented very different scenes. Mrs. Belcher found, through the neighborly services of Mrs. Dillingham, that her home was all prepared for her, even to the selection and engagement of her domestic service. A splendid dinner was ready to be served, for which Mr. Belcher, who had been in constant communication with his convenient and most officious friend, had brought the silver; and the first business was to dispose of it. Mrs. Dillingham led the mistress of the house to her seat, distributed the children, and amused them all by the accounts she gave them of her efforts to make their entrance and welcome satisfactory. Mrs. Belcher observed her quietly, acknowledged to herself the woman's personal charms—her beauty, her wit, her humor, her sprightliness, and her more than neighborly service; but her quick, womanly instincts detected something which she did not like. She saw that Mr. Belcher was fascinated by her, and that he felt that she had rendered him and the family a service for which great gratitude was due; but she saw that the object of his admiration was selfish—that she loved power, delighted in having things her own way, and, more than all, was determined to place the mistress of the house under obligations to her. It would have been far more agreeable to Mrs. Belcher to find everything in confusion, than to have her house brought into habitable order by a stranger in whom she had no trust, and upon whom she had no claim. Mr. Belcher had bought the house without her knowledge; Mrs. Dillingham had arranged it without her supervision. She seemed to herself to be simply a child, over whose life others had assumed the offices of administration.

Mrs. Belcher was weary, and she would have been delighted to be alone with her family, but here was an intruder whom she could not dispose of. She would have been glad to go over the house alone, and to have had the privilege of discovery, but she must go with one who was bent on showing her everything, and giving her reasons for all that had been done.

Mrs. Dillingham was determined to play her cards well with Mrs. Belcher. She was sympathetic, confidential, most respectful; but she found that lady very quiet. Mr. Belcher followed them from room to room with wider eyes for Mrs. Dillingham than for the details of his new home. Now he could see them together—the mother of his children, and the woman who had already won his heart away from her. The shapely lady, with her queenly ways, her vivacity, her graceful adaptiveness to persons and circumstances, was sharply contrasted with the matronly figure, homely manners, and unresponsive mind of his wife. He pitied his wife, he pitied himself, he pitied his children, he almost pitied the dumb walls and the beautiful furniture around him.

Was Mrs. Dillingham conscious of the thoughts which possessed him? Did she know that she was leading him around his house, in her assumed confidential intimacy with his wife, as she would lead a spaniel by a silken cord? Was she aware that, as she moved side by side with Mrs. Belcher, through the grand rooms, she was displaying herself to the best advantage to her admirer, and that, yoked with the wifehood and motherhood of the house, she was dragging, while he held, the plough that was tilling the deep carpets for tares that might be reaped in harvests of unhappiness? Would she have dropped the chain if she had? Not she.

To fascinate, and make a fool of, a man who was strong and cunning in his own sphere; to have a hand —gloved in officious friendship—in other lives, furnished the zest of her unemployed life. She could introduce discord into a family without even acknowledging to herself that she had done it wittingly. She could do it, and weep over the injustice that charged her with it. Her motives were always pure! She had always done her best to serve her friends! and what were her rewards? So the victories which she won by her smiles, she made permanent by her tears. So the woman by whose intrigues the mischief came was transformed into a victim, from whose shapely shoulders the garment of blame slipped off, that society might throw over them the robes of its respectful commiseration, and thus make her more interesting and lovely than before!

Mrs. Belcher measured very carefully, or apprehended very readily, the kind of woman she had to deal with, and felt at once that she was no match for her. She saw that she could not shake her off, so long as it was her choice to remain. She received from her no direct offence, except the offence of her uninvited presence; but the presence meant service, and so could not be resented. And Mrs. Belcher could be of so much service to her! Her life was so lonely—so meaningless! It would be such a joy to her, in a city full of shams, to have one friend who would take her good offices, and so help to give to her life a modicum of significance!

After a full survey of the rooms, and a discussion of the beauties and elegancies of the establishment, they all descended to the dining-room, and, in response to Mrs. Dillingham's order, were served with tea.

"You really must excuse me, Mrs. Belcher," said the beautiful lady deprecatingly, "but I have been here for a week, and it seems so much like my own home, that I ordered the tea without thinking that I am the guest and you are the mistress."

"Certainly, and I am really very much obliged to you;" and then feeling that she had been a little untrue to herself, Mrs. Belcher added bluntly: "I feel myself in a very awkward situation—obliged to one on whom I have no claim, and one whom I can never repay."

"The reward of a good deed is in the doing, I assure you," said Mrs. Dillingham. sweetly. "All I ask is that you make me serviceable to you. I know all about the city, and all about its ways. You can call upon me for anything; and now let's talk about the house. Isn't it lovely?"

"Yes," said Mrs. Belcher, "too lovely. While so many are poor around us, it seems almost like an insult to them to live in such a place, and flaunt our wealth in their faces. Mr. Belcher is very generous toward his family, and I have no wish to complain, but I would exchange it all for my little room in Sevenoaks."

Mr. Belcher, who had been silent and had watched with curious and somewhat anxious eyes the introductory passage of this new acquaintance, was rasped by Mrs. Belcher's remark into saying: "That's Mrs. Belcher, all over! that's the woman, through and through! As if a man hadn't a right to do what he chooses with his money! If men are poor, why don't they get rich? They have the same chance I had; and there isn't one of 'em but would be glad to change places with me, and flaunt his wealth in my face. There's a precious lot of humbug about the poor which won't wash with me. We're all alike."

Mrs. Dillingham shook her lovely head.

"You men are so hard," she said; "and Mrs. Belcher has the right feeling; but I'm sure she takes great comfort in helping the poor. What would you do, my dear, if you had no money to help the poor with?"

"That's just what I've asked her a hundred times," said Mr. Belcher. "What would she do? That's something she never thinks of."

Mrs. Belcher shook her head, in return, but made no reply. She knew that the poor would have been better off if Mr. Belcher had never lived, and that the wealth which surrounded her with luxuries was taken from the poor. It was this, at the bottom, that made her sad, and this that had filled her for many years with discontent.

When the tea was disposed of, Mrs. Dillingham rose to go. She lived a few blocks distant, and it was necessary for Mr. Belcher to walk home with her. This he was glad to do, though she assured him that it was entirely unnecessary. When they were in the street, walking at a slow pace, the lady, in her close, confiding way, said:

"Do you know, I take a great fancy to Mrs. Belcher?"

"Do you, really?"

"Yes, indeed. I think she's lovely; but I'm afraid she doesn't like me. I can read—oh, I can read pretty well. She certainly didn't like it that I had arranged everything, and was there to meet her. But wasn't she tired? Wasn't she very tired? There certainly was something that was wrong."

"I think your imagination had something to do with it," said Mr. Belcher, although he knew that she was right.

"No, I can read;" and Mrs. Dillingham's voice trembled. "If she could only know how honestly I have tried to serve her, and how disappointed I am that my service has not been taken in good part, I am sure that her amiable heart would forgive me."

Mrs. Dillingham took out her handkerchief, near a street lamp, and wiped her eyes.

What could Mr. Belcher do with this beautiful, susceptible, sensitive creature? What could he do but reassure her? Under the influence of her emotion, his wife's offence grew flagrant, and he began by apologizing for her, and ended by blaming her.

"Oh! she was tired—she was very tired. That was all. I've laid up nothing against her; but you know I was disappointed, after I had done so much. I shall be all over it in the morning, and she will see it differently then. I don't know but I should have been troubled to find a stranger in my house. I think I should. Now, you really must promise not to say a word of all this talk to your poor wife. I wouldn't have you do it for the world. If you are my friend (pressing his arm), you will let the matter drop just where it is. Nothing would induce me to be the occasion of any differences in your home."

So it was a brave, true, magnanimous nature that was leaning so tenderly upon Mr. Belcher's arm! And he felt that no woman who was not either shabbily perverse, or a fool, could misinterpret her. He knew that his wife had been annoyed at finding Mrs. Dillingham in the house. He dimly comprehended, too, that her presence was an indelicate intrusion, but her intentions were so good!

Mrs. Dillingham knew exactly how to manipulate the coarse man at her side, and her relations to him and his wife. Her bad wisdom was not the result of experience, though she had had enough of it, but the product of an instinct which was just as acute, and true, and serviceable, ten years earlier in her life as it was then. She timed the walk to her purpose; and when Mr. Belcher parted with her, he went back leisurely to his great house, more discontented with his wife than he had ever been. To find such beauty, such helpfulness, such sympathy, charity, forbearance, and sensitiveness, all combined in one woman, and that woman kind and confidential toward him, brought back to him the days of his youth, in the excitement of a sentiment which he had supposed was lost beyond recall.

He crossed the street on arriving at his house, and took an evening survey of his grand mansion, whose lights were still flaming through the windows. The passengers jostled him as he looked up at his dwelling, his thoughts wandering back to the woman with whom he had so recently parted.

He knew that his heart was dead toward the woman who awaited his return. He felt that it was almost painfully alive toward the one he had left behind him, and it was with the embarrassment of conscious guilt that he rang the bell at his own door, and stiffened himself to meet the honest woman who had borne his children. Even the graceless touch of an intriguing woman's power —even the excitement of something like love toward one who was unworthy of his love—had softened him, so that his conscience could move again. He felt that his eyes bore a secret, and he feared that his wife could read it. And yet, who was to blame? Was anybody to blame? Could anything that had happened have been helped or avoided?

He entered, determining to abide by Mrs. Dillingham's injunction of silence. He found the servants extinguishing the lights, and met the information that Mrs. Belcher had retired. His huge pile of trunks had come during his absence, and remained scattered in the hall. The sight offended him, but, beyond a muttered curse, he said nothing, and sought his bed.

Mr. Belcher was not in good humor when he rose the next morning. He found the trunks where he left them on the previous evening; and when he called for the servants to carry them upstairs, he was met by open revolt. They were not porters, and they would not lift boxes; that sort of work was not what they were engaged for. No New York family expected service of that kind from those who were not hired for it.

The proprietor, who had been in the habit of exacting any service from any man or woman in his employ that he desired, was angry. He would have turned every one of them out of the house, if it had not been so inconvenient for him to lose them then. Curses trembled upon his lips, but he curbed them, inwardly determining to have his revenge when the opportunity should arise. The servants saw his eyes, and went back to their work somewhat doubtful as to whether they had made a judicious beginning. They were sure they had not, when, two days afterward, every one of them was turned out of the house, and a new set installed in their places.

He called for Phipps, and Phipps was at the stable. Putting on his hat, he went to bring his faithful servitor of Sevenoaks, and bidding him find a porter in the streets and remove the trunks at Mrs. Belcher's direction, he sat down at the window to watch for a passing newsboy. The children came down, cross and half sick with their long ride and their late dinner. Then it came on to rain in a most dismal fashion, and he saw before him a day of confinement and ennui. Without mental resource—unable to find any satisfaction except in action and intrigue—the prospect was anything but pleasant. The house was large, and, on a dark day, gloomy. His humor was not sweetened by noticing evidences of tears on Mrs. Belcher's face. The breakfast was badly cooked, and he rose from it exasperated. There was no remedy but to go out and call upon Mrs. Dillingham. He took an umbrella, and, telling his wife that he was going out on business, he slammed the door behind him and went down the steps.

As he reached the street, he saw a boy scudding along under an umbrella, with a package under his arm. Taking him for a newsboy, he called: "Here, boy! Give me some papers." The lad had so shielded his face from the rain and the house that he had not seen Mr. Belcher; and when he looked up he turned pale, and simply said: "I'm not a newsboy;" and then he ran away as if he were frightened.

There was something in the look that arrested Mr. Belcher's attention. He was sure he had seen the lad before, but where, he could not remember. The face haunted him—haunted him for hours, even when in the cheerful presence of Mrs. Dillingham, with whom he spent a long and delightful hour. She was rosy, and sweet, and sympathetic in her morning wrapper—more charming, indeed, than he had ever seen her in evening dress. She inquired for Mrs. Belcher and the children, and heard with great good humor his account of his first collision with his New York servants. When he went out from her inspiring and gracious presence he found his self-complacency restored. He had simply been hungry for her; so his breakfast was complete. He went back to his house with a mingled feeling of jollity and guilt, but the moment he was with his family the face of the boy returned. Where had he seen him? Why did the face give him uneasiness? Why did he permit himself to be puzzled by it? No reasoning, no diversion could drive it from his mind. Wherever he turned during the long day and evening that white, scared face obtruded itself upon him. He had noticed, as the lad lifted his umbrella, that he carried a package of books under his arm, and naturally concluded that, belated by the rain, he was on his way to school. He determined, therefore, to watch him on the following morning, his own eyes reinforced by those of his oldest boy.

The dark day passed away at last, and things were brought into more homelike order by the wife of the house, so that the evening was cozy and comfortable; and when the street lamps were lighted again and the stars came out, and the north wind sounded its trumpet along the avenue, the spirits of the family rose to the influence.

On the following morning, as soon as he had eaten his breakfast, he, with his boy, took a position at one of the windows, to watch for the lad whose face had so impressed and puzzled him. On the other side of the avenue a tall man came out, with a green bag under his arm, stepped into a passing stage, and rolled away. Ten minutes later two lads emerged with their books slung over their shoulders, and crossed toward them.

"That's the boy—the one on the left," said Mr. Belcher. At the same moment the lad looked up, and apparently saw the two faces watching him, for he quickened his pace.

"That's Harry Benedict," exclaimed Mr. Belcher's son and heir. The words were hardly out of his mouth when Mr. Belcher started from his chair, ran down-stairs with all the speed possible within the range of safety, and intercepted the lads at a side door, which opened upon the street along which they were running.

"Stop, Harry, I want to speak to you," said the proprietor, sharply.

Harry stopped, as if frozen to the spot in mortal terror.

"Come along," said Thede Balfour, tugging at his hand, "you'll be late at school."

Poor Harry could no more have walked than he could have flown. Mr. Belcher saw the impression he had made upon him, and became soft and insinuating in his manner.

"I'm glad to see you, my boy," said Mr. Belcher. "Come into the house, and see the children. They all remember you, and they are all homesick. They'll be glad to look at anything from Sevenoaks."

Harry was not reassured: he was only more intensely frightened. A giant, endeavoring to entice him into his cave in the woods, would not have terrified him more. At length he found his tongue sufficiently to say that he was going to school, and could not go in.

It was easy for Mr. Belcher to take his hand, limp and trembling with fear, and under the guise of friendliness to lead him up the steps, and take him to his room. Thede watched them until they disappeared, and then ran back to his home, and reported what had taken place. Mrs. Balfour was alone, and could do nothing. She did not believe that Mr. Belcher would dare to treat the lad foully, with the consciousness that his disappearance within his house had been observed, and wisely determined to do nothing but sit down at her window and watch the house

Placing Harry in a chair, Mr. Belcher sat down opposite to him, and said:

"My boy, I'm very glad to see you. I've wanted to know about you more than any boy in the world. I suppose you've been told that I am a very bad man, but I'll prove to you that I'm not. There, put that ten-dollar gold piece in your pocket. That's what they call an eagle, and I hope you'll have a great many like it when you grow up."

The lad hid his hands behind his back, and shook his head.

"You don't mean to say that you won't take it!" said the proprietor in a wheedling tone.

The boy kept his hands behind him, and shook his head.

"Well, I suppose you are not to blame for disliking me; and now I want you to tell me all about your getting away from the poor-house, and who helped you out, and where your poor, dear father is, and all about it. Come, now, you don't know how much we looked for you, and how we all gave you up for lost. You don't know what a comfort it is to see you again, and to know that you didn't die in the woods."

The boy simply shook his head.

"Do you know who Mr. Belcher is? Do you know he is used to having people mind him? Do you know that you're here in my house, and that you *must* mind me? Do you know what I do to little boys when they disobey me? Now, I want you to answer my questions, and do it straight. Lying won't go down with me. Who helped you and your father to get out of the poor-house?"

Matters had proceeded to a desperate pass with the lad. He had thought very fast, and he had determined that no bribe and no threat should extort a word of information from him. His cheeks grew hot and flushed, his eyes burned, and he straightened himself in his chair as if he expected death or torture, and was prepared to meet either, as he replied :

" I won't tell you."

" Is your father alive ? Tell me, you dirty little whelp ? Don't say that you won't do what I bid you to do again. I have a great mind to choke you. Tell me —is your father alive ? "

" I won't tell you, if you kill me."

The wheedling had failed ; the threatening had failed. Then Mr. Belcher assumed the manner of a man whose motives had been misconstrued, and who wished for information that he might do a kind act to the lad's father.

" I should really like to help your father, and if he is poor, money would do him a great deal of good. And here is the little boy who does not love his father well enough to get money for him, when he can have it and welcome ? The little boy is taken care of. He has plenty to eat, and good clothes to wear, and lives in a fine house, but his poor father can take care of himself. I think such a boy as that ought to be ashamed of himself. I think he ought to kneel down and say his prayers. If I had a boy who could do that, I should be sorry that he'd ever been born."

Harry was proof against this mode of approach also, and was relieved, because he saw that Mr. Belcher was baffled. His instincts were quick, and they told him that he was the victor. In the meantime Mr. Belcher was getting hot. He had closed the door of his room, while a huge coal fire was burning in the grate. He rose and opened the door. Harry watched the movement, and descried the grand staircase beyond his persecutor, as the door swung back. He had looked into the house while passing, during the previous week, and knew the relations of the staircase to the entrance on the avenue. His determination was instantaneously made, and Mr. Belcher was conscious of a swift figure that passed under his arm, and was half down the staircase before he could move or say a word. Before he cried " stop him ! " Harry's hand was on the fastening of the door, and when he reached the door, the boy was half across the street.

He had calculated on smoothing over the rough places of the interview, and preparing a better report of the visit of the lad's friends on the other side of the avenue, but the matter had literally slipped through his fingers. He closed the door after the retreating boy, and went back to his room without deigning to answer the inquiries that were excited by his loud command to " stop him."

Sitting down, and taking to himself his usual solace, and smoking furiously for a while, he said : "D——n!" Into this one favorite and familiar expletive he poured his anger, his vexation, and his fear. He believed at the moment that the inventor was alive. He believed that if he had been dead his boy would, in some way, have revealed the fact. Was he still insane ? Had he powerful friends ? It certainly appeared so. Otherwise, how could the lad be where he had discovered him ? Was it rational to suppose that he was far from his father ? Was it rational to suppose that the lad's friends were not equally the friends of the inventor ? How could he know that Robert Belcher himself had not un wittingly come to the precise locality where he would be under constant surveillance ? How could he know that a deeply laid plot was not already at work to undermine and circumvent him ? The lad's reticence, determined and desperate, showed that he knew the relations that existed between his father and the proprietor, and seemed to show that he had acted under orders.

Something must be done to ascertain the residence of

Paul Benedict, if still alive, or to assure him of his death, if it had occurred. Something must be done to secure the property which he was rapidly accumulating. Already foreign governments were considering the advantages of the Belcher rifle, as an arm for the military service, and negotiations were pending with more than one of them. Already his own Government, then in the first years of its great civil war, had experimented with it, with the most favorable results. The business was never so promising as it then appeared, yet it never had appeared so insecure.

In the midst of his reflections, none of which were pleasant, and in a sort of undefined dread of the consequences of his indiscretions in connection with Harry Benedict, the bell rang, and Mr. and Mrs. Talbot were announced. The factor and his gracious lady were in fine spirits, and full of their congratulations over the safe removal of the family to their splendid mansion. Mrs. Talbot was sure that Mrs. Belcher must feel that all the wishes of her heart were gratified. There was really nothing like the magnificence of the mansion. Mrs. Belcher could only say that it was all very fine, but Mr. Belcher, finding himself an object of envy, took great pride in showing his visitors about the house.

Mrs. Talbot, who in some way had ascertained that Mrs. Dillingham had superintended the arrangement of the house, said, in an aside to Mrs. Belcher: "It must have been a little lonely to come here and find no one to receive you—no friend, I mean."

"Mrs. Dillingham was here," remarked Mrs. Belcher, quietly.

"But she was no friend of yours."

"No; Mr. Belcher had met her."

"How strange! How very strange!"

"Do you know her well?"

"I'm afraid I do; but now, really, I hope you won't

permit yourself to be prejudiced against her. I suppose she means well, but she certainly does the most unheard-of things. She's a restless creature—not quite right, you know, but she has been immensely flattered. She's an old friend of mine, and I don't join the hue and cry against her at all, but she does such imprudent things! What did she say to you?"

Mrs. Belcher detected the spice of pique and jealousy in this charitable speech, and said very little in response—nothing that a mischief-maker could torture into an offence.

Having worked her private pump until the well whose waters she sought refused to give up its treasures, Mrs. Talbot declared she would no longer embarrass the new house-keeping by her presence. She had only called to bid Mrs. Belcher welcome, and to assure her that if she had no friends in the city, there were hundreds of hospitable hearts that were ready to greet her. Then she and her husband went out, waved their adieus from their snug little coupé, and drove away.

The call had diverted Mr. Belcher from his sombre thoughts, and he summoned his carriage, and drove down town, where he spent his day in securing the revolution in his domestic service already alluded to, in talking business with his factor, and in making acquaintances on 'Change.

"I'm going to be in the middle of this thing, one of those days," said he to Talbot as they strolled back to the counting-room of the latter after a long walk among the brokers and bankers of Wall Street. "If anybody supposes that I've come here to lie still, they don't know me. They'll wake up some fine morning and find a new hand at the bellows."

Twilight found him at home again, where he had the supreme pleasure of turning his very independent servants out of his house into the street, and installing a set who knew from the beginning the kind of man they had to deal with, and conducted themselves accordingly.

While enjoying his first cigar after dinner, a note was handed to him, which he opened and read. It was dated at the house across the avenue. He had expected and dreaded it, but he did not shrink like a coward from its perusal. It read thus :

"MR. ROBERT BELCHER : I have been informed of the shameful manner in which you treated a member of my family this morning—Master Harry Benedict. The bullying of a small boy is not accounted a dignified business for a man in the city which I learn you have chosen for your home, however it may be regarded in the little town from which you came. I do not propose to tolerate such conduct toward any dependent of mine. I do not ask for your apology, for the explanation was in my hands before the outrage was committed. I perfectly understand your relations to the lad, and trust that the time will come when the law will define them, so that the public will also understand them. Meantime, you will consult your own safety by letting him alone, and never presuming to repeat the scene of this morning.

"Yours, JAMES BALFOUR,
"Counsellor-at-Law."

"Hum! ha!" exclaimed Mr. Belcher, compressing his lips, and spitefully tearing the letter into small strips and throwing them into the fire. "Thank you, kind sir ; I owe you one," said he, rising, and walking his room. "*That* doesn't look very much as if Paul Benedict were alive. He's a counsellor-at-law, he is ; and he has inveigled a boy into his keeping, who, he supposes, has a claim on me ; and he proposes to make some money out of it. Sharp game!"

Mr. Belcher was interrupted in his reflections and his soliloquy by the entrance of a servant, with the information that there was a man at the door who wished to see him.

"Show him up."

The servant hesitated, and finally said : "He doesn't smell very well, sir."

"What does he smell of?" inquired Mr. Belcher, laughing.

"Rum, sir, and several things."

"Send him away, then."

"I tried to, sir, but he says he knows you, and wants to see you on particular business."

"Take him into the basement, and tell him I'll be down soon."

Mr. Belcher exhausted his cigar, tossed the stump into the fire, and, muttering to himself, "Who the devil!" went down to meet his caller.

As he entered a sort of lobby in the basement that was used as a servants' parlor, his visitor rose, and stood with great shame-facedness before him. He did not extend his hand, but stood still, in his seedy clothes and his coat buttoned to his chin, to hide his lack of a shirt. The blue look of the cold street had changed to a hot purple under the influence of a softer atmosphere ; and over all stood the wreck of a good face, and a head still grand in its outline.

"Well, you look as if you were waiting to be damned," said Mr. Belcher, roughly.

"I am, sir," responded the man solemnly.

"Very well ; consider the business done, so far as I am concerned, and clear out."

"I am the most miserable of men, Mr. Belcher."

"I believe you ; and you'll excuse me if I say that your appearance corroborates your statement."

"And you don't recognize me? Is it possible?" And the maudlin tears came into the man's rheumy eyes and rolled down his cheeks. "You knew me in better days, sir ;" and his voice trembled with weak emotion.

"No ; I never saw you before. That game won't work, and now be off."

"And you don't remember Yates?—Sam Yates—and the happy days we spent together in childhood?" And the man wept again, and wiped his eyes with his coat-sleeve.

"Do you pretend to say that you are Sam Yates, the lawyer?"

"The same, at your service."

"What brought you to this?"

"Drink, and bad company, sir."

"And you want money?"

"Yes!" exclaimed the man, with a hiss as fierce as if he were a serpent.

"Do you want to earn money?"

"Anything to get it."

"Anything to get drink, I suppose. You said 'anything.' Did you mean that?"

The man knew Robert Belcher, and he knew that the last question had a great deal more in it than would appear to the ordinary listener.

"Lift me out of the gutter," said he, "and keep me out, and—command me."

"I have a little business on hand," said Mr. Belcher, "that you can do, provided you will let your drink alone—a business that I am willing to pay for. Do you remember a man by the name of Benedict—a shiftless, ingenious dog, who once lived in Sevenoaks?"

"Very well."

"Should you know him again, were you to see him?"

"I think I should."

"Do you know you should? I don't want any thinking about it. Could you swear to him?"

"Yes. I don't think it would trouble me to swear to him."

"If I were to show you some of his handwriting, do you suppose that would help you any?"

"It—might."

"I don't want any 'mights.' Do you know it would?"

"Yes."

"Do you want to sell yourself—body, soul, brains, legal knowledge, everything—for money?"

"I've sold myself already at a smaller price, and I don't mind withdrawing from the contract for a better."

Mr. Belcher summoned a servant, and ordered something to eat for his visitor. While the man eagerly devoured his food, and washed it down with a cup of tea, Mr. Belcher went to his room, and wrote an order on his tailor for a suit of clothes, and a complete respectable outfit for the legal "dead beat" who was feasting himself below. When he descended, he handed him the paper, and gave him money for a bath and a night's lodging.

"To-morrow morning I want you to come here clean, and dressed in the clothes that this paper will give you. If you drink one drop before that time I will strip the clothes from your back. Come to this room and get a decent breakfast. Remember that you can't fool me, and that I'll have none of your nonsense. If you are to serve me, and get any money out of it, you must keep sober."

"I can keep sober—for a while—any way," said the man, hesitatingly and half-despairingly.

"Very well, now be off; and mind, if I ever hear a word of this, or any of our dealings outside, I'll thrash you as I would a dog. If you are true to me I can be of use to you. If you are not, I will kick you into the street."

The man tottered to his feet, and said: "I am ashamed to say that you may command me. I should have scorned it once, but my chance is gone, and I could be loyal to the devil himself—for a consideration."

The next morning Mr. Belcher was informed that Yates had breakfasted, and was awaiting orders. He descended to the basement, and stood confronted with a respectable-looking gentleman, who greeted him in a courtly way, yet with a deprecating look in his eyes, which said, as plainly as words could express: "Don't humiliate me any more than you can help! Use me, but spare the little pride I have, if you can."

The deprecatory look was lost upon Mr. Belcher. "Where did you get your clothes?" he inquired. "Come, now; give me the name of your tailor. I'm green in the city, you see."

The man tried to smile, but the effort was a failure.

"What did you take for a night-cap last night, eh?"

"I give you my word of honor, sir, that I have not taken a drop since I saw you."

"Word of honor! ha! ha! ha! Do you suppose I want your word of honor? Do you suppose I want a man of honor, any way? If you have come here to talk about honor, you are no man for me. That's a sort of nonsense that I have no use for."

"Very well; my word of dishonor," responded the man, desperately.

"Now you talk. There's no use in such a man as you putting on airs, and forgetting that he wears my clothes and fills himself at my table."

"I do not forget it, sir, and I see that I am not likely to."

"Not while you do business with me; and now, sit down and hear me. The first thing you are to do is to ascertain whether Paul Benedict is dead. It isn't necessary that you should know my reasons. You are to search every insane hospital, public and private, in the city, and every almshouse. Put on your big airs and play philanthropist. Find all the records of the past year—the death records of the city—everything that will help to determine that the man is dead, as I believe he is. This will give you all you want to do for the present.

The man's son is in the city, and the boy and the man left the Sevenoaks poor-house together. If the man is alive, he is likely to be near him. If he is dead, he probably died near him. Find out, too, if you can, when his boy came to live at Balfour's over the way, and where he came from. You may stumble upon what I want very soon, or it may take you all winter. If you should fail then, I shall want you to take the road from here to Sevenoaks, and even to Number Nine, looking into all the almshouses on the way. The great point is to find out whether he is alive or dead, and to know, if he is dead, where, and exactly when, he died. In the meantime, come to me every week with a written report of what you have done, and get your pay. Come always after dark, so that none of Balfour's people can see you. Begin the business and carry it on in your own way. You are old and sharp enough not to need any aid from me, and now be off."

The man took a roll of bills that Mr. Belcher handed him, and walked out of the door without a word. As he rose to the sidewalk, Mr. Balfour came out of the door opposite to him, with the evident intention of taking a passing stage. He nodded to Yates, whom he had not only known in other days, but had many times befriended, and the latter sneaked off down the street, while he, standing for a moment as if puzzled, turned, and with his latch-key re-entered his house. Yates saw the movement, and knew exactly what it meant. He only hoped that Mr. Belcher had not seen it, as, indeed, he had not, having been at the moment on his way upstairs.

Yates knew that, with his good clothes on, the keen lawyer would give but one interpretation to the change, and that any hope or direct plan he might have with regard to ascertaining when the boy was received into the family, and where he came from, was nugatory. He would not tell Mr. Belcher this.

Mr. Balfour called his wife to the window, pointed out the retreating form of Yates, gave utterance to his suspicions, and placed her upon her guard. Then he went to his office, as well satisfied that there was a mischievous scheme on foot as if he had overheard the conversation between Mr. Belcher and the man who had consented to be his tool.

CHAPTER XIV.

WHICH TELLS OF A GREAT PUBLIC MEETING IN SEVENOAKS, THE BURNING IN EFFIGY OF MR. BELCHER, AND THAT GENTLEMAN'S INTERVIEW WITH A REPORTER.

MR. BALFOUR, in his yearly journeys through Sevenoaks, had made several acquaintances among the citizens, and had impressed them as a man of ability and integrity; and, as he was the only New York lawyer of their acquaintance, they very naturally turned to him for information and advice. Without consulting each other, or informing each other of what they had done, at least half a dozen wrote to him the moment Mr. Belcher was out of the village, seeking information concerning the Continental Petroleum Company. They told him frankly about the enormous investments that they and their neighbors had made, and of their fears concerning the results. With a friendly feeling toward the people, he undertook, as far as possible, to get at the bottom of the matter, and sent a man to look up the property, and to find the men who nominally composed the company.

After a month had passed away and no dividend was announced, the people began to talk more freely among themselves. They had hoped against hope, and fought their suspicions until they were tired, and then they sought in sympathy to assuage the pangs of their losses and disappointments.

It was not until the end of two months after Mr. Belcher's departure that a letter was received at Sevenoaks from Mr. Balfour, giving a history of the company, which confirmed their worst fears. This history is already in the possession of the reader, but to that which has been detailed was added the information that, practically, the operations of the company had been discontinued, and the men who formed it were scattered. Nothing had ever been earned, and the dividends which had been disbursed were taken out of the pockets of the principals, from moneys which they had received for stock. Mr. Belcher had absorbed half that had been received, at no cost to himself whatever, and had added the grand total to his already bulky fortune. It was undoubtedly a gross swindle, and was, from the first, intended to be such; but it was under the forms of law, and it was doubtful whether a penny could ever be recovered.

Then, of course, the citizens held a public meeting—the great panacea for all the ills of village life in America. Nothing but a set of more or less impassioned speeches and a string of resolutions could express the indignation of Sevenoaks. A notice was posted for several days, inviting all the resident stockholders in the Continental to meet in council, to see what was to be done for the security of their interests.

The little town-hall was full, and, scattered among the boisterous throng of men, were the pitiful faces and figures of poor women who had committed their little all to the grasp of the great scoundrel who had so recently despoiled and deserted them.

The Rev. Mr. Snow was there, as became the pastor

of a flock in which the wolf had made its ravages, and the meeting was opened with prayer, according to the usual custom. Considering the mood and temper of the people, a prayer for the spirit of forgiveness and fortitude would not have been out of place, but it is to be feared that it was wholly a matter of form. It is noticeable that at political conventions, on the eve of conflicts in which personal ambition and party chicanery play prominent parts; on the inauguration of great business enterprises in which local interests meet in the determined strifes of selfishness, and at a thousand gatherings whose objects leave God forgotten and right and justice out of consideration, the blessing of the Almighty is invoked, while men who are about to rend each other's reputations, and strive, without conscience, for personal and party masteries, bow reverent heads and mumble impatient "Amens."

But the people of Sevenoaks wanted their money back, and that, certainly, was worth praying for. They wanted, also, to find some way to wreak their indignation upon Robert Belcher; and the very men who bowed in prayer after reaching the hall walked under an effigy of that person on their way thither, hung by the neck and dangling from a tree, and had rare laughter and gratification in the repulsive vision. They were angry, they were indignant, they were exasperated, and the more so because they were more than half convinced of their impotence, while wholly conscious that they had been decoyed to their destruction, befooled and overreached by one who knew how to appeal to a greed which his own ill-won successes and prosperities had engendered in them.

After the prayer, the discussion began. Men rose, trying their best to achieve self-control, and to speak judiciously and judicially, but they were hurled, one fter another, into the vortex of indignation, and cheer upon cheer shook the hall as they gave vent to the real feeling that was uppermost in their hearts.

After the feeling of the meeting had somewhat expended itself, Mr. Snow rose to speak. In the absence of the great shadow under which he had walked during all his pastorate, and under the blighting influence of which his manhood had shrivelled, he was once more independent. The sorrows and misfortunes of his people had greatly moved him. A sense of his long humiliation shamed him. He was poor, but he was once more his own ; and he owed a duty to the mad multitude around him which he was bound to discharge. "My friends," said he, "I am with you, for better or for worse. You kindly permit me to share in your prosperity, and now, in the day of your trial and adversity, I will stand by you. There has gone out from among us an incarnate evil influence, a fact which calls for our profound gratitude. I confess with shame that I have not only felt it, but have shaped myself, though unconsciously, to it. It has vitiated our charities, corrupted our morals, and invaded even the house of God. We have worshipped the golden calf. We have bowed down to Moloch. We have consented to live under a will that was base and cruel, in all its motives and ends. We have been so dazzled by a great worldly success, that we have ceased to inquire into its sources. We have done daily obeisance to one who neither feared God nor regarded man. We have become so pervaded with his spirit, so demoralized by his foul example, that when he held out even a false opportunity to realize something of his success, we made no inquisition of facts or processes, and were willing to share with him in gains that his whole history would have taught us were more likely to be unfairly than fairly won. I mourn for your losses, for you can poorly afford to suffer them; but to have that man forever removed from us; to be released from his debasing influence; to be untrammelled in our action and in the development of our resources; to be free men and free women, and to become content with our lot and with such gains as we may win in a legitimate way, is worth all that it has cost us. We needed a severe lesson, and we have had it. It falls heavily upon some who are innocent. Let us, in kindness to these, find a balm for our own trials. And, now, let us not degrade ourselves by hot words and impotent resentments. They can do no good. Let us be men—Christian men, with detestation of the rascality from which we suffer, but with pity for the guilty man, who, sooner or later, will certainly meet the punishment he so richly deserves. 'Vengeance is mine; I will repay,' saith the Lord."

The people of Sevenoaks had never before heard Mr. Snow make such a speech as this. It was a manly confession, and a manly admonition. His attenuated form was straight and almost majestic, his pale face was flushed, his tones were deep and strong, and they saw that one man, at least, breathed more freely, now that the evil genius of the place was gone. It was a healthful speech. It was an appeal to their own conscious history, and to such remains of manhood as they possessed, and they were strengthened by it.

A series of the most objurgatory resolutions had been prepared for the occasion, yet the writer saw that it would be better to keep them in his pocket. The meeting was at a stand, when little Dr. Radcliffe, who was sore to his heart's core with his petty loss, jumped up and declared that he had a series of resolutions to offer. There was a world of unconscious humor in his freak—unconscious, because his resolutions were intended to express his spite, not only against Mr. Belcher, but against the villagers, including Mr. Snow. He began by reading in his piping voice the first resolution passed at the previous meeting which so pleasantly dismissed the proprietor to the commercial metropolis of the country. The reading of this resolution was so sweet a sarcasm on the proceedings of that occasion, that it was received with peals of laughter and deafening cheers, and as he went bitterly on, from resolution to resolution, raising his voice to overtop the jargon, the scene became too ludicrous for description. The resolutions, which never had any sincerity in them, were such a confirmation of all that Mr. Snow had said, and such a comment on their own duplicity and moral debasement, that there was nothing left for them but to break up and go home.

The laugh did them good, and complemented the corrective which had been administered to them by the minister. Some of them still retained their anger, as a matter of course, and when they emerged upon the street and found Mr. Belcher's effigy standing upon the ground, surrounded by fagots ready to be lighted, they yelled: "Light him up, boys!" and stood to witness the sham *auto-da-fé* with a crowd of village urchins dancing around it.

Of course, Mr. Belcher had calculated upon indignation and anger, and rejoiced in their impotence. He knew that those who had lost so much would not care to risk more in a suit at law, and that his property at Sevenoaks was so identified with the life of the town—that so many were dependent upon its preservation for their daily bread—that they would not be foolhardy enough to burn it.

Forty-eight hours after the public meeting, Mr. Belcher, sitting comfortably in his city home, received from the postman a large handful of letters. He looked them over, and as they were all blazoned with the Sevenoaks post-mark, he selected that which bore the handwriting of his agent, and read it. The agent had not dared to attend the meeting, but he had had his spies there, who reported to him fully the authorship and drift of all the speeches in the hall, and the unseemly proceedings of the street. Mr. Belcher did not laugh, for his vanity was wounded. The thought that a town in which he had ruled so long had dared to burn his effigy in the open street was a humiliation ; particularly so, as he did not see how he could revenge himself upon the perpetrators of it without compromising his own interests. He blurted out his favorite expletive, lighted a new cigar, walked his room, and chafed like a caged tiger.

He was not in haste to break the other seals, but at last he sat down to the remainder of his task, and read a series of pitiful personal appeals that would have melted any heart but his own. They were from needy men and women whom he had despoiled. They were a detail of suffering and disappointment, and in some cases they were abject prayers for restitution. He read them all, to the last letter and the last word, and then quietly tore them into strips, and threw them into the fire.

His agent had informed him of the sources of the public information concerning the Continental Company, and he recognized James Balfour as an enemy. He had a premonition that the man was destined to stand in his way, and that he was located just where he could overlook his operations and his life. He would not have murdered him, but he would have been glad to hear that he was dead. He wondered whether he was incorruptible, and whether he, Robert Belcher, could afford to buy him—whether it would not pay to make his acquaintance—whether, indeed, the man were not endeavoring to force him to do so. Every bad motive which could exercise a man, he understood ; but he was puzzled in endeavoring to make out what form of selfishness had moved Mr. Balfour to take such an interest in the people of Sevenoaks.

At last he sat down at his table and wrote a letter to his agent, simply ordering him to establish a more thorough watch over his property, and directing him to visit all the newspaper offices of the region, and keep the reports of the meeting and its attendant personal indignities from publication.

Then, with an amused smile upon his broad face, he wrote the following letter:

"TO THE REVEREND SOLOMON SNOW—

"*Dear Sir:* I owe an apology to the people of Sevenoaks for never adequately acknowledging the handsome manner in which they endeavored to assuage the pangs of parting on the occasion of my removal. The resolutions passed at their public meeting are cherished among my choicest treasures, and the cheers of the people as I rode through their ranks on the morning of my departure, still ring in my ears more delightfully than any music I ever heard. Thank them, I pray you, for me, for their overwhelming friendliness. I now have a request to make of them, and I make it the more boldly because, during the past ten years, I have never been approached by any of them in vain when they have sought my benefactions. The Continental Petroleum Company is a failure, and all the stock I hold in it is valueless. Finding that my expenses in the city are very much greater than in the country, it has occurred to me that perhaps my friends there would be willing to make up a purse for my benefit. I assure you that it would be gratefully received; and I apply to you because, from long experience, I know that you are accomplished in the art of begging. Your graceful manner in accepting gifts from me has given me all the hints I shall need in that respect, so that the transaction will not be accompanied by any clumsy details. My butcher's bill will be due in a few days, and despatch is desirable.

"With the most cordial compliments to Mrs. Snow, whom I profoundly esteem, and to your accomplished daughters, who have so long been spared to the protection of the paternal roof,

"I am your affectionate parishioner,

"ROBERT BELCHER."

Mr. Belcher had done what he considered a very neat and brilliant thing. He sealed and directed the letter, rang his bell, and ordered it posted. Then he sat back in his easy chair, and chuckled over it. Then he rose and paraded himself before his mirror.

"When you get ahead of Robert Belcher, drop us a line. Let it be brief and to the point. Any information thankfully received. Are you, sir, to be bothered by this pettifogger? Are you to sit tamely down and be undermined? Is that your custom? Then, sir, you are a base coward. Who said coward? Did you, sir? Let this right hand, which I now raise in air, and clench in awful menace, warn you not to repeat the damning accusation. Sevenoaks howls, and it is well. Let every man who stands in my path take warning. I button my coat; I raise my arms; I straighten my form, and they flee away—flee like the mists of the morning, and over yonder mountain-top, fade in the far blue sky. And now, my dear sir, don't make an ass of yourself, but sit down. Thank you, sir. I make you my obeisance. I retire."

Mr. Belcher's addresses to himself were growing less frequent among the excitements of new society. He had enough to occupy his mind without them, and found sufficient competition in the matter of dress to modify in some degree his vanity of person; but the present occasion was a stimulating one, and one whose excitements he could not share with another.

His missive went to its destination, and performed a thoroughly healthful work, because it destroyed all hope of any relief from his hands, and betrayed the cruel contempt with which he regarded his old townsmen and friends.

He slept as soundly that night as if he had been an innocent infant; but on the following morning, sipping leisurely and luxuriously at his coffee, and glancing over the pages of his favorite newspaper, he discovered a letter with startling headings, which displayed his own name and bore the date of Sevenoaks. The "R" at its foot revealed Dr. Radcliffe as the writer, and the peppery doctor had not miscalculated in deciding that *The New York Tattler* would be the paper most affected by Mr. Belcher—a paper with more enterprise than brains, more brains than candor, and with no conscience at all; a paper which manufactured hoaxes and vended them for news, bought and sold scandals by the sheet as if they were country ginger-bread, and damaged reputations one day for the privilege and profit of mending them the next.

He read anew, and with marvellous amplification, the story with which the letter of his agent had already made him familiar. This time he had received a genuine wound, with poison upon the barb of the arrow that had pierced him. He crushed the paper in his hand and ascended to his room. All Wall Street would see it, comment upon it, and laugh over it. Balfour would read it and smile. New York and all the country would gossip about it. Mrs. Dillingham would peruse it. Would it change her attitude toward him? This was a serious matter, and it touched him to the quick.

The good angel who had favored him all his life, and brought him safe and sound out of every dirty difficulty of his career, was already on his way with assistance, although he did not know it. Sometimes this angel had assumed the form of a lie, sometimes that of a charity, sometimes that of a palliating or deceptive circumstance; but it had always appeared at the right moment; and this time it came in the form of an interviewing reporter. His bell rang, and a servant appeared with the card of "Mr. Alphonse Tibbets, of *The New York Tattler*."

A moment before, he was cursing *The Tattler* for publishing the record of his shame, but he knew instinctively that the way out of his scrape had been opened to him.

"Show him up," said the proprietor at once. He had

hardly time to look into his mirror, and make sure that his hair and his toilet were all right, before a dapper little fellow, with a professional manner, and a portfolio under his arm, was ushered into the room. The air of easy good nature and good fellowship was one which Mr. Belcher could assume at will, and this was the air that he had determined upon as a matter of policy in dealing with a representative of *The Tattler* office. He expected to meet a man with a guilty look, and a deprecating, fawning smile. He was, therefore, very much surprised to find in Mr. Tibbets a young gentleman without the slightest embarrassment in his bearing, or the remotest consciousness that he was in the presence of a man who might possibly have cause of serious complaint against *The Tattler*. In brief, Mr. Tibbets seemed to be a man who was in the habit of dealing with rascals, and liked them. Would Mr. Tibbets have a cup of coffee sent up to him? Mr. Tibbets had breakfasted, and, therefore, declined the courtesy. Would Mr. Tibbets have a cigar? Mr. Tibbets would, and, on the assurance that they were nicer than he would be apt to find elsewhere, Mr. Tibbets consented to put a handful of cigars into his pocket. Mr. Tibbets then drew up to the table, whittled his pencil, straightened out his paper, and proceeded to business, looking much, as he faced the proprietor, like a Sunday-school teacher on a rainy day, with one pupil before him who had braved the storm because he had his lesson at his tongue's end.

As the substance of the questions and answers appeared in the next morning's *Tattler*, hereafter to be quoted, it is not necessary to recite them here. At the close of the interview, which was very friendly and familiar, Mr. Belcher rose, and with the remark: "You fellows must have a pretty rough time of it," handed the reporter a twenty-dollar bank-note, which that gentleman pocketed without a scruple, and without any remarkable effusiveness of gratitude. Then Mr. Belcher wanted him to see the house, and so walked over it with him. Mr. Tibbets was delighted. Mr. Tibbets congratulated him. Mr. Tibbets went so far as to say that he did not believe there was another such mansion in New York. Mr. Tibbets did not remark that he had been kicked out of several of them, only less magnificent, because circumstances did not call for the statement. Then Mr. Tibbets went away, and walked off hurriedly down the street to write out his report.

The next morning Mr. Belcher was up early in order to get his *Tattler* as soon as it was dropped at his door. He soon found, on opening the reeking sheet, the column which held the precious document of Mr. Tibbets, and read:

"The Riot at Sevenoaks!!!
"An interesting Interview with Col. Belcher!
"The original account grossly Exaggerated!
"The whole matter an outburst of Personal Envy!
"The Palgrave Mansion in a fume!
"Tar, feathers and fagots!
"A Tempest in a Teapot!
"Petroleum in a blaze, and a thousand fingers burnt!!!
"Stand out from under!!!"

The headings came near taking Mr. Belcher's breath away. He gasped, shuddered, and wondered what was coming. Then he went on and read the report of the interview:

"A *Tattler* reporter visited yesterday the great proprietor of Sevenoaks, Colonel Robert Belcher, at his splendid mansion on Fifth Avenue. That gentleman had evidently just swallowed his breakfast, and was comforting himself over the report he had read in the *Tattler* of that morning, by inhaling the fragrance of one of his choice Havanas. He is evidently a devotee of the seductive weed, and knows a good article when he sees it

A copy of the *Tattler* lay on the table, which bore unmistakable evidences of having been spitefully crushed in the hand. The iron had evidently entered the Colonel's righteous soul, and the reporter, having first declined the cup of coffee hospitably tendered to him and accepted (as he always does when he gets a chance) a cigar, proceeded at once to business.

"*Reporter:* Col. Belcher, have you seen the report in this morning's *Tattler* of the riot at Sevenoaks, which nominally had your dealings with the people for its occasion?

"*Answer:* I have, and a pretty mess was made of it.

"*Reporter:* Do you declare the report to be incorrect?

"*Answer:* I know nothing about the correctness or the incorrectness of the report, for I was not there.

"*Reporter:* Were the accusations made against yourself correct, presuming that they were fairly and truthfully reported?

"*Answer:* They were so far from being correct that nothing could be more untruthful or more malicious.

"*Reporter:* Have you any objection to telling me the true state of the case in detail.

"*Answer:* None at all. Indeed, I have been so foully misrepresented, that I am glad of an opportunity to place myself right before a people with whom I have taken up my residence. In the first place, I made Sevenoaks. I have fed the people of Sevenoaks for more than ten years. I have carried the burden of their charities; kept their dirty ministers from starving; furnished employment for their women and children, and run the town. I had no society there, and of course, got tired of my humdrum life. I had worked hard, been successful, and felt that I owed it to myself and my family to go somewhere and enjoy the privileges, social and educational, which I had the means to command. I came to New York without consulting anybody, and bought this house. The people protested, but ended by holding a public meeting, and passing a series of resolutions complimentary to me, of which I very naturally felt proud; and when I came away, they assembled at the roadside and gave me the friendliest cheers.

"*Reporter:* How about the petroleum?

"*Answer:* Well, that is an unaccountable thing. I went into the Continental Company, and nothing would do for the people but to go in with me. I warned them—every man of them—but they would go in; so I acted as their agent in procuring stock for them. There was not a share of stock sold on any persuasion of mine. They were mad, they were wild, for oil. You wouldn't have supposed there was half so much money in the town as they dug out of their old stockings to invest in oil. I was surprised, I assure you. Well, the Continental went up, and they had to be angry with somebody ; and although I held more stock than any of them, they took a fancy that I had defrauded them, and so they came together to wreak their impotent spite on me. That's the sum and substance of the whole matter.

"*Reporter :* And that is all you have to say ?

"*Answer :* Well, it covers the ground. Whether I shall proceed in law against these scoundrels for maligning me, I have not determined. I shall probably do nothing about it. The men are poor, and even if they were rich, what good would it do me to get their money ? I've got money enough, and money with me can never offset a damage to character. When they get cool and learn the facts, if they ever do learn them, they will be sorry. They are not a bad people at heart, though I am ashamed, as their old fellow-townsman, to say that they have acted like children in this matter. There's a half-crazy, half-silly old doctor there by the name of Radcliffe, and an old parson by the name of Snow, whom I have helped to feed for years, who lead them into difficulty. But they're not a bad people, now, and I am sorry for their sake that this thing has got into the papers. It'll hurt the town. They have been badly led, inflamed over false information, and they have disgraced themselves.

"This closed the interview, and then Col. Belcher politely showed the *Tattler* reporter over his palatial abode. 'Taken for all in all,' he does not expect 'to look upon its like again.'

"'None see it but to love it,
None name it but to praise.'

"It was 'linked sweetness long drawn out,' and must have cost the gallant Colonel a pile of stamps. Declining an invitation to visit the stables—for our new millionaire is a lover of horse-flesh, as well as the narcotic weed—and leaving that gentleman to 'witch the world with wondrous horsemanship,' the *Tattler* reporter withdrew, 'pierced through with Envy's venomed darts,' and satisfied that his courtly entertainer had been 'more sinned against than sinning.'"

Col. Belcher read the report with genuine pleasure, and then, turning over the leaf, read upon the editorial page the following :

"COL. BELCHER ALL RIGHT.—We are satisfied that the letter from Sevenoaks, published in yesterday's *Tattler*, in regard to our highly respected fellow-citizen, Colonel Robert Belcher, was a gross libel upon that gentleman, and intended, by the malicious writer, to injure an honorable and innocent man. It is only another instance of the ingratitude of rural communities toward their benefactors. We congratulate the redoubtable Colonel on his removal from so pestilent a neighborhood to a city where his sterling qualities will find 'ample scope and verge enough,' and where those who suffer 'the slings and arrows of outrageous fortune' will not lay them to the charge of one who can, with truthfulness, declare 'Thou canst not say I did it.'"

When Mr. Belcher concluded, he muttered to himself, "Twenty dollars!—cheap enough." He had remained at home the day before; now, he could go upon 'Change with a face cleared of all suspicion. A cloud of truth had overshadowed him, but it had been dissipated by the genial sunlight of falsehood. His self-complacency was fully restored when he received a note, in the daintiest text on the daintiest paper, congratulating him on the triumphant establishment of his innocence before the New York public, and bearing as its signature a name so precious to him that he took it to his own room before destroying it and kissed it.

CHAPTER XV.

WHICH TELLS ABOUT MRS. DILLINGHAM'S CHRISTMAS AND THE NEW YEAR'S RECEPTION AT THE PALGRAVE MANSION.

A BRILLIANT Christmas morning shone in at Mrs. Dillingham's window, where she sat quietly sunning the better side of her nature. Her parlor was a little paradise, and all things around her were in tasteful keeping with her beautiful self. The Christmas chimes were deluging the air with music; throngs were passing by on their way to and from church, and exchanging the greetings of the day; wreaths of holly were in her own windows and in those of her neighbors; and the influences of the hour—half-poetical, half-religious—held the unlovely and the evil within her in benign though temporary thrall. The good angel was dominant within her, while the bad angel slept.

Far down the vista of the ages, she was looking into a stable where a baby lay, warm in its swaddling-clothes, the mother bending over it. She saw above the stable a single star, which, palpitating with prophecy, shook its long rays out into the form of a cross, then drew them in until they circled into a blazing crown. Far above the star the air was populous with lambent forms and resonant with shouting voices, and she heard the words: "Peace on earth, good-will to men!" The chimes melted into her reverie; the kindly sun encouraged it; the voices of happy children fed it, and she was moved to tears.

What could she do now but think over her past life—a life that had given her no children—a life that had been filled neither by peace nor good-will? She had married an old man for his money; had worried him out of his life, and he had gone and left her childless. She would not charge herself with the crime of hastening to the grave her father and mother, but she knew she had not been a comfort to them. Her wilfulness; her love of money and of power; her pride of person and accomplishments; her desire for admiration; her violent passions, had made her a torment to others and to herself. She knew that no one loved her for anything good that she possessed, and knew that her own heart was barren of love for others. She felt that a little child who would call her "mother," clinging to her hand, or nestling in her bosom, could redeem her to her better self; and how could she help thinking of the true men who, with their hearts in their fresh, manly hands, had prayed for her love in the dawn of her young beauty, and been spurned from her presence—men now in the honorable walks of life with their little ones around them? Her relatives had forsaken her. There was absolutely no one to whom she could turn for the sympathy which in that hour she craved.

In these reflections, there was one person of her own blood recalled to whom she had been a curse, and of whom, for a single moment, she could not bear to think. She had driven him from her presence—the one who, through all her childhood, had been her companion, her admirer, her loyal follower. He had dared to love and marry one whom she did not approve, and she had angrily banished him from her side. If she only had him to love, she felt that she should be better and happier, but she had no hope that he would ever return to her.

She felt now, with inexpressible loathing, the unworthiness of the charms with which she fascinated the base men around her. The only sympathy she had was from these, and the only power she possessed was over them, and through them. The aim of her life was to fascinate them; the art of her life was to keep them fascinated without the conscious degradation of herself, and, so, to lead them whithersoever she would. Her business was the manufacture of slaves—slaves to her personal charms and her imperious will. Each slave carried around his own secret, treated her with distant deference in society, spoke of her with respect, and congratulated himself on possessing her supreme favor. Not one of them had her heart, or her confidence. With a true woman's instinct, she knew that no man who would be untrue to his wife would be true to her. So she played with them as with puppies that might gambol around her, and fawn before her, but might not smutch her robes with their dirty feet, or get the opportunity to bite her hand.

She had a house, but she had no home. Again and again the thought came to her that in a million homes that morning the air was full of music—hearty greetings between parents and children, sweet prattle from lips unstained, merry laughter from bosoms without a care. With a heart full of tender regrets for the mistakes and errors of the past, with unspeakable contempt for the life she was living, and with vain yearnings for something better, she rose and determined to join the throngs that were pressing into the churches. Hastily prepared for the street, she went out, and soon, her heart responding to the Christmas music, and her voice to the Christmas utterances from the altar, she strove to lift her heart in devotion. She felt the better for it. It was an old habit, and the spasm was over. Having done a good thing, she turned her ear away from the suggestions of her good angel, and, in turning away, encountered the suggestions of worldliness from the other side, which came back to her with their old music. She came out of the church as one comes out of a theatre, where for hours he has sat absorbed in the fictitious passion of a play, to the grateful rush and roar of Broadway, the flashing of the lights, and the shouting of the voices of the real world.

Mr. Belcher called that evening, and she was glad to see him. Arrayed in all her loveliness, sparkling with vivacity and radiant with health, she sat and wove her toils about him. She had never seemed lovelier in his eyes, and, as he thought of the unresponsive and quiet woman he had left behind him, he felt that his home was not on Fifth Avenue, but in the house where he then sat. Somehow—he could not tell how—she had always kept him at a distance. He had not dared to be familiar with her. Up to a certain point he could carry his gallantries, but no further. Then the drift of conversation would change. Then something called her away. He grew mad with the desire to hold her hand, to touch her, to unburden his heart of its passion for her, to breathe his hope of future possession; but always, when the convenient moment came, he was gently repelled, tenderly hushed, adroitly diverted. He knew the devil was in her; he believed that she was fond of him, and thus knowing and believing, he was at his wit's end to guess why she should be so persistently perverse. He had drank that day, and was not so easily managed as usual, and she had a hard task to hold him to his proprieties. There was only one way to do this, and that was to assume the pathetic.

Then she told him of her lonely day, her lack of employment, her wish that she could be of some use in the world, and, finally, she wondered whether Mrs. Belcher would like to have her, Mrs. Dillingham, receive with her on New Year's Day. If that lady would not consider it an intrusion, she should be happy to shut her own house, and thus be able to present all the gentlemen of the city worth knowing, not only to Mrs. Belcher, but to her husband.

To have Mrs. Dillingham in the house for a whole day, and particularly to make desirable acquaintances so easily, was a rare privilege. He would speak to Mrs. Belcher about it, and he was sure there could be but one answer. To be frank about it, he did not intend there should be but one answer; but, for form's sake, it would be best to consult her. Mr. Belcher did not say—what was the truth—that the guilt in his heart made him more careful to consult Mrs. Belcher in the matter than he otherwise would have been; but now that his loyalty to her had ceased, he became more careful to preserve its semblance. There was a tender quality in Mrs. Dillingham's voice as she parted with him for the evening, and a half-returned, suddenly relinquished response to the pressure of his hand, which left the impression that she had checked an eager impulse. Under the influence of these, the man went out from her presence, flattered to his heart's core, and with his admiration of her self-contained and prudent passion more exalted than ever.

Mr. Belcher went directly home, and into Mrs. Belcher's room. That good lady was alone, quietly reading. The children had retired, and she was spending her time after her custom.

"Well, Sarah, what sort of a Christmas have you had?"

Mrs. Belcher bit her lip, for there was something in her husband's tone which conveyed the impression that he was preparing to wheedle her into some scheme upon which he had set his heart, and which he felt or feared, would not be agreeable to her. She had noticed a change in him. He was tenderer toward her than he had been for years, yet her heart detected the fact that the tenderness was a sham. She could not ungraciously repel it, yet she felt humiliated in accepting it. So, as she answered his question with the words: "Oh, much the same as usual," she could not look into his face with a smile upon her own.

"I've just been over to call on Mrs. Dillingham," said he.

"Ah?"

"Yes; I thought I would drop in and give her the compliments of the season. She's rather lonely, I fancy."

"So am I."

"Well now, Sarah, there's a difference; you know there is. You have your children, and ——"

"And she my husband."

"Well, she's an agreeable woman, and I must go out sometimes. My acquaintance with agreeable women in New York is not very large."

"Why don't you ask your wife to go with you? I'm fond of agreeable women too."

"You are not fond of her, and I'm afraid she suspects it."

"I should think she would. Women who are glad to receive alone the calls of married men, always do suspect their wives of disliking them."

"Well, it certainly isn't her fault that men go to see her without their wives. Don't be unfair now, my dear."

"I don't think I am," responded Mrs. Belcher. "I notice that women never like other women who are great favorites with men; and there must be some good reason for it. Women like Mrs. Dillingham, who abound in physical fascinations for men, have no liking for the society of their own sex. I have never heard a woman speak well of her, and I have never heard her speak well of any other woman."

"I have, and, more than that, I have heard her speak well of you. I think she is shamefully belied. Indeed, I do not think that either of us has a better friend than she, and I have a proposition to present to you which proves it. She is willing to come to us on New Year's Day, and receive with you—to bring all her acquaintances into your house, and make them yours and mine."

"Is it possible?"

"Yes; and I think we should be most ungrateful and discourteous to her, as well as impolitic with relation to ourselves and to our social future, not to accept the proposition."

"I don't think I care to be under obligations to Mrs. Dillingham for society, or care for the society she will bring us. I am not pleased with a proposition of this kind that comes through my husband. If she were my friend it would be a different matter, but she is not. If I were to feel myself moved to invite some lady to come here and receive with me, it would be well enough; but this proposition is a stroke of patronage as far as I am concerned, and I don't like it. It is like Mrs. Dillingham and all of her kind. Whatever may have been her motives, it was an indelicate thing to do, and she ought to be ashamed of herself for doing it."

Mr. Belcher knew in his heart that his wife was right. He knew that every word she had spoken was the truth. He knew that he should never call on Mrs. Dillingham with his wife, save as a matter of policy; but this did not modify his determination to have his own way.

"You place me in a very awkward position, my dear," said he, determined, as long as possible, to maintain an amiable mood.

"And she has placed me in one which you are helping to fasten upon me, and not at all helping to relieve me from."

"I don't see how I cán, my dear. I am compelled to go back to her with some answer; and, as I am determined to have my house open, I must say whether you accept or decline her courtesy; for courtesy it is, and not patronage at all."

Mrs. Belcher felt the chain tightening, and knew that she was to be bound, whether willing or unwilling. The consciousness of her impotence did not act kindly upon her temper, and she burst out:

"I do not want her here. I wish she would have done with her officious helpfulness. Why can't she mind her own business, and let me alone?"

Mr. Belcher's temper rose to the occasion; for although he saw in Mrs. Belcher's petulance and indignation that his victory was half won, he could not quite submit to the abuse of his brilliant pet.

"I have some rights in this house myself, my dear, and I fancy that my wishes are deserving of respect, at least."

"Very well. If it's your business, why did you come

to me with it? Why didn't you settle it before you left the precious lady, who is so much worthier your consideration than your wife? Now go, and tell her that it is your will that she shall receive with me, and that I tamely submit."

"I shall tell her nothing of the kind."

"You can say no less, if you tell her the truth."

"My dear, you are angry. Let's not talk about it any more to-night. You will feel differently about it in the morning."

Of course, Mrs. Belcher went to bed in tears, cried over it until she went to sleep, and woke in the morning submissive, and quietly determined to yield to her husband's wishes. Of course, Mr. Belcher was not late in informing Mrs. Dillingham that his wife would be most happy to accept her proposition. Of course, Mrs. Dillingham lost no time in sending her card to all the gentlemen she had ever met, with the indorsement, "Receives on New Year's with Mrs. Col. Belcher, —— Fifth Avenue." Of course, too, after the task was accomplished, she called on Mrs. Belcher to express her gratitude for the courtesy, and to make suggestions about the entertainment. Was it quite of course that Mrs. Belcher, in the presence of this facile woman, overflowing with kind feeling, courteous deference, pleasant sentiment and sparkling conversation, should feel half ashamed of herself, and wonder how one so good and bright and sweet could so have moved her to anger?

The day came at last, and at ten Mrs Dillingham entered the grand drawing-room in her queenly apparelling. She applauded Mrs. Belcher's appearance, she kissed the children, all of whom thought her the loveliest lady they had ever seen, and in an aside to Mr. Belcher cautioned him against partaking too bountifully of the wines he had provided for his guests. "Let us have a nice thing of it," she said, "and nothing to be sorry for."

Mr. Belcher was faithfully in her leading. It would have been no self-denial for him to abstain entirely for her sake. He would do anything she wished.

There was one thing noticeable in her treatment of the lads of the family, and in their loyalty to her. She could win a boy's heart with a touch of her hand, a smile and a kiss. They clung to her whenever in her presence. They hung charmed upon all her words. They were happy to do anything she desired ; and as children see through shams more quickly than their elders, it could not be doubted that she had a genuine affection for them. A child addressed the best side of her nature, and evoked a passion that had never found rest in satisfaction, while her heartiness and womanly beauty appealed to the boy nature with charms to which it yielded unbounded admiration and implicit confidence.

The reception was a wonderful success. Leaving out of the account the numbers of gentlemen who came to see the revived glories of the Palgrave mansion, there was a large number of men who had been summoned by Mrs. Dillingham's cards—men who undoubtedly ought to have been in better business or in better company. They were men in good positions—clergymen, merchants, lawyers, physicians, young men of good families—men whose wives and mothers and sisters entertained an uncharitable opinion of that lady ; but for this one courtesy of a year the men would not be called to account. Mrs. Dillingham knew them all at sight, called each man promptly by name, and presented them all to her dear friend Mrs. Belcher, and then to Col. Belcher, who, dividing his attention between the drawing-room and the dining-room, played the host with rude heartiness and large hospitality.

Mrs. Belcher was surprised by the presence of a number of men whose names were familiar with the public —members of Congress, representatives of the city government, clergymen even, who were generally supposed to be "at home" on that day. Why had these made their appearance? She could only come to one conclusion, which was, that they regarded Mrs. Dillingham as a show. Mrs. Dillingham in a beautiful house, arranged for self-exhibition, was certainly more attractive than Mary, Queen of Scots, in wax, in a public hall; and she could be seen for nothing.

It is doubtful whether Mrs. Belcher's estimate of their sex was materially raised by their tribute to her companion's personal attractions, but they furnished her with an interesting study. She was comforted by certain observations, viz., that there were at least twenty men among them who, by their manner and their little speeches, which only a woman could interpret, showed that they were entangled in the same meshes that had been woven around her husband; that they were as foolish, as fond, as much deceived, and as treacherously entertained as he.

She certainly was amused. Puffy old fellows with nosegays in their button-holes grew gallant and young in Mrs. Dillingham's presence, filled her ears with flatteries, received the grateful tap of her fan, and were immediately banished to the dining-room, from which they emerged redder in the face and puffier than ever. Dapper young men arriving in cabs threw off their overcoats before alighting, and ran up the steps in evening dress, went through their automatic greeting and leave-taking, and ran out again to get through their task of making almost numberless calls during the day. Steady old men like Mr. Tunbridge and Mr. Schoonmaker, who had had the previous privilege of meeting Mr. Belcher, were turned over to Mrs. Belcher, with whom they sat down and had a quiet talk. Mrs. Dillingham seemed to know exactly how to apportion the constantly arriving and departing guests. Some were entertained by herself, some were given to Mr. Belcher, some to the hostess, and others were sent directly to the refreshment tables to be fed.

Mr. Belcher was brought into contact with men of his own kind, who did not fail to recognize him as a congenial spirit, and to express the hope of seeing more of him, now that he had become "one of us." Each one knew some other one whom he would take an early opportunity of presenting to Mr. Belcher. They were all glad he was in New York. It was the place for him. Everything was open to such a man as he, in such a city, and they only wondered why he had been content to remain so long shut away from his own kind.

These expressions of brotherly interest were very pleasant to Mr. Belcher. They flattered him and paved the way for a career. He would soon be hand-in-glove with them all. He would soon find the ways of their prosperity, and make himself felt among them.

The long afternoon wore away, and just as the sun was setting, Mrs. Belcher was called from the drawing-room by some family care, leaving Mr. Belcher and Mrs. Dillingham together.

"Don't be gone long," said the latter to Mrs. Belcher, as she left the room.

"Be gone till to-morrow morning," said Mr. Belcher, in a whisper at Mrs. Dillingham's ear.

"You're a wretch," said the lady.

"You're right—a very miserable wretch. Here you've been playing the devil with a hundred men all day, and I've been looking at you. Is there any article of your apparel that I can have the privilege of kissing?"

Mrs. Dillingham laughed him in his face. Then she took a wilted rose-bud from a nosegay at her breast, and gave it to him.

"My roses are all faded," she said—"worth nothing to me—worth nothing to anybody—except you."

Then she passed to the window; to hide her emotion? to hide her duplicity? to change the subject? to give Mr. Belcher a glance at her gracefully retreating figure? to show herself, framed by the window, into a picture for the delight of his devouring eyes?

Mr. Belcher followed her. His hand lightly touched her waist, and she struck it down, as if her own were the velvet paw of a lynx.

"You startled me so!" she said.

"Are you always to be startled so easily?"

"Here? yes."

"Everywhere?"

"Yes. Perhaps so."

"Thank you."

"For what?"

"For the perhaps."

"You are easily pleased and grateful for nothing; and, now, tell me who lives opposite to you?"

"A lawyer by the name of James Balfour."

"James Balfour? Why, he's one of my old flames. He ought to have been here to-day. Perhaps he'll be in this evening."

"Not he."

"Why?"

"He has the honor to be an enemy of mine, and knows that I would rather choke him than eat my dinner."

"You men are such savages; but aren't those nice boys on the steps?"

"I happen to know one of them, and I should like to know why he is there, and how he came there. Between you and me, now—strictly between you and me—that boy is the only person that stands between me and —and—a pile of money."

"Is it possible? Which one, now?"

"The larger."

"But, isn't he lovely?"

"He's a Sevenoaks pauper."

"You astonish me."

"I tell you the truth, and Balfour has managed, in some way, to get hold of him, and means to make money out of me by it. I know men. You can't tell me anything about men; and my excellent neighbor will have his hands full, whenever he sees fit to undertake his job."

"Tell me all about it now," said Mrs. Dillingham, her eyes alight with genuine interest.

"Not now, but I'll tell you what I would like to have you do. You have a way of making boys love you, and men too—for that matter—and precious little do they get for it."

"Candid and complimentary," she sighed.

"Well, I've seen you manage with my boys, and I would like to have you try it with him. Meet him in the street, manage to speak to him, get him into your house, make him love you. You can do it. You are bold enough, ingenious enough, and subtle enough to do anything of that kind you will undertake. Some time, if you have him under your influence, you may be of use to me. Some time, he may be glad to hide in your house. No harm can come to you in making his acquaintance."

"Do you know that you are talking very strangely to me?"

"No. I'm talking business. Is that a strange thing to a woman?"

Mrs. Dillingham made no reply, but stood and watched the boys, as they ran up and down the steps in play, with a smile of sympathy upon her face, and genuine admiration of the graceful motions and handsome face and figure of the lad of whom Mr. Belcher had been talking. Her curiosity was piqued, her love of intrigue was appealed to, and she determined to do, at the first convenient opportunity, what Mr. Belcher desired her to do.

Then Mrs. Belcher returned, and the evening, like the afternoon, was devoted to the reception of guests, and when, at last, the clock struck eleven, and Mrs. Dillingham stood bonneted and shawled ready to go home in the carriage that waited at the door, Mrs. Belcher kissed her, while Mr. Belcher looked on in triumph.

" Now, Sarah, haven't we had a nice day ? " said he.

" Very pleasant, indeed."

" And haven't I behaved well ? Upon my word, I believe I shall have to stand treat to my own abstinence, before I go to bed."

" Yes, you've been wonderfully good," remarked his wife.

" Men are such angels ! " said Mrs. Dillingham.

Then Mr. Belcher put on his hat and overcoat, led Mrs. Dillingham to her carriage, got in after her, slammed the door, and drove away.

No sooner were they in the carriage than Mrs. Dillingham went to talking about the little boy, in the most furious manner. Poor Mr. Belcher could not divert her, could not induce her to change the subject, could not get in a word edgewise, could not put forward a single apology for the kiss he intended to win, did not win his kiss at all. The little journey was ended, the carriage door thrown open by her own hand, and she was out without his help.

" Good-night ; don't get out," and she flew up the steps and rang the bell.

Mr. Belcher ordered the coachman to drive him home, and then sank back on his seat, and crowding his lips together, and compressing his disappointment into his familiar expletive, he rode back to his house as rigid in every muscle as if he had been frozen.

"Is there any such thing as a virtuous devil, I wonder," he muttered to himself, as he mounted his steps. "I doubt it; I doubt it."

The next day was icy. Men went slipping along upon the sidewalks as carefully as if they were trying to follow a guide through the galleries of Versailles. And in the afternoon a beautiful woman called a boy to her, and begged him to give her his shoulder and help her home. The request was so sweetly made, she expressed her obligations so courteously, she smiled upon him so beautifully, she praised him so ingenuously, she shook his hand at parting so heartily, that he went home all aglow from his heart to his fingers' ends.

Mrs. Dillingham had made Harry Benedict's acquaintance, which she managed to keep alive by bows in the street and bows from the window—managed to keep alive until the lad worshipped her as a sort of divinity, and, to win her smiling recognition, would go out of his way a dozen blocks on any errand about the city.

He recognized her—knew her as the beautiful woman he had seen in the great house across the street before Mr. Belcher arrived in town. Recognizing her as such, he kept the secret of his devotion to himself, for fear that it would be frowned upon by his good friends the Balfours. Mr. Belcher, however, knew all about it, rejoiced in it, and counted upon it as a possible means in the accomplishment of his ends.

CHAPTER XVI.

WHICH GIVES AN ACCOUNT OF A VOLUNTARY AND AN INVOLUNTARY VISIT OF SAM YATES TO NUMBER NINE.

MR. BELCHER followed up the acquaintance which he had so happily made on New Year's Day with many of the leading operators of Wall Street, during the remainder of the winter, and, by the careful and skilful manipulation of the minor stocks of the market, not only added to his wealth by sure and steady degrees, but built up a reputation for sagacity and boldness. He struck at them with a strong hand, and gradually became a recognized power on 'Change. He knew that he would not be invited into any combinations until he had demonstrated his ability to stand alone. He understood that he could not win a leading position in any of the great financial enterprises until he had shown that he had the skill to manage them. He was playing for two stakes—present profit and future power and glory; and he played with brave adroitness.

During the same winter the work at Number Nine went on according to contract. Mike Conlin found his second horse and the requisite sled, and, the river freezing solidly and continuously, he was enabled not only to draw the lumber to the river, but up to the very point where it was to be used, and where Jim and Mr. Benedict were hewing and framing their timber, and pursuing their trapping with unflinching industry. Number Ten was transformed into a stable, where Mike kept his horses on the nights of his arrival. Two trips a week were all that he could accomplish, but the winter was so long, and he was so industrious, that before the ice broke up, everything for the construction of the house had been delivered, even to the bricks for the chimney, the lime for the plastering, and the last clapboard and shingle. The planning, the chaffing, the merry stories of which Number Nine was the scene that winter, the grand, absorbing interest in the enterprise in which these three men were engaged, it would be pleasant to recount, but they may safely be left to the reader's imagination. What was Sam Yates doing?

He lived up to the letter of his instructions. Finding himself in the possession of an assured livelihood, respectably dressed and engaged in steady employment, his appetite for drink loosened its cruel hold upon him, and he was once more in possession of himself. All the week long he was busy in visiting hospitals, almshouses and lunatic asylums, and in examining their records and the mortuary records of the city. Sometimes he presented himself at the doors of public institutions as a philanthropist, preparing, by personal inspection, for writing some book, or getting statistics, or establishing an institution on behalf of a public benefactor. Sometimes he went in the character of a lawyer, in search of a man who had fallen heir to a fortune. He had always a plausible story to tell, and found no difficulty in obtaining an entrance at all the doors to which his inquisition led him. He was treated everywhere so courteously that his self-respect was wonderfully nourished, and he began to feel as if it were possible for him to become a man again.

On every Saturday night, according to Mr. Belcher's command, he made his appearance in the little basement-room of the grand residence, where he was first presented to the reader. On these occasions he always brought a clean record of what he had done during the week, which he read to Mr. Belcher, and then passed into that gentleman's hands, to be filed away and preserved. On every visit, too, he was made to feel that he was a slave. As his self-respect rose from week to week, the coarse and brutal treatment of the proprietor was increased. Mr. Belcher feared that the man was getting above his business, and that, as the time approached when he might need something very different from these harmless investigations, his instrument might become too fine for use.

Besides the ministry to his self-respect which his labors rendered, there was another influence upon Sam Yates that tended to confirm its effects. He had in his investigations come into intimate contact with the results of all forms of vice. Idiocy, insanity, poverty, moral debasement, disease in a thousand repulsive forms, all these had frightened and disgusted him. On the direct road to one of these terrible goals he had been travelling. He knew it, and, with a shudder many times repeated, felt it. He had been arrested in the downward road, and, God helping him, he would never resume it. He had witnessed brutal cruelties and neglect among officials that maddened him. The professional indifference of keepers and nurses toward those who, if vicious, were still unfortunate and helpless, offended and outraged all of manhood there was left in him.

One evening, early in the spring, he made his customary call upon Mr. Belcher, bringing his usual report. He had completed the canvas of the city and its environs, and had found no testimony to the death or recent presence of Mr. Benedict. He hoped that Mr. Belcher was done with him, for he saw that his brutal will was the greatest obstacle to his reform. If he could get away from his master, he could begin life anew; for his professional brothers, who well remembered his better days, were ready to throw business into his hands, now that he had become himself again.

"I suppose this ends it," said Yates, as he read his report, and passed it over into Mr. Belcher's hands.

"Oh, you do!"

"I do not see how I can be of further use to you."

"Oh, you don't!"

"I have certainly reason to be grateful for your assistance, but I have no desire to be a burden upon your hands. I think I can get a living now in my profession."

"Then we've found that we have a profession, have we? We've become highly respectable."

"I really don't see what occasion you have to taunt me. I have done my duty faithfully, and taken no more than my just pay for the labor I have performed."

"Sam Yates, I took you out of the gutter. Do you know that?"

"I do, sir."

"Did you ever hear of my doing such a thing as that before?"

"I never did."

"What do you suppose I did it for?"

"To serve yourself."

"You are right; and now let me tell you that I am not done with you yet, and I shall not be done with you until I have in my hands a certificate of the death of Paul Benedict, and an instrument drawn up in legal form, making over to me all his right, title, and interest in every patented invention of his which I am now using in my manufactures. Do you hear that?"

"I do."

"What have you to say to it? Are you going to live up to your pledge, or are you going to break with me?"

"If I could furnish such an instrument honorably, I would do it."

"H'm! I tell you, Sam Yates, this sort of thing won't do."

Then Mr. Belcher left the room, and soon returned with a glass and a bottle of brandy. Setting them upon the table, he took the key from the outside of the door, inserted it upon the inside, turned it, and then withdrew it, and put it in his pocket. Yates rose and watched him, his face pale, and his heart thumping at his side like a tilt-hammer.

"Sam Yates," said Mr. Belcher, "you are getting altogether too virtuous. Nothing will cure you but a good, old-fashioned drunk. Dip in, now, and take your fill. You can lie here all night if you wish to."

Mr. Belcher drew the cork, and poured out a tumblerful of the choice old liquid. Its fragrance filled the little room. It reached the nostrils of the poor slave, who shivered as if an ague had smitten him. He hesitated, advanced toward the table, retreated, looked at Mr. Belcher, then at the brandy, then walked the room, then paused before Mr. Belcher, who had coolly watched the struggle from his chair. The victim of this passion was in the supreme of torment. His old thirst was roused to fury. The good resolutions of the preceding weeks, the moral strength he had won, the motives that had come to life within him, the promise of a better future, sank away into blank nothingness. A patch of fire burned on either cheek. His eyes were bloodshot.

"Oh, God! Oh, God!" he exclaimed, and buried his face in his hands.

"Fudge!" said Mr. Belcher. "What do you make an ass of yourself for?"

"If you'll take these things out of the room, and see that I drink nothing to-night, I'll do anything. They are hell and damnation to me. Don't you see? Have you no pity on me? Take them away!"

Mr. Belcher was surprised, but he had secured the promise he was after, and so he coolly rose and removed the offensive temptation.

Yates sat down as limp as if he had had a sunstroke. After sitting a long time in silence, he looked up, and begged for the privilege of sleeping in the house. He did not dare to trust himself in the street until sleep had calmed and strengthened him.

There was a lounge in the room, and, calling a servant, Mr. Belcher ordered blankets to be brought down. "You can sleep here to-night, and I will see you in the morning," said he, rising, and leaving him without even the common courtesy of a "good-night."

Poor Sam Yates had a very bad night indeed. He was humiliated by the proof of his weakness, and maddened by the outrage which had been attempted upon him and his good resolutions. In the morning he met Mr. Belcher, feeble and unrefreshed, and with seeming acquiescence received his directions for future work.

"I want you to take the road from here to Sevenoaks, stopping at every town on the way. You can be sure of this : he is not near Sevenoaks. The whole county, and in fact the adjoining counties, were all ransacked to find him. He cannot have found asylum there ; so he must be either between here and Sevenoaks, or must have gone into the woods beyond. There's a trapper there, one Jim Fenton. He may have come across him in the woods, alive or dead, and I want you to go to his camp and find out whether he knows anything. My impression is that he knew Benedict well, and that Benedict used to hunt with him. When you come back to me, after a faithful search, with the report that you can find nothing of him, or with the report of his death, we shall be ready for decisive operations. Write me when you have anything to write, and if you find it necessary to spend money to secure any very desirable end, spend it."

Then Mr. Belcher put into the hands of his agent a roll of bank notes, and armed him with a check that might be used in case of emergency, and sent him off.

It took Yates six long weeks to reach Sevenoaks. He labored daily with the same faithfulness that had characterized his operations in the city, and, reaching Sevenoaks, he found himself for a few days free from care, and at liberty to resume the acquaintance with his early home, where he and Robert Belcher had been boys together.

The people of Sevenoaks had long before heard of the fall of Sam Yates from his early rectitude. They had once been proud of him, and when he left them for the city, they expected to hear great things of him. So when they learned that, after entering upon his profession with brilliant promise, he had ruined himself with drink, they bemoaned him for a while, and at last forgot him. His relatives never mentioned him, and when, well dressed, dignified, self-respectful, he appeared among them again, it was like receiving one from the dead. The rejoicing of his relatives, the cordiality of his old friends and companions, the reviving influences of the scenes of his boyhood, all tended to build up his self-respect, reinforce his strength, and fix his determination for a new life.

Of course he did not make known his business, and of course he heard a thousand inquiries about Mr. Belcher, and listened to the stories of the proprietor's foul dealings with the people of his native town. His own relatives had been straitened or impoverished by the man's rascalities, and the fact was not calculated to strengthen his loyalty to his employer. He heard also the whole story of the connection of Mr. Belcher with Benedict's insanity, of the escape of the latter from the poor-house, and of the long and unsuccessful search that had been made for him.

He spent a delightful week among his friends in the old village, learned about Jim Fenton and the way to reach him, and on a beautiful spring morning, armed with fishing-tackle, started from Sevenoaks for a fortnight's absence in the woods. The horses were fresh, the air sparkling, and at mid-afternoon he found himself standing by the river-side, with a row of ten miles before him in a birch canoe, whose hiding-place Mike Conlin had revealed to him during a brief call at his house. To his unused muscles it was a serious task to undertake, but he was not a novice, and it was entered upon deliberately and with a prudent husbandry of his power of endurance. Great was the surprise of Jim and Mr. Benedict, as they sat eating their late supper, to hear the sound of the paddle down the river, and to see approaching them a city gentleman, who, greeting them courteously, drew up in front of their cabin, took out his luggage, and presented himself.

"Where's Jim Fenton?" said Yates.

"That's me. Them as likes me calls me Jim, and them as don't like me—wall, they don't call."

"Well, I've called, and I call you Jim."

"All right; let's see yer tackle," said Jim.

Jim took the rod that Yates handed to him, looked it over, and then said: "When ye come to Sevenoaks ye didn't think o' goin' a fishin'. This 'ere tackle wasn't brung from the city, and ye ain't no old fisherman. This is the sort they keep down to Sevenoaks."

"No," said Yates, flushing; "I thought I should find near you the tackle used here, so I didn't burden myself."

"That seems reasomble," said Jim, "but it ain't. A trout's a trout anywhere, an' ye hain't got no reel. Ye never fished with anything but a white birch pole in yer life."

Yates was amused, and laughed. Jim did not laugh. He was just as sure that Yates had come on some errand, for which his fishing-tackle was a cover, as that he had come at all. He could think of but one motive that would bring the man into the woods, unless he came for sport, and for sport he did not believe his visitor had come at all. He was not dressed for it. None but old sportsmen, with nothing else to do, ever came into the woods at that season.

"Jim, introduce me to your friend," said Yates, turning to Mr. Benedict, who had dropped his knife and fork, and sat uneasily witnessing the meeting, and listening to the conversation.

"Well, I call 'im Number Ten. His name's Williams; an' now if ye ain't too tired, perhaps ye'll tell us what they call ye to home."

"Well, I'm Number Eleven, and my name's Williams, too."

"Then, if yer name's Williams, an' ye're Number 'leven, ye want some supper. Set down an' help yerself."

Before taking his seat, Yates turned laughingly to Mr. Benedict, shook his hand, and "hoped for a better acquaintance."

Jim was puzzled. The man was no ordinary man; he was good-natured; he was not easily perturbed; he was there with a purpose, and that purpose had nothing to do with sport.

After Yates had satisfied his appetite with the coarse food before him, and had lighted his cigar, Jim drove directly at business.

"What brung ye here?" said he.

"A pair of horses and a birch canoe."

"Oh! I didn't know but 'twas a mule and a bandanner hankercher," said Jim; "and whar be ye goin' to sleep to-night?"

"In the canoe, I suppose, if some hospitable man doesn't invite me to sleep in his cabin."

"An' if ye sleep in his cabin, what be ye goin' to do to-morrer?"

"Get up."

"An' clear out?"

"Not a bit of it."

"Well, I love to see folks make themselves to home;

but ye don't sleep in no cabin o' mine till I know who ye be, an' what ye're arter."

"Jim, did you ever hear of entertaining angels unaware?" and Yates looked laughingly into his face.

"No, but I've hearn of angels entertainin' theirselves on tin-ware, an' I've had 'em here."

"Do you have tin peddlers here?" inquired Yates, looking around him.

"No, but we have paupers sometimes," and Jim looked Yates directly in the eye.

"What paupers?"

"From Sevenoaks."

"And do they bring tin-ware?"

"Sartin they do; leastways, one on 'em did, an' I never seen but one in the woods, an' he come here one night tootin' on a tin horn, an' blowin' about bein' the angel Gabr'el. Do you see my har?"

"Rather bushy, Jim."

"Well, that's the time it come up, an' it's never been tired enough to lay down sence."

"What became of Gabriel?"

"I skeered 'im, and he went off into the woods pertendin' he was tryin' to catch a bullet. That's the kind o' ball I allers use when I have a little game with a rovin' angel that comes kadoodlin' round me."

"Did you ever see him afterward?" inquired Yates.

"Yes, I seen him. He laid down one night under a tree, an' he wasn't called to breakfast, an' he never woke up. So I made up my mind he'd gone to play angel somewheres else, an' I dug a hole an' put 'im into it, an' he hain't never riz, if so be he wasn't Number 'leven, an' his name was Williams."

Yates did not laugh, but manifested the most eager interest.

"Jim," said he, "can you show me his bones, and swear to your belief that he was an escaped pauper?"

"Easy."

"Was there a man lost from the poor-house about that time?"

"Yes, an' there was a row about it, an' arterward old Buffum was took with knowin' less than he ever knowed afore. He always did make a fuss about breathin', so he give it up."

"Well, the man you buried is the man I'm after."

"Yes, an' old Belcher sent ye. I knowed it. I smelt the old feller when I heern yer paddle. When a feller works for the devil it ain't hard to guess what sort of a angel *he* is. Ye must feel mighty proud o' yer belongin's."

"Jim, I'm a lawyer; it's my business. I do what I'm hired to do."

"Well," responded Jim, "I don't know nothin' about lawyers, but I'd rather be a natural born cuss nor a hired one."

Yates laughed, but Jim was entirely sober. The lawyer saw that he was unwelcome, and that the sooner he was out of Jim's way, the better that freely speaking person would like it. So he said quietly:

"Jim, I see that I am not welcome, but I bear you no ill-will. Keep me to-night, and to-morrow show me this man's bones, and sign a certificate of the statements you have made to me, and I will leave you at once"

The woodsman made no more objection, and the next morning, after breakfast, the three men went together and found the place of the pauper's burial. It took but a few minutes to disinter the skeleton, and, after a silent look at it, it was again buried, and all returned to the cabin. Then the lawyer, after asking further questions, drew up a paper certifying to all the essential facts in the case, and Jim signed it.

"Now, how be ye goin' to get back to Sevenoaks?" inquired Jim.

" I don't know. The man who brought me in is not to come for me for a fortnight."

" Then ye've got to huff it," responded Jim.

" It's a long way."

" Ye can do it as fur as Mike's, an' he'll be glad to git back some o' the hundred dollars that old Belcher got out of him."

" The row and the walk will be too much."

" I'll take ye to the landing," said Jim.

" I shall be glad to pay you for the job," responded Yates.

" An' ef ye do," said Jim, " there'll be an accident, an' two men'll get wet, an' one on 'em'll stan' a chance to be drownded."

" Well, have your own way," said Yates.

It was not yet noon, and Jim hurried off his visitor. Yates bade good-by to Benedict, jumped into Jim's boat, and was soon out of sight down the stream. The boat fairly leaped through the water under Jim's strong and steady strokes, and it seemed that only an hour had passed when the landing was discovered.

They made the whole distance in silence. Jim, sitting at his oars, with Yates in the stern, had watched the lawyer with a puzzled expression. He could not read him. The man had not said a word about Benedict. He had not once pronounced his name. He was evidently amused with something, and had great difficulty in suppressing a smile. Again and again the amused expression suffused the lawyer's face, and still, by an effort of will, it was smothered. Jim was in torture. The man seemed to be in possession of some great secret, and looked as if he only waited an opportunity beyond observation to burst into a laugh.

" What the devil be ye thinkin' on ? " inquired Jim at last.

Yates looked him in the eyes, and replied coolly :

"I was thinking how well Benedict is looking."

Jim stopped rowing, holding his oars in the air. He was dumb. His face grew almost livid, and his hair seemed to rise and stand straight all over his head. His first impulse was to spring upon the man and throttle him, but a moment's reflection determined him upon another course. He let his oars drop into the water, and then took up the rifle, which he always carried at his side. Raising it to his eye, he said:

"Now, Number 'leven, come an' take my seat. Ef ye make any fuss, I'll tip ye into the river, or blow yer brains out. Any man that plays traitor with Jim Fenton, gits traitor's fare."

Yates saw that he had made a fatal mistake, and that it was too late to correct it. He saw that Jim was dangerously excited, and that it would not do to excite him further. He therefore rose, and with feigned pleasantry said he should be very glad to row to the landing.

Jim passed him and took a seat in the stern of the boat. Then, as Yates took up the oars, Jim raised his rifle, and, pointing it directly at the lawyer's breast, said:

"Now, Sam Yates, turn this boat round."

Yates was surprised in turn, bit his lips, and hesitated.

"Turn this boat round, or I'll fix ye so't I can see through ye plainer nor I do now."

"Surely, Jim, you don't mean to have me row back. I haven't harmed you."

"Turn this boat round, quicker nor lightnin'."

"There, it's turned," said Yates, assuming a smile.

"Now row back to Number Nine."

"Come, Jim," said Yates, growing pale with vexation and apprehension, "this fooling has gone far enough."

"Not by ten mile," said Jim.

"You surely don't mean to take me back. You have no right to do it. I can prosecute you for this."

"Not if I put a bullet through ye, or drown ye."

"Do you mean to have me row back to Number Nine?"

"I mean to have you row back to Number Nine, or go to the bottom leakin'," responded Jim.

Yates thought a moment, looked angrily at the determined man before him, as if he were meditating some rash experiment, and then dipped his oars and rowed up stream.

Great was the surprise of Mr. Benedict late in the afternoon to see Yates slowly rowing toward the cabin, and landing under cover of Jim's rifle, and the blackest face that he had ever seen above his good friend's shoulders.

CHAPTER XVII.

IN WHICH JIM CONSTRUCTS TWO HAPPY DAVIDS, RAISES HIS HOTEL, AND DISMISSES SAM YATES.

WHEN the boat touched the bank, Jim, still with his rifle pointed at the breast of Sam Yates, said:

"Now git out, an' take a bee line for the shanty, an' see how many paces ye make on't."

Yates was badly blown by his row of ten miles on the river, and could hardly stir from his seat; but Mr. Benedict helped him up the bank, and then Jim followed him on shore.

Benedict looked from one to the other with mingled surprise and consternation, and then said:

"Jim, what does this mean?"

"It means," replied Jim, "that Number 'leven, an' his name is Williams, forgot to 'tend to his feelin's over old Tilden's grave, an' I've axed 'im to come back an' use up his clean hankerchers. He was took with a fit o knowin' somethin', too, an' I'm goin' to see if I can cure 'im. It's a new sort o' sickness for him, an' it may floor 'im."

"I suppose there is no use in carrying on this farce any longer," said Yates. "I knew you, Mr. Benedict, soon after arriving here, and it seems that you recognized me; and now, here is my hand. I never meant you ill, and I did not expect to find you alive. I have tried my best to make you out a dead man, and so to report you; but Jim has compelled me to come back and make sure that you are alive."

"No, I didn't," responded Jim. "I wanted to let ye know that I'm alive, and that I don't 'low no hired cusses to come snoopin' round my camp, an' goin' off with a haw-haw buttoned up in their jackets, without a thrashin'."

Benedict, of course, stood thunderstruck and irresolute. He was discovered by the very man whom his old persecutor had sent for the purpose. He had felt that the discovery would be made sooner or later—intended, indeed, that it should be made—but he was not ready.

They all walked to the cabin in moody silence. Jim felt that he had been hasty, and was very strongly inclined to believe in the sincerity of Yates; but he knew it was safe to be on his guard with any man who was in the employ of Mr. Belcher. Turk saw there was trouble, and whined around his master, as if inquiring whether there was anything that he could do to bring matters to an adjustment.

"No, Turk; he's my game," said Jim. "Ye couldn't eat 'im no more nor ye could a muss-rat."

There were just three seats in the cabin—two camp-stools and a chest.

"That's the seat for ye," said Jim to Yates, pointing to the chest. "Jest plant yerself thar. Thar's somethin' in that 'ere chest as'll make ye tell the truth."

Yates looked at the chest and hesitated.

"It ain't powder," said Jim, "but it'll blow ye worse nor. powder, if ye don't tell the truth."

Yates sat down. He had not appreciated the anxiety of Benedict to escape discovery, or he would not have been so silly as to bruit his knowledge until he had left the woods. He felt ashamed of his indiscretion, but, as he knew that his motives were good, he could not but feel that he had been outraged.

"Jim, you have abused me," said he. "You have misunderstood me, and that is the only apology that you can make for your discourtesy. I was a fool to tell you what I knew, but you had no right to serve me as you have served me."

"P'raps I hadn't," responded Jim, doubtfully.

Yates went on :

"I have never intended to play you a trick. It may be a base thing for me to do, but I intended to deceive Mr. Belcher. He is a man to whom I owe no good-will. He has always treated me like a dog, and he will continue the treatment so long as I have anything to do with him ; but he found me when I was very low, and he has furnished me with the money that has made it possible for me to redeem myself. Believe me, the finding of Mr. Benedict was the most unwelcome discovery I ever made."

"Ye talk reasomble," said Jim ; "but how be I goin' to know that ye're tellin' the truth ?"

"You cannot know," replied Yates. "The circumstances are all against me, but you will be obliged to trust me. You are not going to kill me ; you are not going to harm me ; for you would gain nothing by getting my ill-will. I forgive your indignities, for it was natural for you to be provoked, and I provoked you needlessly —childishly, in fact ; but after what I have said, anything further in that line will not be borne."

"I've a good mind to lick ye now," said Jim, on hearing himself defied.

"You would be a fool to undertake it," said Yates.

"Well, what be ye goin' to tell old Belcher, anyway?" inquired Jim.

"I doubt whether I shall tell him anything. I have no intention of telling him that Mr. Benedict is here, and I do not wish to tell him a lie. I have intended to tell him that in all my journey to Sevenoaks I did not find the object of my search, and that Jim Fenton declared that but one pauper had ever come into the woods and died there."

"That's the truth," said Jim. "Benedict ain't no pauper, nor hain't been since he left the poor-house."

"If he knows about old Tilden," said Yates, "and I'm afraid he does, he'll know that I'm on the wrong scent. If he doesn't know about him, he'll naturally conclude that the dead man was Mr. Benedict. That will answer his purpose."

"Old Belcher ain't no fool," said Jim.

"Well," said Yates, "why doesn't Mr. Benedict come out like a man and claim his rights? That would relieve me, and settle all the difficulties of the case."

Benedict had nothing to say for this, for there was what he felt to be a just reproach in it.

"It's the way he's made," replied Jim—"leastways, partly. When a man's be'n hauled through hell by the har, it takes 'im a few days to git over bein' dizzy an' find his legs ag'in; an' when a man sells himself to old Belcher, he mustn't squawk an' try to git another feller to help 'im out of 'is bargain. Ye got into't, an' ye must git out on't the best way ye can."

"What would you have me do?" inquired Yates.

"I want to have ye sw'ar, an' sign a Happy David."

"A what?"

"A Happy David. Ye ain't no lawyer if ye don't know what a Happy David is, and can't make one."

Yates recognized, with a smile, the nature of the instrument disguised in Jim's pronunciation and conception, and inquired :

"What would you have me to swear to?"

"To what I tell ye."

"Very well. I have pen and paper with me, and am ready to write. Whether I will sign the paper will depend upon its contents."

"Be ye ready?"

"Yes."

"Here ye have it, then. 'I solem-ny sw'ar, s'welp me! that I hain't seen no pauper, in no woods, with his name as Benedict.'"

Jim paused, and Yates, having completed the sentence, waited. Then Jim muttered to himself :

"With his name *as* Benedict—with his name *is* Benedict—with his name *was* Benedict."

Then with a puzzled look, he said :

"Yates, can't ye doctor that a little?"

"Whose name was Benedict," suggested Yates.

"Whose name was Benedict," continued Jim. "Now read it over, as fur as ye've got."

"'I solemnly swear that I have seen no pauper in the woods whose name was Benedict.'"

"Now look a-here, Sam Yates! That sort o' thing won't do. Stop them tricks. Ye don't know me, an' ye don't know whar ye're settin', if you think that'll go down."

"Why, what's the matter?"

"I telled ye that Benedict was no pauper, an' ye say that ye've seen no pauper whose name was Benedict. That's jest tellin' that he's here. Oh, ye can't come that game! Now begin ag'in, an' write jest as I give it to ye. 'I solem-ny sw'ar, s'welp me! that I hain't seen no pauper, in no woods, whose name was Benedict.'"

"Done," said Yates, "but it isn't grammar."

"Hang the grammar!" responded Jim; "what I want is sense. Now jine this on: 'An' I solem-ny sw'ar, s'welp me! that I won't blow on Benedict, as isn't a pauper—no more nor Jim Fenton is—an' if so be as I do blow on Benedict—I give Jim Fenton free liberty, out and out—to lick me—without goin' to lor—but takin' the privlidge of self-defence.'"

Jim thought a moment. He had wrought out a large phrase.

"I guess," said he, "that covers the thing. Ye understand, don't ye, Yates, about the privlidge of self-defence?"

"You mean that I may defend myself if I can, don't you?"

"Yes. With the privlidge of self-defence. That's fair, an' I'd give it to a painter. Now read it all over."

Jim put his head down between his knees, the better to measure every word, while Yates read the complete document. Then Jim took the paper, and, handing it to Benedict, requested him to see if it had been read correctly. Assured that it was all right, Jim turned his eyes severely on Yates, and said:

"Sam Yates, do ye s'pose ye've any idee what it is to be licked by Jim Fenton? Do ye know what ye're sw'arin' to? Do ye reelize that I wouldn't leave enough on ye to pay for havin' a funeral?"

Yates laughed, and said that he believed he understood the nature of an oath.

"Then sign yer Happy David," said Jim.

Yates wrote his name, and passed the paper into Jim's hands.

"Now," said Jim, with an expression of triumph on his face, "I s'pose ye don't know that ye've been settin' on a Bible; but it's right under ye, in that chest, an it's hearn and seen the whole thing. If ye don't stand by yer Happy David, there'll be somethin' worse nor Jim

Fenton arter ye, an' when that comes, ye can jest shet yer eyes, and gi'en it up."

This was too much for both Yates and Benedict. They looked into each other's eyes, and burst into a laugh. But Jim was in earnest, and not a smile crossed his rough face.

"Now," said he, "I want to do a little sw'arin' my-self, and I want ye to write it."

Yates resumed his pen, and declared himself to be in readiness.

"I solem-ny sw'ar," Jim began, "s'welp me! that I will lick Sam Yates—as is a lawyer—with the privlidge of self-defence—if he ever blows on Benedict—as is not a pauper—no more nor Jim Fenton is—an' I solem-ny sw'ar, s'welp me! that I'll foller 'im till I find 'im, an' lick 'im—with the privlidge of self-defence."

Jim would have been glad to work in the last phrase again, but he seemed to have covered the whole ground, and so inquired whether Yates had got it all down.

Yates replied that he had.

"I'm a-goin' to sign that, an' ye can take it along with ye. Swap seats."

Yates rose, and Jim seated himself upon the chest.

"I'm a-goin' to sign this, settin' over the Bible. I ain't goin' to take no advantage on ye. Now we're squar'," said he, as he blazoned the document with his coarse and clumsy sign-manual. "Put that in yer pocket, an' keep it for five year."

"Is the business all settled?" inquired Yates.

"Clean," replied Jim.

"When am I to have the liberty to go out of the woods?"

"Ye ain't goin' out o' the woods for a fortnight. Ye're a-goin' to stay here, an' have the best fishin' ye ever had in yer life. It'll do ye good, an' ye can go out when yer man comes arter ye. Ye can stay to the raisin', an'

gi'en us a little lift with the other fellers that's comin'
Ye'll be as strong as a hoss when ye go out."

An announcement more welcome than this could not have been made to Sam Yates; and now that there was no secrecy between them, and confidence was restored, he looked forward to a fortnight of enjoyment. He laid aside his coat, and, as far as possible, reduced his dress to the requirements of camp life. Jim and Mr. Benedict were very busy, so that he was obliged to find his way alone, but Jim lent him his fishing-tackle, and taught him how to use it; and, as he was an apt pupil, he was soon able to furnish more fish to the camp than could be used.

Yates had many a long talk with Benedict, and the two men found many points of sympathy, around which they cemented a lasting friendship. Both, though in different ways, had been very low down in the valley of helpless misfortune; both had been the subjects of Mr. Belcher's brutal will; and both had the promise of a better life before them, which it would be necessary to achieve in opposition to that will. Benedict was strengthened by this sympathy, and became able to entertain plans for the assertion and maintenance of his rights.

When Yates had been at the camp for a week, and had taken on the color and the manner of a woodsman, there came one night to Number Nine a dozen men, to assist in the raising of Jim's hotel. They were from the mill where he had purchased his lumber, and numbered several neighbors besides, including Mike Conlin. They came up the old "tote-road" by the river side, and a herd of buffaloes on a stampede could hardly have made more noise. They were a rough, merry set, and Jim had all he could do to feed them. Luckily, trout were in abundant supply, and they supped like kings, and slept on the ground. The following day was one of the severest labor, but when it closed, the heaviest part of the timber had been brought and put up, and when the second day ended, all the timbers were in their place, including those which defined the outlines of Jim's "cupalo."

When the frame was at last complete, the weary men retired to a convenient distance to look it over; and then they emphasized their approval of the structure by three rousing cheers.

"Be gorry, Jim, ye must make us a spache," said Mike Conlin. "Ye've plenty iv blarney; now out wid it."

But Jim was sober. He was awed by the magnitude of his enterprise. There was the building in open outline. There was no going back. For better or for worse, it held his destiny, and not only his, but that of one other—perhaps of others still.

"A speech! a speech!" came from a dozen tongues.

"Boys," said Jim, "there's no more talk in me now nor there is in one o' them chips. I don't seem to have no vent. I'm full, but it don't run. If I could stick a gimblet in somewhere, as if I was a cider-barrel, I could gi'en ye enough; but I ain't no barrel, an' a gimblet ain't no use. There's a man here as can talk. That's his trade, an' if he'll say what I ought to say, I shall be obleeged to 'im. Yates is a lawyer, an' it's his business to talk for other folks, an' I hope he'll talk for me."

"Yates! Yates!" arose on all sides.

Yates was at home in any performance of this kind, and, mounting a low stump, said:

"Boys, Jim wants me to thank you for the great service you've rendered him. You have come a long distance to do a neighborly deed, and that deed has been generously completed. Here, in these forest shades, you have reared a monument to human civilization. In these old woods you have built a temple to the American household gods. The savage beasts of the wilderness will fly from it, and the birds will gather around it. The winter will be the warmer for the fire that will burn within it, and the spring will come earlier in prospect of a better welcome. The river that washes its feet will be more musical in its flow, because finer ears will be listening. The denizens of the great city will come here, year after year, to renew their wasted strength, and they will carry back with them the sweetest memories of these pure solitudes.

"To build a human home, where woman lives and little children open their eyes upon life, and grow up and marry and die—a home full of love and toil, of pleasure and hope and hospitality, is to do the finest thing that a man can do. I congratulate you on what you have done for Jim, and what so nobly you have done for yourselves. Your whole life will be sweeter for this service, and when you think of a lovely woman presiding over this house, and of all the comfort it will be to the gentle folk that will fill it full, you will be glad that you have had a hand in it."

Yates made his bow and stepped down. His auditors all stood for a moment, under an impression that they were in church and had heard a sermon. Their work had been so idealized for them—it had been endowed with so much meaning—it seemed so different from an ordinary "raising"—that they lost, momentarily, the consciousness of their own roughness and the homeliness of their surroundings.

"Be gorry!" exclaimed Mike, who was the first to break the silence, "I'd 'a' gi'en a dollar if me owld woman could 'a' heard that. Divil a bit does she know what I've done for her. I didn't know mesilf what a purty thing it was whin I built me house. It's betther nor goin' to the church, bedad."

Three cheers were then given to Yates and three to Jim, and, the spell once dissolved, they went noisily back to the cabin and their supper.

That evening Jim was very silent. When they were about lying down for the night, he took his blankets, reached into the chest, and withdrew something that he found there and immediately hid from sight, and said that he was going to sleep in his house. The moon was rising from behind the trees when he emerged from his cabin. He looked up at the tall skeleton of his future home, then approached it, and swinging himself from beam to beam, did not pause until he had reached the cupola. Boards had been placed across it for the convenience of the framers, and on these Jim threw his blankets. Under the little package that was to serve as his pillow he laid his Bible, and then, with his eyes upon the stars, his heart tender with the thoughts of the woman for whom he was rearing a home, and his mind oppressed with the greatness of his undertaking, he lay a long time in a waking dream. "If so be He cares," said Jim to himself—"if so be He cares for a little buildin' as don't make no show 'longside o' His doin's up thar an' down here, I hope He sees that I've got this Bible under my head, an' knows what I mean by it. I hope the thing'll strike 'im favorable, an' that He knows, if He cares, that I'm obleeged to 'im."

At last, slumber came to Jim—the slumber of the toiler, and early the next morning he was busy in feeding his helpers, who had a long day's walk before them. When at last they were all ferried over the river, and had started on their homeward way, Jim ascended to the cupola again, and waved his bandanna in farewell.

Two days afterward, Sam Yates left his host, and rowed himself down to the landing in the same canoe by which he had reached Number Nine. He found his conveyance waiting, according to arrangement, and before night was housed among his friends at Sevenoaks.

While he had been absent in the woods, there had been a conference among his relatives and the principal men of the town, which had resulted in the determination to keep him in Sevenoaks, if possible, in the practice of his profession.

To Yates, the proposition was the opening of a door into safety and peace. To be among those who loved him, and had a certain pride in him; to be released from his service to Mr. Belcher, which he felt could go no farther without involving him in crime and dishonor; to be sustained in his good resolutions by the sympathy of friends, and the absence of his city companions and temptations, gave him the promise of perfect reformation, and a life of modest prosperity and genuine self-respect.

He took but little time in coming to his conclusion, and his first business was to report to Mr. Belcher by letter. He informed that gentleman that he had concluded to remain in Sevenoaks; reported all his investigations on his way thither from New York; inclosed Jim's statement concerning the death of a pauper in the woods; gave an account of the disinterment of the pauper's bones in his presence; inclosed the money unused in expenses and wages, and, with thanks for what Mr. Belcher had done in helping him to a reform, closed his missive in such a manner as to give the impression that he expected and desired no further communication.

Great was Mr. Belcher's indignation when he received this letter. He had not finished with Yates. He had anticipated exactly this result from the investigations. He knew about old Tilden, for Buffum had told him; and he did not doubt that Jim had exhibited to Yates the old man's bones. He believed that Benedict was dead, but he did not know. It would be necessary, therefore, to prepare a document that would be good in any event.

If the reader remembers the opening chapter of this story, he will recall the statement of Miss Butterworth, that Mr. Belcher had followed Benedict to the asylum to procure his signature to a paper. This paper, drawn up in legal form, had been preserved, for Mr. Belcher was a methodical, business man; and when he had finished reading Yates's letter, and had exhausted his expletives after his usual manner, he opened a drawer, and, extracting a paper, read it through. It was more than six years old, and bore its date, and the marks of its age. All it needed was the proper signatures.

He knew that he could trust Yates no longer. He knew, too, that he could not forward his own ends by appearing to be displeased. The reply which Yates received was one that astonished him by its mildness, its expression of satisfaction with his faithful labor, and its record of good wishes. Now that he was upon the spot, Mr. Yates could still serve him, both in a friendly and in a professional way. The first service he could render him was to forward to him autograph letters from the hands of two men deceased. He wished to verify the signatures of these men, he said, but as they were both dead, he, of course, could not apply to them.

Yates did not doubt that there was mischief in this request. He guessed what it was, and he kept the letter; but after a few days he secured the desired autographs, and forwarded them to Mr. Belcher, who filed them away with the document above referred to. After that, the great proprietor, as a relief from the severe pursuits of his life, amused himself by experiments with inks and pens and pencils, and with writing in a hand not his own, the names of "Nicholas Johnson" and "James Ramsey."

CHAPTER XVIII.

IN WHICH MRS. DILLINGHAM MAKES SOME IMPORTANT DISCOVERIES, BUT FAILS TO REVEAL THEM TO THE READER.

MRS. DILLINGHAM was walking back and forth alone through her long drawing-room. She was revolving in her mind a compliment, breathed into her ear by her friend Mrs. Talbot that day. Mrs. Talbot had heard from the mouth of one of Mrs. Dillingham's admirers the statement, confirmed with a hearty, good-natured oath, that he considered the fascinating widow "the best groomed woman in New York."

The compliment conveyed a certain intimation which was not pleasant for her to entertain. She was indebted to her skill in self-"grooming" for the preservation of her youthful appearance. She had been conscious of this, but it was not pleasant to have the fact detected by her friends. Neither was it pleasant to have it bruited in society, and reported to her by one who rejoiced in the delicacy of the arrow which, feathered by friendship, she had been able to plant in the widow's breast.

She walked to her mirror and looked at herself. There were the fine, familiar outlines of face and figure; there were the same splendid eyes; but a certain charm beyond the power of "grooming" to restore was gone. An incipient, almost invisible, brood of wrinkles was gathering about her eyes; there was a loss of freshness of complexion, and an expression of weariness and age, which, in the repose of reflection and inquisition, almost startled her.

Her youth was gone, and, with it, the most potent charms of her person. She was hated and suspected by her own sex, and sought by men for no reason honorable either to her or to them. She saw that it was all, at no distant day, to have an end, and that when the end should come, her life would practically be closed. When the means by which she had held so many men in her power were exhausted, her power would cease. Into the blackness of that coming night she could not bear to look. It was full of hate, and disappointment, and despair. She knew that there was a taint upon her —the taint that comes to every woman, as certainly as death, who patently and purposely addresses, through her person, the sensuous element in men. It was not enough for her to remember that she despised the passion she excited, and contemned the men whom she fascinated. She knew it was better to lead even a swine by a golden chain than by the ears.

She reviewed her relations to Mr. Belcher. That strong, harsh, brutal man, lost alike to conscience and honor, was in her hands. What should she do with him? He was becoming troublesome. He was not so easily managed as the most of her victims. She knew that, in his heart, he was carrying the hope that some time in the future, in some way, she would become his; that she had but to lift her finger to make the Palgrave mansion so horrible a hell that the wife and mother would fly from it in indignant despair. She had no intention of doing this. She wished for no more intimate relation with her victim than she had already established.

There was one thing in which Mr. Belcher had offended and humiliated her. He had treated her as if he had fascinated her. In his stupid vanity, he had fancied that his own personal attractions had won her heart and her allegiance, and that she, and not himself, was the victim. He had tried to use her in the accomplishment of outside purposes; to make a tool of her in carrying forward his mercenary or knavish ends. Other men had striven to hide their unlovely affairs from her, but the new lover had exposed his, and claimed her assistance in carrying them forward. This was a degradation that she could not submit to. It did not flatter her, or minister to her self-respect.

Again and again had Mr. Belcher urged her to get the little Sevenoaks pauper into her confidence, and to ascertain whether his father were still living. She did not doubt that his fear of a man so poor and powerless as the child's father must be, was based in conscious knavery; and to be put to the use of deceiving a lad whose smile of affectionate admiration was one of the sweetest visions of her daily life, disgusted and angered her. The thought, in any man's mind, that she could be so base, in consideration of a guilty affection for him, as to betray the confidence of an innocent child on his behalf, disgraced and degraded her.

And still she walked back and forth in her drawing-room. Her thoughts were uneasy and unhappy; there was no love in her life. That life was leading to no satisfactory consummation. How could it be changed? What could she do?

She raised her eyes, looked across the street, and there saw, loitering along and casting furtive glances at her window, the very lad of whom she had been thinking. He had sought and waited for her recognition, and instead of receiving it in the usual way, saw a beckoning finger. He waited a moment, to be sure that he had not misunderstood the sign, and then, when it was repeated, crossed over, and stood at the door. Mrs. Dillingham admitted the boy, then called the servant, and told him that, while the lad remained, she would not be at home to any one. As soon as the pair were in the drawing-room she stooped and kissed the lad, warming his heart with a smile so sweet, and a manner so cordial and gracious, that he could not have told whether his soul was his own or hers.

She led him to her seat, giving him none, but sitting with her arm around him, as he stood at her side.

"You are my little lover, aren't you?" she said, with an embrace.

"Not so very little!" responded Harry, with a flush.

"Well, you love me, don't you?"

"Perhaps I do," replied he, looking smilingly into her eyes.

"You are a rogue, sir."

"I'm not a bad rogue."

"Kiss me."

Harry put his arms around Mrs. Dillingham's neck and kissed her, and received a long, passionate embrace in return, in which her starved heart expressed the best of its powerful nature.

Nor clouds nor low-born vapors drop the dew. It only gathers under a pure heaven and the tender eyes of stars. Mrs. Dillingham had always held a heart that could respond to the touch of a child. It was dark, its ways were crooked, it was not a happy heart, but for the moment her whole nature was flooded with a tender passion. A flash of lightning from heaven makes the darkest night its own, and gilds with glory the uncouth shapes that grope and crawl beneath its cover.

"And your name is Harry?" she said.

"Yes."

"Do you mind telling me about yourself?"

Harry hesitated. He knew that he ought not to do it. He had received imperative commands not to tell anybody about himself; but his temptation to yield to the beautiful lady's wishes was great, for he was heart-starved like herself. Mrs. Balfour was kind, even affectionate, but he felt that he had never filled the place in her heart of the boy she had lost. She did not take him into her embrace, and lavish caresses upon him. He had hungered for just this, and the impulse to show the whole of his heart and life to Mrs. Dillingham was irresistible.

"If you'll never tell."

"I will never tell, Harry."

"Never, never tell?"

"Never."

"You are Mr. Belcher's friend, aren't you?"

"I know Mr. Belcher."

"If Mr. Belcher should tell you that he would kill you if you didn't tell, what would you do?"

"I should call the police," responded Mrs. Dillingham, with a smile.

Then Harry, in a simple, graphic way, told her all about the hard, wretched life in Sevenoaks, the death of his mother, the insanity of his father, the life in the poor-house, the escape, the recovery of his father's health, his present home, and the occasion of his own removal to New York. The narrative was so wonderful, so full of pathos, so tragic, so out of all proportion in its revelation of wretchedness to the little life at her side, that the lady was dumb. Unconsciously to herself—almost unconsciously to the boy—her arms closed around him, and she lifted him into her lap. There, with his head against her breast, he concluded his story; and there were tears upon his hair, rained from the eyes that bent above him. They sat for a long minute in silence. Then the lady, to keep herself from bursting into hysterical tears, kissed Harry again and again, exclaiming:

"My poor, dear boy! My dear, dear child! And Mr. Belcher could have helped it all! Curse him!"

The lad jumped from her arms as if he had received the thrust of a dagger, and looked at her with great, startled, wondering eyes. She recognized in an instant the awful indiscretion into which she had been betrayed by her fierce and sudden anger, and threw herself upon her knees before the boy, exclaiming:

"Harry, you must forgive me. I was beside myself with anger. I did not know what I was saying. Indeed, I did not. Come to my lap again, and kiss me, or I shall be wretched."

Harry still maintained his attitude and his silence. A furious word from an angel would not have surprised or pained him more than this expression of her anger, that had flashed upon him like a fire from hell.

Still the lady knelt, and pleaded for his forgiveness.

"No one loves me, Harry. If you leave me, and do not forgive me, I shall wish I were dead. You cannot be so cruel."

"I didn't know that ladies ever said such words," said Harry.

"Ladies who have little boys to love them never do," responded Mrs. Dillingham.

"If I love you, shall you ever speak so again?" inquired Harry.

"Never, with you and God to help me," she responded.

She rose to her feet, led the boy to her chair, and once more held him in her embrace.

"You can do me a great deal of good, Harry — a great deal more good than you know, or can understand. Men and women make me worse. There is nobody who can protect me like a child that trusts me. You can trust me."

Then they sat a long time in a silence broken only by Harry's sobs, for the excitement and the reaction had shaken his nerves as if he had suffered a terrible fright.

"You have never told me your whole name, Harry," she said tenderly, with the design of leading him away from the subject of his grief.

"Harry Benedict."

He felt the thrill that ran through her frame, as if it had been a shock of electricity. The arms that held him trembled, and half relaxed their hold upon him. Her heart struggled, intermitted its beat, then throbbed against his reclining head as if it were a hammer. He raised himself, and looked up at her face. It was pale and ghastly ; and her eyes were dimly looking far off, as if unconscious of anything near.

" Are you ill ? "

There was no answer.

" Are you ill ? " with a voice of alarm.

The blood mounted to her face again.

" It was a bad turn," she said. " Don't mind it. I'm better now."

" Isn't it better for me to sit in a chair ? " he inquired, trying to rise.

She tightened her grasp upon him.

" No, no. I am better with you here. I wish you were never to leave me."

Again they sat a long time in silence. Then she said:

" Harry, can you write ? "

" Yes."

" Well, there is a pencil on the table, and paper. Go and write your father's name. Then come and give me a kiss, and then go home. I shall see you again, perhaps to-night. I suppose I ought to apologize to Mrs. Balfour for keeping you so long."

Harry did her bidding. She did not look at him, but turned her eyes to the window. There she saw Mr. Belcher, who had just been sent away from the door. He bowed, and she returned the bow, but the smile she summoned to her face by force of habit, failed quickly, for her heart had learned to despise him.

Harry wrote the name, left it upon the table, and then came to get his kiss. The caress was calmer and tenderer than any she had given him. His instinct detected the change ; and, when he bade her a good-night, it seemed as if she had grown motherly—as if a new life had been developed in her that subordinated the old—as if, in her life, the sun had set, and the moon had risen.

She had no doubt that as Harry left the door Mr. Belcher would see him, and seek admission at once on his hateful business, for, strong as his passion was for Mrs. Dillingham, he never forgot his knavish affairs, in which he sought to use her as a tool. So when she summoned the servant to let Harry out, she told him that if Mr. Belcher should call, he was to be informed that she was too ill to see him.

Mr. Belcher did call within three minutes after the door closed on the lad. He had a triumphant smile on his face, as if he did not doubt that Mrs. Dillingham had been engaged in forwarding his own dirty work. His face blackened as he received her message, and he went wondering home, with ill-natured curses on his lips that will not bear repeating.

Mrs. Dillingham closed the doors of her drawing-room, took the paper on which Harry had written, and resumed her seat. For the hour that lay between her and her dinner, she held the paper in her cold, wet hand. She knew the name she should find there, and she determined that before her eye should verify the prophecy of her heart, she would achieve perfect self-control.

Excited by the interview with the lad, and the prescience of its waiting *dénouement*, her mind went back into his and his father's history. Mr. Belcher could have alleviated that history; nay, prevented it altogether. What had been her own responsibility in the case? She could not have foreseen all the horrors of that history; but she, too, could have prevented it. The consciousness of this filled her with self-condemnation; yet she could not acknowledge herself to be on a level with Mr. Belcher. She was ready and anxious to right all the wrongs she had inflicted; he was bent on increasing and confirming them. She cursed him in her heart for his injustice and cruelty, and almost cursed herself.

But she dwelt most upon the future which the discoveries of the hour had rendered possible to herself. She had found a way out of her hateful life. She had found a lad who admired, loved, and trusted her, upon whom she could lavish her hungry affections—one, indeed, upon whom she had a right to lavish them. The life which she had led from girlhood was like one of those deep cañons in the far West, down which her beautiful boat had been gliding between impassable walls that gave her only here and there glimpses of the heaven above. The uncertain stream had its fascinations. There were beautiful shallows over which she had glided smoothly and safely, rocks and rapids over which she had shot swiftly amid attractive dangers, crooked courses that led she did not know whither, landing-places where she could enjoy an hour of the kindly sun. But all the time she knew she was descending. The song of the waterfalls was a farewell song to scenes that could never be witnessed again. Far away perhaps, perhaps near, waited the waters of the gulf that would drink the sparkling stream into its sullen depths, and steep it in its own bitterness. It was beautiful all the way, but it was going down, down, down. It was seeking the level of its death; and the little boat that rode so buoyantly over the crests which betrayed the hidden rocks, would be but a chip among the waves of the broad, wild sea that waited at the end.

Out of the fascinating roar that filled her ears; out of the sparkling rapids and sheeny reaches, and misty cataracts that enchanted her eyes; and out of the relentless drift toward the bottomless sea, she could be lifted! The sun shone overhead. There were rocks to climb where her hands would bleed ; there were weary heights to scale ; but she knew that on the top there were green pastures and broad skies, and the music of birds—places where she could rest, and from which she could slowly find her way back, in loving companionship, to the mountains of purity from which she had come.

She revolved the possibilities of the future ; and, provided the little paper in her hand should verify her expectations, she resolved to realize them. During the long hour in which she sat thinking, she discounted the emotion which the little paper in her hand held for her, so that, when she unfolded it and read it, she only kissed it, and placed it in her bosom.

After dinner, she ordered her carriage. Then, thinking that it might be recognized by Mr. Belcher, she changed her order, and sent to a public stable for one that was not identified with herself ; and then, so disguising her person that in the evening she would not be known, she ordered the driver to take her to Mr. Balfour's.

Mrs. Dillingham had met Mr. Balfour many times, but she had never, though on speaking terms with her, cultivated Mrs. Balfour's acquaintance, and that lady did not fail to show the surprise she felt when her visitor was announced.

"I have made the acquaintance of your little ward," said Mrs. Dillingham, "and we have become good friends. I enticed him into my house to-day, and as I kept him a long time, I thought I would come over and apologize for his absence."

"I did not know that he had been with you," said Mrs. Balfour, coolly.

"He could do no less than come to me when I asked him to do so," said Mrs. Dillingham ; "and I was entirely to blame for his remaining with me so long. You ladies who have children cannot know how sweet their society sometimes is to those who have none."

Mrs. Balfour was surprised. She saw in her visitor's eyes the evidence of recent tears, and their was a moisture in them then, and a subdued and tender tone to her voice which did not harmonize at all with her conception of Mrs. Dillingham's nature and character. Was she trying her arts upon her? She knew of her intimacy with Mr. Belcher, and naturally connected the visit with that unscrupulous person's schemes.

Mrs. Balfour was soon relieved by the entrance of her husband, who greeted Mrs. Dillingham in the old, stereotyped, gallant way in which gentlemen were accustomed to address her. How did she manage to keep herself so young? Would she be kind enough to give Mrs. Balfour the name of her hair-dresser? What waters had she bathed in, what airs had she breathed, that youth should clothe her in such immortal fashion?

Quite to his surprise, Mrs. Dillingham had nothing to say to this badinage. She seemed either not to hear it at all, or to hear it with impatience. She talked in a listless way, and appeared to be thinking of anything but what was said.

At last, she asked Mr. Balfour if she could have the liberty to obtrude a matter of business upon him. She did not like to interfere with his home enjoyments, but he would oblige her much by giving her half an hour of private conversation. Mr. Balfour looked at his wife, received a significant glance, and invited the lady into his library.

It was a long interview. Nine o'clock, ten o'clock, eleven o'clock sounded, and then Mrs. Balfour went upstairs. It was nearly midnight when Mrs. Dillingham emerged from the door. She handed a bank-note to the impatient coachman, and ordered him to drive her home. As she passed Mr. Belcher's corner of the street, she saw Phipps helping his master to mount the steps. He had had an evening of carousal among some of his new acquaintances. "Brute!" she said to herself, and withdrew her head from the window.

Admitted at her door, she went to her room in her unusual wrappings, threw herself upon her knees, and buried her face in her bed. She did not pray; she hardly lifted her thoughts. She was excessively weary. Why she knelt she did not know; but on her knees she thought over the occurrences of the evening. Her hungry soul was full—full of hopes, plans, purposes. She had found something to love.

What is that angel's name who, shut away from ten thousand selfish, sinful lives, stands always ready, when the bearers of those lives are tired of them, and are longing for something better, to open the door into a new realm? What patience and persistence are his! Always waiting, always prepared, cherishing no resentments, willing to lead, anxious to welcome, who is he, and whence came he? If Mrs. Dillingham did not pray, she had a vision of this heavenly visitant, and kissed the hem of his garments.

She rose and walked to her dressing-table. There she found a note in Mrs. Belcher's handwriting, inviting her to a drive in the Park with her and Mr. Belcher on the following afternoon. Whether the invitation was self-moved, or the result of a suggestion from Mr. Belcher, she did not know. In truth, she did not care. She had wronged Mrs. Belcher in many ways, and she would go.

Why was it that when the new and magnificent carriage rolled up to her door the next afternoon, with its wonderful horses and showy equipage, and appointments calculated to attract attention, her heart was smitten with disgust? She was to be stared at; and, during all the drive, she was to sit face to face with a man who believed that he had fascinated her, and who was trying to use her for all the base purposes in which it was possible for her to serve his will. What could she do with him?

How, in the new relations of her life to him, should she carry herself?

The drive was a quiet one. Mr. Belcher sat and feasted his greedy, exultant eyes on the woman before him, and marvelled at the adroitness with which, to use his own coarse phrase, she "pulled the wool" over the eyes of his wife. In what a lovely way did she hide her passion for him! How sweetly did she draw out the sympathy of the deceived woman at her side! Ah! he could trust her! Her changed, amiable, almost pathetic demeanor was attributed by him to the effect of his power upon her, and her own subtle ingenuity in shielding from the eyes of Mrs. Belcher a love that she deemed hopeless. In his own mind it was not hopeless. In his own determination, it should not be!

As for Mrs. Belcher, she had never so much enjoyed Mrs. Dillingham's society before. She blamed herself for not having understood her better; and when she parted with her for the day, she expressed in hearty terms her wish that she might see more of her in the future.

Mrs. Dillingham, on the return, was dropped at her own door first. Mr. Belcher alighted, and led her up the steps. Then, in a quiet voice, he said:

"Did you find out anything of the boy?"

"Yes, some things, but none that it would be of advantage to you to know."

"Well, stick to him, now that you have got hold of him."

"I intend to."

"Good for you!"

"I imagine that he has been pretty well drilled," said Mrs. Dillingham, "and told just what he may and must not say to any one."

"You can work it out of him. I'll risk you."

Mrs. Dillingham could hardly restrain her impatience, but said quietly:

"I fancy I have discovered all the secrets I shall ever discover in him. I like the boy, and shall cultivate his acquaintance; but, really, it will not pay you to rely upon me for anything. He is under Mr. Balfour's directions, and very loyal."

Mr. Belcher remembered his own interview with the lad, and recognized the truth of the statement. Then he bade her good-by, rejoined his wife, and rode home.

CHAPTER XIX.

IN WHICH MR. BELCHER BECOMES PRESIDENT OF THE CROOKED VALLEY RAILROAD, WITH LARGE "TERMINAL FACILITIES," AND MAKES AN ADVENTURE INTO A LONG-MEDITATED CRIME.

MR. BELCHER had never made money so rapidly as during the summer following his removal to New York. The tides of wealth rolled in faster than he could compute them. Twenty regiments in the field had been armed with the Belcher rifle, and the reports of its execution and its popularity among officers and men, gave promise of future golden harvests to the proprietor. Ten thousand of them had been ordered by the Prussian Government. His agents in France, Russia, Austria, and Italy, all reported encouragingly concerning their attempts to introduce the new arm into the military service of those countries. The civil war had advanced the price of, and the demand for, the products of his mills at Sevenoaks. The people of that village had never before received so good wages, or been so fully employed. It seemed as if there were work for every man, woman, and child, who had hands willing to work. Mr. Belcher bought stocks upon a rising market, and unloaded again and again, sweeping into his capacious coffers his crops of profits. Bonds that early in the war could be bought for a song, rose steadily up to par. Stocks that had been kicked about the market for years, took on value from day to day, and asserted themselves as fair investments. From these, again and again, he harvested the percentage of advance, until his greed was gorged.

That he enjoyed his winnings, is true; but the great trouble with him was that, beyond a certain point, he could show nothing for them. He lived in a palace, surrounded by every appointment of luxury that his wealth could buy. His stables held the choicest horseflesh that could be picked out of the whole country, from Maine to Kentucky. His diamond shirt-studs were worth thousands. His clothes were of the most expensive fabrics, made at the top of the style. His wife and children had money lavished upon them without stint. In the direction of show, he could do no more. It was his glory to drive in the Park alone, with his servants in livery and his four horses, fancying that he was the observed of all observers, and the envied of all men.

Having money still to spend, it must find a market in other directions. He gave lavish entertainments at his club, at which wine flowed like water, and at which young and idle men were gathered in and debauched, night after night. He was surrounded by a group of flatterers who laughed at his jokes, repeated them to the public, humored his caprices, and lived upon his hospitalities. The plain "Colonel Belcher" of his first few months in New York, grew into "the General," so that Wall Street knew him, at last, by that title, without the speaking of his name. All made way for "the General" whenever he appeared. "The General" was "bulling" this stock, and "bearing" that. All this was honey to his palate, and he was enabled to forget something of his desire for show in his love of glory. Power was sweet, as well as display.

Of course, "the General" had forsaken, somewhat, his orderly habits of life—those which kept him sound and strong in his old country home. He spent few evenings with his family. There was so genuine a passion in his heart for Mrs. Dillingham, that he went into few excesses which compromised a fair degree of truthfulness to her; but he was in the theatres, in the resorts of fast men, among the clubs, and always late in his bed. Phipps had a hard time in looking after and waiting upon him, but had a kind of sympathetic enjoyment in it all, because he knew there was more or less of wickedness connected with it.

Mr. Belcher's nights began to tell upon his days. It became hard for him to rise at his old hours; so, after a while, he received the calls of his brokers in bed. From nine to ten, Mr. Belcher, in his embroidered dressing-gown, with his breakfast at his side, gave his orders for the operations of the day. The bedroom became the General's head-quarters, and there his staff gathered around him. Half a dozen cabs and carriages at his door in the morning became a daily recurring vision to residents and habitual passengers.

Mr. Talbot, not a regular visitor at this hour, sometimes mingled with the brokers, though he usually came late for the purpose of a private interview. He had managed to retain the General's favor, and to be of such use to him that that gentleman, in his remarkable prosperity, had given up the idea of reducing his factor's profits.

One morning, after the brokers and the General's lawyer were gone, Talbot entered, and found his principal still in bed.

"Toll, it's a big thing," said Mr. Belcher.

"I believe you."

"Toll, what did I tell you? I've always worked to a

programme, and exactly this was my programme when I came here. How's your wife?"

"Quite well."

"Why don't we see more of her?"

"Well, Mrs. Talbot is a quiet woman, and knows her place. She isn't quite at home in such splendors as yours, you know, and she naturally recognizes my relations to you."

"Oh, nonsense, nonsense, Toll! She mustn't feel that way. I like her. She is a devilish handsome woman."

"I shall tell her that you say so," said the obsequious Mr. Talbot.

"Toll, my boy, I've got an idea."

"Cherish it, General; you may never have another."

"Good for you. I owe you one."

"Not at all, General. I'm only paying off old debts."

"Toll, how are you doing now? Getting a living?"

"Thanks to you, General, I am thriving in a modest way. I don't aspire to any such profits as you seem to win so easily, so I have no fault to find."

"The General has been a godsend to you, hasn't he, eh? Happy day when you made his acquaintance, eh? Well, go ahead; it's all right. Pile it up while you can."

"But you haven't told me about your idea," Mr. Talbot suggested.

"Well, Toll, I'm pining for a railroad. I'm crying nights for a railroad. A fellow must have amusements you know. Health must be taken care of, eh? All the fellows have railroads. It's well enough to keep horses and go to the theatre. A steamship line isn't bad, but the trouble is, a man can't be captain of his own vessels. No, Toll; I need a railroad. I'm yearning for engines, and double tracks, and running over my own line."

"You might buy up a European kingdom or two, at a pinch, General."

"Yes; but, Toll, you don't know what terminal facili ties I've got for a railroad."

"Your pocket will answer for one end," said Talbot, laughing.

"Right, the first time," responded the General, "and glory will answer for the other. Toll, do you know what I see at the other end?"

"No."

"I see a man of about the size of Robert Belcher in the chair of an alderman. I see him seated on a horse, riding down Broadway at the head of a regiment. I see him Mayor of the city of New York. I see him Governor of the State. I see him President of the United States. I see no reason why he cannot hold any one, or all these offices. All doors yield to a golden key. Toll, I haven't got to go as far as I have come, to reach the top. Do you know it? Big thing! Yes, Toll, I must have a railroad."

"Have you selected the toy you propose to purchase?" inquired Talbot.

"Well, I've looked about some; but the trouble is, that all the best of 'em are in hands that can hold them. I must buy a poor one and build it up, or make it build me up."

"That's a pity."

"I don't know about that. The big ones are hard to handle, and I'm not quite big enough for them yet. What do you say to the Crooked Valley?"

"Poor road, and wants connections."

"Those are exactly the points. I can buy it for a song, issue bonds, and build the connections—issue plenty of bonds, and build plenty of connections. Terminal facilities large—do you understand? Eh, Toll?"

Mr. Talbot laughed.

"I don't think you need any suggestions from me," he said.

"No; the General can manage this thing without help. He only wanted to open your eyes a little, and get you ready for your day's work. You fellows who fiddle around with a few goods need waking up occasionally. Now, Toll, go off and let the General get up. I must have a railroad before night, or I shall not be able to sleep a wink. By-by!"

Talbot turned to leave the room, when Mr. Belcher arrested him with the question:

"Toll, would you like an office in the Crooked Valley corporation?"

Talbot knew that the corporation would have a disgraceful history, and a disastrous end—that it would be used by the General for the purposes of stealing, and that the head of it would not be content to share the plunder with others. He had no wish to be his principal's cat's-paw, or to be identified with an enterprise in which, deprived of both will and voice, he should get neither profit nor credit. So he said:

"No, I thank you; I have all I can do to take care of your goods, and I am not ambitious."

"There'll be nothing for you to do, you know. I shall run the whole thing."

"I can serve you better, General, where I am."

"Well, by-by; I won't urge you."

After Talbot left, Mr. Belcher rose and carefully dressed himself. Phipps was already at the door with the carriage, and, half an hour afterward, the great proprietor, full of his vain and knavish projects, took his seat in it, and was whirled off down to Wall Street. His brokers had already been charged with his plans, and, before he reached the ground, every office where the Crooked Valley stock was held had been visited, and every considerable deposit of it ascertained, so that, before night, by one grand swoop, the General had absorbed a controlling interest in the corporation.

A few days afterward, the annual meeting was held, Mr. Belcher was elected President, and every other office was filled by his creatures and tools. His plans for the future of the road gradually became known, and the stock began to assume a better position on the list. Weak and inefficient corporations were already in existence for completing the various connections of the road, and of these he immediately, and for moderate sums, bought the franchises. Within two months, bonds were issued for building the roads, and the roads themselves were put under contract. The "terminal facilities" of one end of every contract were faithfully attended to by Mr. Belcher. His pockets were still capacious and absorbent. He parted with so much of his appreciated stock as he could spare without impairing his control, and so, at the end of a few months, found himself in the possession of still another harvest. Not only this, but he found his power increased. Men watched him, and followed him into other speculations. They hung around him, anxious to get indications of his next movement. They flattered him; they fawned upon him; and to those whom he could in any way use for his own purposes, he breathed little secrets of the market from which they won their rewards. People talked about what "the General" was doing, and proposed to do, as if he were a well-recognized factor in the financial situation.

Whenever he ran over his line, which he often did for information and amusement, and for the pleasure of exercising his power, he went in a special car, at breakneck speed, by telegraph, always accompanied by a body of friends and toadies, whom he feasted on the way. Everybody wanted to see him. He was as much a lion as if he had been an emperor or a murderer. To emerge upon a platform at a way-station, where there were hundreds of country people who had flocked in to witness the exhibition, was his great delight. He spoke to them familiarly and good-naturedly; transacted his business with a rush; threw the whole village into tumult; waved his hand; and vanished in a cloud of dust. Such enterprise, such confidence, such strength, such interest in the local prosperities of the line, found their natural result in the absorption of the new bonds. They were purchased by individuals and municipal corporations. Freight was diverted from its legitimate channels, and drawn over the road at a loss; but it looked like business. Passes were scattered in every direction, and the passenger traffic seemed to double at once. All was bustle, drive, business. Under a single will, backed by a strong and orderly executive capacity, the dying road seemed to leap into life. It had not an *employé* who did not know and take off his hat to the General. He was a kind of god, to whom they all bowed down; and to be addressed or chaffed by him was an honor to be reported to friends, and borne home with self-gratulations to wives and children.

The General, of course, had moments of superlative happiness. He never had enjoyed anything more than he enjoyed his railroad. His notoriety with the common people along the line—the idea which they cherished that he could do anything he wished to do; that he had only to lift his hand to win gold to himself or to bear it to them—these were pleasant in themselves; but to have their obeisance witnessed by his city friends and associates, while they discussed his champagne and boned turkey from the abounding hampers which always furnished "the President's car"—this was the crown of his pleasure. He had a pleasure, too, in business. He never had enough to do, and the railroad which would have loaded down an ordinary man with an ordinary conscience, was only a pleasant diversion to him. Indeed, he was wont to reiterate, when rallied upon his new enterprise : "The fact was, I had to do something for my health, you know."

Still, the General was not what could be called a thoroughly happy man. He knew the risks he ran on 'Change. He had been reminded, by two or three mortifying losses, that the sun did not always shine on Wall Street. He knew that his railroad was a bubble, and that sooner or later it would burst. Times would change, and, after all, there was nothing that would last like his manufactures. With a long foresight, he had ordered the funds received from the Prussian sales of the Belcher rifle to be deposited with a European banking house at interest, to be drawn against in his foreign purchases of material ; yet he never drew against this deposit. Self-confident as he was, glutted with success as he was, he had in his heart a premonition that some time he might want that money just where it was placed. So there it lay, accumulating interest. It was an anchor to windward, that would hold him if ever his bark should drift into shallow or dangerous waters.

The grand trouble was, that he did not own a single patent by which he was thriving in both branches of his manufactures. He had calculated upon worrying the inventor into a sale, and had brought his designs very nearly to realization, when he found, to his surprise and discomfiture, that he had driven him into a mad-house. Rich as he was, therefore, there was something very unsubstantial in his wealth, even to his own apprehension. Sometimes it all seemed like a bubble, which a sudden breath would wreck. Out of momentary despondencies, originating in visions like these, he always rose with determinations that nothing should come between him and his possessions and prosperities which his hand, by fair means or foul, could crush.

Mr. Balfour, a lawyer of faultless character and undoubted courage, held his secret. He could not bend him or buy him. He was the one man in all the world whom he was afraid of. He was the one man in New York who knew whether Benedict was alive or not. He had Benedict's heir in his house, and he knew that by him the law would lay its hand on him and his possessions. He only wondered that the action was delayed. Why was it delayed? Was he, Mr. Belcher, ready for it? He knew he was not, and he saw but one way by which he could become so. Over this he hesitated, hoping that some event would occur which would render his projected crime unnecessary.

Evening after evening, when every member of his family was in bed, he shut himself in his room, looked behind every article of furniture to make himself sure that he was alone, and then drew from its drawer the long unexecuted contract with Mr. Benedict, with the accompanying autograph letters, forwarded to him by Sam Yates. Whole quires of paper he traced with the names of "Nicholas Johnson" and "James Ramsey." After he had mastered the peculiarities of their signs-manual, he took up that of Mr. Benedict. Then he wrote the three names in the relations in which he wished them to appear on the document. Then he not only burned all the paper he had used, in the grate, but pulverized its ashes.

Not being able to ascertain whether Benedict were alive or dead, it would be necessary to produce a document which would answer his purpose in either case. Of course, it would be requisite that its date should anticipate the inventor's insanity. He would make one more effort to ascertain a fact that had so direct a relation to his future security.

Accordingly, one evening after his railroad scheme was fairly inaugurated, he called on Mrs. Dillingham, determined to obtain from her what she knew. He had witnessed for months her fondness for Harry Benedict. The boy had, apparently with the consent of the Balfours, been frequently in her house. They had taken long drives together in the Park. Mr. Belcher felt that there was a peculiar intimacy between the two, yet not one satisfactory word had he ever heard from the lady about her new pet. He had become conscious, too, of a certain change in her. She had been less in society, was more quiet than formerly, and more reticent in his presence, though she had never repulsed him. He had caught fewer glimpses of that side of her nature and character which he had once believed was sympathetic with his own. Misled by his own vanity into the constant belief that she was seriously in love with himself, he was determined to utilize her passion for his own purposes. If she would not give kisses, she should give confidence.

"Mrs. Dillingham," he said, "I have been waiting to hear something about your pauper *protégé*, and I have come to-night to find out what you know about him and his father."

"If I knew of anything that would be of real advantage to you, I would tell you, but I do not," she replied.

"Well, that's an old story. Tell that to the marines. I'm sick of it."

Mrs. Dillingham's face flushed.

"I prefer to judge for myself, if it's all the same to you," pursued the proprietor. "You've had the boy in your hands for months, and you know him, through and through, or else you are not the woman I have taken you for."

"You have taken me for, Mr. Belcher?"

"Nothing offensive. Don't roll up your pretty eyes in that way."

Mrs. Dillingham was getting angry.

"Please don't address me in that way again," she said.

"Well, what the devil have you to do with the boy anyway, if you are not at work for me? That's what I'd like to know."

"I like him, and he is fond of me."

"I don't see how that helps me," responded Mr. Belcher.

"It is enough for me that I enjoy it."

"Oh, it is!"

"Yes, it is," with an emphatic nod of the head.

"Perhaps you think that will go down with me. Perhaps you are not acquainted with my way of doing business."

"Are you doing business with me, Mr. Belcher? Am I a partner of yours? If I am, perhaps you will be kind enough to tell me—business-like enough to tell me—why you wish me to worm secrets out of this boy."

It was Mr. Belcher's turn to color.

"No, I will not. I trust no woman with my affairs. I keep my own councils."

"Then do your own business," snappishly.

"Mrs. Dillingham, you and I are friends—destined, I trust, to be better friends—closer friends—than we have ever been. This boy is of no consequence to you, and you cannot afford to sacrifice a man who can serve you more than you seem to know, for him."

"Well," said the lady, "there is no use in acting under a mask any longer. I would not betray the confidence of a child to serve any man I ever saw. You have been kind to me, but you have not trusted me. The lad loves me, and trusts me, and I will never betray him. What I tell you is true. I have learned nothing from him that can be of any genuine advantage to you. That is all the answer you will ever get from me. If you choose to throw away our friendship, you can take the responsibility," and Mrs. Dillingham hid her face in her handkerchief.

Mr. Belcher had been trying an experiment, and he had not succeeded—could not succeed ; and there sat the beautiful, magnanimous woman before him, her heart torn as he believed with love for him, yet loyal to her ideas of honor as they related to a confiding child ! How beautiful she was ! Vexed he certainly was, but there was a balm for his vexation in these charming revelations of her character.

"Well," he said, rising, and in his old good-natured tone, "there's no accounting for a woman. I'm not going to bother you."

He seized her unresisting hand, pressed it to his lips, and went away. He did not hear the musical giggle that followed him into the street, but, absorbed by his purpose, went home and mounted to his room. Locking the door, and peering about among the furniture, according to his custom, he sat down at his desk, drew out the old contract, and started at his usual practice. "Sign it," he said to himself, "and then you can use it or not —just as you please. It's not the signing that will trouble you ; it's the using."

He tried the names all over again, and then, his heart beating heavily against the desk, he spread the document and essayed his task. His heart jarred him. His hand trembled. What could he do to calm himself? He rose and walked to his mirror, and found that he was pale. "Are you afraid ?" he said to himself. "Are you a coward ? Ha ! ha ! ha ! ha ! Did I laugh ? My God ! how it sounded ! Aren't you a pretty King of Wall Street ! Aren't you a lovely President of the Crooked Valley Railroad ! Aren't you a sweet sort of a nabob ! You *must* do it. Do you hear ? You *must* do it ! Eh ? do you hear ? Sit down, sir ! Down with you, sir ! and don't you rise again until the thing is done."

The heart-thumping passed away. The reaction, under the strong spur and steady push of will, brought his nerves up to steadiness, and he sat down, took his pencils and pens that had been selected for the service, and wrote first the name of Paul Benedict, and then, as witnesses, the names of Nicholas Johnson and James Ramsey.

So the document was signed, and witnessed by men whom he believed to be dead. The witnesses whose names he had forged he knew to be dead. With this document he believed he could defend his possession of all the patent rights on which the permanence of his fortune depended. He permitted the ink to dry, then folded the paper, and put it back in its place. Then he shut and opened the drawer, and took it out again. It had a genuine look.

Then he rang his bell and called for Phipps. When Phipps appeared, he said :

" Well, Phipps, what do you want ? "

" Nothing, sir," and Phipps smiled.

" Very well ; help yourself."

" Thank you, sir," and Phipps rubbed his hands.

" How are you getting along in New York, Phipps ? "

" Very well, sir."

" Big thing to be round with the General, isn't it ? It's a touch above Sevenoaks, eh ? "

" Yes, sir."

" Get enough to eat down-stairs ? "

" Plenty."

" Good clothes to wear ? "

" Very good," and Phipps looked down upon his toilet with great satisfaction.

" Stolen mostly from the General, eh ? "

Phipps giggled.

" That's all ; you can go. I only wanted to see if you were in the house, and well taken care of."

Phipps started to go. " By the way, Phipps, have you a good memory ?—first-rate memory ? "

"Yes, sir."

"Can you remember everything that happened, a—say, six years ago?"

"I can try," said Phipps, with an intelligent glance into Mr. Belcher's eyes.

"Do you remember a day, about six years ago, when Paul Benedict came into my house at Sevenoaks, with Nicholas Johnson and James Ramsey, and they all signed a paper together?"

"Very well," replied Phipps.

"And do you remember that I said to you, after they were gone, that that paper gave me all of Benedict's patent rights?"

Phipps looked up at the ceiling, and then said:

"Yes, sir, and I remember that I said, 'It will make you very rich, won't it, Mr. Belcher?'"

"And what did I reply to you?"

"You said, 'That remains to be seen.'"

"All right. Do you suppose you should know that paper if you were to see it?"

"I think I should—after I'd seen it once."

"Well, there it is—suppose you take a look at it."

"I remember it by two blots in the corner, and the red lines down the side."

"You didn't write your own name, did you?"

"It seems to me I did."

"Suppose you examine the paper, under James Ramsey's name, and see whether yours is there."

Mr. Belcher walked to his glass, turning his back upon Phipps. The latter sat down, and wrote his name upon the spot thus blindly suggested.

"It is here, sir."

"Ah! So you have found it! You distinctly remember writing it on that occasion, and can swear to it, and to the signatures of the others?"

"Oh yes, sir."

" And all this was done in my library, wasn't it ? "

" Yes, sir."

" How did you happen to be there when these other men were there ? "

" You called me in, sir."

" All right ! You never smoke, Phipps ? "

" Never in the stable, sir."

" Well, lay these cigars away where you have laid the rest of 'em, and go to bed."

Phipps took the costly bundle of cigars that was handed to him, carried them by habit to his nose, said " Thank you, sir," and went off down the stairs, felicitating himself on the ease with which he had won so choice a treasure.

The effect of Phipps' signature on Mr. Belcher's mind was a curious illustration of the self-deceptions in which a human heart may indulge. Companionship in crime, the sharing of responsibility, the fact that the paper was to have been signed at the time it was drawn, and would have been signed but for the accident of Benedict's insanity ; the fact that he had paid moneys with the expectation of securing a title to the inventions he was using—all these gave to the paper an air of genuineness which surprised even Mr. Belcher himself.

When known evil seems absolutely good to a man, and conscious falsehood takes on the semblance and the authority of truth, the Devil has him fast.

CHAPTER XX.

IN WHICH "THE LITTLE WOMAN" ANNOUNCES HER ENGAGEMENT TO JIM FENTON AND RECEIVES THE CONGRATULATIONS OF HER FRIENDS.

AFTER the frame of Jim's hotel was up, at Number Nine, and those who had assisted in its erection were out of the woods, he and his architect entered with great industry upon the task of covering it. Under Mr. Benedict's direction, Jim became an expert in the work, and the sound of two busy hammers kept the echoes of the forests awake from dawn until sunset, every day. The masons came at last and put up the chimneys; and more and more, as the days went on, the building assumed the look of a dwelling. The grand object was to get their enterprise forwarded to a point that would enable them to finish everything during the following winter, with such assistance as it might be necessary to import from Sevenoaks. The house needed to be made habitable for workmen while their work was progressing, and to this end Mr. Benedict and Jim pushed their efforts without assistance.

Occasionally, Jim found himself obliged to go to Sevenoaks for supplies, and for articles and tools whose necessity had not been anticipated. On these occasions, he always called Mike Conlin to his aid, and always managed to see "the little woman" of his hopes. She was busy with her preparations, carried on in secret; and he always left her with his head full of new plans and his heart brimming with new satisfactions. It was arranged that they should be married in the following spring, so as to be ready for city boarders; and all his efforts were bent upon completing the house for occupation.

During the autumn, Jim took from the Sevenoaks Post-Office a letter for Paul Benedict, bearing the New York post-mark, and addressed in the handwriting of a lady. The letter was a great puzzle to Jim, and he watched its effect upon his companion with much curiosity. Benedict wept over it, and went away where he could weep alone. When he came back, he was a transformed man. A new light was in his eye, a new elasticity in all his movements.

"I cannot tell you about it, Jim," he said; "at least I cannot tell you now; but a great burden has been lifted from my life. I have never spoken of this to you, or to anybody; but the first cruel wound that the world ever gave me has been healed by a touch."

"It takes a woman to do them things," said Jim. "I knowed when ye gin up the little woman, as was free from what happened about an hour arter, that ye was firin' low an' savin' yer waddin'. Oh, ye can't fool me, not much!"

"What do you think of that, Jim?" said Benedict, smiling, and handing him a check for five hundred dollars that the letter had inclosed.

Jim looked it over and read it through with undisguised astonishment.

"Did she gin it to ye?" he inquired.

"Yes."

"An' be ye a goin' to keep it?"

"Yes, I'm going to keep it."

Jim was evidently doubtful touching the delicacy both of tendering and receiving such a gift.

"If that thing had come to me from the little woman," said he, "I should think she was gittin' oneasy, an' a little dubersome about my comin' to time. It don't seem jest the thing for a woman to shell out money to a man. My nater goes agin it. I feel it all over me, an' I vow, I b'lieve that if the little woman had did that thing to me, I sh'd rub out my reckonin' an' start new."

"It's all right, though, Jim," responded Benedict, good-naturedly—"right for the woman to give it, and right for me to receive it. Don't trouble yourself at all about it."

Benedict's assurance did little to relieve Jim's bewilderment, who still thought it a very improper thing to receive money from a woman. He did not examine himself far enough to learn that Benedict's independence of his own care and provision was partly the cause of his pain. Five hundred dollars in the woods was a great deal of money. To Jim's apprehension, the man had become a capitalist. Some one beside himself—some one richer and more powerful than himself—had taken the position of benefactor toward his friend. He was glad to see Benedict happy, but sorry that he could not have been the agent in making him so.

"Well, I can't keep ye forever'n' ever, but I was a hopin' ye'd hang by till I git hold of the little woman," said Jim.

"Do you suppose I would leave you now, Jim?"

"Well, I knowed a yoke o' cattle couldn't start ye, with a hoss ahead on 'em; but a woman, Mr. Benedict"—and Jim's voice sunk to a solemn and impressive key—"a woman with the right kind of an eye, an' a takin' way, is stronger nor a steam Injun. She can snake ye 'round anywhere; an' the queerest thing about it is that a feller's willin' to go, an' thinks it's purty. She tells ye to come, an' ye come smilin'; and then she tells ye to go, an' ye go smilin'; and then she winds ye 'round her finger, and ye feel as limber an' as willin' as if ye was a whip-lash, an' hadn't nothin' else to do."

"Nevertheless, I shall stay with you, Jim."

"Well, I hope ye will; but don't ye be too sartin; not that I'm goin' to stan' atween ye an' good luck, but if ye calc'late that a woman's goin' to let ye do jest as ye think ye will—leastways a woman as has five hundred dollars in yer pocket—yer eddication hasn't been well took care on. If I was sitooated like you, I'd jest walk up to the pastur'-bars like a hoss, an' whinner to git in, an' expect to be called with a corn-cob when she got ready to use me."

"Still, I shall stay with you, Jim."

"All right; here's hopin', an' here's my hand."

Benedict's letter, besides the check, held still another inclosure—a note from Mr. Balfour. This he had slipped into his pocket, and, in the absorption of his attention produced by the principal communication, forgotten. At the close of his conversation with Jim, he remembered it, and took it out and read it. It conveyed the intelligence that the lawyer found it impossible to leave the city according to his promise, for an autumn vacation in the woods. Still, he would find some means to send up Harry if Mr. Benedict should insist upon it. The boy was well, and progressing satisfactorily in his studies. He was happy, and found a new reason for happiness in his intimacy with Mrs. Dillingham, with whom he was spending a good deal of his leisure time. If Mr. Benedict would consent to a change of plans, it was his wish to keep the lad through the winter, and then, with all his family, to go up to Number Nine in the spring, be present at Jim's wedding, and assist in the inauguration of the new hotel.

Mr. Benedict was more easily reconciled to this change of plan than he would have believed possible an hour previously. The letter, whose contents had so mystified and disturbed Jim, had changed the whole aspect of his life. He replied to this letter during the day, and wrote another to Mr. Balfour, consenting to his wishes, and acquiescing in his plans. For the first time in many years, he could see through all his trials, into the calm daylight. Harry was safe and happy in a new association with a woman who, more than any other, held his life in her hands. He was getting a new basis for life in friendship and love. Shored up by affection and sympathy, and with a modest competence in his hands for all present and immediately prospective needs, his dependent nature could once more stand erect.

Henceforward he dropped his idle dreaming and became interested in his work, and doubly efficient in its execution. Jim once more had in possession the old friend whose cheerfulness and good-nature had originally won his affection ; and the late autumn and winter which lay before them seemed full of hopeful and happy enterprise.

Miss Butterworth, hearing occasionally through Jim of the progress of affairs at Number Nine, began to think it about time to make known her secret among her friends. Already they had begun to suspect that the little tailoress had a secret, out of which would grow a change in her life. She had made some astonishing purchases at the village shops, which had been faithfully reported. She was working early and late in her little room. She was, in the new prosperity of the villagers, collecting her trifling dues. She had given notice of the recall of her modest loans. There were many indications that she was preparing to leave the town.

"Now, really," said Mrs. Snow to her one evening, when Miss Butterworth was illuminating the parsonage by her presence—"now, really, you must tell us all about it. I'm dying to know."

"Oh, it's too ridiculous for anything," said Miss Butterworth, laughing herself almost into hysterics.

"Now, what, Keziah? What's too ridiculous? You *are* the most provoking person!"

"The idea of my getting married!"

Mrs. Snow jumped up and seized Miss Butterworth's hands, and said :

"Why, Keziah Butterworth! You don't tell me! You wicked, deceitful creature!"

The three Misses Snow all jumped up with their mother, and pressed around the merry object of their earnest congratulations.

"So unexpected and strange, you know," said the oldest.

"So very unexpected!" said the second.

"And so very strange, too!" echoed Number Three.

"Well, it *is* too ridiculous for anything," Miss Butterworth repeated. "The idea of my living to be an old maid, and, what's more, making up my mind to it, and then"—and then Miss Butterworth plunged into a new fit of merriment.

"Well, Keziah, I hope you'll be very happy. Indeed I do," said Mrs. Snow, becoming motherly.

"Happy all your life," said Miss Snow.

"Very happy," said Number Two.

"All your life long," rounded up the complement of good wishes from the lips of the youngest of the trio.

"Well, I'm very much obliged to you—to you all"—said Miss Butterworth, wiping her eyes; "but it certainly is the most ridiculous thing. I say to myself sometimes: 'Keziah Butterworth! You little old fool! What *are* you going to do with that man? How *are* you going to live with him?' Goodness knows that I've racked my brain over it until I'm just about crazy. Don't mention it, but I believe I'll use him for a watch-dog—tie him up daytimes, and let him out nights, you know!"

"Why, isn't he nice?" inquired Mrs. Snow.

"Nice! He's as rough as a hemlock tree."

"What do you marry him for?" inquired Mrs. Snow in astonishment.

"I'm sure I don't know. I've asked myself the question a thousand times."

"Don't you want to marry him?"

"I don't know. I guess I do."

"My dear," said Mrs. Snow, soberly, "this is a very solemn thing."

"I don't see it in that light," said Miss Butterworth, indulging in a new fit of laughter. "I wish I could, but it's the funniest thing. I wake up laughing over it, and I go to sleep laughing over it, and I say to myself, 'What are you laughing at, you ridiculous creature?'"

"Well, I believe you are a ridiculous creature," said Mrs. Snow.

"I know I am, and if anybody had told me a year ago that I should ever marry Jim Fenton, I——"

"Jim Fenton!" exclaimed the whole Snow family.

"Well, what is there so strange about my marrying Jim Fenton?" and the little tailoress straightened in her chair, her eyes flashing, and the color mounting to her face.

"Oh, nothing; but you know—it's such a surprise—he's so—he's so—well he's a—not cultivated—never has seen much society, you know; and lives almost out of the world, as it were."

"Oh, no! He isn't cultivated! He ought to have been brought up in Sevenoaks and polished! He ought to have been subjected to the civilizing and refining influences of Bob Belcher!"

"Now, you mustn't be offended, Keziah. We are all your friends, and anxious for your welfare."

"But you think Jim Fenton is a brute."

"I have said nothing of the kind."

"But you think so."

"I think you ought to know him better than I do."

"Well, I do, and he is just the loveliest, manliest, noblest, splendidest old fellow that ever lived. I don't care if he does live out of the world. I'd go with him, and live with him, if he used the North Pole for a back log. Fah! I hate a slick man. Jim has spoiled me for anything but a true man in the rough. There's more pluck in his old shoes than you can find in all the men of Sevenoaks put together. And he's as tender—Oh, Mrs. Snow! Oh, girls! He's as tender as a baby—just as tender as a baby! He has said to me the most wonderful things! I wish I could remember them. I never can, and I couldn't say them as he does if I could. Since I became acquainted with him, it seems as if the world had been made all over new. I'd become kind o' tired of human nature, you know. It seemed sometimes as if it was just as well to be a cow as a woman; but I've become so much to him, and he has become so much to me, that all the men and women around me have grown beautiful. And he loves me in a way that is so strong—and so protecting—and so sweet and careful—that—now don't you laugh, or you'll make me angry—I'd feel safer in his arms than I would in a church!"

"Well, I'm sure!" exclaimed Mrs. Snow.

"Isn't it remarkable!" said Miss Snow.

"Quite delightful!" exclaimed the second sister, whose enthusiasm could not be crammed into Miss Snow's expression.

"Really charming," added Number Three.

"You are quite sure you don't know what you want to marry him for?" said Mrs. Snow, with a roguish twinkle in her eye. "You are quite sure you don't love him?"

"Oh, I don't know," said Miss Butterworth. "It's something. I wish you could hear him talk. His grammar would kill you. It would just kill you. You'd never breathe after it. Such awful nominative cases as that man has! And you can't beat him out of them. And such a pronunciation! His words are just as rough as he is, and just like him. They seem to have a great deal more meaning in them than they do when they have good clothes on. You don't know how I enjoy hearing him talk."

"I'm inclined to think you love him," said Mrs. Snow, smiling.

"I don't know. Isn't it the most ridiculous thing now?"

"No; it isn't ridiculous at all," said Mrs. Snow, soberly.

Miss Butterworth's moon was sailing high that evening. There were but few clouds in her heaven, but occasionally a tender vapor passed across the silver disc, and one passed at this moment. Her eyes were loaded with tears as she looked up in Mrs. Snow's face, and said:

"I was very lonely, you know. Life had become very tame, and I saw nothing before me different from my daily experience, which had grown to be wearisome. Jim came and opened a new life to me, offered me companionship, new circumstances, new surroundings. It was like being born again. And, do you know, I don't think it is natural for a woman to carry her own life. I got very tired of mine, and when this strong man came, and was willing to take it up, and bear it for me as the greatest pleasure I could bestow upon him, what could I do—now, what could I do? I don't think I'm proud of him, but I belong to him, and I'm glad; and that's all there is about it;" and Miss Butterworth sprang to her feet as if she were about to leave the house.

"You are not going," said Mrs. Snow, catching her by both shoulders, "so sit down."

"I've told you the whole: there's nothing more. I suppose it will be a great wonder to the Sevenoaks people, and that they'll think I'm throwing myself away; but I do hope they will let me alone."

"When are you to be married?"

"In the spring."

"Where?"

"Oh! anywhere. No matter where. I haven't thought about that part of it."

"Then you'll be married right here, in this house. You shall have a nice little wedding."

"Oh! and orange-blossoms!" exclaimed Miss Snow, clapping her hands.

"And a veil!" added Number Two.

"And a ——" Number Three was not so familiar with such occasions as to be able to supply another article, so she clapped her hands.

They were all in a delicious flutter. It would be so nice to have a wedding in the house! It was a good sign. Did the young ladies think that it might break a sort of electric spell that hung over the parsonage, and result in a shower which would float them all off? Perhaps so. They were, at least, very happy about it.

Then they all sat down again, to talk over the matter of clothes. Miss Butterworth did not wish to make herself ridiculous.

"I've said a thousand times, if I ever said it once," she remarked, "that there's no fool like an old fool. Now, I don't want to hear any nonsense about orange-blossoms, or about a veil. If there's anything that I do despise above board, it's a bridal veil on an old maid. And I'm not going to have a lot of things made up that I can't use. I'm just going to have a snug, serviceable set of clothes, and in three days I'm going to look as if I'd been married ten years."

"It seems to me," said Miss Snow, "that you ought to do something. I'm sure, if I were in your place, that I should want to do something."

The other girls tittered.

"Not that I ever expect to be in your place, or anything like it," she went on, "but it does seem to me as if something extra ought to be done—white kid gloves or something."

"And white satin gaiters," suggested the youngest sister.

"I guess you'd think Jim Fenton was extra enough if you knew him," said Miss Butterworth, laughing. "There's plenty that's extra, goodness knows! without buying anything."

"Well," persisted the youngest Miss Snow, "I'd have open-worked stockings, and have my hair frizzed, any way."

"Oh, I speak to do your hair," put in the second daughter.

"You're just a lot of chickens, the whole of you," said the tailoress.

Miss Snow, whose age was hovering about the confines of mature maidenhood, smiled a deprecating smile, and said that she thought she was about what they sold for chickens sometimes, and intimated that she was anything but tender.

"Well, don't be discouraged; that's all I have to say," remarked Miss Butterworth. "If I can get married, anybody can. If anybody had told me that—well isn't it too ridiculous for anything? Now, isn't it?" And the little tailoress went off into another fit of laughter. Then she jumped up and said she really must go.

The report that Jim Fenton was soon to lead to the hymeneal altar the popular village tailoress, spread with great rapidity, and as it started from the minister's family, it had a good send-off, and was accompanied by information that very pleasantly modified its effect upon the public mind. The men of the village who knew Jim a great deal better than the women, and who, in various ways, had become familiar with his plans for a hotel, and recognized the fact that his enterprise would make Sevenoaks a kind of thoroughfare for his prospective city-boarders, decided that she had "done well." Jim was enterprising, and, as they termed it, "forehanded." His habits were good, his industry indefatigable, his common sense and good nature unexampled. Everybody liked Jim. To be sure, he was rough and uneducated, but he was honorable and true. He would make a good "provider." Miss Butterworth might have gone further and fared worse. On the whole, it was a good thing; and they were glad for Jim's sake and for Miss Butterworth's that it had happened.

The women took their cue from the men. They thought, however, that Miss Butterworth would be very lonesome, and found various pegs on which to hang out their pity for a public airing. Still, the little tailoress was surprised at the heartiness of their congratulations, and often melted to tears by the presents she received from the great number of families for whom, every year, she had worked. No engagement had occurred in Sevenoaks for a long time that created so much interest, and enlisted so many sympathies. They hoped she would be very happy. They would be exceedingly sorry to lose her. Nobody could ever take her place. She had always been one whom they could have in their families "without making any difference," and she never tattled.

So Miss Butterworth found herself quite a heroine, but whenever Jim showed himself, the women all looked out of the windows, and made their own comments. After all, they couldn't see exactly what Miss Butterworth could find to like in him. They saw a tall, strong, rough, good-natured-looking man, whom all the men and all the boys greeted with genuine heartiness. They saw him pushing about his business with the air of one who owned the whole village; but his clothes were rough, and his boots over his trowsers. They hoped it would all turn out well. There was "no doubt that he needed a woman badly enough."

Not only Miss Butterworth but Jim became the subject of congratulation. The first time he entered Sevenoaks after the announcement of his engagement, he was hailed from every shop, and button-holed at every corner. The good-natured chaffing to which he was subjected he met with his old smile.

"Much obleeged to ye for leavin' her for a man as knows a genuine creetur when he sees her," he said, to one and another, who rallied him upon his matrimonial intentions.

"Isn't she rather old?" inquired one whose manners were not learned of Lord Chesterfield.

"I dunno," he replied; "she's hearn it thunder enough not to be skeered, an' she's had the measles an' the whoopin' cough, an' the chicken-pox, an' the mumps, an' got through with her nonsense."

CHAPTER XXI.

IN WHICH JIM GETS THE FURNITURE INTO HIS HOUSE, AND MIKE CONLIN GETS ANOTHER INSTALMENT OF ADVICE INTO JIM.

JIM had a weary winter. He was obliged to hire and to board a number of workmen, whom it was necessary to bring in from Sevenoaks, to effect the finishing of his house. His money ran low at last, and Mr. Benedict was called upon to write a letter to Mr. Balfour on his behalf, accepting that gentleman's offer of pecuniary assistance. This was a humiliating trial to Jim, for he had hoped to enter upon his new life free from the burden of debt; but Mr. Balfour assured him that he did not regard his contribution to the building-fund as a loan—it was only the payment for his board in advance.

Jim was astonished to learn the extent of Miss Butterworth's resources. She proposed to furnish the house from the savings of her years of active industry. She had studied it so thoroughly during its progress, though she had never seen it, that she could have found every door and gone through every apartment of it in the dark. She had received from Mr. Benedict the plan and dimensions of every room. Carpets were made, matting was purchased, sets of furniture were procured, crockery, glass, linen, mirrors, curtains, kitchen utensils, everything necessary to house-keeping, were bought and placed in store, so that, when the spring came, all that remained necessary was to give her order to forward them, and write her directions for their bestowal in the house.

The long-looked for time came at last. The freshets of spring had passed away; the woods were filling with birds; the shad-blossoms were reaching their flat sprays out over the river, and looking at themselves in the sunny waters; and the thrush, standing on the deck of the New Year, had piped all hands from below, and sent them into the rigging to spread the sails.

Jim's heart was glad. His house was finished, and nothing remained but to fill it with the means and appliances of life, and with that precious life to which they were to be devoted. The enterprise by which it was to be supported lay before him, and was a burden upon him; but he believed in himself, and was not afraid.

One morning, after he had gone over his house for the thousandth time, and mounted to the cupola for a final survey, he started for Sevenoaks to make his arrangements for the transportation of the furniture. Two new boats had been placed on the river by men who proposed to act as guides to the summer visitors, and these he engaged to aid in the water transportation of the articles that had been provided by "the little woman."

After his arrival in Sevenoaks, he was in consultation with her every day; and every day he was more impressed by the method which she had pursued in the work of furnishing his little hotel.

"I knowed you was smarter nor lightnin'," he said to her; "but I didn't know you was smarter nor a man."

In his journeys, Jim was necessarily thrown into the company of Mike Conlin, who was officiously desirous to place at his disposal the wisdom which had been acquired by long years of intimate association with the feminine element of domestic life, and the duties and practices of house-keeping. When the last load of furniture was on its way to Number Nine, and Jim had stopped at Mike's house to refresh his weary team, Mike saw that his last opportunity for giving advice had come, and he determined to avail himself of it.

"Jim," he said, "ye're jist nothing but a babby, an' ye must ax me some quistions. I'm an owld house-kaper, an' I kin tell ye everything, Jim."

Jim was tired with his work, and tired of Mike. The great event of his life stood so closely before him, and he was so much absorbed by it, that Mike's talk had a harsher effect upon his sensibilities than the grating of a saw-mill.

"Ah! Mike! shut up, shut up!" he said. "Ye mean well, but ye're the ignorantest ramus I ever seen. Ye know how to run a shanty an' a pig-pen, but what do ye know about keepin' a hotel?"

"Bedad, if that's where ye are, what do ye know about kapin' a hotel yersilf? Ye'll see the time, Jim, when ye'll be sorry ye turned the cold shoolder to the honest tongue of Mike Conlin."

"Well, Mike, ye understand a pig-pen better nor I do. I gi'en it up," said Jim, with a sigh that showed how painfully Mike was boring him.

"Yes, Jim, an' ye think a pig-pen is benathe ye, for-gittin' a pig is the purtiest thing in life. Ah, Jim! whin ye git up in the marnin', a falin' shtewed, an' niver a bit o' breakfast in ye, an' go out in the djew barefut, as ye was borrn, lavin' yer coat kapin' company wid yer ugly owld hat, waitin' for yer pork and pertaties, an' see yer pig wid his two paws an' his dirty nose rachin' oover the pin, an' sayin' 'good-marnin' to ye,' an' squalin' away wid his big v'ice for his porridge, ye'll remimber what I say. An' Jim, whin ye fade 'im, ah! whin ye fade 'im! an' he jist lays down continted, wid his belly full, an' ye laugh to hear 'im a groontin' an' a shwearin' to 'imself to think he can't ate inny more, an' yer owld woman calls ye to breakfast, ye'll go in jist happy—jist happy, now. Ah, ye can't tell me! I'm an' owld house-kaper, Jim."

"Ye're an old pig-keeper; that's what you be," said Jim. "Ye're a reg'lar Paddy, Mike. Ye're a good fellow, but I'd sooner hearn a loon nor a pig."

"Divil a bit o' raison have ye got in ye, Jim. Ye can't ate a loon no more nor ye can ate a boot."

Mike was getting impatient with the incorrigible character of Jim's prejudices, and Jim saw that he was grieving him.

"Well, I persume I sh'll have to keep pigs, Mike," he said, in a compromising tone; "but I shan't dress 'em in calliker, nor larn 'em to sing Old Hundred. I sh'll jest let 'em rampage round the woods, and when I want one on 'em, I'll shoot 'im."

"Yis, bedad, an' thin ye'll shkin 'im, an' throw the rist of 'im intil the river," responded Mike, contemptuously.

"No, Mike; I'll send for ye to cut 'im up an' pack 'im."

"Now ye talk," said Mike; and this little overture of friendly confidence became a door through which he could enter a subject more profoundly interesting to him than that which related to his favorite quadruped.

"What kind of an owld woman have ye got, Jim? Jist open yer heart like a box o' tobacky, Jim, an' lit me hilp ye. There's no man as knows more about a woman nor Mike Conlin. Ah, Jim! ye ought to 'ave seed me wid the girrls in the owld counthry! They jist rin afther me as if I'd been stalin' their little hearrts. There was a twilvemonth whin they tore the very coat tails aff me back. Be gorry I could 'ave married me whole neighborhood, an' I jist had to marry the first one I could lay me honest hands on, an' take mesilf away wid her to Ameriky."

This was too much for Jim. His face broadened into his old smile.

"Mike," said he, "ye haven't got an old towel or a hoss blanket about ye, have ye? I feel as if I was a goin' to cry?"

"An' what the divil be ye goin' to cry for?"

"Well, Mike, this is a world o' sorrer, an' when a feller comes to think of a lot o' women as is so hard pushed that they hanker arter Mike Conlin, it fetches me. It's worse nor bein' without victuals, an' beats the cholery out o' sight."

"Oh, ye blaggard! Can't ye talk sinse whin yer betthers is thryin' to hilp ye? What kind of an owld woman have ye got, now?"

"Mike," said Jim, solemnly, "ye don't know what ye're talkin' about. If ye did, ye wouldn't call her an old woman. She's a lady, Mike. She isn't one o' your kind, an' I ain't one o' your kind, Mike. Can't ye see there's the difference of a pig atween us? Don't ye know that if I was to go hazin' round in the mornin' without no clo'es to speak on, an' takin' comfort in a howlin' pig, that I shouldn't be up to keepin' a hotel? Don't be unreasomble; and, Mike, don't ye never speak to me about my old woman. That's a sort o' thing that won't set on her."

Mike shook his head in lofty pity.

"Ah, Jim, I can see what ye're comin' to."

Then, as if afraid that his "owld woman" might overhear his confession, he bent toward Jim, and half whispered:

"The women is all smarter nor the men, Jim; but ye mustn't let 'em know that ye think it. Ye've got to call 'em yer owld women, or ye can't keep 'em where ye want 'em. Be gorry! I wouldn't let me owld woman know what I think of 'er fur fifty dollars. I couldn't kape me house over me head inny time at all at all, if I should whishper it. She's jist as much of a leddy as there is in Sevenoaks, bedad, an' I have to put on me big airs, an' thrash around wid me two hands in me breeches pockets, an' shtick out me lips like a lorrd, an' promise to raise the divil wid her whiniver she gets a fit o' high flyin', an' ye'll have to do the same, Jim, or jist lay down an' let 'er shtep on ye. Git a good shtart, Jim. Don't ye gin 'er the bit for five minutes. She'll rin away wid ye. Ye can't till me anything about women."

"No, nor I don't want to. Now you jest shut up, Mike. I'm tired a hearin' ye. This thing about women is one as has half the fun of it in larnin' it as ye go along. Ye mean well enough, Mike, but yer eddication is poor; an' if it's all the same to ye, I'll take my pudden straight an' leave yer sarce for them as likes it."

Jim's utter rejection of the further good offices of Mike, in the endeavor to instruct him in the management of his future relations with the little woman, did not sink very deep into the Irishman's sensibilities. Indeed, it could not have done so, for their waters were shallow, and, as at this moment Mike's "owld woman" called both to dinner, the difference was forgotten in the sympathy of hunger and the satisfactions of the table.

Jim felt that he was undergoing a change—had undergone one, in fact. It had never revealed itself to him so fully as it did during his conversation with Mike. The building of the hotel, the study of the wants of another grade of civilization than that to which he had been accustomed, the frequent conversations with Miss Butterworth, the responsibilities he had assumed, all had tended to lift him; and he felt that Mike Conlin was no longer a tolerable companion. The shallowness of the Irishman's mind and life disgusted him, and he knew that the time would soon come when, by a process as natural as the falling of the leaves in autumn, he should drop a whole class of associations, and stand where he could look down upon them—where they would look up to him. The position of principal, the command of men, the conduct of, and the personal responsibility for, a great enterprise, had given him conscious growth. His old life and his old associations were insufficient to contain him.

After dinner they started on, for the first time accompanied by Mike's wife. Before her marriage she had lived the life common to her class—that of cook and housemaid in the families of gentlemen. She knew the duties connected with the opening of a house, and could bring its machinery into working order. She could do a thousand things that a man either could not do, or would not think of doing; and Jim had arranged that she should be house-keeper until the mistress of the establishment should be installed in her office.

The sun had set before they arrived at the river, and the boats of the two guides, with Jim's, which had been brought down by Mr. Benedict, were speedily loaded with the furniture, and Mike, picketing his horses for the night, embarked with the rest, and all slept at Number Nine.

In three days Jim was to be married, and his cage was

ready for his bird. The stoop with its "settle," the ladder for posies, at the foot of which the morning-glories were already planted, and the "cupalo," had ceased to be dreams, and become realities. Still, it all seemed a dream to Jim. He waked in the morning in his own room, and wondered whether he were not dreaming. He went out upon his piazza, and saw the cabin in which he had spent so many nights in his old simple life, then went off and looked up at his house or ranged through the rooms, and experienced the emotion of regret so common to those in similar circumstances, that he could never again be what he had been, or be contented with what he had been—that he had crossed a point in his life which his retiring feet could never repass. It was the natural reaction of the long strain of expectation which he had experienced, and would pass away; but while it was upon him he mourned over the death of his old self, and the hopeless obliteration of his old circumstances.

Mr. Balfour had been written to, and would keep his promise to be present at the wedding, with Mrs. Balfour and the boys. Sam Yates, at Jim's request, had agreed to see to the preparation of an appropriate outfit for the bridegroom. Such invitations had been given out as Miss Butterworth dictated, and the Snow family was in a flutter of expectation. Presents of a humble and useful kind had been pouring in upon Miss Butterworth for days, until, indeed, she was quite overwhelmed. It seemed as if the whole village were in a conspiracy of beneficence.

In a final conference with Mrs. Snow, Miss Butterworth said:

"I don't know at all how he is going to behave, and I'm not going to trouble myself about it; he shall do just as he pleases. He has made his way with me, and if he is good enough for me, he is good enough for other people. I'm not going to badger him into nice manners, and I'm going to be just as much amused with him as anybody is. He isn't like other people, and if he tries to act like other people, it will just spoil him. If there's anything that I do despise above board, it's a woman trying to train a man who loves her. If I were the man, I should hate her."

CHAPTER XXII.

IN WHICH JIM GETS MARRIED, THE NEW HOTEL RECEIVES ITS MISTRESS, AND BENEDICT CONFERS A POWER OF ATTORNEY.

THERE was great commotion in the little Sevenoaks tavern. It was Jim's wedding morning, and on the previous evening there had been a sufficient number of arrivals to fill every room. Mr. and Mrs. Balfour, with the two boys, had come in by the evening stage; Jim and Mr. Benedict had arrived from Number Nine. Friends of Miss Butterworth from adjoining towns had come, so as to be ready for the ceremony of the morning. Villagers had thronged the noisy bar-room until midnight, scanning and discussing the strangers, and speculating upon the event which had called them together. Jim had moved among them, smiling, and returning their good-natured badinage with imperturbable coolness, so far as appearances went, though he acknowledged to Mr. Balfour that he felt very much as he did about his first moose.

"I took a good aim," said he, "restin' acrost a stump, but the stump was oneasy like; an' then I blazed away, an' when I obsarved the moose sprawlin', I was twenty feet up a tree, with my gun in the snow; an' if they don't find me settin' on the parson's chimbly about nine o'clock to-morrer mornin', it won't be on account o' my not bein' skeered."

But the wedding morning had arrived. Jim had had an uneasy night, with imperfect sleep and preposterous dreams. He had been pursuing game. Sometimes it was a bear that attracted his chase, sometimes it was a deer, sometimes it was a moose, but all the time it was Miss Butterworth, flying and looking back, with robes and ribbons vanishing among the distant trees, until he shot and killed her, and then he woke in a great convulsion of despair, to hear the singing of the early birds, and to the realization of the fact that his days of bachelor life were counted.

Mr. Benedict, with his restored boy in his arms, occupied the room next to his, a door opening between them. Both were awake, and were busy with their whispered confidences, when they became aware that Jim was roused and on his feet. In a huge bundle on the table lay Jim's wedding garments, which he eyed from time to time as he busied himself at his bath.

"Won't ye be a purty bird with them feathers on! This makin' crows into bobolinks'll do for oncet, but, my! won't them things spin when I git into the woods agin?"

Benedict and Harry knew Jim's habit, and the measure of excitement that was upon him, and lay still, expecting to be amused by his soliloquies. Soon they heard him say:

"Oh, lay down, lay down, lay *down*, ye misable old mop!"

It was an expression of impatience and disgust.

"What's the matter, Jim?" Mr. Benedict called.

"Here's my har," responded Jim, "actin' as if it was a piece o' woods or a hay-lot, an' there ain't no lodgin' it with nothin' short of a harricane. I've a good mind to git it shingled and san'-papered."

Then, shifting his address to the object of his care and anxiety, he went on :

" Oh, stick up, stick up, if you want to! Don't lay down on my 'count. P'rhaps ye want to see what's goin' on. P'rhaps ye're goin' to stand up with me. P'rhaps ye want to skeer somebody's hosses. If I didn't look no better nor you, I sh'd want to lay low ; an', if I'd 'a slep as poor as ye did last night, I'd lop down in the fust bed o' bear's grease I could find. *Hain't* ye got no manners ? "

This was too much for Harry, who, in his happy mood, burst into the merriest laughter.

This furnished Jim with just the apology he wanted for a frolic, and rushing into the adjoining bed-room, he pulled Harry from his bed, seated him on the top of his head, and marched with him struggling and laughing about the room. After he had performed sundry acrobatic feats with him, he carried him back to his bed. Then he returned to his room, and entered seriously upon the task of arraying himself in his wedding attire. To get on his collar and neck tie properly, he was obliged to call for Mr. Benedict's assistance.

Jim was already getting red in the face.

" What on arth folks want to tie theirselves up in this way for in hot weather, is more nor I know," he said. " How do ye s'pose them Mormons live, as is doin' this thing every three days ? "

Jim asked this question with his nose in the air, patiently waiting the result of Mr. Benedict's manipulations at his throat. When he could speak again, he added :

" I vow, if I was doin' a big business in this line, I'd git some tin things, an' have 'em soddered on, an' sleep in 'em."

This sent Harry into another giggle, and, with many soliloquies and much merriment, the dressing in both rooms went on, until, in Jim's room, all became still. When Benedict and his boy had completed their toilet, they looked in upon Jim, and found him dressed and seated on his trunk.

"Good morning, Mr. Fenton," said Benedict, cheerfully.

Jim, who had been in deep thought, looked up, and said :

" Do ye know that that don't seem so queer to me as it used to ? It seems all right fur pertickler friends to call me Jim, but clo'es is what puts the Mister into a man. I felt it comin' when I looked into the glass. Says I to myself : 'Jim, that's Mr. Fenton as is now afore ye. Look at 'im sharp, so that, if so be ye ever seen 'im agin' ye'll know 'im.' I never knowed exactly where the Mister come from afore. Ye have to be measured for't. A pair o' shears, an' a needle an' thread, an' a hot goose is what changes a man into a Mister. It's a nice thing to find out, but it's uncomf'table. It ain't so bad as it would be if ye couldn't strip it off when ye git tired on't, an' it's a good thing to know."

" Do clothes make Belcher a gentleman ? " inquired Mr. Benedict.

" Well, it's what makes him a Mister, any way. When ye git his clo'es off thar ain't nothin' left of 'im. Dress 'im up in my old clo'es, as has got tar enough on 'em to paint a boat, an' there wouldn't be enough man in 'im to speak to."

How long Jim would have indulged in his philosophy of the power of dress had he not been disturbed will never be known, for at this moment Mr. Balfour knocked at his door, and was admitted. Sam Yates followed, and both looked Jim over and pronounced him perfect. Even these familiar friends felt the power of dress, and treated Jim in a way to which he had been unaccustomed. The stalwart figure, developed in every mus cle, and becomingly draped, was well calculated to ex cite their admiration. The refractory hair which had given its possessor so much trouble, simply made his head impressive and picturesque. There was a man before them—humane, brave, bright, original. All he wanted was culture. Physical and mental endowments were in excess, and the two men, trained in the schools, had learned to love—almost to revere him. Until he spoke, they did not feel at home with him in his new disguise.

They all descended to breakfast together. Jim was quiet under the feeling that his clothes were an unnatural expression of himself, and that his words would make them a mockery. He was awed, too, by the presence of Mrs. Balfour, who met him at the table for the first time in her life. The sharp-eyed, smiling Yankee girls who waited at the meal, were very much devoted to Jim, who was ashamed to receive so much attention. On the whole, it was the most uncomfortable breakfast he had ever eaten, but his eyes were quick to see all that was done, for he was about to open a hotel, and wished particularly to learn the details of the table service.

There was great excitement, too, at the parsonage that morning. The Misses Snow were stirred by the romance of the occasion. They had little enough of this element in their lives, and were disposed to make the most of it when it came. The eldest had been invited to accompany the bride to Number Nine, and spend a few weeks with her there. As this was accounted a great privilege by the two younger sisters, they quietly shelved her, and told her that they were to have their own way at home ; so Miss Snow became ornamental and critical. Miss Butterworth had spent the night with her, and they had talked like a pair of school-girls until the small hours of the morning. The two younger girls had slept together, and discussed at length the duties of their respective offices. One was to do the bride's hair and act as the general supervisor of her dress, the other was to arrange the flowers and take care of the guests. Miss Butterworth's hair was not beautiful, and how it was to be made the most of was the great question that agitated the hair-dresser. All the possibilities of braid and plait and curl were canvassed. If she only had a switch, a great triumph could be achieved, but she had none, and, what was worse, would have none. A neighbor had sent in a potted white rose, full of buds and bloom, and over this the sisters quarrelled. The hair would not be complete without the roses, and the table would look "shameful" if the pot did not stand upon it, unshorn of a charm. The hair-dresser proposed that the stems which she was bent on despoiling should have some artificial roses tied to them, but the disgraceful project was rejected with scorn. They wrangled over the dear little rose-bush and its burden until they went to sleep—the one to dream that Miss Butterworth had risen in the morning with a new head of hair that reached to her knee, in whose luxuriance she could revel with interminable delight, and the other that the house was filled with roses; that they sprouted out of the walls, fluttered with beads of dew against the windows, strewed the floor, and filled the air with odor.

Miss Butterworth was not to step out of the room—not to be seen by any mortal eye—until she should come forth as a bride. Miss Snow was summarily expelled from the apartment, and only permitted to bring in Miss Butterworth's breakfast, while her self-appointed lady's maid did her hair, and draped her in her new gray silk.

"Make just as big a fool of me, my dear, as you choose," said the prospective bride to the fussy little girl who fluttered about her. "It's only for a day, and I don't care."

Such patient manipulation, such sudden retiring for the study of effects, such delicious little experiments with a curl, such shifting of hair-pins, such dainty adjustments of ruffles and frills as were indulged in in that little room can only be imagined by the sex familiar with them. And then, in the midst of it all, came a scream of delight that stopped everything. Mrs. Balfour had sent in a great box full of the most exquisite flowers, which she had brought all the way from the city. The youngest Miss Snow was wild with her new wealth, and there were roses for Miss Butterworth's hair, and her throat, and a bouquet for her hand. And after this came wonderful accessions to the refreshment table. Cake, with Miss Butterworth's initials; tarts, marked "Number Nine," and Charlotte de Russe, with a "B" and an "F" hopelessly twisted together in a monogram. The most excited exclamations reached Miss Butterworth's ears in her imprisonment:

"Goodness, gracious me!"

"If there isn't another cake as big as a flour barrel!"

"Tell your mother she's an angel. She's coming down to help us eat it, I hope."

"Just look at this basket of little cakes! I was saying to mother this minute that that was all we wanted."

So the good things came, and the cheerful givers went, and Miss Butterworth took an occasional sip at her coffee, with a huge napkin at her throat, and tears in her eyes, not drawn forth by the delicate tortures in progress upon her person. She thought of her weary years of service, her watchings by sick-beds, her ministry to the poor, her long loneliness, and acknowledged to herself that her reward had come. To be so loved and petted, and cared for, and waited upon, was payment for every sacrifice and every service, and she felt that she and the world were at quits.

Before the finishing touches to her toilet were given,

there was a tumult at the door. She could hear new voices. The guests were arriving. She heard laughter and merry greetings ; and still they poured in, as if they had come in a procession. Then there was a hush, followed by the sound of a carriage, the letting down of steps, and a universal murmur. Jim had arrived, with Mr. and Mrs. Balfour and the boys. They had had great difficulty in getting him into the one hackney coach which the village possessed, on account of his wish to ride with the driver, " a feller as he knowed ;" but he was overruled by Mrs. Balfour, who, on alighting, took his arm. He came up the garden walk, smiling in the faces and eyes of those gathered around the door and clustered at the windows. In his wedding dress he was the best figure in the crowd, and many were the exclamations of feminine admiration.

On entering the door, he looked about him, saw the well-dressed and expectant company, the dainty baskets of flowers, the bountifully loaded table in the little dining-room, all the preparations for his day of happiness, but he saw nowhere the person who gave to him the significance of the occasion.

Mr. Snow greeted him cordially, and introduced him to those who stood near.

" Well, parson, where's the little woman ? " he said at last, in a voice so loud that all heard the startling question. Miss Butterworth heard him, and laughed.

" Just hear him ! " she exclaimed to the busy girl, whose work was now hurrying to a close. " If he doesn't astonish them before he gets through, I shall be mistaken. I do think it's the most ridiculous thing. Now isn't it ! The idea ! "

Miss Snow, in the general character of outside manager and future companion of the bride, hurried to Jim's side at once, and said :

" Oh, Mr. Fenton ! "

"Jest call me Jim."

"No, no, I won't. Now, Mr. Fenton, really! you can't see her until she is ready!"

"Oh, can't I!" and Jim smiled.

Miss Snow had the impression, prevalent among women, that a bridegroom has no rights so long as they can keep him out of them, and that it is their privilege to fight him up to the last moment.

"Now, really, Mr. Fenton, you *must* be patient," she said, in a whisper. "She is quite delicate this morning, and she's going to look so pretty that you'll hardly know her."

"Well," said Jim, "if you've got a ticket into the place whar she's stoppin', tell her that kingdom-come is here an' waitin'."

A ripple of laughter went around the circle, and Jim, finding the room getting a little close, beckoned Mr. Snow out of the doors. Taking him aside and removing his hat, he said:

"Parson, do you see my har?"

"I do," responded the minister, good-naturedly.

"That riz last night," said Jim, solemnly.

"Is it possible?" and Mr. Snow looked at the intractable pile with genuine concern.

"Yes, riz in a dream. I thought I'd shot 'er. I was follerin' 'er all night. Sometimes she was one thing an' sometimes she was another, but I drew a bead on 'er, an' down she went, an' up come my har quicker nor lightnin'. I don't s'pose it looks very purty, but I can't help it."

"Have you tried anything on it?" inquired Mr. Snow with a puzzled look.

"Yis, everything but a hot flat-iron, an' I'm a little afraid o' that. If wust comes to wust, it'll have to be did, though. It may warm up my old brains a little, but if my har is well sprinkled, and the thing is handled lively, it'll pay for tryin'."

The perfect candor and coolness of Jim's manner were too much for the unsuspicious spirit of the minister, who thought it all very strange. He had heard of such things, but this was the first instance he had ever seen.

"Parson," said Jim, changing the topic, "what's the damage for the sort o' thing ye're drivin' at this mornin'?"

"The what?"

"The damage—what's the—well—damage? What do ye consider a fa'r price?"

"Do you mean the marriage fee?"

"Yes, I guess that's what ye call it."

"The law allows us two dollars, but you will permit me to perform the ceremony for nothing. It's a labor of love, Mr. Fenton. We are all very much interested in Miss Butterworth, as you see."

"Well, I'm a little interested in 'er myself, an' I'm a goin' to pay for the splice. Jest tuck that X into yer jacket, an' tell yer neighbors as ye've seen a man as was five times better nor the law."

"You are very generous."

"No; I know what business is, though. Ye have to get somethin' to square the buryins an' baptizins with. When a man has a weddin', he'd better pay the whole thing in a lump. Parsons have to live, but how the devil they do it in Sevenoaks is more nor I know."

"Mr. Fenton! excuse me!" said Mr. Snow, coloring, "but I am not accustomed to hearing language of that kind."

"No, I s'pose not," said Jim, who saw too late that he had made a mistake. "Your sort o' folks knuckle to the devil more nor I do. A good bein' I take to, but a bad bein' I'm careless with; an' I don't make no more o' slingin' his name round nor I do kickin' an old boot."

Mr. Snow was obliged to laugh, and half a dozen others, who had gathered about them, joined in a merry chorus.

Then Miss Snow came out and whispered to her father, and gave a roguish glance at Jim. At this time the house was full, and the little yard was full, and there was a crowd of boys at the gate. Mr. Snow took Jim by the arm and led him in. They pressed through the crowd at the door, Miss Snow making way for them, and so, in a sort of triumphal progress, they went through the room, and disappeared in the apartment where "the little woman," flushed and expectant, waited their arrival.

It would be hard to tell which was the more surprised as they were confronted by the meeting. Dress had wrought its miracle upon both of them, and they hardly knew each other.

"Well, little woman, how fare ye?" said Jim, and he advanced, and took her cheeks tenderly between his rough hands, and kissed her.

"Oh, don't! Mr. Fenton! You'll muss her hair!" exclaimed the nervous little lady's maid of the morning, dancing about the object of her delightful toils and anxieties, and readjusting a rose, and pulling out the fold of a ruffle.

"A purty job ye've made on't! The little woman 'll never look so nice again," said Jim.

"Perhaps I shall—when I'm married again," said Miss Butterworth, looking up into Jim's eyes, and laughing.

"Now, ain't that sassy!" exclaimed Jim, in a burst of admiration. "That's what took me the first time I seen 'er."

Then Miss Snow Number Two came in, and said it really was time for the ceremony to begin. Such a job as she had had in seating people!

Oh, the mysteries of that little room! How the people outside wondered what was going on there! How the girls inside rejoiced in their official privileges!

Miss Snow took Jim by the button-hole :

"Mr. Fenton, you must take Miss Butterworth on your arm, you know, and lead her in front of the sofa, and turn around, and face father, and then do just what he tells you, and remember that there's nothing for you to say."

The truth was, that they were all afraid that Jim would not be able to hold his tongue.

"Are we all ready ?" inquired Mr. Snow, in a pleasant, official tone.

All were ready, and then Mr. Snow, going out with a book in his hand, was followed by Jim and his bride, the little procession being completed by the three Misses Snow, who, with a great deal of care upon their faces, slipped out of the door, one after another, like three white doves from a window. Mr. Snow took his position, the pair wheeled and faced him, and the three Misses Snow supported Miss Butterworth as impromptu bridesmaids. It was an impressive tableau, and when the good pastor said : "Let us pray," and raised his thin, white hands, a painter in search of a subject could have asked for nothing better.

When, at the close of his prayer, the pastor inquired if there were any known obstacles to the union of the pair before him in the bonds of holy matrimony, and bade all objectors to speak then, or forever after hold their peace, Jim looked around with a defiant air, as if he would like to see the man who dared to respond to the call. No one did respond, and the ceremony proceeded.

"James," said Mr. Snow.

"Jest call me ——"

Miss Butterworth pinched Jim's arm, and he recalled Miss Snow's injunction in time to arrest his sentence in mid-passage.

"James," the pastor repeated, and then went on to

ask him, in accordance with the simple form of his sect, whether he took the woman whom he was holding by the hand to be his lawful and wedded wife, to be loved and cherished in sickness and health, in prosperity and adversity, cleaving to her, and to her only.

"Parson," said Jim, "that's jest what I'm here for."

There would have been a titter if any other man had said it, but it was so strong and earnest, and so much in character, that hardly a smile crossed a face that fronted him.

Then "Keziah" was questioned in the usual form, and bowed her response, and Jim and the little woman were declared to be one. "What God hath joined together, let not man put asunder."

And then Mr. Snow raised his white hands again, and pronounced a formal benediction. There was a moment of awkwardness, but soon the pastor advanced with his congratulations, and Mrs. Snow came up, and the three Misses Snow, and the Balfours, and the neighbors; and there were kisses and hand-shakings and good wishes. Jim beamed around upon the fluttering and chattering groups like a great, good-natured mastiff upon a playful collection of silken spaniels and smart terriers. It was the proudest moment of his life. Even when standing on the cupola of his hotel, surveying his achievements, and counting his possessions, he had never felt the thrill which moved him then. The little woman was his, and his forever. His manhood had received the highest public recognition, and he was as happy as if it had been the imposition of a crown.

"Ye made purty solemn business on't Parson," said Jim.

"It's a very important step, Mr. Fenton," responded the clergyman.

"Step!" exclaimed Jim. "That's no name for't; it's a whole trip. But I sh'll do it. When I said it I meaned it. I sh'll take care o' the little woman, an' atween you an' I, Parson, it's about the best thing as a man can do. Takin' care of a woman is the nateral thing for a man, an' no man ain't much as doesn't do it, and glad o' the job."

The capacity of a country assembly for cakes, pies, and lemonade, is something quite unique, especially at a morning festival. If the table groaned at the beginning, it sighed at the close. The abundance that asserted itself in piles of dainties was left a wreck. It faded away like a bank of snow before a drift of southern vapor. Jim, foraging among the solids, found a mince-pie, to which he devoted himself.

"This is the sort o' thing as will stan' by a man in trouble," said he, with a huge piece in his hand.

Then, with a basket of cake, he vanished from the house, and distributed his burden among the boys at the gate.

"Boys, I know ye're hungry, 'cause ye've left yer breakfast on yer faces. Now git this in afore it rains."

The boys did not stand on the order of the service, but helped themselves greedily, and left his basket empty in a twinkling.

"It beats all nater," said Jim, looking at them sympathetically, "how much boys can put down when they try. If the facks could be knowed, without cuttin' into 'em, I'd be willin' to bet somethin' that their legs is holler."

While Jim was absent, the bride's health was drunk in a glass of lemonade, and when he returned, his own health was proposed, and Jim seemed to feel that something was expected of him.

"My good frens," said he, "I'm much obleeged to ye. Ye couldn't 'a' treated me better if I'd 'a' been the President of this country. I ain't used to yer ways, but I know when I'm treated well, an' when the little woman is treated well. I'm obleeged to ye on her 'count. I'm a goin' to take 'er into the woods, an' take care on 'er. We are goin' to keep a hotel—me and the little woman—an' if so be as any of ye is took sick by overloadin' with cookies 'arly in the day, or bein' thinned out with lemonade, ye can come into the woods, an' I'll send ye back happy."

There was a clapping of hands and a flutter of handkerchiefs, and a merry chorus of laughter, and then two vehicles drove up to the door. The bride bade a tearful farewell to her multitude of friends, and poured out her thanks to the minister's family, and in twenty minutes thereafter, two happy loads of passengers went pounding over the bridge, and off up the hill on the way to Number Nine. The horses were strong, the morning was perfect, and Jim was in possession of his bride. They, with Miss Snow, occupied one carriage, while Mr. Benedict and the Balfours filled the other. Not a member of the company started homeward until the bridal party was seen climbing the hill in the distance, but waited, commenting upon the great event of the morning, and speculating upon the future of the pair whose marriage they had witnessed. There was not a woman in the crowd who did not believe in Jim; and all were glad that the little tailoress had reached so pleasant and stimulating a change in her life.

When the voyagers had passed beyond the scattered farm-houses into the lonely country, Jim, with his wife's help, released himself from the collar and cravat that tormented him, and once more breathed freely. On they sped, shouting to one another from carriage to carriage, and Mike Conlin's humble house was reached in a two hours' drive. There was chaffing at the door and romping among the trees while the horses were refreshed, and then they pushed on again with such speed as was possible with poorer roads and soberer horses;

and two hours before sunset they were at the river. The little woman had enjoyed the drive. When she found that she had cut loose from her old life, and was entering upon one unknown and untried, in pleasant companionship, she was thoroughly happy. It was all like a fairy story; and there before her rolled the beautiful river, and, waiting on the shore, were the trunks and remnants of baggage that had been started for their destination before daylight, and the guides with their boats, and with wild flowers in their hat-bands.

The carriages were dismissed to find their way back to Mike Conlin's that night, while Jim, throwing off his coat, assisted in loading the three boats. Mr. Balfour had brought along with him, not only a large flag for the hotel, but half a dozen smaller ones for the little fleet. The flags were soon mounted upon little rods, and set up at either end of each boat, and when the luggage was all loaded, and the passengers were all in their places—Jim taking his wife and Miss Snow in his own familiar craft—they pushed out into the stream, and started for a race. Jim was the most powerful man of the three, and was aching for work. It was a race all the way, but the broader chest and harder muscles won. It was a regatta without spectators, but as full of excitement as if the shores had been fringed with a cheering crowd.

The two women chatted together in the stern of Jim's boat, or sat in silence, as if they were enchanted, watching the changing shores, while the great shadows of the woods deepened upon them. They had never seen anything like it. It was a new world—God's world, which man had not marred.

At last they heard the barking of a dog, and, looking far up among the woods, they caught the vision of a new building. The boys in the boats behind yelled with delight. Ample in its dimensions and fair in its outlines, there stood the little woman's home. Her eyes filled with tears, and she hid them on Miss Snow's shoulder.

"Be ye disap'inted, little woman?" inquired Jim, tenderly.

"Oh, no."

"Feelin's a little too many fur ye?"

The little woman nodded, while Miss Snow put her arm around her neck and whispered.

"A woman is a curi's bein'," said Jim. "She cries when she's tickled, an' she laughs when she's mad."

"I'm not mad," said the little woman, bursting into a laugh, and lifting her tear-burdened eyes to Jim.

"An' then," said Jim, "she cries and laughs all to oncet, an' a feller don't know whether to take off his jacket or put up his umberell."

This quite restored the "little woman," and her eyes were dry and merry as the boat touched the bank, and the two women were helped on shore. Before the other boats came up, they were in the house, with the delighted Turk at their heels, and Mike Conlin's wife courtseying before them.

It was a merry night at Number Nine. Jim's wife became the mistress at once. She knew where everything was to be found, as well as if she had been there for a year, and played the hostess to Mr. and Mrs. Balfour as agreeably as if her life had been devoted to the duties of her establishment.

Mr. Balfour could not make a long stay in the woods, but had determined to leave his wife there with the boys. His business was pressing at home, and he had heard something while at Sevenoaks that made him uneasy on Mr. Benedict's account. The latter had kept himself very quiet while at the wedding, but his intimacy with one of Mr. Balfour's boys had been observed, and there were those who detected the likeness of this boy, though much changed by growth and better conditions, to the little Harry Benedict of other days. Mr. Balfour had overheard the speculations of the villagers on the strange Mr. Williams who had for so long a time been housed with Jim Fenton, and the utterance of suspicions that he was no other than their old friend, Paul Benedict. He knew that this suspicion would be reported by Mr. Belcher's agent at once, and that Mr. Belcher would take desperate steps to secure himself in his possessions. What form these measures would take—whether of fraud or personal violence—he could not tell.

He advised Mr. Benedict to give him a power of attorney to prosecute Mr. Belcher for the sum due him on the use of his inventions, and to procure an injunction on his further use of them, unless he should enter into an agreement to pay such a royalty as should be deemed equitable by all the parties concerned. Mr. Benedict accepted the advice, and the papers were executed at once.

Armed with this document, Mr. Balfour bade good-bye to Number Nine and its pleasant company, and hastened back to the city, where he took the first opportunity to report to his friends the readiness of Jim to receive them for the summer.

It would be pleasant to follow them into their forest pastimes, but more stirring and important matters will hold us to the city.

CHAPTER XXIII.

IN WHICH MR. BELCHER EXPRESSES HIS DETERMINATION TO BECOME A "FOUNDER," BUT DROPS HIS NOUN IN FEAR OF A LITTLE VERB OF THE SAME NAME.

MRS. DILLINGHAM had a difficult rôle to play. She could not break with Mr. Belcher without exposing her motives and bringing herself under unpleasant suspicion and surveillance. She felt that the safety of her protégé and his father would be best consulted by keeping peace with their enemy ; yet every approach of the great scoundrel disgusted and humiliated her. That side of her nature which had attracted and encouraged him was sleeping, and, under the new motives which were at work within her, she hoped that it would never wake. She looked down the devious track of her past, counted over its unworthy and most unwomanly satisfactions, and wondered. She looked back to a great wrong which she had once inflicted on an innocent man, with a self-condemnation so deep that all the womanhood within her rose into the purpose of reparation.

The boy whom she had called to her side, and fastened by an impassioned tenderness more powerful even than her wonderful art, had become to her a fountain of pure motives. She had a right to love this child. She owed a duty to him beyond any woman living. Grasping her right, and acknowledging her duty—a right and duty accorded to her by his nominal protector—she would not have forfeited them for the world. They soon became all that gave significance to her existence, and to them she determined that her life should be devoted. To stand well with this boy, to be loved, admired and respected by him, to be to him all that a mother could be, to be guided by his pure and tender conscience toward her own reformation, to waken into something like life and nourish into something like strength the starved motherhood within her—these became her dominant motives.

Mr. Belcher saw the change in her, but was too gross in his nature, too blind in his passion, and too vain in his imagined power, to comprehend it. She was a woman, and had her whims, he thought. Whims were evanescent, and this particular whim would pass away. He was vexed by seeing the boy so constantly with her. He met them walking together in the street, or straying in the park, hand in hand, or caught the lad looking at him from her window. He could not doubt that all this intimacy was approved by Mr. Balfour. Was she playing a deep game? Could she play it for anybody but himself—the man who had taken her heart by storm? Her actions, however, even when interpreted by his self-conceit, gave him uneasiness. She had grown to be very kind and considerate toward Mrs. Belcher. Had this friendship moved her to crush the passion for her husband? Ah! if she could only know how true he was to her in his untruthfulness!—how faithful he was to her in his perjury!—how he had saved himself for the ever-vanishing opportunity!

Many a time the old self-pity came back to the successful scoundrel. Many a time he wondered why the fate which had been so kind to him in other things would not open the door to his wishes in this. With this unrewarded passion gnawing at his heart, and with the necessity of treating the wife of his youth with constantly increasing consideration, in order to cover it from her sight, the General was anything but a satisfied and happy man. The more he thought upon it, the more morbid he grew, until it seemed to him that his wife must look through his hypocritical eyes into his guilty heart. He grew more and more guarded in his speech. If he mentioned Mrs. Dillingham's name, he always did it incidentally, and then only for the purpose of showing that he had no reason to avoid the mention of it.

There was another thought that preyed upon him. He was consciously a forger. He had not used the document he had forged, but he had determined to do so. Law had not laid its finger upon him, but its finger was over him. He had not yet crossed the line that made him legally a criminal, but the line was drawn before him, and only another step would be necessary to place him beyond it. A brood of fears was gathering around him. They stood back, glaring upon him from the distance; but they only waited another act in his career of dishonor to crowd in and surround him with menace. Sometimes he shrank from his purpose, but the shame of being impoverished and beaten spurred him renewedly to determination. He became conscious that what there was of bravery in him was sinking into bravado. His self-conceit, and what little he possessed of self-respect, were suffering. He dimly apprehended the fact that he was a rascal, and it made him uncomfortable. It ceased to be enough for him to assure himself that he was no more a rascal than those around him. He reached out on every side for means to maintain his self-respect. What good thing could he do to counterbalance his bad deeds? How could he shore himself up by public praise, by respectable associations, by the obligations of the public for deeds of beneficence? It is the most natural thing in the world for the dishonest steward, who cheats his lord, to undertake to win consideration against contingencies with his lord's money.

On the same evening in which the gathering at the Sevenoaks tavern occurred, preceding Jim's wedding, Mr. Belcher sat in his library, looking over the document which nominally conveyed to him the right and title of Paul Benedict to his inventions. He had done this many times since he had forged three of the signatures, and secured a fraudulent addition to the number from the hand of Phipps. He had brought himself to believe, to a certain extent, in their genuineness, and was wholly sure that they were employed on behalf of justice. The inventions had cost Benedict little or no money, and he, Mr. Belcher, had developed them at his own risk. Without his money and his enterprise they would have amounted to nothing. If Benedict had not lost his reason, the document would have been legally signed. The cause of Benedict's lapse from sanity did not occur to him. He only knew that if the inventor had not become insane, he should have secured his signature at some wretched price, and out of this conviction he reared his self-justification.

"It's right!" said Mr. Belcher. "The State prison may be in it, but it's right!"

And then, confirming his foul determination by an oath, he added:

"I'll stand by it."

Then he rang his bell, and called for Phipps.

"Phipps," said he, as his faithful and plastic servitor appeared, "come in, and close the door."

When Phipps, with a question in his face, walked up to where Mr. Belcher was sitting at his desk, with the forged document before him, the latter said:

"Phipps, did you ever see this paper before?"

"Yes, sir."

"Now, think hard—don't be in a hurry—and tell me when you saw it before. Take it in your hand, and look it all over, and be sure."

"I can't tell, exactly," responded Phipps, scratching his head; "but I should think it might have been six years ago, or more. It was a long time before we came from Sevenoaks."

"Very well; is that your signature?"

"It is, sir."

"Did you see Benedict write his name? Did you see Johnson and Ramsey write their names?"

"I did, sir."

"Do you remember all the circumstances—what I said to you, and what you said to me—why you were in the room?"

"Yes, sir."

"Phipps, do you know that if it is ever found out that you have signed that paper within a few weeks, you are as good as a dead man?"

"I don't know what you mean, sir," replied Phipps, in evident alarm.

"Do you know that that signature is enough to send you to the State prison?"

"No, sir."

"Well, Phipps, it is just that, provided it isn't stuck to. You will have to swear to it, and stand by it. I know the thing is coming. I can feel it in my bones. Why it hasn't come before, the Lord only knows."

Phipps had great faith in the might of money, and entire faith in Mr. Belcher's power to save him from any calamity. His master, during all his residence with and devotion to him, had shown himself able to secure every end he had sought, and he believed in him, or believed in his power, wholly.

"Couldn't you save me, sir, if I were to get into trouble?" he inquired, anxiously.

"That depends upon whether you stand by me, Phipps. It's just here, my boy. If you swear, through thick and thin, that you saw these men sign this paper, six years ago or more, that you signed it at the same time, and stand by your own signature, you will sail through all right, and do me a devilish good turn. If you balk, or get twisted up in your own reins, or throw off your seat, down goes your house. If you stand by me, I shall stand by you. The thing is all right, and just as it ought to be, but it's a little irregular. It gives me what belongs to me, but the law happens to be against it."

Phipps hesitated, and glanced suspiciously, and even menacingly, at the paper. Mr. Belcher knew that he would like to tear it in pieces, and so, without unseemly haste, he picked it up, placed it in its drawer, locked it in, and put the key in his pocket.

"I don't want to get into trouble," said Phipps.

"Phipps," said Mr. Belcher, in a conciliatory tone, "I don't intend that you shall get into trouble."

Then, rising, and patting his servant on the shoulder, he added:

"But it all depends on your standing by me, and standing by yourself. You know that you will lose nothing by standing by the General, Phipps; you know me."

Phipps was not afraid of crime; he was only afraid of its possible consequences; and Mr. Belcher's assurance of safety, provided he should remember his story and adhere to it, was all that he needed to confirm him in the determination to do what Mr. Belcher wished him to do.

After Phipps retired, Mr. Belcher took out his document again, and looked it over for the hundredth time. He recompared the signatures which he had forged with their originals. Consciously a villain, he regarded himself still as a man who was struggling for his rights. But something of his old, self-reliant courage was gone. He recognized the fact that there was one thing in the world more powerful than himself. The law was against him. Single-handed, he could meet men; but the great power which embodied the justice and strength of the State awed him, and compelled him into a realization of his weakness.

The next morning Mr. Belcher received his brokers and operators in bed in acccordance with his custom. He was not good-natured. His operations in Wall Street had not been prosperous for several weeks. In some way, impossible to be foreseen by himself or his agents, everything had worked against him. He knew that if he did not rally from this passage of ill-luck, he would, in addition to his loss of money, lose something of his prestige. He had a stormy time with his advisers and tools, swore a great deal, and sent them off in anything but a pleasant frame of mind.

Talbot was waiting in the drawing-room when the brokers retired, and followed his card upstairs, where he found his principal with an ugly frown upon his face.

"Toll," he whimpered, "I'm glad to see you. You're the best of 'em all, and in the long run, you bring me the most money."

"Thank you," responded the factor, showing his white teeth in a gratified smile.

"Toll, I'm not exactly ill, but I'm not quite myself. How long it will last I don't know, but just this minute the General is devilish unhappy, and would sell himself cheap. Things are not going right. I don't sleep well."

"You've got too much money," suggested Mr. Talbot.

"Well, what shall I do with it?"

"Give it to me."

"No, I thank you; I can do better. Besides, you are getting more than your share of it now."

"Well, I don't ask it of you," said Talbot, "but if you wish to get rid of it, I could manage a little more of it without trouble."

"Toll, look here! The General wants to place a little money where it will bring him some reputation with the highly respectable old dons—our spiritual fathers, you know—and the brethren. Understand?"

"General, you are deep; you'll have to explain."

"Well, all our sort of fellows patronize something or other. They cheat a man out of his eye-teeth one day, and the next, you hear of them endowing something or other, or making a speech to a band of old women, or figuring on a top-lofty list of directors. That's the kind of thing I want."

"You can get any amount of it, General, by paying for it. All they want is money; they don't care where it comes from."

"Toll, shut up. I behold a vision. Close your eyes now, and let me paint it for you. I see the General—General Robert Belcher, the millionnaire—in the aspect of a great public benefactor. He is dressed in black, and sits upon a platform, in the midst of a lot of seedy men in white chokers. They hand him a programme. There is speech-making going on, and every speech makes an allusion to 'our benefactor,' and the brethren and sisters cheer. The General bows. High old doctors of divinity press up to be introduced. They are all after more. They flatter the General; they coddle him. They give him the highest seat. They pretend to respect him. They defend him from all slanders. They are proud of the General. He is their man. I look into the religious newspapers, and in one column I behold a curse on the stock-jobbing of Wall Street, and in the next, the praise of the beneficence of General Robert Belcher. I see the General passing down Wall Street the next day. I see him laughing out of the corner of his left eye, while his friends punch him in the ribs. Oh, Toll! it's delicious! Where are your feelings, my boy? Why don't you cry?"

"Charming picture, General! Charming! but my handkerchief is fresh, and I must save it. I may have a cold before night."

"Well, now, Toll, what's the thing to be done?"

"What do you say to soup-kitchens for the poor? They don't cost so very much, and you get your name in the papers."

"Soup-kitchens be hanged! That's Mrs. Belcher's job. Besides, I don't want to get up a reputation for helping the poor. They're a troublesome lot and full of bother; I don't believe in 'em. They don't associate you with anybody but themselves. What I want is to be in the right sort of a crowd."

"Have you thought of a hospital?"

"Yes, I've thought of a hospital, but I don't seem to hanker after it. To tell the truth, the hospitals are pretty well taken up already. I might work into a board of directors by paying enough, I suppose, but it is too much the regular thing. What I want is ministers—something religious, you know."

"You might run a church-choir," suggested Talbot, "or, better than that, buy a church, and turn the crank."

"Yes, but they are not quite large enough. I tell you what it is, Toll, I believe I'm pining for a theological seminary. Ah, my heart! my heart! If I could only tell you, Toll, how it yearns over the American people! Can't you see, my boy, that the hope of the nation is in educated and devoted young men? Don't you see that we are going to the devil with our thirst for filthy lucre? Don't you understand how noble a thing it would be for one of fortune's favorites to found an institution with his wealth, that would bear down its blessings to unborn millions? What if that institution should also bear his name? What if that name should be forever associated with that which is most hallowed in our national history? Wouldn't it pay? Eh, Toll?"

Mr. Talbot laughed.

"General, your imagination will be the death of you, but there is really nothing impracticable in your plan. All these fellows want is your money. They will give you everything you want for it in the way of glory."

"I believe you; and wouldn't it be fun for the General? I vow I must indulge. I'm getting tired of horses; and these confounded suppers don't agree with me. It's a theological seminary or nothing. The tides of my destiny, Toll—you understand—the tides of my destiny tend in that direction, and I resign my bark to their sway. I'm going to be a founder, and I feel better already."

It was well that he did, for at this moment a dispatch was handed in which gave him a shock, and compelled him to ask Talbot to retire while he dressed.

"Don't go away, Toll," he said; "I want to see you again."

The dispatch that roused the General from his dream of beneficence was from his agent at Sevenoaks, and read thus: "Jim Fenton's wedding occurred this morning. He was accompanied by a man whom several old citizens firmly believe to be Paul Benedict, though he passed under another name. Balfour and Benedict's boy were here, and all are gone up to Number Nine. Will write particulars."

The theological seminary passed at once into the realm of dimly remembered dreams, to be recalled or forgotten as circumstances should determine. At present, there was something else to occupy the General's mind.

Before he had completed his toilet, he called for Talbot.

"Toll," said he, "if you were in need of legal advice of the best kind, and wanted to be put through a thing straight, whether it were right or not, to whom would you apply? Now mind, I don't want any milksops."

"I know two or three lawyers here who have been

through a theological seminary," Talbot responded, with a knowing smile.

"Oh, get out! There's no joke about this. I mean business now."

"Well, I took pains to show you your man, at my house, once. Don't you remember him?"

"Cavendish?"

"Yes."

"I don't like him."

"Nor do I. He'll bleed you; but he's your man."

"All right; I want to see him."

"Get into my coupé, and I'll take you to his office."

Mr. Belcher went to the drawer that contained his forged document. Then he went back to Talbot, and said:

"Would Cavendish come here?"

"Not he! If you want to see him, you must go where he is. He wouldn't walk into your door to accommodate you if he knew it."

Mr. Belcher was afraid of Cavendish, as far as he could be afraid of any man. The lawyer had bluffed everybody at the dinner-party, and, in his way, scoffed at everybody. He had felt in the lawyer's presence the contact of a nature which possessed more self-assertion and self-assurance than his own. He had felt that Cavendish could read him, could handle him, could see through his schemes. He shrank from exposing himself, even to the scrutiny of this sharp man, whom he could hire for any service. But he went again to the drawer, and, with an excited and trembling hand, drew forth the accursed document. With this he took the autographs on which his forgeries were based. Then he sat down by himself, and thought the matter all over, while Talbot waited in another room. It was only by a desperate determination that he started at last, called Talbot downstairs, put on his hat, and went out.

It seemed to the proprietor, as he emerged from his house, that there was something weird in the morning light. He looked up, and saw that the sky was clear. He looked down, and the street was veiled in a strange shadow. The boys looked at him as if they were half startled. Inquisitive faces peered at him from a passing omnibus. A beggar laughed as he held out his greasy hand. Passengers paused to observe him. All this attention, which he once courted and accepted as flattery and fame, was disagreeable to him.

"Good God! Toll, what has happened since last night?" he said, as he sank back upon the satin cushions of the coupé.

"General, I don't think you're quite well. Don't die now. We can't spare you yet."

"Die? Do I look like it?" exclaimed Mr. Belcher, slapping his broad chest. "Don't talk to me about dying. I haven't thought about that yet."

"I beg your pardon. You know I didn't mean to distress you."

Then the conversation dropped, and the carriage wheeled on. The roll of vehicles, the shouting of drivers, the panoramic scenes, the flags swaying in the morning sky, the busy throngs that went up and down Broadway, were but the sights and sounds of a dimly apprehended dream. He was journeying toward guilt. What would be its end? Would he not be detected in it at the first step? How could he sit before the hawk-eyed man whom he was about to meet without in some way betraying his secret?

When the coupé stopped, Talbot roused his companion with difficulty.

"This can't be the place, Toll. We haven't come half a mile."

"On the contrary, we have come three miles."

"It can't be possible, Toll. I must look at your horse. I'd no idea you had such an animal."

Then Mr. Belcher got out, and looked the horse over He was a connoisseur, and he stood five minutes on the curbstone, expatiating upon those points of the animal that pleased him.

" I believe you came to see Mr. Cavendish," suggested Talbot with a laugh.

" Yes, I suppose I must go up. I hate lawyers, anyway."

They climbed the stairway. They knocked at Mr. Cavendish's door. A boy opened it, and took in their cards. Mr. Cavendish was busy, but would see them in fifteen minutes. Mr. Belcher sat down in the anteroom, took a newspaper from his pocket, and began to read. Then he took a pen and scribbled, writing his own name with three other names, across which he nervously drew his pen. Then he drew forth his knife, and tremblingly dressed his finger-nails. Having completed this task, he took out a large pocket-book, withdrew a blank check, filled and signed it, and put it back. Realizing, at last, that Talbot was waiting to go in with him, he said:

" By the way, Toll, this business of mine is private."

" Oh, I understand," said Talbot; " I'm only going in to make sure that Cavendish remembers you."

What Talbot really wished to make sure of was, that Cavendish should know that he had brought him his client.

At last they heard a little bell which summoned the boy, who soon returned to say that Mr. Cavendish would see them. Mr. Belcher looked around for a mirror, but discovering none, said:

" Toll, look at me! Am I all right? Do you see anything out of the way?"

Talbot having looked him over, and reported favorably, they followed the boy into the penetralia of the great office, and into the presence of the great man. Mr. Cavendish did not rise, but leaned back in his huge carved chair, and rubbed his hands, pale in their morning whiteness, and said, coldly :

" Good morning, gentlemen ; sit down."

Mr. Talbot declined. He had simply brought to him his friend, General Belcher, who, he believed, had a matter of business to propose. Then, telling Mr. Belcher that he should leave the coupé at his service, he retired.

Mr. Belcher felt that he was already in court. Mr. Cavendish sat behind his desk in a judicial attitude, with his new client fronting him. The latter fell, or tried to force himself, into a jocular mood and bearing, according to his custom on serious occasions.

" I am likely to have a little scrimmage," said he, " and I shall want your help, Mr. Cavendish."

Saying this, he drew forth a check for a thousand dollars, which he had drawn in the ante-room, and passed it over to the lawyer. Mr. Cavendish took it up listlessly, held it by its two ends, read its face, examined its back, and tossed it into a drawer, as if it were a suspicious sixpence.

" It's a thousand dollars," said Mr. Belcher, surprised that the sum had apparently made no impression.

" I see—a retainer—thanks ! "

All the time the hawk-eyes were looking into Mr. Belcher. All the time the scalp was moving backward and forward, as if he had just procured a new one, that might be filled up before night, but for the moment was a trifle large. All the time there was a subtle scorn upon the lips, the flavor of which the finely curved nose apprehended with approval.

" What's the case, General ? "

The General drew from his pocket his forged assignment, and passed it into the hand of Mr. Cavendish.

" Is that a legally constructed document ? " he inquired.

Mr. Cavendish read it carefully, every word. He

looked at the signatures. He looked at the blank page on the back. He looked at the tape with which it was bound. He fingered the knot with which it was tied. He folded it carefully, and handed it back.

"Yes—absolutely perfect," he said. "Of course I know nothing about the signatures. Is the assignor living?"

"That is precisely what I don't know," replied Mr. Belcher. "I supposed him to be dead for years. I have now reason to suspect that he is living."

"Have you been using these patents?"

"Yes, and I've made piles of money on them."

"Is your right contested?"

"No; but I have reason to believe that it will be."

"What reason?" inquired Mr. Cavendish, sharply.

Mr. Belcher was puzzled.

"Well, the man has been insane, and has forgotten, very likely, what he did before his insanity. I have reason to believe that such is the case, and that he intends to contest my right to the inventions which this paper conveys to me.

"What reason, now?"

Mr. Belcher's broad expanse of face crimsoned into a blush, and he simply answered:

"I know the man."

"Who is his lawyer?"

"Balfour."

Mr. Cavendish gave a little start.

"Let me see that paper again," said he.

After looking it through again, he said, dryly:

"I know Balfour. He is a shrewd man, and a good lawyer: and unless he has a case, or thinks he has one, he will not fight this document. What deviltry there is in it, I don't know, and I don't want you to tell me. I can tell you that you have a hard man to fight. Where are these witnesses?"

"Two of them are dead. One of them is living, and is now in the city."

"What can he swear to?"

"He can swear to his own signature, and to all the rest. He can relate and swear to all the circumstances attending the execution of the paper."

"And you know that these rights were never previously conveyed."

"Yes, I know they never were."

"Then, mark you, General, Balfour has no case at all —provided this isn't a dirty paper. If it is a dirty paper, and you want me to serve you, keep your tongue to yourself. You've recorded it, of course."

"Recorded it?" inquired Mr. Belcher in an alarm which he did not attempt to disguise.

"You don't mean to tell me that this paper has been in existence more than six years, and has not been recorded?"

"I didn't know it was necessary."

Mr. Cavendish tossed the paper back to the owner of it with a sniff of contempt.

"It isn't worth that!" said he, snapping his fingers.

Then he drew out the check from his drawer, and handed it back to Mr. Belcher.

"There's no case, and I don't want your money," said he.

"But there is a case!" said Mr. Belcher, fiercely, scared out of his fear. "Do you suppose I am going to be cheated out of my rights without a fight? I'm no chicken, and I'll spend half a million before I'll give up my rights."

Mr. Cavendish laughed.

"Well, go to Washington," said he, "and if you don't find that Balfour or somebody else has been there before you, I shall be mistaken. Balfour isn't very much of a chicken, and he knows enough to know that the first as signment recorded there holds. Why has he not been down upon you before this? Simply because he saw that you were making money for his client, and he preferred to take it all out of you in a single slice. I know Balfour, and he carries a long head. Chicken!"

Mr. Belcher was in distress. The whole game was as obvious and real to him as if he had assured himself of its truth. He staggered to his feet. He felt the hand of ruin upon him. He believed that while he had been perfecting his crime he had been quietly overreached. He lost his self-command, and gave himself up to profanity and bluster, at which Mr. Cavendish laughed.

"There's no use in that sort of thing, General," said he. "Go to Washington. Ascertain for yourself about it, and if you find it as I predict, make the best of it. You can make a compromise of some sort. Do the best you can."

There was one thing that Mr. Cavendish had noticed. Mr. Belcher had made no response to him when he told him that if the paper was a dirty one he did not wish to know it. He had made up his mind that there was mischief in it, somewhere. Either the consideration had never been paid, or the signatures were fraudulent, or perhaps the paper had been executed when the assignor was demonstrably of unsound mind. Somewhere, he was perfectly sure, there was fraud.

"General," said he, "I have my doubts about this paper. I'm not going to tell you why. I understand that there is one witness living who will swear to all these signatures."

"There is."

"Is he a credible witness? Has he ever committed a crime? Can anything wrong be proved against him?"

"The witness," responded Mr. Belcher, "is my man Phipps; and a more faithful fellow never lived. I've known him for years, and he was never in an ugly scrape in his life."

"Well, if you find that no one is before you on the records, come back; and when you come you may as well multiply that check by ten. When I undertake a thing of this kind, I like to provide myself against all contingencies."

Mr. Belcher groaned, and tore up the little check that seemed so large when he drew it, and had shrunk to such contemptible dimensions in the hands of the lawyer.

"You lawyers put the lancet in pretty deep."

"Our clients never do!" said Mr. Cavendish through his sneering lips.

Then the boy knocked, and came in. There was another gentleman who wished to see the lawyer.

"I shall go to Washington to-day, and see you on my return," said Mr. Belcher.

Then, bidding the lawyer a good-morning, he went out, ran down the stairs, jumped into Mr. Talbot's waiting coupé, and ordered himself driven home. Arriving there, he hurriedly packed a satchel, and, announcing to Mrs. Belcher that he had been unexpectedly called to Washington, went out, and made the quickest passage possible to Jersey City. As he had Government contracts on hand, his wife asked no questions, and gave the matter no thought.

The moment Mr. Belcher found himself on the train, and in motion, he became feverishly excited. He cursed himself that he had not attended to this matter before. He had wondered why Balfour was so quiet. With Benedict alive and in communication, or with Benedict dead, and his heir in charge, why had he made no claim upon rights which were the basis of his own fortune? There could be but one answer to these questions, and Cavendish had given it!

He talked to himself, and attracted the attention of those around him. He walked the platforms at all the stations where the train stopped. He asked the conductor a dozen times at what hour the train would arrive in Washington, apparently forgetting that he had already received his information. He did not reach his destination until evening, and then, of course, all the public offices were closed. He met men whom he knew, but he would not be tempted by them into a debauch. He went to bed early, and, after a weary night of sleeplessness, found himself at the Patent Office before a clerk was in his place.

When the offices were opened, he sought his man, and revealed his business. He prepared a list of the patents in which he was interested, and secured a search of the records of assignment. It was a long time since the patents had been issued, and the inquisition was a tedious one ; but it resulted, to his unspeakable relief, in the official statement that no one of them had ever been assigned. Then he brought out his paper, and, with a blushing declaration that he had not known the necessity of its record until the previous day, saw the assignment placed upon the books.

Then he was suddenly at ease. Then he could look about him. A great burden was rolled from his shoulders, and he knew that he ought to be jolly ; but somehow his spirits did not rise. As he emerged from the Patent Office, there was the same weird light in the sky that he had noticed the day before, on leaving his house with Talbot. The great dome of the Capitol swelled in the air like a bubble, which seemed as if it would burst. The broad, hot streets glimmered as if a volcano were breeding under them. Everything looked unsubstantial. He found himself watching for Balfour, and expecting to meet him at every corner. He was in a new world, and had not become wonted to it—the world of conscious crime—the world of outlawry. It had a sun of its own, fears of its own, figures and aspects of its own. There was a new man growing up within him, whom he wished to hide. To this man's needs his face had not yet become hardened, his words had not yet been trained beyond the danger of betrayal, his eyes had not adjusted their pupils for vision and self-suppression.

He took the night train home, breakfasted at the Astor, and was the first man to greet Mr. Cavendish when that gentleman entered his chambers. Mr. Cavendish sat listlessly, and heard his story. The lawyer's hands were as pale, his scalp as uneasy, and his lips as redolent of scorn as they were two days before, while his nose bent to sniff the scorn with more evident approval than then. He apprehended more thoroughly the character of the man before him, saw more clearly the nature of his business, and wondered with contemptuous incredulity that Balfour had not been sharper and quicker.

After Mr. Belcher had stated the facts touching the Washington records, Mr. Cavendish said:

"Well, General, as far as appearances go, you have the lead. Nothing but the overthrow of your assignment can damage you, and, as I told you the day before yesterday, if the paper is dirty, don't tell me of it—that is, if you want me to do anything for you. Go about your business, say nothing to anybody, and if you are prosecuted, come to me."

Still Mr. Belcher made no response to the lawyer's suggestion touching the fraudulent nature of the paper; and the latter was thoroughly confirmed in his original impression that there was something wrong about it.

Then Mr. Belcher went out upon Wall Street, among his brokers, visited the Exchange, visited the Gold Room, jested with his friends, concocted schemes, called upon Talbot, wrote letters, and filled up his day. Going home to dinner, he found a letter from his agent at Sevenoaks, giving in detail his reasons for supposing not only that Benedict had been in the village, but that, from the time of his disappearance from the Sevenoaks poor-house, he had been living at Number Nine with Jim Fenton. Balfour had undoubtedly found him there, as he was in the habit of visiting the woods. Mike Conlin must also have found him there, and worst of all, Sam Yates must have discovered him. The instruments that he had employed, at a considerable cost, to ascertain whether Benedict were alive or dead had proved false to him. The discovery that Sam Yates was a traitor made him tremble. It was from him that he had procured the autographs on which two of his forgeries were based. He sat down immediately, and wrote a friendly letter to Yates, putting some business into his hands, and promising more. Then he wrote to his agent, telling him of his interest in Yates, and of his faithful service, and directing him to take the reformed man under his wing, and, as far as possible, to attach him to the interests of the concern.

Two days afterward, he looked out of his window and saw Mr. Balfour descending the steps of his house with a travelling satchel in his hand. Calling Phipps, he directed him to jump into the first cab, or carriage, pay double price, and make his way to the ferry that led to the Washington cars, see if Balfour crossed at that point, and learn, if possible, his destination. Phipps returned in an hour and a half with the information that the lawyer had bought a ticket for Washington.

Then Mr. Belcher knew that trouble was brewing, and braced himself to meet it. In less than forty-eight hours, Balfour would know, either that he had been deceived by Benedict, or that a forgery had been committed. Balfour was cautious, and would take time to settle this question in his own mind.

CHAPTER XXIV.

WHEREIN THE GENERAL LEAPS THE BOUNDS OF LAW, FINDS HIMSELF IN A NEW WORLD, AND BECOMES THE VICTIM OF HIS FRIENDS WITHOUT KNOWING IT.

FOR several weeks the General had been leading a huge and unscrupulous combination for "bearing" International Mail. The stock had ruled high for a long time—higher than was deemed legitimate by those familiar with its affairs—and the combination began by selling large blocks of the stock for future delivery, at a point or two below the market. Then stories about the corporation began to be circulated upon the street, of the most damaging character—stories of fraud, peculation, and rapidly diminishing business—stories of maturing combinations against the company—stories of the imminent retirement of men deemed essential to the management. The air was full of rumors. One died only to make place for another, and men were forced to believe that where there was so much smoke there must be some fire. Still the combination boldly sold. The stock broke, and went down, down, down, day after day, and still there were strong takers for all that offered. The operation had worked like a charm to the point where it was deemed prudent to begin to repurchase, when there occurred one of those mysterious changes in the market which none could have foreseen. It was believed that the market had been oversold, and the holders held. The combination was short, and up went the stock by the run. The most frantic efforts were made to cover, but without avail, and as the contracts matured, house after house went down with a crash that startled the country. Mr. Belcher, the heaviest man of them all, turned the cold shoulder to his confrères in the stupendous mischief, and went home to his dinner one day, conscious that half a million dollars had slipped through his fingers. He ate but little, walked his rooms for an hour like a caged tiger, muttered and swore to himself, and finally went off to his club. There seemed to be no way in which he could drown his anger, disappointment, and sense of loss, except by a debauch, and he was brought home by his faithful Phipps at the stage of confidential silliness.

When his brokers appeared at ten the next morning, he drove them from the house, and then, with such wits as he could muster, in a head still tortured by his night's excesses, thought over his situation. A heavy slice of his ready money had been practically swept out of existence. If he was not crippled, his wings were clipped. His prestige was departed. He knew that men would thereafter be wary of following him, or trusting to his sagacity. Beyond the power of his money, and his power to make money, he knew that he had no consideration on 'Change—that there were five hundred men who would laugh to see the General go down—who had less feeling for him, personally, than they entertained toward an ordinary dog. He knew this because so far, at least, he understood himself. To redeem his position was now the grand desideratum. He would do it or die!

There was one direction in which the General had permitted himself to be shortened in, or rather, one in which he had voluntarily crippled himself for a consideration. He had felt himself obliged to hold large quantities of the stock of the Crooked Valley Railroad, in order to maintain his seat at the head of its management. He had parted with comparatively little of it since his first huge purchase secured the place he sought, and though the price he gave was small, the quantity raised the aggregate to a large figure. All this was unproductive. It simply secured his place and his influence.

No sooner had he thoroughly realized the great loss he had met with, in connection with his Wall Street conspiracy, than he began to revolve in his mind a scheme which he had held in reserve from the first moment of his control of the Crooked Valley Road. He had nourished in every possible way the good-will of those who lived along the line. Not only this, but he had endeavored to show his power to do anything he pleased with the stock.

The people believed that he only needed to raise a finger to carry up the price of the stock in the market, and that the same potent finger could carry it down at will. He had already wrought wonders. He had raised a dead road to life. He had invigorated business in every town through which it passed. He was a king, whose word was law and whose will was destiny. The rumors of his reverses in Wall Street did not reach them, and all believed that, in one way or another, their fortunes were united with his.

The scheme to which he reverted in the first bitter moments of his loss could have originated in no brain less unscrupulous than his own. He would repeat the game that had been so successful at Sevenoaks. To do this, he only needed to call into action his tools on the street and in the management.

In the midst of his schemes, the bell rang at the door, and Talbot was announced. Mr. Belcher was always glad to see him, for he had no association with his speculations. Talbot had uniformly been friendly and ready to serve him. In truth, Talbot was almost his only friend.

"Toll, have you heard the news?"

"About the International Mail?"

"Yes."

"I've heard something of it, and I've come around

this morning to get the facts. I shall be bored about them all day by your good friends, you know."

"Well, Toll, I've had a sweat."

"You're not crippled?"

"No, but I've lost every dollar I have made since I've been in the city. Jones has gone under; Pell has gone under. Cramp & Co. will have to make a statement, and get a little time, but they will swim. The General is the only man of the lot who isn't shaken. But, Toll, it's devilish hard. It scares me. A few more such slices would spoil my cheese."

"Well, now, General, why do you go into these things at all? You are making money fast enough in a regular business."

"Ah, but it's tame, tame, tame! I must have excitement. Theatres are played out, horses are played out, and suppers raise the devil with me."

"Then take it easy. Don't risk so much. You used to do this sort of thing well—used to do it right every time. You got up a good deal of reputation for foresight and skill."

"I know, and every man ruined in the International Mail will curse me. I led them into it. I shall have a sweet time in Wall Street when I go there again. But it's like brandy; a man wants a larger dose every time, and I shall clean them out yet."

Talbot's policy was to make the General last. He wanted to advise him for his good, because his principal's permanent prosperity was the basis of his own. He saw that he was getting beyond control, and, under an exterior of compliance and complaisance, he was genuinely alarmed.

"Toll," said Mr. Belcher, "you are a good fellow."

"Thank you, General," said the factor, a smile spreading around his shining teeth. "My wife will be glad to know it."

" By the way—speaking of your wife—have you seen anything of Mrs. Dillingham lately ? "

" Nothing. She is commonly supposed to be absorbed by the General."

" Common Supposition is a greater fool than I wish it were."

" That won't do, General. There never was a more evident case of killing at first sight than that."

" Well, Toll, I believe the woman is fond of me, but she has a queer way of showing it. I think she has changed. It seems so to me, but she's a devilish fine creature. Ah, my heart ! my heart ! Toll."

" You were complaining of it the other day. It was a theological seminary then. Perhaps that is the name you know her by."

" Not much theological seminary about her ! " with a laugh.

" Well, there's one thing that you can comfort yourself, with, General ; she sees no man but you."

" Is that so ? " inquired Mr. Belcher, eagerly.

" That is what everybody says."

Mr. Belcher rolled this statement as a sweet morsel under his tongue. She must be hiding her passion from him under an impression of its hopelessness ! Poor woman ! He would see her at the first opportunity.

" Toll," said Mr. Belcher, " after a moment of delicious reflection, " you're a good fellow."

" I think I've heard that remark before."

" Yes, you're a good fellow, and I'd like to do something for you."

" You've done a great deal for me already, General."

" Yes, and I'm going to do something more."

" Will you put it in my hand or my hat ? " inquired Talbot, jocularly.

" Toll, how much Crooked Valley stock have you ? "

" A thousand shares."

"What did you buy it for?"

"To help you."

"What have you kept it for?"

"To help keep the General at the head of the management."

"Turn about is fair play, isn't it?"

"That's the adage," responded Talbot.

"Well, I'm going to put that stock up; do you understand?"

"How will you do it?"

"By saying I'll do it. I want it whispered along the line that the General is going to put that stock up within a week. They're all greedy. They are all just like the rest of us. They know it isn't worth a continental copper, but they want a hand in the General's speculations, and the General wants it understood that he would like to have them share in his profits."

"I think I understand," said Talbot.

"Toll, I've got another vision. Hold on now! I behold a man in the General's confidence—a reliable, business man—who whispers to his friend that he heard the General say that he had all his plans laid for putting up the Crooked Valley stock within a week. This friend whispers it to another friend. No names are mentioned. It goes from friend to friend. It is whispered through every town along the line. Everybody gets crazy over it, and everybody quietly sends in an order for stock. In the meantime the General and his factor, yielding to the pressure—melted before the public demand—gently and tenderly unload! The vision still unrolls. Months later I behold the General buying back the stock at his own price, and with it maintaining his place in the management. Have you followed me?"

"Yes, General, I've seen it all. I comprehend it, and I shall unload with all the gentleness and tenderness possible."

Then the whimsical scoundrel and his willing lieutenant laughed a long, heartless laugh.

"Toll, I feel better, and I believe I'll get up," said the General. "Let this vision sink deep into your soul. Then give it wings, and speed it on its mission. Remember that this is a vale of tears, and don't set your affections on things below. By-by!"

Talbot went downstairs, drawing on his gloves, and laughing. Then he went out into the warm light, buttoned up his coat instinctively, as if to hide the plot he carried, jumped into his coupé, and went to his business.

Mr. Belcher dressed himself with more than his usual care, went to Mrs. Belcher's room and inquired about his children, then went to his library and drew forth from a secret drawer a little book. He looked it over for a few minutes, then placed it in his pocket, and went out. The allusion that had been made to Mrs. Dillingham, and the assurance that he was popularly understood to be her lover, and the only man who was regarded by her with favor, intoxicated him, and his old passion came back upon him.

It was a strange manifestation of his brutal nature that at this moment of his trouble, and this epoch of his cruelty and crime, he longed for the comfort of a woman's sympathy. He was too much absorbed by his affairs to be moved by that which was basest in his regard for his beautiful idol. If he could feel her hand upon his forehead; if she could tell him that she was sorry for him; if he could know that she loved him; ay, if he could be assured that this woman, whom he had believed to be capable of guilt, had prayed for him, it would have been balm to his heart. He was sore with struggle, and guilt, and defeat. He longed for love and tenderness. As if he were a great bloody dog, just coming from the fight of an hour, in which he had been worsted, and seeking for a tender hand to pat his head, and call him "poor, good old fellow," the General longed for a woman's loving recognition. He was in his old mood of self-pity. He wanted to be petted, smoothed, commiserated, reassured; and there was only one woman in all the world from whom such ministry would be grateful.

He knew that Mrs. Dillingham had heard of his loss, for she heard of and read everything. He wanted her to know that it had not shaken him. He would not for the world have her suppose that he was growing poor. Still to appear to her as a person of wealth and power; still to hold her confidence as a man of multiplied resources, was, perhaps, the deepest ambition that moved him. He had found that he could not use her in the management of his affairs. Though from the first, up to the period of her acquaintance with Harry Benedict, she had led him on to love her by every charm she possessed, and every art she knew, she had always refused to be debased by him in any way.

When he went out of his house, at the close of his interviews with Talbot and Mrs. Belcher, it was without a definitely formed purpose to visit the charming widow. He simply knew that his heart was hungry. The sunflower is gross, but it knows the sun as well as the morning-glory, and turns to it as naturally. It was with like unreasoning instinct that he took the little book from its drawer, put on his hat, went down his steps, and entered the street that led him toward Mrs. Dillingham's house. He could not keep away from her. He would not if he could, and so, in ten minutes, he was seated with her, *vis à vis.*

"You have been unfortunate, Mr. Belcher," she said, sympathetically. "I am very sorry for you. It is not so bad as I heard, I am sure. You are looking very well."

"Oh! it is one of those things that may happen any

day, to any man, operating as I do," responded Mr. Belcher with a careless laugh. "The General never gets in too deep. He is just as rich to-day as he was when he entered the city."

"I am so glad to hear it—gladder than I can express," said Mrs. Dillingham, with heartiness.

Her effusiveness of good feeling and her evident relief from anxiety, were honey to him.

"Don't trouble yourself about me," said he, musingly. "The General knows what he's about, every time. He has the advantage of the rest of them, in his regular business."

"I can't understand how it is," responded Mrs. Dillingham, with fine perplexity. "You men are so different from us. I should think you would be crazy with your losses."

Now, Mr. Belcher wished to impress Mrs. Dillingham permanently with a sense of his wisdom, and to inspire in her an inextinguishable faith in his sagacity and prudence. He wanted her to believe in his power to retain all the wealth he had won. He would take her into his confidence. He had never done this with relation to his business, and under that treatment she had drifted away from him. Now that he found how thoroughly friendly she was, he would try another method, and bind her to him. The lady read him as plainly as if he had been a book, and said:

"Oh, General! I have ascertained something that may be of use to you. Mr. Benedict is living. I had a letter from his boy this morning—dear little fellow—and he tells me how well his father is, and how pleasant it is to be with him again."

Mr. Belcher frowned.

"Do you know I can't quite stomach your whim—about that boy? What under heaven do you care for him?"

"Oh, you mustn't touch that whim, General," said Mrs. Dillingham, laughing. "I am a woman, and I have a right to it. He amuses me, and a great deal more than that. I wouldn't tell you a word about him, or what he writes to me, if I thought it would do him any harm. He's my pet. What in the world have I to do but to pet him? How shall I fill my time? I'm tired of society, and disgusted with men—at least, with my old acquaintances—and I'm fond of children. They do me good. Oh, you mustn't touch my whim!"

"There is no accounting for tastes!" Mr. Belcher responded, with a laugh that had a spice of scorn and vexation in it.

"Now, General, what do you care for that boy? If you are a friend to me, you ought to be glad that he interests me."

"I don't like the man who has him in charge. I believe Balfour is a villain."

"I'm sure I don't know," said the lady. "He never has the courtesy to darken my door. I once saw something of him. He is like all the rest, I suppose; he is tired of me."

Mrs. Dillingham had played her part perfectly, and the man before her was a blind believer in her loyalty to him.

"Let the boy go, and Balfour too," said the General. "They are not pleasant topics to me, and your whim will wear out. When is the boy coming back?"

"He is to be away all summer, I believe."

"Good!"

Mrs. Dillingham laughed.

"Why, I am glad of it, if you are," she said.

Mr. Belcher drew a little book from his pocket.

"What have you there?" the lady inquired.

"Women have great curiosity," said Mr. Bercher slapping his knee with the little volume.

"And men delight to excite it," she responded.

"The General is a business man, and you want to know how he does it," said he.

"I do, upon my word," responded the lady.

"Very well, the General has two kinds of business, and he never mixes one with the other."

"I don't understand."

"Well, you know he's a manufacturer—got his start in that way. So he keeps that business by itself, and when he operates in Wall Street, he operates outside of it. He never risks a dollar that he makes in his regular business in any outside operation."

"And you have it all in the little book?"

"Would you like to see it?"

"Yes."

"Very well, you shall, when I've told you all about it. I suppose that it must have been ten years ago that a man came to Sevenoaks who was full of all sorts of inventions. I tried some of them, and they worked well; so I went on furnishing money to him, and, at last, I furnished so much that he passed all his rights into my hands—sold everything to me. He got into trouble, and lost his head—went into an insane hospital, where I supported him for more than two years. Then he was sent back as incurable, and, of course, had to go to the poor-house. I couldn't support him always, you know. I'd paid him fairly, run all the risk, and felt that my hands were clean."

"He had sold everything to you, hadn't he?" inquired Mrs. Dillingham, sympathetically.

"Certainly, I have the contract, legally drawn, signed, and delivered."

"People couldn't blame you, of course."

"But they did."

"How could they, if you paid him all that belonged to him?"

"That's Sevenoaks. That's the thing that drove me

away. Benedict escaped, and they all supposed he was dead, and fancied that because I had made money out of him, I was responsible for him in some way. But I punished them. They'll remember me."

And Mr. Belcher laughed a brutal laugh that rasped Mrs. Dillingham's sensibilities almost beyond endurance.

"And, now," said the General, resuming, "this man Balfour means to get these patents, that I've owned and used for from seven to ten years, out of me. Perhaps he will do it, but it will be after the biggest fight that New York ever saw."

Mrs. Dillingham eyed the little book. She was very curious about it. She was delightfully puzzled to know how these men who had the power of making money managed their affairs. Account-books were such conundrums to her!

She took a little hassock, placed it by Mr. Belcher's chair, and sat down, leaning by the weight of a feather against him. It was the first approach of the kind she had ever made, and the General appreciated it.

"Now you shall show me all about it," she said

The General opened the book. It contained the results, in the briefest space, of his profits from the Benedict inventions. It showed just how and where all those profits had been invested and re-invested. Her admiration of the General's business habits and methods was unbounded. She asked a thousand silly questions, with one, occasionally, which touched an important point. She thanked him for the confidence he reposed in her. She was delighted to know his system, which seemed to her to guard him from the accidents so common to those engaged in great enterprises ; and Mr. Belcher drank in her flatteries with supreme satisfaction. They comforted him. They were balm to his disappointments. They soothed his wounded vanity. They assured him of perfect trust where he most tenderly wanted it.

In the midst of these delightful confidences, they were interrupted. A servant appeared who told Mr. Belcher that there was a messenger at the door who wished to see him on urgent business. Mrs. Dillingham took the little book to hold while he went to the door. After a few minutes, he returned. It seemed that Phipps, who knew his master's habits, had directed the messenger to inquire for him at Mrs. Dillingham's house, and that his brokers were in trouble and desired his immediate presence in Wall Street. The General was very much vexed with the interruption, but declared that he should be obliged to follow the messenger.

"Leave the little book until you come back," insisted Mrs. Dillingham, sweetly. "It will amuse me all day."

She held it to her breast with both hands, as if it were the sweetest treasure that had ever rested there.

"Will you take care of it?"

"Yes."

He seized her unresisting hand and kissed it.

"Between this time and dinner I shall be back. Then I must have it again," he said.

"Certainly."

Then the General retired, went to his house and found his carriage waiting, and, in less than an hour, was absorbed in ravelling the snarled affairs connected with his recent disastrous speculation. The good-nature engendered by his delightful interview with Mrs. Dillingham lasted all day, and helped him like a cordial.

The moment he was out of the house, and had placed himself beyond the possibility of immediate return, the lady called her servant, and told him that she should be at home to nobody during the day. No one was to be admitted but Mr. Belcher, on any errand whatsoever.

Then she went to her room, and looked the little book over at her leisure. There was no doubt about the business skill and method of the man who had made every entry. There was no doubt in her own mind that it was a private book, which no eye but that of its owner had ever seen, before it had been opened to her.

She hesitated upon the point of honor as to what she would do with it. It would be treachery to copy it, but it would be treachery simply against a traitor. She did not understand its legal importance, yet she knew it contained the most valuable information. It showed, in unmistakable figures, the extent to which Benedict had been wronged. Perfectly sure that it was a record of the results of fraud against a helpless man and a boy in whom her heart was profoundly interested, her hesitation was brief. She locked her door, gathered her writing materials, and, by an hour's careful and rapid work, copied every word of it.

After completing the copy, she went over it again and again, verifying every word and figure. When she had repeated the process to her entire satisfaction, and even to weariness, she took her pen, and after writing: "This is a true copy of the records of a book this day lent to me by Robert Belcher," she affixed the date and signed her name.

Then she carefully wrapped Mr. Belcher's book in a sheet of scented paper, wrote his name and the number and street of his residence upon it, and placed it in her pocket. The copy was consigned to a drawer and locked in, to be recalled and re-perused at pleasure.

She understood the General's motives in placing these records and figures in her hands. The leading one, of course, related to his standing with her. He wanted her to know how rich he was, how prudent he was, how invincible he was. He wanted her to stand firm in her belief in him, whatever rumors might be afloat upon the street. Beyond this, though he had made no allusion to it, she knew that he wanted the use of her tongue among his friends and enemies alike. She was a talking woman, and it was easy for her, who had been so much at home in the General's family, to strengthen his reputation wherever she might touch the public. He wanted somebody to know what his real resources were—somebody who could, from personal knowledge of his affairs, assert their soundness without revealing their details. He believed that Mrs. Dillingham would be so proud of the possession of his confidence, and so prudent in showing it, that his general business reputation, and his reputation for great wealth, would be materially strengthened by her. All this she understood, because she knew the nature of the man, and appreciated the estimate which he placed upon her.

Nothing remained for her that day but the dreaded return of Mr. Belcher. She was now more than ever at a loss to know how she should manage him. She had resumed, during her interview with him, her old arts of fascination, and seen how easily she could make him the most troublesome of slaves. She had again permitted him to kiss her hand. She had asked a favor of him and he had granted it. She had committed a breach of trust; and though she justified herself in it, she felt afraid and half ashamed to meet the man whom she had so thoroughly befooled. She was disgusted with the new intimacy with him which her own hand had invited, and heartily wished that the long game of duplicity were concluded.

The General found more to engage his attention than he had anticipated, and after a few hours' absence from the fascinations of his idol, he began to feel uneasy about his book. It was the first time it had ever left his hands. He grew nervous about it at last, and was haunted by a vague sense of danger. As soon, therefore, as it became apparent to him that a second call upon Mrs. Dillingham that day would be impracticable, he sent Phipps to her with a note apprising her of the fact, and asking her to deliver to him the little account book he had left with her.

It was with a profound sense of relief that she handed it to the messenger, and realized that, during that day and evening at least, she should be free, and so able to gather back her old composure and self assurance. Mr. Belcher's note she placed with her copy of the book, as her authority for passing it into other hands than those of its owner.

While these little things, which were destined to have large consequences, were in progress in the city, an incident occurred in the country, of no less importance in the grand outcome of events relating to Mr. Belcher and his victim.

It will be remembered that after Mr. Belcher had been apprised by his agent at Sevenoaks that Mr. Benedict was undoubtedly alive, and that he had lived, ever since his disappearance, at Number Nine, he wrote to Sam Yates, putting profitable business into his hands, and that he also directed his agent to attach him, by all possible means, to the proprietor's interests. His motive, of course, was to shut the lawyer's mouth concerning the autograph letters he had furnished. He knew that Yates would remember the hints of forgery which he had breathed into his ear during their first interview in the city, and would not be slow to conclude that those autographs were procured for some foul purpose. He had been careful, from the first, not to break up the friendly relations that existed between them, and now that he saw that the lawyer had played him false, he was more anxious than ever to conciliate him.

Yates attended faithfully to the business intrusted to him, and, on reporting results to Mr. Belcher's agent, according to his client's directions, was surprised to find him in a very friendly and confidential mood, and ready with a proposition for further service. There were tangled affairs in which he needed the lawyer's assistance. and, as he did not wish to have the papers pertaining to them leave his possession, he invited Yates to his house, where they could work together during the brief evenings, when he would be free from the cares of the mill.

So, for two or three weeks, Sam Yates occupied Mr. Belcher's library—the very room in which that person was first introduced to the reader. There, under the shade of the old Seven Oaks, he worked during the day. and there, in the evening, he held his consultations with the agent.

One day, during his work, he mislaid a paper, and in his search for it, had occasion to examine the structure of the grand library table at which he wrote. The table had two sides, finished and furnished exactly alike, with duplicate sets of drawers opposite to each other. He pulled out one of these drawers completely, to ascertain whether his lost paper had not slipped through a crack and lodged beyond it. In reaching in, he moved, or thought he moved, the drawer that met him from the opposite side. On going to the opposite side, however, he found that he had not moved the drawer at all. He then pulled that out, and, endeavoring to look through the space thus vacated by both drawers, found that it was blocked by some obstacle that had been placed between them. Finding a cane in a corner of the room, he thrust it in, and pushed through to the opposite side a little secret drawer, unfurnished with a knob, but covered with a lid.

He resumed his seat, and held the little box in his hand. Before he had time to think of what he was doing, or to appreciate the fact that he had no right to open a secret drawer, he had opened it. It contained but one article, and that was a letter directed to Paul Benedict. The letter was sealed, so that he was measurably relieved from the temptation to examine its contents. Of one thing he felt sure : that if it contained anything prejudicial to the writer's interests—and it was addressed in the handwriting of Robert Belcher—it had been forgotten. It might be of great importance to the inventor. The probabilities were, that a letter which was deemed of sufficient importance to secrete in so remarkable a manner was an important one.

To Sam Yates, as to Mrs. Dillingham, with the little book in her hand, arose the question of honor at once. His heart was with Benedict. He was sure that Belcher had some foul purpose in patronizing himself, yet he went through a hard struggle before he could bring himself to the determination that Benedict and not Belcher should have the first handling of the letter. Although the latter had tried to degrade him, and was incapable of any good motive in extending patronage to him, he felt that he had unintentionally surrounded him with influences which had saved him from the most disgraceful ruin. He was at that very moment in his employ. He was eating every day the bread which his patronage provided.

After all, was he not earning his bread ? Was he under any obligation to Mr. Belcher which his honest and faithful labor did not discharge ? Mr. Belcher had written and addressed the letter. He would deliver it, and Mr. Benedict should decide whether, under all the circumstances, the letter was rightfully his. He put it in his pocket, placed the little box back in its home, replaced the drawers which hid it, and went on with his work.

Yates carried the letter around in his pocket for several days. He did not believe the agent knew either of the existence of the letter or the drawer in which it was hidden. There was, in all probability, no man but himself in the world who knew anything of the letter. If it was a paper of no importance to anybody, of course Mr. Belcher had forgotten it. If it was of great importance to Mr. Benedict, Mr. Belcher believed that it had been destroyed.

He had great curiosity concerning its contents, and determined to deliver it into Mr. Benedict's hand; so, at the conclusion of his engagement with Mr. Belcher's agent, he announced to his friends that he had accepted Jim Fenton's invitation to visit the new hotel at Number Nine, and enjoy a week of sport in the woods.

Before he returned, he became entirely familiar with the contents of the letter, and, if he brought it back with him on his return to Sevenoaks, it was for deposit in the post-office, directed to James Balfour in the handwriting of Paul Benedict.

The contents of this note were of such importance in the establishment of justice, that Yates, still doubtful of the propriety of his act, was able to justify it to his conscience. Under the circumstances, it belonged to the man to whom it was addressed, and not to Mr. Belcher at all. His own act might be doubtful, but it was in the interest of fair dealing, and in opposition to the schemes of a consummate rascal, to whom he owed neither respect nor good-will. He would stand by it, and take the consequences of it.

Were Mrs. Dillingham and Sam Yates justifiable in their treachery to Mr. Belcher? A nice question this, in casuistry! Certainly they had done as they would have been done by, had he been in their circumstances and they in his. He, at least, who had tried to debauch both of them, could reasonably find no fault with them. Their act was the natural result of his own influence. It was fruit from seeds of his own sowing. Had he ever approached them with a single noble and unselfish motive, neither of them could have betrayed him.

CHAPTER XXV.

IN WHICH THE GENERAL GOES THROUGH A GREAT MANY TRIALS, AND MEETS AT LAST THE ONE HE HAS SO LONG ANTICIPATED.

THE fact that the General had deposited the proceeds of his foreign sales of arms with a European banking house, ostensibly subject to draft for the materials of his manufactures, has already been alluded to. This deposit had been augmented by subsequent sales, until it amounted to an imposing sum, which Mrs. Dillingham ascertained, from the little account-book, to be drawing a low rate of interest. With the proprietor, this heavy foreign deposit was partly a measure of personal safety, and partly a measure of projected iniquity. He had the instinct to provide against any possible contingencies of fortune or crime.

Two or three days after his very agreeable call upon Mrs. Dillingham, he had so far mastered his difficulties connected with the International Mail that he could find time for another visit, to which he had looked forward with eager anticipation.

"I was very much interested in your little book, Mr. Belcher," said the lady, boldly.

"The General is one of the ablest of our native authors, eh?" responded that facetious person, with a jolly laugh.

"Decidedly," said Mrs. Dillingham, "and so very terse and statistical."

"Interesting book, wasn't it?"

"Very! And it was so kind of you, General, to let me see how you men manage such things!"

"We men!" and the General shrugged his shoulders.

"One man, then," said the lady, on seeing that he

was disposed to claim a monopoly in the wisdom of business.

"Do you remember one little item—a modest little item—concerning my foreign deposits? Eh?"

"Little item, General! What are you doing with so much money over there?"

"Nothing, or next to nothing. That's my anchor to windward."

"It will hold," responded the lady, "if weight is all that's needed."

"I intend that it shall hold, and that it shall be larger before it is smaller."

"I don't understand it;" and Mrs. Dillingham shook her pretty head.

Mr. Belcher sat and thought. There was a curious flush upon his face, as he raised his eyes to hers, and looked intensely into them, in the endeavor to read the love that hid behind them. He was desperately in love with her. The passion, a thousand times repelled by her, and a thousand times diverted by the distractions of his large affairs, had been raised to new life by his last meeting with her; and the determinations of his will grew strong, almost to fierceness. He did not know what to say, or how to approach the subject nearest to his heart. He had always frightened her so easily; she had been so quick to resent any approach to undue familiarity; she had so steadily ignored his insinuations, that he was disarmed.

"What are you thinking about, General?"

"You've never seen me in one of my trances, have you?" inquired Mr. Belcher, with trembling lips and a forced laugh.

"No! Do you have trances?"

"Trances? Yes; and visions of the most stunning character. Talbot has seen me in two or three of them."

"Are they dangerous?"

"Not at all. The General's visions are always of a celestial character—warranted not to injure the most delicate constitution! I feel one of them coming on now. Don't disturb me."

"Shall I fan you?"

"Do, please!"

The General closed his eyes. He had never before betrayed such excitement in her presence, and had never before appeared so dangerous. While she determined that this should be her last exposure to his approaches, she maintained her brave and unsuspecting demeanor, and playfully waved her fan toward him.

"I behold," said the General, "a business man of great ability and great wealth, who discovers too late that his wife is unequally yoked with an unbeliever. Love abides not in his home, and his heart is afloat on the fierce, rolling sea. He leaves his abode in the country, and seeks in the tumultuous life of the metropolis to drown his disappointments. He there discovers a beautiful woman, cast in Nature's finest mould, and finds himself, for the first time, matched. Gently this heavenly creature repels him, though her heart yearns toward him with unmistakable tenderness. She is a prudent woman. She has a position to maintain. She is alone. She is a friend to the wife of this unfortunate gentleman. She is hindered in many ways from giving rein to the impulses of her heart. This man of wealth deposits a magnificent sum in Europe. This lady goes thither for health and amusement, and draws upon this sum at will. She travels from capital to capital, or hides herself in Alpine villages, but is found at last by him who has laid his wealth at her feet."

The General revealed his vision with occasional glances through half-closed eyes at the face that hung bowed before him. It was a desperate step, but he had determined to take it when he entered the house. Humiliated, tormented, angry, Mrs. Dillingham sat before him, covering from his sight as well as she could the passion that raged within her. She knew that she had invited the insult. She was conscious that her treatment of him, from the first, though she had endeavored to change her relations with him without breaking his friendship, had nursed his base passion and his guilty purpose. She was undergoing a just punishment, and acknowledged to herself the fact. Once she would have delighted in tormenting him. Once she would not have hesitated to drive him from her door. Once—but she was changed. A little boy who had learned to regard her as a mother, was thinking of her in the distant woods. She had fastened to that childish life the hungry instincts of her motherly nature. She had turned away forever from all that could dishonor the lad, or hinder her from receiving his affection without an upbraiding conscience.

Mr. Belcher's instincts were quick enough to see that his vision had not prospered in the mind to which he had revealed it; and yet, there was a hesitation in the manner of the woman before him which he could not explain to himself, if he admitted that his proposition had been wholly offensive. Mrs. Dillingham's only wish was to get him out of the house. If she could accomplish this without further humiliation, it was all she desired.

"General," she said, at last, "you must have been drinking. I do not think you know what you have said to me."

"On the contrary, I am perfectly sober," said he, rising and approaching her.

"You must not come near me. Give me time! give me time!" she exclaimed, rising and retreating.

Mr. Belcher was startled by the alarmed and angry

look in her eyes. "Time!" he said, fiercely; "Eternity, you mean."

"You pretend to care for me, and yet you disobey what you know to be my wish. Prove your friendship by leaving me. I wish to be alone."

"Leave you, with not so much as the touch of your hand?" he said.

"Yes."

The General turned on his heel, took up his hat, paused at the door as if hesitating what to do; then, without a word, he went downstairs and into the street, overwhelmed with self-pity. He had done so much, risked so much, and accomplished so little! That she was fond of him there was no question in his own mind; but women were so different from men! Yet the villain knew that if she had been easily won his heart would have turned against her. The prize grew more precious through the obstacles that came between him and its winning. The worst was over, at least; she knew his project; and it would all come right in time!

As soon as he was out of the house, Mrs. Dillingham burst into a fit of uncontrollable weeping. She had passed through the great humiliation of her life. The tree which she had planted and nursed through many years of unworthy aims had borne its natural fruit. She groaned under the crushing punishment. She almost cursed herself. Her womanly instincts were quick to apprehend the fact that only by her own consent or invitation, could any man reach a point so near to any woman that he could coolly breathe in her ear a base proposition. Yet, with all her self-loathing and self-condemnation, was mingled a hatred of the vile man who had insulted her, which would have killed him had it been possible for him to know and realize it.

After her first passion had passed away, the question concerning her future came up for settlement. She could not possibly remain near Mr. Belcher. She must not be exposed to further visits from him. The thought that in the little account-book which she had copied there was a record that covered a design for her own destruction. stung her to the quick. What should she do? She would consult Mr. Balfour.

She knew that on that evening Mr. Belcher would not be at home, that after the excitements and disappointments of that day he would seek for solace in any place but that which held his wife and children. So, muffled in a slight disguise, and followed by her servant, she stole out of her house during the evening, and sought the house of the lawyer. To him she poured out her heart. To him she revealed all that had passed between her and the proprietor, and to him she committed the care of the precious document of which she had possessed herself, and the little note that accompanied it.

Mr. Balfour advised her to leave the city at once, and to go to some place where Mr. Belcher would not be able to find her. He knew of no place so fit for her in every respect as Number Nine, with his own family and those most dear to her. Her boy and his father were there; it was health's own home; and she could remain away as long as it might be necessary. She would be wanted as a witness in a few months, at furthest, in a suit which he believed would leave her persecutor in a position where, forgetting others, he would be absorbed in the effort to take care of himself.

Her determination was taken at once. Mr. Balfour accompanied her home, and gave her all the necessary directions for her journey; and that night she packed a single trunk in readiness for it. In the morning, leaving her house to the care of trusty servants, she rode to the station, while Mr. Belcher was lolling feverishly in his bed, and in an hour was flying northward toward the place that was to be her summer home, and into a region that was destined to be associated with her future life, through changes and revolutions of which she did not dream.

After her thirty-six hours of patient and fatiguing travel, the company at Jim Fenton's hotel, eager for letters from the city, stood on the bank of the river, waiting the arrival of the guide who had gone down for the mail, and such passengers as he might find in waiting. They saw, as he came in sight, a single lady in the stern of the little boat, deeply veiled, whose name they could not guess. When she debarked among them, and looked around upon the waiting and curious group, Harry was the first to detect her, and she smothered him with kisses. Mr. Benedict stood pale and trembling. Harry impulsively led her toward him, and in a moment they were wrapped in a tender embrace. None but Mrs. Balfour, of all who were present, understood the relation that existed between the two, thus strangely reunited; but it soon became known, and the little romance added a new charm to the life in the woods.

It would be pleasant to dwell upon the happy days and the pleasant doings of the summer that followed—the long twilights that Mr. Benedict and Mrs. Dillingham spent upon the water, their review of the events of the past, the humble confessions of the proud lady, the sports and diversions of the wilderness, and the delights of society brought by circumstances into the closest sympathy. It would be pleasant to remain with Jim and "the little woman," in their new enterprise and their new house-keeping; but we must return to the city, to follow the fortunes of one who, if less interesting than those we leave behind, is more important in the present stage and ultimate resolution of our little drama.

Soon after Mrs. Dillingham's departure from the city, Mr. Belcher missed her. Not content with the position in which he had left his affairs with her, he called at her house three days after her disappearance, and learned that the servants either did not know or would not tell whither she had gone. In his blind self-conceit, he could not suppose that she had run away from him. He could not conclude that she had gone to Europe, without a word of her purpose breathed to him. Still, even that was possible. She had hidden somewhere, and he should hear from her. Had he frightened her? Had he been too precipitate? Much as he endeavored to explain her sudden disappearance to his own advantage, he was left unsatisfied and uneasy.

A few days passed away, and then he began to doubt. Thrown back upon himself, deprived of the solace of her society, and released from a certain degree of restraint that she had always exercised upon him, he indulged more freely in drink, and entered with more recklessness upon the excitements of speculation.

The General had become conscious that he was not quite the man that he had been. His mind was darkened and dulled by crime. He was haunted by vague fears and apprehensions. With his frequent and appalling losses of money, he had lost a measure of his faith in himself. His coolness of calculation had been diminished; he listened with readier credulity to rumors, and yielded more easily to the personal influences around him. Even the steady prosperity which attended his regular business became a factor in his growing incapacity for the affairs of the street. His reliance on his permanent sources of income made him more reckless in his speculations.

His grand schemes for "gently" and "tenderly" unloading his Crooked Valley stock upon the hands of his trusting dupes along the line, worked, however, to perfection. It only required rascality, pure and simple, under the existing conditions, to accomplish this scheme, and he found in the results nothing left to be desired

They furnished him with a capital of ready money, but his old acquaintances discovered the foul trick he had played, and gave him a wide berth. No more gigantic combinations were possible to him, save with swindlers like himself, who would not hesitate to sacrifice him as readily and as mercilessly as he had sacrificed his rural victims.

Mrs. Dillingham had been absent a month when he one day received a polite note from Mr. Balfour, as Paul Benedict's attorney, requesting him, on behalf of his principal, to pay over to him an equitable share of the profits upon his patented inventions, and to enter into a definite contract for the further use of them.

The request came in so different a form from what he had anticipated, and was so tamely courteous, that he laughed over the note in derision. "Milk for babes!" he exclaimed, and laughed again. Either Balfour was a coward, or he felt that his case was a weak one. Did he think the General was a fool?

Without taking the note to Cavendish, who had told him to bring ten thousand dollars when he came again, and without consulting anybody, he wrote the following note in answer:

"TO JAMES BALFOUR, ESQ.:

"Your letter of this date received, and contents noted. Permit me to say in reply:

"1st. That I have no evidence that you are Paul Benedict's attorney.

"2d. That I have no evidence that Paul Benedict is living, and that I do not propose to negotiate in any way, on any business, with a fraud, or a man of straw.

"3d. That I am the legal assignee of all the patents originally issued to Paul Benedict, which I have used and am now using. I hold his assignment in the desk on which I write this letter, and it stands duly recorded in Washington, though, from my ignorance of the law, it has only recently been placed upon the books in the Patent Office.

"Permit me to say, in closing, that, as I bear you no malice, I will show you the assignment at your pleasure, and thus relieve you from the danger of entering upon a conspiracy to defraud me of rights which I propose, with all the means at my disposal, to defend.

"Yours, ROBERT BELCHER."

Mr. Belcher read over this letter with great satisfaction. It seemed to him very dignified and very wise. He had saved his ten thousand dollars for a while, at least, and bluffed, as he sincerely believed, his dreaded antagonist.

Mr. Balfour did more than to indulge in his professional smile, over the frank showing of the General's hand, and the voluntary betrayal of his line of defence. He filed away the note among the papers relating to the case, took his hat, walked across the street, rang the bell, and sent up his card to Mr. Belcher. That self-complacent gentleman had not expected this visit, although he had suggested it. Instead, therefore, of inviting Mr. Balfour to his library, he went down to the drawing-room, where he found his visitor, quietly sitting with his hat in his hand. The most formal of courtesies opened the conversation, and Mr. Balfour stated his business at once. "You were kind enough to offer to show me the assignment of Mr. Benedict's patents," he said. "I have called to see it."

"I've changed my mind," said the General.

"Do you suspect me of wishing to steal it?" inquired Mr. Balfour.

"No, but the fact is, I wrote my note to you without consulting my lawyer."

"I thought so," said Mr. Balfour. "Good-day, sir."

"No offence, I hope," said Mr. Belcher, with a peculiar toss of the head, and a laugh.

"Not the least," said the lawyer, passing out of the door.

The General felt that he had made a mistake He was in the habit of making mistakes in those days. The habit was growing upon him. Indeed, he suspected that he had made a mistake in not boldly exhibiting his assignment. How to manage a lie, and not be managed by it, was a question that had puzzled wiser heads than that of the General. He found an egg in his possession that he was not ready to eat, though it was too hot to be held long in either hand, and could not be dropped without disaster.

For a week, he was haunted with the expectation of a suit, but it was not brought, and then he began to breathe easier, and to feel that something must be done to divert his mind from the subject. He drank freely, and was loud-mouthed and blustering on the street. Poor Talbot had a hard time, in endeavoring to shield him from his imprudences. He saw that his effort to make his principal "last" was not likely to be successful.

Rallied by his "friends" on his ill-luck, the General declared that he only speculated for fun. He knew what he was about. He never risked any money that he could not afford to lose. Everybody had his amusement, and this was his.

He was secure for some months in his seat as President of the Crooked Valley Railroad, and calculated, of course, on buying back his stock in his own time, at his own price. In the meantime, he would use his position for carrying on his private schemes.

The time came at last when he wanted more ready money. A grand combination had been made, among his own unprincipled set, for working up a "corner" in the Muscogee Air Line, and he had been invited into it. He was flattered by the invitation, and saw in it a chance for redeeming his position, though, at bottom, the scheme was one for working up a corner in Robert Belcher.

Under the plea that he expected, at no distant day, to go to Europe, for rest and amusement, he mortgaged his house, in order, as he declared, that he might handle it the more easily in the market. But Wall Street knew the fact at once, and made its comments. Much to the proprietor's disgust, it was deemed of sufficient importance to find mention in the daily press.

But even the sum raised upon his house, united with that which he had received from unloading his Crooked Valley stock, was not sufficient to give him the preponderance in the grand combination which he desired.

He still held a considerable sum in Crooked Valley bonds, for these were valuable. He had already used these as collaterals, in the borrowing of small sums at short time, to meet emergencies in his operations. It was known by money-lenders that he held them. Now, the General was the manufacturer of these bonds. The books of the corporation were under his control, and he intended that they should remain so. It was very easy for him to make an over-issue, and hard for him to be detected in his fraud by any one who would be dangerous to him. The temptation to make this issue was one which better men than he had yielded to in a weak moment, and, to the little conscience which he possessed, the requisite excuses were ready. He did not intend that any one should lose money by these bonds. He only proposed a temporary relief to himself. So he manufactured the bonds, and raised the money he wanted.

Meantime, the members of the very combination in which he had engaged, having learned of his rascally operation with the stock, were secretly buying it back from the dupes along the road, at their own figures, with the purpose of ousting him from the management, and taking the road to themselves. Of this movement he did not learn until it was too late to be of use to him.

It was known, in advance, by the combination, that

the working up of the corner in Muscogee Air Line would be a long operation. The stock had to be manipulated with great care, to avoid exciting a suspicion of the nature of the scheme, and the General had informed the holders of his notes that it might be necessary for him to renew them before he should realize from his operations. He had laid all his plans carefully, and looked forward with an interest which none but he and those of his kind could appreciate, to the excitements, intrigues, marches and countermarches of the mischievous campaign.

And then came down upon him the prosecution which he had so long dreaded, and for which he had made the only preparation consistent with his greedy designs. Ten thousand dollars of his ready money passed at once into the hands of Mr. Cavendish, and Mr. Cavendish was satisfied with the fee, whatever may have been his opinion of the case. After a last examination of his forged assignment, and the putting of Phipps to an exhaustive and satisfactory trial of his memory with relation to it, he passed it into the lawyer's hands, and went about his business with uncomfortable forebodings of the trial and its results.

It was strange, even to him, at this point of his career, that he felt within himself no power to change his course. No one knew better than he, that there was money enough in Benedict's inventions for both inventor and manufacturer. No one knew better than he, that there was a prosperous course for himself inside the pale of equity and law, yet he found no motive to walk there. For the steps he had taken, there seemed no retreat. He must go on, on, to the end. The doors that led back to his old life had closed behind him. Those which opened before were not inviting, but he could not stand still. So he hardened his face, braced his nerves, stiffened his determination, and went on.

Of course he passed a wretched summer. He had intended to get away for rest, or, rather, for an exhibition of himself and his equipage at Newport, or Saratoga, or Long Branch ; but through all the burning days of the season he was obliged to remain in the city, while other men were away and off their guard, to watch his Wall Street operations, and prepare for the *coup de grace* by which he hoped to regain his lost treasure and his forfeited position. The legal trial that loomed up before him, among the clouds of autumn, could not be contemplated without a shiver and a sinking of the heart. His preparations for it were very simple, as they mainly related to the establishment of the genuineness of his assignment.

The months flew away more rapidly with the proprietor than with any of the other parties interested in the suit, and when, at last, only a fortnight was wanting to the time of the expected trial, Mr. Balfour wrote to Number Nine, ordering his family home, and requiring the presence of Mr. Benedict, Mrs. Dillingham, Harry and Jim.

Just at this time, the General found himself in fresh difficulty. The corner in Muscogee Air Line was as evasive as a huckleberry in a mouth bereft of its armament. Indeed, to use still further the homely but suggestive figure, the General found that his tongue was in more danger than his huckleberry. His notes, too, secured by fraudulent collaterals, were approaching a second and third maturity. He was without ready money for the repurchase of his Crooked Valley stock, and had learned, in addition, that the stock had already changed hands, in the execution of a purpose which he more than suspected. Large purchases of material for the execution of heavy contracts in his manufactures had drained his ready resources, in the department of his regular business. He was getting short, and into a tight place. Still he was desperate, and determined to sacrifice nothing.

Mr. Benedict and Jim, on their arrival in the city, took up their residence in Mrs. Dillingham's house, and the landlord of Number Nine spent several days in making the acquaintance of the city, under the guidance of his old companion, who was at home. Jim went through a great mental convulsion. At first, what seemed to him the magnitude of the life, enterprise, and wealth of the city, depressed him. He declared that he "had be'n growin' smaller an' smaller every minute" since he left Sevenoaks. "I felt as if I'd allers be'n a fly, crawlin' 'round on the edge of a pudden," he said, when asked whether he enjoyed the city. But, before the trial came on, he had fully recovered his old equanimity. The city grew smaller the more he explored it, until, when compared with the great woods, the lonely rivers, and the broad solitudes in which he had spent his life, it seemed like a toy ; and the men who chaffered in the market, and the women who thronged the avenues, or drove in the park, or filled the places of amusement, came to look like children, engaged in frolicsome games. He felt that people who had so little room to breathe in must be small ; and before the trial brought him into practical contact with them, he was himself again, and quite ready to meet them in any encounter which required courage or address.

CHAPTER XXVI.

IN WHICH THE CASE OF "BENEDICT *vs.* BELCHER" FINDS ITSELF IN COURT, AN INTERESTING QUESTION OF IDENTITY IS SETTLED, AND A MYSTERIOUS DISAPPEARANCE TAKES PLACE.

"OYEZ! *Oyez! All-persons-having-business-to-do-with-the-Circuit-Court-of-the-United-States-for-the-Southern-District-of-New-York,-draw-near,-give-your-attention,-and-you-shall-be-heard.*"

"That's the crier," whispered Mr. Benedict to Jim.

"What's the matter of 'im?" inquired the latter.

"That's the way they open the court."

"Well, if he opens it with cryin', he'll have a tough time a shuttin' on it," responded Jim, in a whisper so loud that he attracted attention.

There within the bar sat Mr. Balfour, calmly examining his papers. He looked up among the assembled jurors, witnesses, and idlers, and beckoned Benedict to his side. There sat Robert Belcher with his counsel. The great rascal was flashily dressed, with a stupendous show of shirt-front, over which fell, down by the side of the diamond studs, a heavy gold chain. Brutality, vulgarity, self-assurance and an overbearing will, all expressed themselves in his broad face, bold eyes and heavy chin. Mr. Cavendish, with his uneasy scalp, white hands, his scornful lips and his thin, twitching nostrils, looked the very impersonation of impatience and contempt. If the whole court-room had been thronged with vermin instead of human beings, among which he was obliged to sit, he could not have appeared more disgusted. Quite retired among the audience, and deeply veiled, sat Mrs. Dillingham. Mr. Belcher detected her, and, though he could not see her face, felt that he could not be mistaken as to her identity. Why was she there? Why, but to notice the progress and issue of the trial, in her anxiety for him? He was not glad to see her there.

He beckoned for Phipps, who sat uneasily, with a scared look upon his face, among the crowd.

"Is that Mrs. Dillingham?" he asked in a whisper.

Phipps assured him that it was. Then Mr. Belcher wrote upon his card the words: "Do not, for my sake, remain in this room."

"Give this to her," he said to his servant.

The card was delivered, but the lady, quite to his surprise, did not stir. He thought of his little book, but it seemed impossible that his idol, who had so long been hidden from his sight and his knowledge, could betray him.

A jury was empanelled, the case of Benedict *vs.* Belcher was called, and the counsel of both parties declared themselves ready for the trial.

The suit was for damages, in the sum of half a million dollars, for the infringement of patents on machines, implements, and processes, of which it was declared that the plaintiff was the first and only inventor. The answer to the complaint alleged the disappearance and death of Benedict, and declared the plaintiff to be an impostor, averred the assignment of all the patents in question to the defendant, and denied the profits.

The judge, set somewhat deep in his shirt-collar, as if his head and his heart were near enough together to hold easy communication, watched the formal proceedings listlessly, out of a pair of pleasant eyes, and when they were completed, nodded to Mr. Balfour, in indication that he was ready to proceed.

Mr. Balfour, gathering his papers before him, rose to make the opening for the prosecution.

"May it please the Court," he said, "and gentlemen

of the jury, I have to present to you a case, either issue of which it is not pleasant for me to contemplate. Either my client or the defendant will go out of this court, at the conclusion of this case, a blackened man ; and as I have a warm friendship for one of them, and bear no malice to the other, I am free to confess that, while I seek for justice, I shrink from the results of its vindication."

Mr. Cavendish jumped up and interjected spitefully: "I beg the gentleman to spare us his hypothetical sentiment. It is superfluous, so far as my client is concerned, and offensive."

Mr. Balfour waited calmly for the little explosion and the clearing away of the smoke, and then resumed. "I take no pleasure in making myself offensive to the defendant and his counsel," said he, "but, if I am interrupted, I shall be compelled to call things by their right names, and to do something more than hint at the real status of this case. I see other trials, in other courts, at the conclusion of this action—other trials with graver issues. I could not look forward to them with any pleasure, without acknowledging myself to be a knave. I could not refrain from alluding to them, without convicting myself of carelessness and frivolity. Something more than money is involved in the issue of this action. Either the plaintiff or the defendant will go out of this court wrecked in character, blasted in reputation, utterly ruined. The terms of the bill and the answer determine this result."

Mr. Cavendish sat through this exordium as if he sat on nettles, but wisely held his tongue, while the brazen-faced proprietor leaned carelessly over, and whispered to his counsel. Phipps, on his distant seat, grew white around the lips, and felt that he was on the verge of the most serious danger of his life.

"The plaintiff in this case," Mr. Balfour went on,

"brings an action for damages for the infringement of various patent-rights. I shall prove to you that these patents were issued to him, as the first and only inventor; that he has never assigned them to any one; that they have been used by the defendant for from seven to ten years, to his great profit; that he is using them still without a license, and without rendering a just consideration for them. I shall prove to you that the defendant gained his first possession of these inventions by a series of misrepresentations, false promises, oppressions and wrongs, and has used them without license in consequence of the weakness, illness, poverty and defencelessness of their rightful owner. I shall prove to you that their owner was driven to insanity by these perplexities and the persecutions of the defendant, and that even after he became insane, the defendant tried to secure the execution of the assignment which he had sought in vain during the sanity of the patentee.

"I will not characterize by the name belonging to it the instrument which is to be presented in answer to the bill filed in this case, further than to say that it has no legal status whatsoever. It is the consummate fruit of a tree that was planted in fraud; and if I do not make it so to appear, before the case is finished, I will beg pardon of the court, of you, gentlemen of the jury, and especially of the defendant and his honorable counsel. First, therefore, I offer in evidence certified copies of the patents in question."

Mr. Balfour read these documents, and they were examined both by Mr. Cavendish and the court.

The name of Paul Benedict was then called, as the first witness.

Mr. Benedict mounted the witness-stand. He was pale and quiet, with a pink tinge on either cheek. He had the bearing and dress of a gentleman, and contrasted strangely with the coarse, bold man to whom he had been indebted for so many wrongs and indignities. He was at last in the place to which he had looked forward with so much dread, but there came to him a calmness and a self-possession which he had not anticipated. He was surrounded by powerful friends. He was menaced, too, by powerful enemies, and all his manhood was roused.

"What is your name?" asked Mr. Balfour.

"Paul Benedict."

"Where were you born?"

"In the city of New York."

"Are you the inventor of the machines, implements, and processes named in the documents from the Patent Office which have just been read in your hearing?"

"I am, sir."

"And you are the only owner of all these patent-rights?"

"I am, sir."

"What is your profession?"

"I was trained for a mechanical engineer."

"What has been your principal employment?"

"Invention."

"When you left New York, whither did you go?"

"To Sevenoaks."

"How many years ago was that?"

"Eleven or twelve, I suppose."

"Now I want you to tell to the Court, in a plain, brief way, the history of your life in Sevenoaks, giving, with sufficient detail, an account of all your dealings with the defendant in this case, so that we may perfectly understand how your inventions came into Mr. Belcher's hands, and why you have never derived any benefit from them."

It was a curious illustration of the inventor's nature that, at this moment, with his enemy and tormentor before him, he shrank from giving pain. Mr. Cavendish noticed his hesitation, and was on his feet in an instant. "May it please the Court," said he, "there is a question concerning identity that comes up at this point, and I beg the privilege of asking it here."

The judge looked at Mr. Balfour, and the latter said: "Certainly."

"I would like to ask the witness," said Mr. Cavendish, "whether he is the Paul Benedict who left the city about the time at which he testifies that he went away, in consequence of his connection with a band of counterfeiters. Did you, sir, invent their machinery, or did you not?"

"I did not," answered the witness—his face all aflame. The idea that he could be suspected, or covertly charged, with crime, in the presence of friends and strangers, was so terrible that the man tottered on his feet.

Mr. Cavendish gave a significant glance at his client, whose face bloomed with a brutal smile, and then sat down.

"Is that all?" inquired Mr. Balfour.

"All, for the present," responded Mr. Cavendish, sneeringly, and with mock courtesy.

"May it please the Court," said Mr. Balfour, "I hope I may be permitted to say that the tactics of the defendant are worthy of his cause." Then turning to Mr. Benedict, he said, "I trust the witness will not be disturbed by the insult that has been gratuitously offered him, and will tell the history which I have asked him to tell."

Mr. Cavendish had made a mistake. At this insult, and the gratification which it afforded Mr. Belcher, the inventor's pity died out of him, and he hardened to his work.

"When I went to Sevenoaks," said he, "I was very poor, as I have always been since. I visited Mr. Belcher's mill, and saw how great improvements could be made in his machines and processes; and then I visited him, and told him what I could do for him. He furnished me with money for my work, and for securing the patents on my inventions, with the verbal promise that I should share in such profits as might accrue from their use. He was the only man who had money; he was the only man who could use the inventions; and he kept me at work, until he had secured everything that he wished for. In the meantime, I suffered for the lack of the necessaries of life, and was fed from day to day, and month to month, and year to year, on promises. He never rendered me any returns, declared that the patents were nearly useless to him, and demanded, as a consideration for the money he had advanced to me, the assignment of all my patents to him. My only child was born in the midst of my early trouble, and such were the privations to which my wife was subjected that she never saw a day of health after the event. She died at last, and in the midst of my deepest troubles Mr. Belcher pursued me with his demands for the assignment of my patents. He still held me to him by the bestowal of small sums, which necessity compelled me to accept. He always had a remarkable power over me, and I felt that he would lead me to destruction. I saw the hopes of years melting away, and knew that in time he would beat down my will, and, on his own terms, possess himself of all the results of my years of study and labor. I saw nothing but starvation before me and my child, and went down into a horror of great darkness."

A cold shiver ran over the witness, and his face grew pale and pinched, at this passage of his story. The court-house was as still as midnight. Even the General lost his smile, and leaned forward, as if the narration concerned some monster other than himself.

"What then?" inquired Mr. Balfour.

"I hardly know. Everything that I remember after

that was confused and terrible. For years I was insane I went to the hospital, and was there supported by Mr. Belcher. He even followed me there, and endeavored to get my signature to an assignment, but was positively forbidden by the superintendent of the asylum. Then, after being pronounced incurable, I was sent back to the Sevenoaks almshouse, where, for a considerable time, my boy was also kept; and from that horrible place, by the aid of a friend, I escaped. I remember it all as a long dream of torture. My cure came in the woods, at Number Nine, where I have ever since lived, and where twice I have been sought and found by paid emissaries of Mr. Belcher, who did not love him well enough to betray me. And, thanks to the ministry of the best friends that God ever raised up to a man, I am here to-day to claim my rights."

"These rights," said Mr. Balfour, "these rights which you hold in your patented inventions, for all these years used by the defendant, you say you have never assigned."

"Never."

"If an assignment executed in due form should be presented to you, what should you say?"

"I object to the question," said Mr. Cavendish, leaping to his feet. "The document has not yet been presented to him."

"The gentleman is right," said Mr. Balfour; "the witness has never seen it. I withdraw the question; and now tell me what you know about Mr. Belcher's profits on the use of these inventions."

"I cannot tell much," replied Mr. Benedict. "I know the inventions were largely profitable to him; otherwise he would not have been so anxious to own them. I have never had access to his books, but I know he became rapidly rich on his manufactures, and that, by the cheapness with which he produced them, he was able to hold the market, and to force his competitors into bankruptcy."

"May it please the Court," said Mr. Balfour, "I am about done with this witness, and I wish to say, just here, that if the defendant stands by his pleadings, and denies his profits, I shall demand the production of his books in court. We can get definite information from them, at least." Then bowing to Mr. Benedict, he told him that he had no further questions to ask.

The witness was about to step down, when the judge turned to Mr. Cavendish, with the question: "Does the counsel for the defendant wish to cross-examine the witness?"

"May it please the Court," said Mr. Cavendish, rising, "the counsel for the defence regards the examination so far simply as a farce. We do not admit that the witness is Paul Benedict, at all—or, rather, the Paul Benedict named in the patents, certified copies of which are in evidence. The Paul Benedict therein named has long been regarded as dead. This man has come and gone for months in Sevenoaks, among the neighbors of the real Paul Benedict, unrecognized. He says he has lived for years within forty miles of Sevenoaks, and at this late day puts forward his claims. There is nobody in court, sir. We believe the plaintiff to be a fraud, and this prosecution a put-up job. In saying this, I would by no means impugn the honor of the plaintiff's counsel. Wiser men than he have been deceived and duped, and he may be assured that he is the victim of the villanies or the hallucinations of an impostor. There are men in this room, ready to testify in this case, who knew Paul Benedict during all his residence in Sevenoaks; and the witness stands before them at this moment unrecognized and unknown. I cannot cross-examine the witness without recognizing his identity with the Paul Benedict named in the patents. There is nothing but a pretender in court, may it please your honor, and I decline to have anything to do with him."

Mr. Cavendish sat down, with the air of a man who believed he had blasted the case in the bud, and that there was nothing left to do but to adjourn.

"It seems to the Court, gentlemen," said the judge in a quiet tone, "that this question of identity should be settled as an essential preliminary to further proceedings."

"May it please your honor," said Mr. Balfour, rising, "I did not suppose it possible, after the plaintiff had actually appeared in court, and shown himself to the defendant, that this question of identity would be mooted or mentioned. The defendant must know that I have witnesses here—that I would not appear here without competent witnesses—who will place his identity beyond question. It seems, however, that this case is to be fought inch by inch, on every possible ground. As the first witness upon this point, I shall call for James Fenton."

"Jest call me Jim," said the individual named, from his distant seat.

"James Fenton" was called to the stand, and Mr. Benedict stepped down. Jim advanced through the crowd, his hair standing very straight in the air, and his face illumined by a smile that won every heart in the house, except those of the defendant and his counsel. A war-horse going into battle, or a hungry man going to his dinner, could not have manifested more rampant alacrity.

"Hold up your right hand," said the clerk.

"Sartin," said Jim. "Both on 'em if ye say so."

"You solemnly swear m-m-m-m-m-m-m-m- so help you God!"

"I raally wish, if ye ain't too tired, that ye'd say that over ag'in," said Jim. "If I'm a-goin' to make a Happy David, I want to know what it is."

The clerk hesitated, and the judge directed him to repeat the form of the oath distinctly. When this was done, Jim said : " Thank ye ; there's nothin' like startin' squar."

" James Fenton," said Mr. Balfour, beginning a question.

" Jest call me Jim : I ain't no prouder here nor I be at Number Nine," said the witness.

" Very well, Jim," said Mr. Balfour, smiling, " tell us who you are."

" I'm Jim Fenton, as keeps a hotel at Number Nine. My father was an Englishman, my mother was a Scotchman, I was born in Ireland, an' raised in Canady, an' I've lived in Number Nine for more nor twelve year, huntin', trappin' an' keepin' a hotel. I hain't never be'n eddicated, but I can tell the truth when it's necessary, an' I love my friends and hate my enemies."

" May it please the Court," said Mr. Cavendish with a sneer, " I beg to suggest to the plaintiff's counsel that the witness should be required to give his religious views."

Mr. Belcher laughed, and Mr. Cavendish sniffed his lips, as if they had said a good thing.

" Certainly," responded Mr. Balfour. " What are your religious views, Jim ? "

" Well," said Jim, " I hain't got many, but I sh'd be s'prised if there wasn't a brimstone mine on t'other side, with a couple o' picks in it for old Belcher an' the man as helps 'im."

The laugh was on Mr. Cavendish. The Court smiled, the audience roared, and order was demanded.

" That will do," said Mr. Cavendish. " The religious views of the witness are definite and satisfactory."

" Jim, do you know Paul Benedict ? " inquired Mr. Balfour.

" Well, I do," said Jim. " I've knowed 'im ever sence he come to Sevenoaks."

"How did you make his acquaintance?"

"He used to come into the woods, fishin' an' huntin'. Him an' me was like brothers. He was the curisest cree-tur I ever seen, an' I hope he takes no 'fence in hearin' me say so. Ye've seen his tackle, Mr. Balfour, an' that split bamboo o' his, but the jedge hasn't seen it. I wish I'd brung it along. Fond of fishin', sir?" And Jim turned blandly and patronizingly to the Court.

The Judge could not repress a little ripple of amuse-ment, which, from a benevolent mouth, ran out over his face. Biting his lips, he said: "The witness had bet-ter be confined to the matter in hand."

"An' Jedge—no 'fence—but I like yer looks, an' if ye'll come to Number Nine—it's a little late now—I'll—"

Mr. Cavendish jumped up and said fiercely: "I ob-ject to this trifling."

"Jim," said Mr. Balfour, "the defendant's counsel objects to your trifling. He has a right to do so, par-ticularly as he is responsible for starting it. Now, tell me whether the Paul Benedict you knew was the only man of the name who has lived in Sevenoaks since you have lived in Number Nine?"

"He was the only one I ever hearn on. He was the one as invented Belcher's machines, anyway. He's talked about 'em with me a thousand times."

"Is he in the room?"

"Mostly," said Jim, with his bland smile.

"Give me a direct answer, now."

"Yis, he's in this room, and he's a settin' there by you, an' he's been a stannin' where I stan' now."

"How do you know that this is the same man who used to visit you in the woods, and who invented Mr. Belcher's machines?"

"Well, it's a long story. I don't mind tellin' on it, if it wouldn't be too triflin'," with a comical wink at Mr Cavendish.

"Go on and tell it," said Mr. Balfour.

"I knowed Benedict up to the time when he lost his mind, an' was packed off to the 'Sylum, an' I never seen 'im ag'in till I seen 'im in the Sevenoaks poor-house. I come acrost his little boy one night on the hill, when I was a-trampin' home. He hadn't nothin' on but rags, an' he was as blue an' hungry as a spring bar. The little feller teched me, ye know—teched my feelins—an' I jest sot down to comfort 'im. He telled me his ma was dead, and that his pa was at old Buffum's, as crazy as a loon. Well, I stayed to old Buffum's that night, an' went into the poor-house in the mornin', with the doctor. I seen Benedict thar, an' knowed him. He was a lyin' on the straw, an' he hadn't clothes enough on 'im to put in tea. An', says I, 'Mr. Benedict, give us your benediction;' an', says he, 'Jim!' That floored me, an' I jest cried and swar'd to myself. Well, I made a little 'rangement with him an' his boy, to take 'im to Abram's bosom. Ye see he thought he was in hell, an' it was a reasomble thing in 'im too; an' I telled 'im that I'd got a settlement in Abram's bosom, an' I axed 'im over to spend the day. I took 'im out of the poor-house an' carried 'im to Number Nine, an' I cured 'im. He's lived there ever sence, helped me build my hotel, an' I come down with 'im, to 'tend this court, an' we brung his little boy along too, an' the little feller is here, an' knows him better nor I do."

"And you declare, under oath, that the Paul Benedict whom you knew in Sevenoaks, and at Number Nine—before his insanity—the Paul Benedict who was in the poor-house at Sevenoaks and notoriously escaped from that institution—escaped by your help, has lived with you ever since, and has appeared here in court this morning," said Mr. Balfour.

"He's the same feller, an' no mistake, if so be he hain't slipped his skin," said Jim, "an' no triflin'. I make my Happy David on't."

"Did Mr. Belcher ever send into the woods to find him?"

"Yis," said Jim, laughing, "but I choked 'em off."

"How did you choke them off?"

"I telled 'em both I'd lick 'em if they ever blowed. They didn't want to blow any, to speak on, but Mike Conlin come in with a hundred dollars of Belcher's money in his jacket, an' helped me nuss my man for a week; an' I got a Happy David out o' Sam Yates, an' ther's the dockyment;" and Jim drew from his pocket the instrument with which the reader is already familiar.

Mr. Balfour had seen the paper, and told Jim that it was not necessary in the case. Mr. Belcher looked very red in the face, and leaned over and whispered to his lawyer.

"That is all," said Mr. Balfour.

Mr. Cavendish rose. "You helped Mr. Benedict to escape, did you, Jim?"

"I said so," replied Jim.

"Did you steal the key when you were there first?"

"No; I borrowed it, an' brung it back an' left it in the door."

"Did you undo the fastenings of the outside door?"

"Yis, an' I did 'em up ag'in."

"Did you break down the grated door?"

"I remember about somethin' squeakin' an' givin' 'way," replied Jim, with a smile. "It was purty dark, an' I couldn't see 'xactly what was a-goin' on."

"Oh, you couldn't! We have your confession, then, that you are a thief and a burglar, and that you couldn't see the man you took out."

"Well, now, Squar, that won't help ye any. Benedict is the man as got away, an' I saved the town the board of two paupers an' the cost of two pine coffins, an' sent old Buffum where he belonged, an' nobody cried but his pertickler friend as sets next to ye."

"I beg the Court's protection for my client, against the insults of this witness," said Mr. Cavendish.

"When a man calls Jim Fenton a thief an' a buggler, he must take what comes on't," said Jim. "Ye may thank yer everlastin' stars that ye didn't say that to me in the street, for I should 'a licked ye. I should 'a fastened that slippery old scalp o' yourn tighter nor a drum-head."

"Witness," said the judge, peremptorily, "you forget where you are, sir. You must stop these remarks."

"Jedge, look 'ere! When a man is insulted by a lawyer in court, what can he do? I'm a reasomble man, but I can't take anybody's sarse. It does seem to me as if a lawyer as snubs a witness and calls 'im names, wants dressin' down too. Give Jim Fenton a fair shake, an' he's all right."

Jim's genial nature and his irrepressible tongue were too much for the Court and the lawyers together. Mr. Cavendish writhed in his seat. He could do nothing with Jim. He could neither scare nor control him, and saw that the witness was only anxious for another encounter. It was too evident that the sympathy of the jury and the increasing throng of spectators was with the witness, and that they took delight in the discomfiture of the defendant's counsel.

"May it please the Court," said Mr. Cavendish, "after the disgraceful confessions of the witness, and the revelation of his criminal character, it will not comport with my own self-respect to question him further."

"Paddlin' off, eh?" said Jim, with a comical smile.

"Witness," said the judge, "be silent and step down."

"No 'fence, Jedge, I hope?"

"Step down, sir."

Jim saw that matters were growing serious. He liked the judge, and had intended, in some private way, to explain the condition of his hair as attributable to his fright on being called into court as a witness, but he was obliged to relinquish his plan, and go back to his seat. The expression of his face must have been most agreeable to the spectators, for there was a universal giggle among them which called out the reproof of the Court.

"Helen Dillingham" was next called for. At the pronunciation of her name, and her quiet progress through the court-room to the stand, there was a hush in which nothing was heard but the rustle of her own drapery. Mr. Belcher gasped, and grew pale. Here was the woman whom he madly loved. Here was the woman whom he had associated with his scheme of European life, and around whom, more and more, as his difficulties increased and the possibilities of disaster presented themselves, he had grouped his hopes and gathered his plans. Had he been the dupe of her cunning? Was he to be the object of her revenge? Was he to be betrayed? Her intimacy with Harry Benedict began to take on new significance. Her systematic repulses of his blind passion had an explanation other than that which he had given them. Mr. Belcher thought rapidly while the formalities which preceded her testimony were in progress.

Every man in the court-room leaned eagerly forward to catch her first word. Her fine figure, graceful carriage and rich dress had made their usual impression.

"Mrs. Dillingham," said the judge, with a courteous bow and gesture, "will you have the kindness to remove your veil?"

The veil was quietly raised over her hat, and she stood revealed. She was not pale; she was fresh from the woods, and in the glory of renewed health. A murmur of admiration went around the room like the stirring of leaves before a vagrant breeze.

"Mrs. Dillingham," said Mr. Balfour, "where do you reside?"

"In this city, sir."

"Have you always lived here?"

"Always."

"Do you know Paul Benedict?"

"I do, sir."

"How long have you known him?"

"From the time I was born until he left New York, after his marriage."

"What is his relation to you?"

"He is my brother, sir."

Up to this answer, she had spoken quietly, and in a voice that could only be heard through the room by the closest attention; but the last answer was given in a full, emphatic tone.

Mr. Belcher entirely lost his self-possession. His face grew white, his eyes were wild, and raising his clenched fist, he brought it down with a powerful blow upon the table before him, and exclaimed: "My God!"

The court-room became in an instant as silent as death. The judge uttered no reprimand, but looked inquiringly, and with unfeigned astonishment, at the defendant.

Mr. Cavendish rose and begged the Court to overlook his client's excitement, as he had evidently been taken off his guard.

"Paul Benedict is your brother, you say?" resumed Mr. Balfour.

"He is, sir."

"What was his employment before he left New York?"

"He was an inventor from his childhood, and received a careful education in accordance with his mechanical genius."

"Why did he leave New York?"

"I am ashamed to say that he left in consequence of my own unkindness."

"What was the occasion of your unkindness."

"His marriage with one whom I did not regard as his own social equal or mine."

"What was her name?"

"Jane Kendrick."

"How did you learn that he was alive?"

"Through his son, whom I invited into my house, after he was brought to this city by yourself."

"Have you recently visited the cemetery at Sevenoaks?"

"I have, sir."

"Did you see the grave of your sister-in-law?"

"I did."

"Was there a headstone upon the grave?"

"There was a humble one."

"What inscription did it bear?"

"Jane Kendrick, wife of Paul Benedict."

"When and where did you see your brother first, after your separation?"

"Early last summer, at a place called Number Nine."

"Did you recognize him?"

"I did, at once."

"Has anything occurred, in the intercourse of the summer, to make you suspect that the man whom you recognized as your brother was an impostor?"

"Nothing. We have conversed with perfect familiarity on a thousand events and circumstances of our early life. I know him to be my brother as well as I know my own name, and my own identity."

"That is all," said Mr. Balfour.

"Mrs. Dillingham," said Mr. Cavendish, after holding a long whispered conversation with his client, "you were glad to find your brother at last, were you not?"

"Very glad, sir."

"Why?"

"Because I was sorry for the misery which I had inflicted upon him, and to which I had exposed him."

"You were the victim of remorse, as I understand you?"

"Yes, sir; I suppose so."

"Were you conscious that your condition of mind unfitted you to discriminate? Were you not so anxious to find your brother, in order to quiet your conscience, that you were easily imposed upon?"

"No, sir, to both questions."

"Well, madam, such things have happened. Have you been in the habit of receiving Mr. Belcher at your house?"

"I have."

"You have been in the habit of receiving gentlemen rather indiscriminately at your house, haven't you?"

"I object to the question," said Mr. Balfour quickly. "It carries a covert insult to the witness."

Mrs. Dillingham bowed to Mr. Balfour in acknowledgment of his courtesy, but answered the question. "I have received you, sir, and Mr. Belcher. I may have been indiscriminate in my courtesies. A lady living alone cannot always tell."

A titter ran around the court-room, in which Mr. Belcher joined. His admiration was too much at the moment for his self-interest.

"Did you know, before you went to Number Nine, that your brother was there?" inquired Mr. Cavendish.

"I did, and the last time but one at which Mr. Belcher called upon me I informed him of the fact."

"That your brother was there?"

"No, that Paul Benedict was there."

"How did you know he was there?"

"His little boy wrote me from there, and told me so."

Mr. Cavendish had found more than he sought. He

wanted to harass the witness, but he had been withheld by his client. Baffled on one hand and restrained on the other—for Mr. Belcher could not give her up, and learn to hate her in a moment—he told the witness he had no more questions to ask.

Mrs. Dillingham drew down her veil again, and walked to her seat.

Harry Benedict was next called, and after giving satisfactory answers to questions concerning his understanding of the nature of an oath, was permitted to testify.

"Harry," said Mr. Balfour, "were you ever in Mr. Belcher's house?"

"Yes, sir."

"Tell us how it happened that you were there."

"Mr. Belcher stopped me in the street, and led me up the steps, and then upstairs into his room."

"What question did he ask you?"

"He wanted to know whether my father was alive."

"Did he offer you money if you would tell?"

"Yes, sir; he offered me a great gold piece of money, and told me it was an eagle."

"Did you take it?"

"No, sir."

"Did he threaten you?"

"He tried to scare me, sir."

"Did he tell you that he should like to give your father some money?"

"Yes, sir."

"And did you tell him that your father was alive?"

"No, sir, I ran away;" and Harry could not restrain a laugh at the remembrance of the scene.

"Harry, is your father in this room?"

Harry looked at his father with a smile, and answered, "Yes, sir."

"Now, Harry, I want you to pick him out from all these people. Be sure not to make any mistake. Mr.

Belcher has been so anxious to find him, that I presume he will be very much obliged to you for the information. Go and put your hand on him."

Harry started at a run, and, dodging around the end of the bar, threw himself into his father's arms. The performance seemed so comical to the lad, that he burst into a peal of boyish laughter, and the scene had such a pretty touch of nature in it, that the spectators cheered, and were only checked by the stern reprimand of the judge, who threatened the clearing of the room if such a demonstration should again be indulged in.

"Does the counsel for the defence wish to cross-examine the witness?" inquired the judge.

"I believe not," said Mr. Cavendish, with a nod; and then Harry went to his seat, at the side of Jim Fenton, who hugged him so that he almost screamed. "Ye're a brick, little feller," Jim whispered. "That was a Happy David, an' a Goliar into the barg'in. You've knocked the Ph'listine this time higher nor a kite."

"May it please the Court," said Mr. Cavendish, "I have witnesses here who knew Paul Benedict during all his residence in Sevenoaks, and who are ready to testify that they do not know the person who presents himself here to-day, as the plaintiff in this case. I comprehend the disadvantage at which I stand, with only negative testimony at my command. I know how little value it has, when opposed to such as has been presented here; and while I am convinced that my client is wronged, I shall be compelled, in the end, to accept the identity of the plaintiff as established. If I believed the real Paul Benedict, named in the patents in question, in this case, to be alive, I should be compelled to fight this question to the end, by every means in my power, but the main question at issue, as to whom the title to these patents rests in, can be decided between my client and a man of straw, as well as between him and the real inventor. That is the first practical issue, and to save the time of the Court, I propose to proceed to its trial; and first I wish to cross-examine the plaintiff."

Mr. Benedict resumed the stand.

"Witness, you pretend to be the owner of the patents in question, in this case, and the inventor of the machines, implements, and processes which they cover, do you?" said Mr. Cavendish.

"I object to the form of the question," said Mr. Balfour. "It is an insult to the witness, and a reflection upon the gentleman's own sincerity, in accepting the identity of the plaintiff."

"Very well," said Mr. Cavendish, "since the plaintiff's counsel is so difficult to please! You are the owner of these patents, are you?"

"I am, sir."

"You have been insane, have you, sir?"

"I suppose I have been, sir. I was very ill for a long time, and have no doubt that I suffered from mental alienation."

"What is your memory of things that occurred immediately preceding your insanity?"

Mr. Benedict and his counsel saw the bearings of this question, at once, but the witness would no more have lied than he would have stolen, or committed murder. So he answered: "It is very much confused, sir."

'Oh, it is! I thought so! Then you cannot swear to the events immediately preceding your attack?"

"I am afraid I cannot, sir, at least not in their order or detail."

"No! I thought so!" said Mr. Cavendish, in his contemptuous manner, and rasping voice. "I commend your prudence. Now, witness, if a number of your neighbors should assure you that, on the day before your attack, you did a certain thing, which you do not remember to have done, how should you regard their testimony?"

"If they were credible people, and not unfriendly to me, I should be compelled to believe them."

"Why, sir! you are an admirable witness! I did not anticipate such candor. We are getting at the matter bravely. We have your confession, then, that you do not remember distinctly the events that occurred the day before your attack, and your assertion that you are ready to believe and accept the testimony of credible witnesses in regard to those events."

"Yes, sir."

"Did you ever know Nicholas Johnson and James Ramsey?"

"Yes, sir."

"Where did you see them last?"

"In Mr. Belcher's library."

"On what occasion, or, rather, at what time?"

"I have sad reason to remember both the occasion and the date, sir. Mr. Belcher had determined to get my signature to an assignment, and had brought me to his house on another pretext entirely. I suppose he had summoned these men as witnesses."

"Where are these men now?"

"Unhappily, they are both dead."

"Yes, unhappily indeed—unhappily for my client. Was there anybody else in the room?"

"I believe that Phipps, Mr. Belcher's man, was coming and going."

"Why, your memory is excellent, is it not? And you remember the date of this event too! Suppose you tell us what it was."

"It was the 4th of May, 1860."

"How confused you must have been!" said Mr Cavendish.

"These are things that were burnt into my memory,"

responded the witness. "There were other occurrences that day, of which I have been informed, but of which I have no memory."

"Ah, there are! Well, I shall have occasion to refresh your mind upon still another, before I get through with you. Now, if I should show you an assignment, signed by yourself on the very day you have designated, and also signed by Johnson, Ramsey, and Phipps as witnesses, what should you say to it?"

"I object to the question. The counsel should show the document to the witness, and then ask his opinion of it," said Mr. Balfour.

The Court coincided with Mr. Balfour's view and ruled accordingly.

"Very well," said Mr. Cavendish, "we shall get at that in good time. Now, witness, will you be kind enough to tell me how you remember that all this occurred on the 4th of May, 1860?"

"It happened to be the first anniversary of my wife's death. I went from her grave to Mr. Belcher's house. The day was associated with the saddest and most precious memories of my life."

"What an excellent memory!" said Mr. Cavendish, rubbing his white hands together. "Are you familiar with the signatures of Nicholas Johnson and James Ramsey?"

"I have seen them many times."

"Would you recognize them, if I were to show them to you?"

"I don't know, sir."

"Oh! your memory begins to fail now, does it? How is it that you cannot remember things with which you were familiar during a series of years, when you were perfectly sane, and yet can remember things so well that happened when your mind was confused?"

Mr. Benedict's mind was getting confused again, and

he began to stammer. Mr. Cavendish wondered that, in some way, Mr. Balfour did not come to the relief of his witness; but he sat perfectly quiet, and apparently unconcerned. Mr. Cavendish rummaged among his papers, and withdrew two letters. These he handed to the witness. "Now," said he, "will the witness examine these letters, and tell us whether he recognizes the signatures as genuine?"

Mr. Benedict took the two letters, of which he had already heard through Sam Yates, and very carefully read them. His quick, mechanical eye measured the length and every peculiarity of the signatures. He spent so much time upon them that even the Court grew impatient.

"Take all the time you need, witness," said Mr. Balfour.

"All day, of course, if necessary," responded Mr. Cavendish raspingly.

"I think these are genuine autograph letters, both of them," said Mr. Benedict.

"Thank you; now please hand them back to me."

"I have special reasons for requesting the Court to impound these letters," said Mr. Balfour. "They will be needed again in the case."

"The witness will hand the letters to the clerk," said the judge.

Mr. Cavendish was annoyed, but acquiesced gracefully. Then he took up the assignment, and said: "Witness, I hold in my hand a document signed, sealed, and witnessed on the fourth day of May, 1860, by which Paul Benedict conveys to Robert Belcher his title to the patents, certified copies of which have been placed in evidence. I want you to examine carefully your own signature, and those of Johnson and Ramsey. Happily, one of the witnesses is still living, and is ready, not only to swear to his own signature, but to yours and to those of the other witnesses."

Mr. Cavendish advanced, and handed Benedict the instrument. The inventor opened it, looked it hurriedly through, and then paused at the signatures. After examining them long, with naked eyes, he drew a glass from his pocket, and scrutinized them with a curious, absorbed look, forgetful, apparently, where he was.

"Is the witness going to sleep?" inquired Mr. Cavendish; but he did not stir. Mr. Belcher drew a large handkerchief from his pocket, and wiped his red, perspiring face. It was an awful moment to him. Phipps, in his seat, was as pale as a ghost, and sat watching his master.

At last Mr. Benedict looked up. He seemed as if he had been deprived of the power of speech. His face was full of pain and fright. "I do not know what to say to this," he said.

"Oh, you don't! I thought you wouldn't! Still, we should like to know your opinion of the instrument," said Mr. Cavendish.

"I don't think you would like to know it, sir," said Benedict, quietly.

"What does the witness insinuate?" exclaimed the lawyer, jumping to his feet. "No insinuations, sir!"

"Insinuations are very apt to breed insinuations," said the judge, quietly. "The witness has manifested no disinclination to answer your direct questions."

"Very well," said Mr. Cavendish. "Is your signature at the foot of that assignment?"

"It is not, sir."

"Perhaps those are not the signatures of the witnesses," said Mr. Cavendish, with an angry sneer.

"Two of them, I have no doubt, are forgeries," responded Mr. Balfour, with an excited voice.

Mr. Cavendish knew that it would do no good to manifest anger; so he laughed. Then he sat down by the side of Mr. Belcher, and said something to him, and they both laughed together.

"That's all," he said, nodding to the witness.

"May it please the Court," said Mr. Balfour, "we got along so well with the question of identity, that, with the leave of the defendant's counsel, I propose, in order to save the time of the Court, that we push our inquiries directly into the validity of this assignment. This is the essential question, and the defendant has only to establish the validity of the instrument to bring the case to an end at once. This done, the suit will be abandoned."

"Certainly," said Mr. Cavendish, rising. "I agree to the scheme with the single provision on behalf of the defendant, that he shall not be debarred from his pleading of a denial of profits, in any event."

"Agreed," said Mr. Balfour.

"Very well," said Mr. Cavendish. "I shall call Cornelius Phipps, the only surviving witness of the assignment."

But Cornelius Phipps did not appear when he was called. A second call produced the same result. He was not in the house. He was sought for in every possible retreat about the house, but could not be found. Cornelius Phipps had mysteriously disappeared.

After consulting Mr. Belcher, Mr. Cavendish announced that the witness who had been called was essential at the present stage of the case. He thought it possible that, in the long confinement of the court-room, Phipps had become suddenly ill, and gone home. He hoped, for the honor of the plaintiff in the case, that nothing worse had happened, and suggested that the court adjourn until the following day.

And the court adjourned, amid tumultuous whispering. Mr. Belcher was apparently oblivious of the fact, and sat and stared, until touched upon the shoulder by his counsel, when he rose and walked out upon a world and into an atmosphere that had never before seemed so strange and unreal.

CHAPTER XXVII.

IN WHICH PHIPPS IS NOT TO BE FOUND, AND THE GENERAL IS CALLED UPON TO DO HIS OWN LYING.

AT the appointed hour on the following morning, the court resumed its session. The plaintiff and defendant were both in their places, with their counsel, and the witnesses of the previous day were all in attendance. Among the little group of witnesses there were two or three new faces—a professional-looking gentleman with spectacles; a thin-faced, carefully dressed, slender man, with a lordly air, and the bearing of one who carried the world upon his shoulders and did not regard it as much of a burden; and, last, our old friend Sam Yates.

There was an appearance of perplexity and gloom on the countenances of Mr. Cavendish and his client. They were in serious conversation, and it was evident that they were in difficulty. Those who knew the occasion of the abrupt adjournment of the court on the previous day looked in vain among the witnesses for the face of Phipps. He was not in the room, and, while few suspected the real state of the case, all understood how essential he was to the defendant in his attempt to establish the genuineness of the assignment.

At the opening of the court, Mr. Cavendish rose to speak. His bold, sharp manner had disappeared. The instrument which he had expected to use had slipped hopelessly out of his hand. He was impotent. "May it please the Court," he said, "the defendant in this case finds himself in a very embarrassing position this morning. It was known yesterday that Cornelius Phipps, the only surviving witness of the assignment, mysteriously disappeared at the moment when his testimony was wanted. Why and how he disappeared, I cannot tell. He has not yet been found. All due diligence has been exercised to discover him, but without success. I make no charges of foul play, but it is impossible for me, knowing what I know about him—his irreproachable character, his faithfulness to my client, and his perfect memory of every event connected with the execution of the paper in question—to avoid the suspicion that he is by some means, and against his will, detained from appearing here this morning. I confess, sir, that I was not prepared for this. It is hard to believe that the plaintiff could adopt a measure so desperate as this for securing his ends, and I will not criminate him ; but I protest that the condition in which the defendant is left by this defection, or this forcible detention—call it what you will—demands the most generous consideration, and compels me to ask the Court for suggestions as to the best course of proceeding. There are now but two men in court who saw the paper executed, namely, the assignor and the assignee. The former has declared, with an effrontery which I have never seen equalled, that he never signed the document which so unmistakably bears his signature, and that the names of two of the witnesses are forgeries. I do not expect that, in a struggle like this, the testimony of the latter will be accepted, and I shall not stoop to ask it."

Mr. Cavendish hesitated, looked appealingly at the judge, and then slowly took his seat, when Mr. Balfour, without waiting for any suggestions from the Court, rose and said :

"I appreciate the embarrassment of the defence, and am quite willing to do all I can to relieve it. His insinuations of foul dealing toward his witness are absurd, of course, and, to save any further trouble, I am willing to receive as a witness, in place of Mr. Phipps, Mr. Belcher himself, and to pledge myself to abide by what he establishes. I can do no more than this, I am sure, and now I challenge him to take the stand."

The judge watched the defendant and his counsel in their whispered consultation for a few minutes, and then said: "It seems to the Court that the defence can reasonably ask for nothing more than this."

Mr. Belcher hesitated. He had not anticipated this turn of the case. There appeared to be no alternative, however, and, at last, he rose with a very red face, and walked to the witness-stand, placing himself just where Mr. Balfour wanted him—in a position to be cross-examined.

It is useless to rehearse here the story which had been prepared for Phipps, and for which Phipps had been prepared. Mr. Belcher swore to all the signatures to the assignment, as having been executed in his presence, on the day corresponding with the date of the paper. He was permitted to enlarge upon all the circumstances of the occasion, and to surround the execution of the assignment with the most ingenious plausibilities. He told his story with a fine show of candor, and with great directness and clearness, and undoubtedly made a profound impression upon the Court and the jury. Then Mr. Cavendish passed him into the hands of Mr. Balfour.

"Well, Mr. Belcher, you have told us a very straight story, but there are a few little matters which I would like to have explained," said Mr. Balfour. "Why, for instance, was your assignment placed on record only a few months ago?"

"Because I was not a lawyer, sir," replied Mr. Belcher, delighted that the first answer was so easy and so plausible. "I was not aware that it was necessary, until so informed by Mr. Cavendish."

"Was Mr. Benedict's insanity considered hopeless from the first?"

"No," replied Mr. Belcher, cheerfully; "we were quite hopeful that we should bring him out of it."

"He had lucid intervals, then."

"Yes, sir."

"Was that the reason why, the next day after the alleged assignment, you wrote him a letter, urging him to make the assignment, and offering him a royalty for the use of his patents?"

"I never wrote any such letter, sir. I never sent him any such letter, sir."

"You sent him to the asylum, did you?"

"I co-operated with others, sir, and paid the bills," said Mr. Belcher, with emphasis.

"Did you ever visit the asylum when he was there?"

"I did, sir."

"Did you apply to the superintendent for liberty to secure his signature to a paper?"

"I do not remember that I did. It would have been an unnatural thing for me to do. If I did, it was a paper on some subordinate affair. It was some years ago, and the details of the visit did not impress themselves upon my memory."

"How did you obtain the letters of Nicholas Johnson and James Ramsey? I ask this, because they are not addressed to you."

"I procured them of Sam Yates, in anticipation of the trial now in progress here. The witnesses were dead, and I thought they would help me in establishing the genuineness of their signatures."

"What reason had you to anticipate this trial?"

"Well, sir, I am accustomed to providing for all contingencies. That is the way I was made, sir. It seemed to me quite probable that Benedict, if living, would forget what he had done before his insanity, and that, if he were dead, some friend of his boy would engage in the suit on his behalf. I procured the autographs after I saw his boy in your hands, sir."

"So you had not seen these particular signatures at the time when the alleged assignment was made?"

"No, sir, I had not seen them."

"And you simply procured them to use as a defence in a suit which seemed probable, or possible, and which now, indeed, is in progress of trial?"

"That is about as clear a statement of the fact as I can make, sir;" and Mr. Belcher bowed and smiled.

"I suppose, Mr. Belcher," said Mr. Balfour, "that it seems very strange to you that the plaintiff should have forgotten his signature."

"Not at all, sir. On the contrary, I regard it as the most natural thing in the world. I should suppose that a man who had lost his mind once would naturally lose his memory of many things."

"That certainly seems reasonable, but how is it that he does not recognize it, even if he does not remember the writing of it?"

"I don't know; a man's signature changes with changing habits, I suppose," responded the witness.

"You don't suppose that any genuine signature of yours could pass under your eye undetected, do you?" inquired Mr. Balfour.

"No, sir, I don't. I'll be frank with you, sir."

"Well, now, I'm going to test you. Perhaps other men, who have always been sane, do sometimes forget their own signatures."

Mr. Balfour withdrew from his papers a note. Mr. Belcher saw it in the distance, and made up his mind that it was the note he had written to the lawyer before the beginning of the suit. The latter folded over the signature so that it might be shown to the witness, independent of the body of the letter, and then he stepped to him holding it in his hand, and asked him to declare it either a genuine signature or a forgery.

"That's my sign-manual, sir."

"You are sure?"

"I know it, sir."

"Very well," said Mr. Balfour, handing the letter to the clerk to be marked. "You are right, I have no doubt, and I believe this is all I want of you, for the present."

"And now, may it please the Court," said Mr. Balfour, "I have some testimony to present in rebuttal of that of the defendant. I propose, practically, to finish up this case with it, and to show that the story to which you have listened is false in every particular. First, I wish to present the testimony of Dr. Charles Barhydt."

At the pronunciation of his name, the man in spectacles arose, and advanced to the witness-stand.

"What is your name?" inquired Mr. Balfour.

"Charles Barhydt."

"What is your profession?"

"I am a physician."

"You have an official position, I believe?"

"Yes, sir; I have for fifteen years been the superintendent of the State Asylum for the Insane."

"Do you recognize the plaintiff in this case, as a former patient in the asylum?"

"I do, sir."

"Was he ever visited by the defendant while in your care?"

"He was, sir."

"Did the defendant endeavor to procure his signature to any document while he was in the asylum?"

"He did, sir."

"Did he apply to you for permission to get this signature, and did he importunately urge you to give him this permission?"

"He did, sir."

"Did you read this document?"

"I did, sir."

"Do you remember what it was?"

"Perfectly, in a general way. It was an assignment

of a number of patent-rights and sundry machines, implements, and processes."

Mr. Balfour handed to the witness the assignment, and then said: "Be kind enough to look that through, and tell us whether you ever saw it before."

After reading the document through, the Doctor said: "This is the identical paper which Mr. Belcher showed me, or a very close copy of it. Several of the patents named here I remember distinctly, for I read the paper carefully, with a professional purpose. I was curious to know what had been the mental habits of my patient."

"But you did not give the defendant liberty to procure the signature of the patentee?"

"I did not. I refused to do so on the ground that he was not of sound mind—that he was not a responsible person."

"When was this?"

"I have no record of the date, but it was after the 12th of May, 1860—the date of Mr. Benedict's admission to the asylum."

"That is all," said Mr. Balfour. Mr. Cavendish tried to cross-examine, but without any result, except to emphasize the direct testimony, though he tried persistently to make the witness remember that, while Mr. Belcher might have shown him the assignment, and that he read it for the purpose which he had stated, it was another paper to which he had wished to secure the patient's signature.

Samuel Yates was next called.

"You are a member of our profession, I believe," said Mr. Balfour.

"I am, sir."

"Have you ever been in the service of the defendant in this case?"

"Yes, sir."

"What have you done for him?"

"I worked many months in the endeavor to ascertain whether Paul Benedict was living or dead."

"It isn't essential that we should go into that; and as the defendant has testified that he procured the autograph letters which are in the possession of the Court from you, I presume you will corroborate his testimony."

"He did procure them of me, sir."

"Did he inform you of the purpose to which he wished to put them?"

"He did, sir. He said that he wished to verify some signatures."

"Were you ever employed in his library at Sevenoaks, by his agent?"

"Yes, sir, I wrote there for several weeks."

"May it please the Court, I have a letter in my hand, the genuineness of whose signature has been recognized by the defendant, written by Robert Belcher to Paul Benedict, which, as it has a direct bearing upon the case, I beg the privilege of placing in evidence. It was written the next day after the date of the alleged assignment, and came inclosed from Benedict's hands to mine."

Mr. Belcher evidently recalled the letter, for he sat limp in his chair, like a man stunned. A fierce quarrel then arose between the counsel concerning the admission of the letter. The judge examined it, and said that he could see no reason why it should not be admitted. Then Mr. Balfour read the following note:

"SEVENOAKS, May 5, 1860.

"*Dear Benedict:*—I am glad to know that you are better. Since you distrust my pledge that I will give you a reasonable share of the profits on the use of your patents, I will go to your house this afternoon, with witnesses, and have an independent paper prepared, to be signed by myself, after the assignment is executed which will give you a definite claim upon me for royalty. We will be there at four o'clock,

"Yours, ROBERT BELCHER."

"Mr. Yates," said Mr. Balfour, "have you ever seen this letter before?"

Yates took the letter, looked it over, and then said: "I have, sir. I found the letter in a drawer of the library-table, in Mr. Belcher's house at Sevenoaks. I delivered it unopened to the man to whom it was addressed, leaving him to decide the question as to whether it belonged to him or the writer. I had no idea of its contents at the time, but became acquainted with them afterward, for I was present at the opening of the letter."

"That is all," said Mr. Balfour.

"So you stole this letter, did you?" inquired Mr. Cavendish.

"I found it while in Mr. Belcher's service, and took it personally to the man to whom it was addressed, as he apparently had the best right to it. I am quite willing to return it to the writer, if it is decided that it belongs to him. I had no selfish end to serve in the affair."

Here the judge interposed. "The Court," said he, "finds this letter in the hands of the plaintiff, delivered by a man who at the time was in the employ of the defendant, and had the contents of the room in his keeping. The paper has a direct bearing on the case, and the Court will not go back of the facts stated."

Mr. Cavendish sat down and consulted his client. Mr. Belcher was afraid of Yates. The witness not only knew too much concerning his original intentions, but he was a lawyer who, if questioned too closely and saucily, would certainly manage to bring in facts to his disadvantage. Yates had already damaged him sadly, and Mr. Belcher felt that it would not do to provoke a re-direct examination. So, after a whispered colloquy with his counsel, the latter told the witness that he was done with him. Then Mr. Belcher and his counsel conversed again for some time, when Mr. Balfour rose and said, addressing the Court:

"The defendant and his counsel evidently need time for consultation, and, as there is a little preliminary work to be done before I present another witness, I suggest that the court take a recess of an hour. In the meantime, I wish to secure photographic copies of the signatures of the two autograph letters, and of the four signatures of the assignment. I ask the Court to place these documents in the keeping of an officer, to be used for this purpose, in an adjoining room, where I have caused a photographic apparatus to be placed, and where a skilful operator is now in waiting. I ask this privilege, as it is essential to a perfect demonstration of the character of the document on which the decision of this case must turn."

The judge acceded to Mr. Balfour's request, both in regard to the recess and the use of the paper, and the assembly broke up into little knots of earnest talkers, most of whom manifested no desire to leave the building.

Mr. Cavendish approached Mr. Balfour, and asked for a private interview. When they had retired to a lobby, he said: "You are not to take any advantage of this conversation. I wish to talk in confidence."

"Very well," said Mr. Balfour.

"My client," said Cavendish, "is in a devilish bad box. His principal witness has run away, his old friends all turn against him, and circumstantial evidence doesn't befriend him. I have advised him to stop this suit right here, and make a compromise. No one wants to kill the General. He's a sharp man, but he is good-natured, and a useful citizen. He can handle these patents better than Benedict can, and make money enough for both of them. What could Benedict do if he had the patents in his hands? He's a simpleton. He's a nobody. Any man capable of carrying on his business would cheat him out of his eye-teeth."

" I am carrying on his business, myself, just at this time," remarked Mr. Balfour, seriously.

" That's all right, of course ; but you know that you and I can settle this business better for these men than they can settle it for themselves."

" I'll be frank with you," said Mr. Balfour. " I am not one who regards Robert Belcher as a good-natured man and a useful citizen, and I, for one—to use your own phrase—want to kill him. He has preyed upon the public for ten years, and I owe a duty not only to my client but to society. I understand how good a bargain I could make with him at this point, but I will make no bargain with him. He is an unmitigated scoundrel, and he will only go out of this court to be arrested for crime ; and I do not expect to drop him until I drop him into a penitentiary, where he can reflect upon his forgeries at leisure."

" Then you refuse any sort of a compromise."

" My dear sir," said Mr. Balfour, warmly, " do you suppose I can give a man a right to talk of terms who is in my hands ? Do you suppose I can compromise with crime ? You know I can't."

" Very well—let it go. I suppose I must go through with it. You understand that this conversation is confidential."

" I do : and you ? "

" Oh, certainly ! "

CHAPTER XXVIII.

IN WHICH A HEAVENLY WITNESS APPEARS WHO CANNOT BE CROSS-EXAMINED, AND BEFORE WHICH THE DEFENCE UTTERLY BREAKS DOWN.

AT the re-assembling of the court, a large crowd had come in. Those who had heard the request of Mr. Balfour had reported what was going on, and, as the promised testimony seemed to involve some curious features, the court-room presented the most crowded appearance that it had worn since the beginning of the trial.

Mr. Belcher had grown old during the hour. His consciousness of guilt, his fear of exposure, the threatened loss of his fortune, and the apprehension of a retribution of disgrace were sapping his vital forces, minute by minute. All the instruments that he had tried to use for his own base purposes were turned against himself. The great world that had glittered around the successful man was growing dark, and, what was worse, there were none to pity him. He had lived for himself; and now, in his hour of trouble, no one was true to him, no one loved him—not even his wife and children!

He gave a helpless, hopeless sigh, as Mr. Balfour called to the witness-stand Prof. Albert Timms.

Prof. Timms was the man already described among the three new witnesses, as the one who seemed to be conscious of bearing the world upon his shoulders, and to find it so inconsiderable a burden. He advanced to the stand with the air of one who had no stake in the contest. His impartiality came from indifference. He had an opportunity to show his knowledge and his skill, and he delighted in it.

"What is your name, witness?" inquired Mr. Balfour.

"Albert Timms, at your service."

"What is your calling, sir?"

"I have at present the charge of a department in the School of Mines. My specialties are chemistry and microscopy."

"You are specially acquainted with these branches of natural science, then?"

"I am, sir."

"Have you been regarded as an expert in the detection of forgery?"

"I have been called as such in many cases of the kind, sir."

"Then you have had a good deal of experience in such things, and in the various tests by which such matters are determined?"

"I have, sir."

"Have you examined the assignment and the autograph letters which have been in your hands during the recess of the court?"

"I have, sir."

"Do you know either the plaintiff or the defendant in this case?"

"I do not, sir. I never saw either of them until to-day."

"Has any one told you about the nature of these papers, so as to prejudice your mind in regard to any of them?"

"No, sir. I have not exchanged a word with any one in regard to them."

"What is your opinion of the two letters?"

"That they are veritable autographs."

"How do you judge this?"

"From the harmony of the signatures with the text of the body of the letters, by the free and natural shaping and interflowing of the lines, and by a general impression of truthfulness which it is very difficult to communicate in words."

"What do you think of the signatures to the assignment?"

"I think they are all counterfeits but one."

"Prof. Timms, this is a serious matter. You should be very sure of the truth of a statement like this. You say you think they are counterfeits: why?"

"If the papers can be handed to me," said the witness, "I will show what leads me to think so."

The papers were handed to him, and, placing the letters on the bar on which he had been leaning, he drew from his pocket a little rule, and laid it lengthwise along the signature of Nicholas Johnson. Having recorded the measurement, he next took the corresponding name on the assignment.

"I find the name of Nicholas Johnson of exactly the same length on the assignment that it occupies on the letter," said he.

"Is that a suspicious circumstance?"

"It is, and, moreover" (going on with his measurements), "there is not the slightest variation between the two signatures in the length of a letter. Indeed, to the naked eye, one signature is the counterpart of the other, in every characteristic."

"How do you determine, then, that it is anything but a genuine signature?"

"The imitation is too nearly perfect."

"How can that be?"

"Well; no man writes his signature twice alike. There is not one chance in a million that he will do so, without definitely attempting to do so, and then he will be obliged to use certain appliances to guide him."

"Now will you apply the same test to the other signature?"

Prof. Timms went carefully to work again with his measure. He examined the form of every letter in detail, and compared it with its twin, and declared, at the close of his examination, that he found the second name as close a counterfeit as the first.

"Both names on the assignment, then, are exact fac-similes of the names on the autograph letters," said Mr. Balfour.

"They are, indeed, sir—quite wonderful reproductions."

"The work must have been done, then, by a very skilful man," said Mr. Balfour.

The professor shook his head pityingly. "Oh, no, sir," he said. "None but bunglers ever undertake a job like this. Here, sir, are two forged signatures. If one genuine signature, standing alone, has one chance in a million of being exactly like any previous signature of the writer, two standing together have not one chance in ten millions of being exact fac-similes of two others brought together by chance."

"How were these fac-similes produced?" inquired Mr. Balfour.

"They could only have been produced by tracing first with a pencil, directly over the signature to be counterfeited."

"Well, this seems very reasonable, but have you any further tests?"

"Under this magnifying glass," said the professor, pushing along his examination at the same time, "I see a marked difference between the signatures on the two papers, which is not apparent to the naked eye. The letters of the genuine autograph have smooth, unhesitating lines; those of the counterfeits present certain minute irregularities that are inseparable from painstaking and slow execution. Unless the Court and the jury are accustomed to the use of a glass, and to examinations of this particular character, they will hardly be able to see just what I describe, but I have an experiment which will convince them that I am right."

"Can you perform this experiment here, and now?"

"I can, sir, provided the Court will permit me to establish the necessary conditions. I must darken the room, and as I notice that the windows are all furnished with shutters, the matter may be very quickly and easily accomplished."

"Will you describe the nature of your experiment?"

"Well, sir, during the recess of the court, I have had photographed upon glass all the signatures. These, with the aid of a solar microscope, I can project upon the wall behind the jury, immensely enlarged, so that the peculiarities I have described may be detected by every eye in the house, with others, probably, if the sun remains bright and strong, that I have not alluded to."

"The experiment will be permitted," said the judge, "and the officers and the janitor will give the professor all the assistance he needs."

Gradually, as the shutters were closed, the room grew dark, and the faces of judge, jury, and the anxious-looking parties within the bar grew weird and wan among the shadows. A strange silence and awe descended upon the crowd. The great sun in heaven was summoned as a witness, and the sun would not lie. A voice was to speak to them from a hundred millions of miles away—a hundred millions of miles near the realm toward which men looked when they dreamed of the Great White Throne.

They felt as a man might feel, were he conscious, in the darkness of the tomb, when waiting for the trump of the resurrection and the breaking of the everlasting day. Men heard their own hearts beat, like the tramp of trooping hosts; yet there was one man who was glad of the darkness. To him the judgment day had come; and the closing shutters were the rocks that covered him. He could see and not be seen. He could behold his own shame and not be conscious that five hundred eyes were upon him.

All attention was turned to the single pair of shutters not entirely closed. Outside of these, the professor had established his heliostat, and then gradually, by the aid of drapery, he narrowed down the entrance of light to a little aperture where a single silver bar entered and pierced the darkness like a spear. Then this was closed by the insertion of his microscope, and, leaving his apparatus in the hands of an assistant, he felt his way back to his old position.

"May it please the Court, I am ready for the experiment," he said.

"The witness will proceed," said the judge.

"There will soon appear upon the wall, above the heads of the jury," said Prof. Timms, "the genuine signature of Nicholas Johnson, as it has been photographed from the autograph letter. I wish the judge and jury to notice two things in this signature—the cleanly cut edges of the letters, and the two lines of indentation produced by the two prongs of the pen, in its down-stroke. They will also notice that, in the up-stroke of the pen, there is no evidence of indentation whatever. At the point where the up-stroke begins, and the down-stroke ends, the lines of indentation will come together and cease."

As he spoke the last word, the name swept through the darkness over an unseen track, and appeared upon the wall, within a halo of amber light. All eyes saw it, and all found the characteristics that had been predicted. The professor said not a word. There was not a whisper in the room. When a long minute had passed, the light was shut off.

"Now," said the professor, "I will show you, in the same place, the name of Nicholas Johnson, as it has been photographed from the signatures to the assignment. What I wish you to notice particularly in this signature is, first, the rough and irregular edges of the lines which constitute the letters. They will be so much magnified as to present very much the appearance of a Virginia fence. Second, another peculiarity which ought to be shown in the experiment—one which has a decided bearing upon the character of the signature. If the light continues strong, you will be able to detect it. The lines of indentation made by the two prongs of the pen will be evident, as in the real signature. I shall be disappointed if there do not also appear a third line, formed by the pencil which originally traced the letters, and this line will not only accompany, in an irregular way, crossing from side to side, the two indentations of the down-strokes of the pen, but it will accompany irregularly the hair-lines. I speak of this latter peculiarity with some doubt, as the instrument I use is not the best which science now has at its command for this purpose, though competent under perfect conditions."

He paused, and then the forged signatures appeared upon the wall. There was a universal burst of admiration, and then all grew still—as if those who had given way to their feelings were suddenly stricken with the consciousness that they were witnessing a drama in which divine forces were playing a part. There were the ragged, jagged edges of the letters ; there was the supplementary line, traceable in every part of them. There was man's lie—revealed, defined, convicted by God's truth !

The letters lingered, and the room seemed almost sensibly to sink in the awful silence. Then the stillness was broken by a deep voice. What lips it came from, no one knew, for all the borders of the room were as dark as night. It seemed, as it echoed from side to side, to come from every part of the house : "*Mene,*

mene, tekel upharsin!" Such was the effect of these words upon the eager and excited, yet thoroughly solemnized crowd, that when the shutters were thrown open, they would hardly have been surprised to see the bar covered with golden goblets and bowls of wassail, surrounded by lordly revellers and half-nude women, with the stricken Belshazzar at the head of the feast. Certainly Belshazzar, on his night of doom, could hardly have presented a more pitiful front than Robert Belcher, as all eyes were turned upon him. His face was haggard, his chin had dropped upon his breast, and he reclined in his chair like one on whom the plague had laid its withering hand.

There stood Prof. Timms in his triumph. His experiment had proved to be a brilliant success, and that was all he cared for.

"You have not shown us the other signatures," said Mr. Balfour.

"False in one thing, false in all," responded the professor, shrugging his shoulders. "I can show you the others; they would be like this; you would throw away your time."

Mr. Cavendish did not look at the witness, but pretended to write.

"Does the counsel for the defence wish to question the witness?" inquired Mr. Balfour, turning to him.

"No," very sharply.

"You can step down," said Mr. Balfour. As the witness passed him, he quietly grasped his hand and thanked him. A poorly suppressed cheer ran around the court-room as he resumed his seat. Jim Fenton, who had never before witnessed an experiment like that which, in the professor's hands, had been so successful, was anxious to make some personal demonstration of his admiration. Restrained from this by his surroundings, he leaned over and whispered: "Professor, you've did a big thing, but it's the fust time I ever knowed any good to come from peekin' through a keyhole."

"Thank you," and the professor nodded sidewise, evidently desirous of shutting Jim off, but the latter wanted further conversation.

"Was it you that said it was mean to tickle yer parson?" inquired Jim.

"What?" said the astonished professor, looking round in spite of himself.

"Didn't you say it was mean to tickle yer parson? It sounded more like a furriner," said Jim.

When the professor realized the meaning that had been attached by Jim to the "original Hebrew," he was taken with what seemed to be a nasal hemorrhage that called for his immediate retirement from the court-room.

What was to be done next? All eyes were turned upon the counsel, who were in earnest conversation. Too evidently the defence had broken down utterly. Mr. Cavendish was angry, and Mr. Belcher sat beside him like a man who expected every moment to be smitten in the face, and who would not be able to resent the blow.

"May it please the Court," said Mr. Cavendish, "it is impossible, of course, for counsel to know what impression this testimony has made upon the Court and the jury. Dr. Barhydt, after a lapse of years, and dealings with thousands of patients, comes here and testifies to an occurrence which my client's testimony makes impossible; a sneak discovers a letter which may have been written on the third or the fifth of May, 1860—it is very easy to make a mistake in the figure—and this stolen letter, never legitimately delivered—possibly never intended to be delivered under any circumstances—is produced here in evidence; and, to crown all, we have had the spectacular drama in a single act by a man who has appealed to the imaginations of us all, and who, by his skill in the management of an experiment with which none of us are familiar, has found it easy to make a falsehood appear like the truth. The counsel for the plaintiff has been pleased to consider the establishment or the breaking down of the assignment as the practical question at issue. I cannot so regard it. The question is, whether my client is to be deprived of the fruits of long years of enterprise, economy, and industry; for it is to be remembered that, by the plaintiff's own showing, the defendant was a rich man when he first knew him. I deny the profits from the use of the plaintiff's patented inventions, and call upon him to prove them. I not only call upon him to prove them, but I defy him to prove them. It will take something more than superannuated doctors, stolen letters, and the performances of a mountebank to do this."

This speech, delivered with a sort of frenzied bravado, had a wonderful effect upon Mr. Belcher. He straightened in his chair, and assumed his old air of self-assurance. He could sympathize in any game of "bluff," and when it came down to a square fight for money his old self came back to him. During the little speech of Mr. Cavendish, Mr. Balfour was writing, and when the former sat down, the latter rose, and, addressing the Court, said: "I hold in my hand a written notice, calling upon the defendant's counsel to produce in court a little book in the possession of his client entitled 'Records of profits and investments of profits from manufactures under the Benedict patents,' and I hereby serve it upon him."

Thus saying, he handed the letter to Mr. Cavendish, who received and read it.

Mr. Cavendish consulted his client, and then rose and said: "May it please the Court, there is no such book in existence."

"I happen to know," rejoined Mr. Balfour, "that there is such a book in existence, unless it has recently been destroyed. This I stand ready to prove by the testimony of Helen Dillingham, the sister of the plaintiff."

"The witness can be called," said the judge.

Mrs. Dillingham looked paler than on the day before, as she voluntarily lifted her veil, and advanced to the stand. She had dreaded the revelation of her own treachery toward the treacherous proprietor, but she had sat and heard him perjure himself, until her own act, which had been performed on behalf of justice, became one of which she could hardly be ashamed.

"Mrs. Dillingham," said Mr. Balfour, "have you been on friendly terms with the defendant in this case?"

"I have, sir," she answered. "He has been a frequent visitor at my house, and I have visited his family at his own."

"Was he aware that the plaintiff was your brother?"

"He was not."

"Has he, from the first, made a confidant of you?"

"In some things—yes."

"Do you know Harry Benedict—the plaintiff's son?"

"I do, sir."

"How long have you known him?"

"I made his acquaintance soon after he came to reside with you, sir, in the city."

"Did you seek his acquaintance?"

"I did, sir."

"From what motive?"

"Mr. Belcher wished me to do it, in order to ascertain of him whether his father were living or dead."

"You did not then know that the lad was your nephew?"

"I did not, sir."

"Have you ever told Mr. Belcher that your brother was alive?"

"I told him that Paul Benedict was alive, at the last interview but one that I ever had with him."

"Did he give you at this interview any reason for his great anxiety to ascertain the facts as to Mr. Benedict's life or death?"

"He did, sir."

"Was there any special occasion for the visit you allude to?"

"I think there was, sir. He had just lost heavily in International Mail, and evidently came in to talk about business. At any rate, he did talk about it, as he had never done before."

"Can you give us the drift or substance of his conversation and statements?"

"Well, sir, he assured me that he had not been shaken by his losses, said that he kept his manufacturing business entirely separate from his speculations, gave me a history of the manner in which my brother's inventions had come into his hands, and, finally, showed me a little account-book, in which he had recorded his profits from manufactures under what he called the Benedict Patents."

"Did you read this book, Mrs. Dillingham?"

"I did, sir."

"Every word?"

"Every word."

"Did you hear me serve a notice on the defendant's counsel to produce this book in court?"

"I did, sir."

"In that notice did I give the title of the book correctly?"

"You did, sir."

"Was this book left in your hands for a considerable length of time?"

"It was, sir, for several hours."

"Did you copy it?"

" I did, sir, every word of it."

" Are you sure that you made a correct copy ? "

" I verified it, sir, item by item, again and again."

" Can you give me any proof corroborative of your statement that this book has been in your hands ? "

" I can, sir."

" What is it ? "

" A letter from Mr. Belcher, asking me to deliver the book to his man Phipps."

" Is that the letter ? " inquired Mr. Balfour, passing the note into her hands.

" It is, sir."

" May it please the Court," said Mr. Balfour, turning to the judge, " the copy of this account-book is in my possession, and if the defendant persists in refusing to produce the original, I shall ask the privilege of placing it in evidence."

During the examination of this witness, the defendant and his counsel sat like men overwhelmed. Mr. Cavendish was angry with his client, who did not even hear the curses which were whispered in his ear. The latter had lost not only his money, but the woman whom he loved. The perspiration stood in glistening beads upon his forehead. Once he put his head down upon the table before him, while his frame was convulsed with an uncontrollable passion. He held it there until Mr. Cavendish touched him, when he rose and staggered to a pitcher of iced water upon the bar, and drank a long draught. The exhibition of his pain was too terrible to excite in the beholders any emotion lighter than pity.

The judge looked at Mr. Cavendish, who was talking angrily with his client. After waiting for a minute or two, he said : " Unless the original of this book be produced, the Court will be obliged to admit the copy. It was made by one who had it in custody from the owner's hands."

"I was not aware," said Mr. Cavendish fiercely, "that a crushing conspiracy like this against my client could be carried on in any court of the United States, under judicial sanction."

"The counsel must permit the Court," said the judge calmly, "to remind him that it is so far generous toward his disappointment and discourtesy as to refrain from punishing him for contempt, and to warn him against any repetition of his offence."

Mr. Cavendish sneered in the face of the judge, but held his tongue, while Mr. Balfour presented and read the contents of the document. All of Mr. Belcher's property at Sevenoaks, his rifle manufactory, the goods in Talbot's hands, and sundry stocks and bonds came into the enumeration, with the enormous foreign deposit, which constituted the General's "anchor to windward." It was a handsome showing. Judge, jury, and spectators were startled by it, and were helped to understand, better than they had previously done, the magnitude of the stake for which the defendant had played his desperate game, and the stupendous power of the temptation before which he had been led to sacrifice both his honor and his safety.

Mr. Cavendish went over to Mr. Balfour, and they held a long conversation, *sotto voce.* Then Mrs. Dillingham was informed that she could step down, as she would not be wanted for cross-examination. Mr. Belcher had so persistently lied to his counsel, and his case had become so utterly hopeless, that even Cavendish practically gave it up.

Mr. Balfour then addressed the Court, and said that it had been agreed between himself and Mr. Cavendish, in order to save the time of the Court, that the case should be given to the jury by the judge, without presentation or argument of counsel.

The judge occupied a few minutes in recounting the

evidence, and presenting the issue, and without leaving their seats the jury rendered a verdict for the whole amount of damages claimed.

The bold, vain-glorious proprietor was a ruined man. The consciousness of power had vanished. The law had grappled with him, shaken him once, and dropped him. He had had a hint from his counsel of Mr. Balfour's intentions, and knew that the same antagonist would wait but a moment to pounce upon him again, and shake the life out of him. It was curious to see how, not only in his own consciousness, but in his appearance, he degenerated into a very vulgar sort of scoundrel. In leaving the court-room, he skulked by the happy group that surrounded the inventor, not even daring to lift his eyes to Mrs. Dillingham. When he was rich and powerful, with such a place in society as riches and power commanded, he felt himself to be the equal of any woman; but he had been degraded and despoiled in the presence of his idol, and knew that he was measurelessly and hopelessly removed from her. He was glad to get away from the witnesses of his disgrace, and the moment he passed the door, he ran rapidly down the stairs, and emerged upon the street.

CHAPTER XXIX.

WHEREIN MR. BELCHER, HAVING EXHIBITED HIS DIRTY RECORD, SHOWS A CLEAN PAIR OF HEELS.

THE first face that Mr. Belcher met upon leaving the court-house was that of Mr. Talbot.

"Get into my coupé," said Talbot. "I will take you home."

Mr. Belcher got into the coupé quickly, as if he were

hiding from some pursuing danger. "Home!" said he, huskily, and in a whimpering voice. "Home! Good God! I wish I knew where it was."

"What's the matter, General? How has the case gone?"

"Gone? Haven't you been in the house?"

"No; how has it gone?"

"Gone to hell," said Mr. Belcher, leaning over heavily upon Talbot, and whispering it in his ear.

"Not so bad as that, I hope," said Talbot, pushing him off.

"Toll," said the suffering man, haven't I always used you well? You are not going to turn against the General? You've made a good thing out of him, Toll."

"What's happened, General? Tell me."

"Toll, you'll be shut up to-morrow. Play your cards right. Make friends with the mammon of unrighteousness."

Talbot sat and thought very fast. He saw that there was serious trouble, and questioned whether he were not compromising himself. Still, the fact that the General had enriched him, determined him to stand by his old principal as far as he could, consistently with his own safety.

"What can I do for you, General?" he said.

"Get me out of the city. Get me off to Europe. You know I have funds there."

"I'll do what I can, General."

"You're a jewel, Toll."

"By the way," said Talbot, "the Crooked Valley corporation held its annual meeting to-day. You are out, and they have a new deal."

"They'll find out something to-morrow, Toll. It all comes together."

When the coupé drove up at Palgrave's Folly, and the General alighted, he found one of his brokers on the steps, with a pale face. "What's the matter?" said Mr. Belcher.

"The devil's to pay."

"I'm glad of it," said he. "I hope you'll get it all out of him."

"It's too late for joking," responded the man seriously. "We want to see you at once. You've been overreached in this matter of the Air Line, and you've got some very ugly accounts to settle."

"I'll be down to-morrow early," said the General.

"We want to see you to-night," said the broker.

"Very well, come here at nine o'clock."

Then the broker went away, and Mr. Belcher and Mr. Talbot went in. They ascended to the library, and there, in a few minutes, arranged their plans. Mrs. Belcher was not to be informed of them, but was to be left to get the news of her husband's overthrow after his departure. "Sarah's been a good wife, Toll," he said, "but she was unequally yoked with an unbeliever and hasn't been happy for a good many years. I hope you'll look after her a little, Toll. Save something for her, if you can. Of course, she'll have to leave here, and it won't trouble her much."

At this moment the merry voices of his children came through an opening door.

The General gave a great gulp in the endeavor to swallow his emotion. After all, there was a tender spot in him. "Toll, shut the door; I can't stand that. Poor little devils! What's going to become of them?"

The General was busy with his packing. In half an hour his arrangements were completed. Then Talbot went to one of the front rooms of the house, and, looking from the window, saw a man talking with the driver of his coupé. It was an officer. Mr. Belcher peeped through the curtain, and knew him. What was to be done? A plan of escape was immediately made and executed. There was a covered passage into the stable from the rear of the house, and through that both the proprietor and Talbot made their way. Now that Phipps had left him, Mr. Belcher had but a single servant who could drive. He was told to prepare the horses at once, and to make himself ready for service. After everything was done, but the opening of the doors, Talbot went back through the house, and, on appearing at the front door of the mansion, was met by the officer, who inquired for Mr. Belcher. Mr. Talbot let him in, calling for a servant at the same time, and went out and closed the door behind him.

Simultaneously with this movement, the stable-doors flew open, and the horses sprang out upon the street, and were half a mile on their way to one of the upper ferries, leading to Jersey City, before the officer could get an answer to his inquiries for Mr. Belcher. Mr. Belcher had been there only five minutes before, but he had evidently gone out. He would certainly be back to dinner. So the officer waited until convinced that his bird had flown, and until the proprietor was across the river in search of a comfortable bed among the obscure hotels of the town.

It had been arranged that Talbot should secure a state-room on the Aladdin to sail on the following day, and make an arrangement with the steward to admit Mr. Belcher to it on his arrival, and assist in keeping him from sight.

Mr. Belcher sent back his carriage by the uppermost ferry, ate a wretched dinner, and threw himself upon his bed, where he tossed his feverish limbs until daybreak. It was a night thronged with nervous fears. He knew that New York would resound with his name on the following day. Could he reach his state-room on the Aladdin without being discovered? He resolved to try it early the next morning, though he knew the steamer would not sail until noon. Accordingly, as the day began to break, he rose and looked out of his dingy window. The milkmen only were stirring. At the lower end of the street he could see masts, and the pipes of the great steamers, and a ferry-boat crossing to get its first batch of passengers for an early train. Then a wretched man walked under his window, looking for something—hoping, after the accidents of the evening, to find money for his breakfast. Mr. Belcher dropped him a dollar, and the man looked up and said feebly: "May God bless you, sir!"

This little benediction was received gratefully. It would do to start on. He felt his way downstairs, called for his reckoning, and when, after an uncomfortable and vexatious delay, he had found a sleepy, half-dressed man to receive his money, he went out upon the street, satchel in hand, and walked rapidly toward the slip where the Aladdin lay asleep.

Talbot's money had done its work well, and the fugitive had only to make himself known to the officer in charge to secure an immediate entrance into the state-room that had been purchased for him. He shut to the door and locked it; then he took off his clothes and went to bed.

Mr. Belcher's entrance upon the vessel had been observed by a policeman, but, though it was an unusual occurrence, the fact that he was received showed that he had been expected. As the policeman was soon relieved from duty, he gave the matter no farther thought, so that Mr. Belcher had practically made the passage from his library to his state-room unobserved.

After the terrible excitements of the two preceding days, and the sleeplessness of the night, Mr. Belcher with the first sense of security fell into a heavy slumber. All through the morning there were officers on the vessel who knew that he was wanted, but his state-room had been engaged for an invalid lady, and the steward assured the officers that she was in the room, and was not to be disturbed.

The first consciousness that came to the sleeper was with the first motion of the vessel as she pushed out from her dock. He rose and dressed, and found himself exceedingly hungry. There was nothing to do, however, but to wait. The steamer would go down so as to pass the bar at high tide, and lay to for the mails and the latest passengers, to be brought down the bay by a tug. He knew that he could not step from his hiding until the last policeman had left the vessel, with the casting off of its tender, and so sat and watched from the little port-hole which illuminated his room the panorama of the Jersey and Staten Island shores.

His hard, exciting life was retiring. He was leaving his foul reputation, his wife and children, his old pursuits and his fondly cherished idol behind him. He was leaving danger behind. He was leaving Sing Sing behind! He had all Europe, with plenty of money, before him. His spirits began to rise. He even took a look into his mirror, to be a witness of his own triumph.

At four o'clock, after the steamer had lain at anchor for two or three hours, the tug arrived, and as his was the leeward side of the vessel, she unloaded her passengers upon the steamer where he could see them. There were no faces that he knew, and he was relieved. He heard a great deal of tramping about the decks, and through the cabin. Once, two men came into the little passage into which his door opened. He heard his name spoken, and the whispered assurance that his room was occupied by a sick woman; and then they went away.

At last, the orders were given to cast off the tug. He saw the anxious looks of officers as they slid by his port-hole, and then he realized that he was free.

The anchor was hoisted, the great engine lifted itself

to its mighty task, and the voyage was begun. They had gone down a mile, perhaps, when Mr. Belcher came out of his state-room. Supper was not ready—would not be ready for an hour. He took a hurried survey of the passengers, none of whom he knew. They were evidently gentle-folk, mostly from inland cities, who were going to Europe for pleasure. He was glad to see that he attracted little attention. He sat down on deck, and took up a newspaper which a passenger had left behind him.

The case of "Benedict *vs*. Belcher" absorbed three or four columns, besides a column of editorial comment, in which the General's character and his crime were painted with a free hand and in startling colors. Then, in the financial column, he found a record of the meeting of the Crooked Valley corporation, to which was added the statement that suspicions were abroad that the retiring President had been guilty of criminal irregularities in connection with the bonds of the company—irregularities which would immediately become a matter of official investigation. There was also an account of his operations in Muscogee Air Line, and a rumor that he had fled from the city, by some of the numerous outgoing lines of steamers, and that steps had already been taken to head him off at every possible point of landing in this country and Europe.

This last rumor was not calculated to increase his appetite, or restore his self-complacency and self-assurance. He looked all these accounts over a second time, in a cursory way, and was about to fold the paper, so as to hide or destroy it, when his eye fell upon a column of foreign dispatches. He had never been greatly interested in this department of his newspaper, but now that he was on his way to Europe, they assumed a new significance; and, beginning at the top, he read them through. At the foot of the column, he read the words:

"Heavy Failure of a Banking House;" and his attention was absorbed at once by the item which followed:

"The house of Tempin Brothers, of Berlin, has gone down. The failure is said to be utterly disastrous, even the special deposits in the hands of the house having been used. The house was a favorite with Americans, and the failure will inevitably produce great distress among those who are travelling for pleasure. The house is said to have no assets, and the members are not to be found."

Mr. Belcher's "anchor to windward" had snapped its cable, and he was wildly afloat, with ruin behind him, and starvation or immediate arrest before. With curses on his white lips, and with a trembling hand, he cut out the item, walked to his state-room, and threw the record of his crime and shame out of the port-hole, Then, placing the little excerpt in the pocket of his waistcoat, he went on deck.

There sat the happy passengers, wrapped in shawls, watching the setting sun, thinking of the friends and scenes they had left behind them, and dreaming of the unknown world that lay before. Three or four elderly gentlemen were gathered in a group discussing Mr. Belcher himself; but none of them knew him. He had no part in the world of honor and of innocence in which all these lived. He was an outlaw. He groaned when the overwhelming consciousness of his disgrace came upon him—groaned to think that not one of all the pleasant people around could know him without shrinking from him as a monster.

He was looking for some one. A sailor engaged in service passed near him. Stepping to his side, Mr. Belcher asked him to show him the captain. The man pointed to the bridge. "There's the Cap'n, sir—the man in the blue coat and brass buttons." Then he went along.

Mr. Belcher immediately made his way to the bridge. He touched his hat to the gruff old officer, and begged his pardon for obtruding himself upon him, but he was in trouble, and wanted advice.

"Very well, out with it; what's the matter?" said the captain.

Mr. Belcher drew out the little item he had saved, and said: "Captain, I have seen this bit of news for the first time since I started. This firm held all the money I have in the world. Is there any possible way for me to get back to my home?"

"I don't know of any," said the captain.

"But I must go back."

"You'll have to swim for it, then."

Mr. Belcher was just turning away in despair, with a thought of suicide in his mind, when the captain said: "There's Pilot-boat Number 10. She's coming round to get some papers. Perhaps I can get you aboard of her, but you are rather heavy for a jump."

The wind was blowing briskly off shore, and the beautiful pilot-boat, with her wonderful spread of canvas, was cutting the water as a bird cleaves the air. She had been beating toward land, but, as she saw the steamer, she rounded to, gave way before the wind, worked toward the steamer's track on the windward side, and would soon run keel to keel with her.

"Fetch your traps," said the captain. "I can get you on board, if you are in time."

Mr. Belcher ran to his state-room, seized his valise, and was soon again on deck. The pilot-boat was within ten rods of the steamer, curving in gracefully toward the monster, and running like a race-horse. The captain had a bundle of papers in his hand. He held them while Mr. Belcher went over the side of the vessel, down the ladder, and turned himself for his jump. There was peril in the venture, but desperation had strung his nerves. The captain shouted, and asked the bluff fellows on the little craft to do him the personal favor to take his passenger on shore, at their convenience. Then a sailor tossed them the valise, and the captain tossed them the papers. Close in came the little boat. It was almost under Mr. Belcher. "Jump!" shouted half a dozen voices together, and the heavy man lay sprawling upon the deck among the laughing crew. A shout and a clapping of hands was heard from the steamer, "Number 10" sheered off, and continued her cruise, and, stunned and bruised, the General crawled into the little cabin, where it took only ten minutes of the new motion to make him so sick that his hunger departed, and he was glad to lie where, during the week that he tossed about in the cruise for incoming vessels, he would have been glad to die.

One, two, three, four steamers were supplied with pilots, and an opportunity was given him on each occasion to go into port, but he would wait. He had told the story of his bankers, given a fictitious name to himself, and managed to win the good-will of the simple men around him. His bottle of brandy and his box of cigars were at their service, and his dress was that of a gentleman. His natural drollery took on a very amusing form during his sickness, and the men found him a source of pleasure rather than an incumbrance.

At length the last pilot was disposed of, and "Number 10" made for home; and on a dark midnight she ran in among the shipping above the Battery, on the North River, and was still.

Mr. Belcher was not without ready money. He was in the habit of carrying a considerable sum, and, before leaving Talbot, he had drained that gentleman's purse. He gave a handsome fee to the men, and, taking his satchel in his hand, went on shore. He was weak and wretched with long sea-sickness and loss of sleep, and staggered as he walked along the wharf like a drunken man. He tried to get one of the men to go with him, and carry his burden, but each wanted the time with his family, and declined to serve him at any price. So he followed up the line of shipping for a few blocks, went by the dens where drunken sailors and river-thieves were carousing, and then turned up Fulton Street toward Broadway. He knew that the city cars ran all night, but he did not dare to enter one of them. Reaching the Astor, he crossed over, and, seeing an up-town car starting off without a passenger, he stepped upon the front platform, where he deposited his satchel and sat down upon it. People came into the car and stepped off, but they could not see him. He was oppressed with drowsiness, yet he was painfully wide awake.

At length he reached the vicinity of his old splendors. The car was stopped, and, resuming his burden, he crossed over to Fifth Avenue, and stood in front of the palace which had been his home. It was dark at every window. Where were his wife and children? Who had the house in keeping? He was tired, and sat down on the curb-stone, under the very window where Mr. Balfour was at that moment sleeping. He put his dizzy head between his hands, and whimpered like a sick boy. "Played out!" said he; "played out!"

He heard a measured step in the distance. He must not be seen by the watch; so he rose and bent his steps toward Mrs. Dillingham's. Opposite to her house, he sat down upon the curb-stone again, and recalled his old passion for her. The thought of her treachery and of his own fatuitous vanity—the reflection that he had been so blind in his self-conceit that she had led him to his ruin, stung him to the quick. He saw a stone at his feet. He picked it up, and, taking his satchel in one hand, went half across the street, and hurled the little missile at her window. He heard the crash of glass and a shrill scream, and then walked rapidly off. Then he heard a watchman running from a distance ; for the noise was peculiar, and resounded along the street. The watchman met him and made an inquiry, but passed on without suspecting the fugitive's connection with the alarm.

As soon as he was out of the street, he quickened his pace, and went directly to Talbot's. Then he rang the door-bell, once, twice, thrice. Mr. Talbot put his head out of the window, looked down, and, in the light of a street-lamp, discovered the familiar figure of his old principal. "I'll come down," he said, "and let you in."

The conference was a long one, and it ended in both going into the street, and making their way to Talbot's stable, two or three blocks distant. There the coachman was roused, and there Talbot gave Mr. Belcher the privilege of sleeping until he was wanted.

Mr. Talbot had assured Mr. Belcher that he would not be safe in his house, that the whole town was alive with rumors about him, and that while some believed he had escaped and was on his way to Europe, others felt certain that he had not left the city.

Mr. Belcher had been a railroad man, and Mr. Talbot was sure that the railroad men would help him. He would secure a special car at his own cost, on a train that would leave on the following night. He would see that the train should stop before crossing Harlem Bridge. At that moment the General must be there. Mr. Talbot would send him up, to sit in his cab until the train should stop, and then to take the last car, which should be locked after him ; and he could go through in it without observation.

A breakfast was smuggled into the stable early, where Mr. Belcher lay concealed, of which he ate greedily. Then he was locked into the room, where he slept all day. At eight o'clock in the evening, a cab stood in the stable, ready to issue forth on the opening of the doors.

Mr. Belcher took his seat in it, in the darkness, and then the vehicle was rapidly driven to Harlem. After ten minutes of waiting, the dazzling head-light of a great train, crawling out of the city, showed down the avenue. He unlatched the door of his cab, took his satchel in his hand, and, as the last car on the train came up to him, he leaped out, mounted the platform, and vanished in the car, closing the door behind him. "All right!" was shouted from the rear; the conductor swung his lantern, and the train thundered over the bridge and went roaring off into the night.

The General had escaped. All night he travelled on, and, some time during the forenoon, his car was shunted from the trunk line upon the branch that led toward Sevenoaks. It was nearly sunset when he reached the terminus. The railroad sympathy had helped and shielded him thus far, but the railroad ended there, and its sympathy and help were cut off short with the last rail.

Mr. Belcher sent for the keeper of a public stable whom he knew, and with whom he had always been in sympathy, through the love of horse-flesh which they entertained in common. As he had no personal friendship to rely on in his hour of need, he resorted to that which had grown up between men who had done their best to cheat each other by systematic lying in the trading of horses.

"Old Man Coates," for that was the name by which the stable-keeper was known, found his way to the car where Mr. Belcher still remained hidden. The two men met as old cronies, and Mr. Belcher said: "Coates, I'm in trouble, and am bound for Canada. How is Old Calamity?"

Now in all old and well-regulated stables there is one horse of exceptional renown for endurance. "Old Calamity" was a roan, with one wicked white eye, that in his best days had done a hundred miles in ten hours. A great deal of money had been won and lost on him, first and last, but he had grown old, and had degenerated into a raw-boned, tough beast, that was resorted to in great emergencies, and relied upon for long stretches of travel that involved extraordinary hardship.

"Well, he's good yet," replied Old Man Coates.

"You must sell him to me, with a light wagon," said Mr. Belcher.

"I could make more money by telling a man who is looking for you in the hotel that you are here," said the old man, with a wicked leer.

"But you won't do it," responded the General. "You can't turn on a man who has loved the same horse with you, old man; you know you can't."

"Well, I can, but in course I won't;" and the stable-keeper went into a calculation of the value of the horse and harness, with a wagon "that couldn't be broke down."

Old Man Coates had Belcher at a disadvantage, and, of course, availed himself of it, and had no difficulty in making a bargain which reduced the fugitive's stock of ready money in a fearful degree.

At half-past nine, that night, "Old Calamity" was driven down to the side of the car by Coates' own hands, and in a moment the old man was out of the wagon and the new owner was in it. The horse, the moment Mr. Belcher took the reins, had a telegraphic communication concerning the kind of man who was behind him, and the nature of the task that lay before him, and struck off up the road toward Sevenoaks with a long, swinging trot that gave the driver a sense of being lifted at every stride.

It was a curious incident in the history of Mr. Belcher's flight to Canada, which practically began when he leaped upon the deck of Pilot-boat Number 10, that he desired to see every spot that had been connected with his previous life. A more sensitive man would have shunned the scenes which had been associated with his prosperous and nominally respectable career, but he seemed possessed with a morbid desire to look once more upon the localities in which he had moved as king.

He had not once returned to Sevenoaks since he left the village for the metropolis; and although he was in bitter haste, with men near him in pursuit, he was determined to take the longer road to safety, in order to revisit the scene of his early enterprise and his first successes. He knew that Old Calamity would take him to Sevenoaks in two hours, and that then the whole village would be in its first nap. The road was familiar, and the night not too dark. Dogs came out from farmhouses as he rattled by, and barked furiously. He found a cow asleep in the road, and came near being upset by her. He encounted one or two tramps, who tried to speak to him, but he flew on until the spires of the little town, where he had once held the supreme life, defined themselves against the sky, far up the river. Here he brought his horse down to a walk. The moment he was still, for he had not yet reached the roar of the falls, he became conscious that a wagon was following him in the distance. Old Man Coates had not only sold him his horse, but he had sold his secret!

Old Calamity was once more put into a trot, and in ten minutes he was by the side of his mill. Seeing the watchman in front, he pulled up, and, in a disguised voice, inquired the way to the hotel. Having received a rough answer, he inquired of the man whose mill he was watching.

"I don't know," responded the man. "It's stopped now. It was old Belcher's once, but he's gone up, they say."

Mr. Belcher started on. He crossed the bridge, and

drove up the steep hill toward his mansion. Arriving at the height, he stood still by the side of the Seven Oaks, which had once been the glory of his country home. Looking down into the town, he saw lights at the little tavern, and, by the revelations of the lantern that came to the door, a horse and wagon. At this moment, his great Newfoundland dog came bounding toward him, growling like a lion. He had alighted to stretch his limbs, and examine into the condition of his horse. The dog came toward him faster and faster, and more and more menacingly, till he reached him, and heard his own name called. Then he went down into the dust, and fawned upon his old master pitifully. Mr. Belcher caressed him. There was still one creature living that recognized him, and acknowledged him as his lord. He looked up at his house and took a final survey of the dim outlines of the village. Then he mounted his wagon, turned his horse around, and went slowly down the hill, calling to his dog to follow. The huge creature followed a few steps, then hesitated, then, almost crawling, he turned and sneaked away, and finally broke into a run and went back to the house, where he stopped and with a short, gruff bark scouted his retiring master.

Mr. Belcher looked back. His last friend had left him.

"Blast the brute!" he exclaimed. "He is like the rest of 'em."

As he came down the road to turn into the main highway, a man stepped out from the bushes and seized Old Calamity by the bridle. Mr. Belcher struck his horse a heavy blow, and the angry beast, by a single leap, not only shook himself clear of the grasp upon his bit, but hurled the intercepting figure upon the ground. A second man stood ready to deal with Mr. Belcher, but the latter in passing gave him a furious cut with his whip, and Old Calamity was, in twenty seconds, as many rods away from both of them, sweeping up the long hill at a trot that none but iron sinews could long sustain.

The huge pile that constituted the Sevenoaks poor-house was left upon his right, and in half an hour he began a long descent, which so far relieved his laboring horse, that when he reached the level he could hardly hold him. The old fire of the brute was burning at its hottest. Mr. Belcher pulled him in, to listen for the pursuit. Half a mile behind, he could hear wheels tearing madly down the hill, and he laughed. The race had, for the time, banished from his mind the history of the previous week, banished the memory of his horrible losses, banished his sense of danger, banished his nervous fears. It was a stern chase, proverbially a long one, and he had the best horse, and knew that he could not be overtaken. The sound of the pursuing wheels grew fainter and fainter, until they ceased altogether.

Just as the day was breaking, he turned from the main road into the woods, and as the occupants of a cabin were rising, he drove up and asked for shelter and a breakfast.

He remained there all day, and, just before night, passed through the forest to another road, and in the early morning was driving quietly along a Canadian highway, surveying his "adopted country," and assuming the character of a loyal subject of the good Queen of England.

CHAPTER XXX.

WHICH GIVES THE HISTORY OF AN ANNIVERSARY, PRESENTS A TABLEAU, AND DROPS THE CURTAIN.

THREE months after Mr. Belcher's escape, the great world hardly remembered that such a man as he had ever lived. Other rascals took his place, and absorbed the public attention, having failed to learn—what even their betters were slow to apprehend—that every strong, active, bad man is systematically engaged in creating and shaping the instruments for his own destruction. Men continued to be dazzled by their own success, until they could see neither the truth and right that lay along their way, nor the tragic end that awaited them.

The execution in satisfaction of the judgment obtained against Mr. Belcher was promptly issued and levied; claimants and creditors of various sorts took all that the execution left; Mrs. Belcher and her children went to their friends in the country; the Sevenoaks property was bought for Mr. Benedict, and a thousand lives were adjusted to the new circumstances; but narrative palls when its details are anticipated. Let us pass them, regarding them simply as memories coming up—sometimes faintly, sometimes freshly—from the swiftly retiring years, and close the book, as we began it, with a picture.

Sevenoaks looks, in its main features, as it looked when the reader first saw it. The river rolls through it with the old song that the dwellers upon its banks have heard through all these changing years. The workmen and workwomen come and go in the mill, in their daily round of duty, as they did when Phipps, and the gray trotters, and the great proprietor were daily visions of the streets. The little tailoress returns twice a year with her thrifty husband, to revisit her old friends; and she brings at last a little one, which she shows with great pride. Sevenoaks has become a summer thoroughfare to the woods, where Jim receives the city-folk in incredible numbers.

We look in upon the village on a certain summer evening, at five years' remove from the first occupation of the Belcher mansion by Mr. Benedict. The mist above the falls cools the air and bathes the trees as it did when Robert Belcher looked upon it as the incense which rose to his lordly enterprise. The nestling cottages, the busy shops, the fresh-looking spires, the distant woods, the more distant mountain, the old Seven Oaks upon the western plateau and the beautiful residence behind them, are the same to-day that they were when we first looked upon them; but a new life and a new influence inform them all. Nature holds her unvarying frame, but the life upon the canvas is what we paint from year to year. The river sings to vice as it sings to virtue. The birds carol the same, whether selfishness or love be listening. The great mountains rejoice in the sun, or drape their brows in clouds, irrespective of the eyes that regard them.

This one fact remains good in Sevenoaks, and the world over. The man who holds the financial power and the social throne of a town, makes that town, in a good degree, what he is. If he is virtuous, noble, unselfish, good, the elements beneath him shape themselves, consciously or unconsciously, to his character. Vice shrinks into disgrace, or flies to more congenial haunts. The greed for gold which grasps and overreaches, becomes ashamed, or changes to neighborly helpfulness. The discontent that springs up in the shadow of an unprincipled and boastful worldly success, dies; and men become happy in the toil that wins a comfortable shelter and daily bread, when he to whom all look up, looks down upon them with friendly and sympathetic eyes, and holds his wealth and power in service of their good.

Paul Benedict is now the proprietor of Sevenoaks; and from the happy day in which he, with his sister and child, came to the occupation of the mansion which his old persecutor had built for himself, the fortunes and character of the town have mended. Even the poor-house has grown more comfortable in its apartments and administration, while year by year its population has decreased. Through these first years, the quiet man has moved around his mill and his garden, his mind teeming with suggestions, and filling with new interest in their work the dull brains that had been worn deep and dry with routine. All eyes turn upon him with affection. He is their brother as well as their master.

In the great house, there is a happy woman. She has found something to love and something to do. These were all she needed to make her supremely self-respectful, happy, and, in the best degree, womanly. Wilful, ambitious, sacrificing her young affections to gold at the first, and wasting years in idleness and unworthy intrigue, for the lack of affection and the absence of motive to usefulness and industry, she has found, at last, the secret of her woman's life, and has accepted it with genuine gratitude. In ministering to her brother and her brother's child, now a stalwart lad, in watching with untiring eyes and helping with ready wit the unused proprietor in his new circumstances, and in assisting the poor around her, she finds her days full of toil and significance, and her nights brief with grateful sleep. She is the great lady of the village, holding high consideration from her relationship to the proprietor, and bestowing importance upon him by her revelation of his origin and his city associations.

The special summer evening to which we allude is one

which has long been looked forward to by all the people in whom our story has made the reader sympathetically interested. It is an anniversary—the fifth since the new family took up their residence in the grand house. Mr. and Mrs. Balfour with their boy are there. Sam Yates is there—now the agent of the mill—a trusty, prosperous man; and by a process of which we have had no opportunity to note the details, he has transformed Miss Snow into Mrs. Yates. The matter was concluded some years ago, and they seem quite wonted to each other. The Rev. Mr. Snow, grown thinner and grayer, and a great deal happier, is there with his wife and his two unmarried daughters. He finds it easier to "take things as they air," than formerly, and, by his old bridge, holds them against all comers. And who is this, and who are these? Jim Fenton, very much smoothed exteriorly, but jolly, acute, outspoken, peculiar as ever. He walks around the garden with a boy on his shoulder. The "little feller" that originally appeared in Mr. Benedict's plans of the new hotel is now in his hands—veritable flesh and blood; and "the little woman," sitting with Mrs. Snow, while Mrs. Dillingham directs the arrangement of the banquet that is being spread in the pagoda, watches the pair, and exclaims: "Look at them! now isn't it ridiculous?"

The warm sun hides himself behind the western hill, though still an hour above his setting. The roar of the falling river rises to their ears, the sound of the factory bell echoes among the hills, and the crowd of grimy workmen and workwomen pours forth, darkening the one street that leads from the mill, and dissipating itself among the waiting cottages. All is tranquillity and beauty, while the party gather to their out-door feast.

It is hardly a merry company, though a very happy one. It is the latest issue of a tragedy in which all have borne more or less important parts. The most thoughtless of them cannot but feel that a more powerful hand than their own has shaped their lives and determined their destinies.

The boys are called in, and the company gather to their banquet, amid conversation and laughter.

Mr. Balfour turns to Jim and says: "How does this compare with Number Nine, Jim? Isn't this better than the woods?"

Jim has been surveying the preparations with a critical and professional eye, for professional purposes. The hotel-keeper keeps himself constantly open to suggestions, and the table before him suggests so much, that his own establishment seems very humble and imperfect.

"I be'n thinkin' about it," Jim responds. "When a man has got all he wants, he's brung up standin' at the end of his road. If thar ain't comfort then, then there ain't no comfort. When he's got more nor he wants, then he's got by comfort, and runnin' away from it. I hearn the women talk about churnin' by, so that the butter never comes, an' a man as has more money nor he wants churns by his comfort, an' spends his life swashin' with his dasher, and wonderin' where his butter is. Old Belcher's butter never come, but he worked away till his churn blowed up, an' he went up with it."

"So you think our good friend Mr. Benedict has got so much that he has left comfort behind," says Mr. Balfour with a laugh.

"I should be afeard he had, if he could realize it was all his'n, but he can't. He hain't got no more comfort here, no way, nor he used to have in the woods." Then Jim leans over to Mr. Balfour's ear, and says: "It's the woman as does it. It's purty to look at, but it's too pertickler for comfort."

Mr. Balfour sees that he and Jim are observed, and so speaks louder. "There is one thing," he says, "that I have learned in the course of this business. It does not lie very deep, but it is at least worth speaking of. I have learned how infinitely more interesting and picturesque vulgar poverty is than vulgar riches. One can find more poetry in a log cabin than in all that wealth ever crowded into Palgrave's Folly. If poor men and poor women, honest and patient workers, could only apprehend the poetical aspects of their own lives and conditions, instead of imagining that wealth holds a monopoly of the poetry of life, they would see that they have the best of it, and are really enviable people."

Jim knows, of course, that his old cabin in the woods is in Mr. Balfour's mind, and feels himself called upon to say something in response. "If so be as ye're 'ludin' at me," says he, "I'm much obleeged to ye, but I perfer a hotel to a log cabin, pertickler with a little woman and a little feller in it, Paul B. by name."

"That's all right, Jim," says Mr. Balfour, "but I don't call that vulgar wealth which is won slowly, by honest industry. A man who has more money than he has brains, and makes his surroundings the advertisement of his possessions, rather than the expression of his culture, is a vulgar man, or a man of vulgar wealth."

"Did ye ever think," says Jim, "that riches rots or keeps accordin' to their natur'?—rots or keeps," he goes on, "accordin' to what goes into 'em when a man is gitten' 'em together? Blood isn't a purty thing to mix with money, an' I perfer mine dry. A golden sweetin' grows quick an' makes a big show, but ye can't keep it through the winter."

"That's true, Jim," responds Mr. Balfour. "Wealth takes into itself the qualities by which it is won. Gathered by crime or fraud, and gathered in haste, it becomes a curse to those who hold it, and falls into ruin by its own corruptions. Acquired by honest toil, manly frugality, patient endurance, and patient waiting, it is full of good, and holds together by a force within itself."

"Poor Mrs. Belcher!" exclaims Mrs. Dillingham, as the reflection comes to her that that amiable lady was once the mistress of the beautiful establishment over which she has been called upon to preside.

"They say she is living nicely," says Mr. Snow, "and that somebody sends her money, though she does not know where it comes from. It is supposed that her husband saved something, and keeps himself out of sight, while he looks after his family."

Mr. Benedict and Mrs. Dillingham exchange significant glances. Jim is a witness of the act, and knows what it means. He leans over to Mr. Benedict, and says: "When I seen sheet-lightnin', I know there's a shower where it comes from. Ye can't fool me about ma'am Belcher's money."

"You will not tell anybody, Jim," says Mr. Benedict, in a low tone.

"Nobody but the little wòman," responds Jim; and then, seeing that his "little feller," in the distance, is draining a cup with more than becoming leisure, he shouts down the table: "Paul B.! Paul B.! Ye can't git that mug on to yer head with the brim in yer mouth. It isn't yer size, an' it doesn't look purty on ye."

"I should like to know where the old rascal is," says Mrs. Snow, going back to the suggestion that Mr. Belcher was supplying his family with money.

"Well, I can tell ye," replies Jim. "I've been a keepin' it in for this very meetin'."

"Oh Jim!" exclaim half a dozen voices, which means: "we are dying to hear all about it."

"Well," says Jim, "there was a feller as come to my hotel a month ago, and says he: 'Jim, did ye ever know what had become of old Belcher?' 'No,' says I, 'I only knowed he cut a big stick, an' slid.' 'Well, says he, 'I seen 'im a month ago, with whiskers enough on 'is ugly face to set up a barberry-bush.' Says I,

'Where did ye seen 'im?' 'Where do ye guess?' says he. 'Swoppin' a blind hoss,' says I, 'fur a decent one, an' gettin' boot.' 'No,' says he, 'guess ag'in.' 'Preachin' at a camp-meetin',' says I, 'an' passin' round a hat arter it.' 'No,' says he, 'I seen 'im jest where he belonged. He was tendin' a little bar, on a S'n' Lor'nce steamboat. He was settin' on a big stool in the middle of 'is bottles, where he could reach 'em all without droppin' from his roost, an' when his customers was out he was a peekin' into a little lookin'-glass, as stood aside of 'im, an' a combin' out his baird.' 'That settles it,' says I, 'you've seen 'im, an' no mistake.' 'Then,' says he, 'I called 'im "General," an' he looked kind a skeered, an' says 'e to me, "Mum's the word! Crooked Valley an' Air Line is played out, an' I'm workin' up a corner in Salt River"—laughin', an' offerin' to treat.' "

"I wonder how he came in such a place as that," says Mrs. Snow.

"That's the funniest part on't," responds Jim. "He found an old friend on the boat, as was much of a gentleman—an old friend as was dressed within an inch of his life, an' sold the tickets."

"Phipps!" "Phipps!" shout half a dozen voices, and a boisterous laugh goes around the group.

"Ye've guessed right the fust time," Jim continues, "an' the gentlemanlest clerk, an' the poplarest man as ever writ names in a book, an' made change on a counter, with no end o' rings an' hankercher-pins, an' presents of silver mugs, an' rampin' resolootions of admirin' passingers. An' there the two fellers be, a sailin' up an' down the S'n' Lor'nce, as happy as two clams in high water, workin' up corners in their wages, an' playin' into one another's hands like a pair of pickpockets; and what do ye think old Belcher said about Phipps?"

"What did he say?" comes from every side.

"Well, I can't tell percisely," responds Jim. "Fust he said it was proverdential as Phipps run away when he did; an' then he put in somethin' that sounded as if it come from a book—somethin' about tunin' the wind to the sheared ram."

Jim is very doubtful about his quotation, and actually blushes scarlet under the fire of laughter that greets him from every quarter.

"I'm glad if it 'muses ye," says Jim, "but it wasn't anything better nor that, considerin' the man as took it to himself."

"Jim, you'll be obliged to read up," says "the little woman," who still stands by her early resolutions to take her husband for what he is, and enjoy his peculiarities with her neighbors.

"I be as I be," he responds. "I can keep a hotel, an' make money on it, an' pervide for my own, but when it comes to books ye can trip me with a feather."

The little banquet draws to a close, and now two or three inquire together for Mr. Yates. He has mysteriously disappeared! The children have already left the table, and Paul B. is romping with a great show of equine spirit about the garden paths, astride of a stick. Jim is looking at him in undisguised admiration. "I do believe," he exclaims, "that the little feller thinks he's a hoss, with a neck more nor three feet long. See 'im bend it over agin the check-rein he's got in his mind! Hear 'im squeal! Now look out for his heels!"

At this moment, there rises upon the still evening air a confused murmur of many voices. All but the children pause and listen. "What is coming?" "Who is coming?" "What is it?" break from the lips of the listeners. Only Mrs. Yates looks intelligent, and she holds her tongue, and keeps her seat. The sound comes nearer, and breaks into greater confusion. It is laughter, and merry conversation, and the jar of tramping feet. Mr. Benedict suspects what it is, and goes off among his vines, in a state of painful unconcern! The boys run out to the brow of the hill, and come back in great excitement, to announce that the whole town is thronging up toward the house. Then all, as if apprehending the nature of the visit, gather about their table again, that being the place where their visitors will expect to find them.

At length, Sam Yates comes in sight, around the corner of the mansion, followed closely by all the operatives of the mill, dressed in their holiday attire. Mrs. Dillingham has found her brother, and with her hand upon his arm she goes out to meet his visitors. They have come to crown the feast, and signalize the anniversary, by bringing their congratulations to the proprietor, and the beautiful lady who presides over his house. There is a great deal of awkwardness among the young men, and tittering and blushing among the young women, with side play of jest and coquetry, as they form themselves in a line, preparatory to something formal, which presently appears.

Mr. Yates, the agent of the mill, who has consented to be the spokesman of the occasion, stands in front, and faces Mr. Benedict and Mrs. Dillingham.

"Mr. Benedict," says he, "this demonstration in your honor is not one originated by myself, but, in some way, these good people who serve you learned that you were to have a formal celebration of this anniversary, and they have asked me to assist them in expressing the honor in which they hold you, and the sympathy with which they enter into your rejoicing. We all know your history. Many of those who now stand before you, remember your wrongs and your misfortunes; and there is not one who does not rejoice that you have received that which your own genius won in the hands of another. There is not one who does not rejoice that the evil influence of this house is departed, and that one now occupies it who thoroughly respects and honors the manhood and womanhood that labor in his service. We are glad to acknowledge you as our master, because we know that we can regard you as our friend. Your predecessor despised poverty—even the poverty into which he was born—and forgot, in the first moment of his success, that he had ever been poor, while your own bitter experiences have made you brotherly. On behalf of all those who now stand before you, let me thank you for your sympathy, for your practical efforts to give us a share in the results of your prosperity, and for the purifying influences which go out from this dwelling into all our humble homes. We give you our congratulations on this anniversary, and hope for happy returns of the day, until, among the inevitable changes of the future, we all yield our places to those who are to succeed us."

Mr. Benedict's eyes are full of tears. He does not turn, however, to Mr. Balfour, for help. The consciousness of power, and, more than this, the consciousness of universal sympathy, give him self-possession and the power of expression.

"Mr. Yates," says Mr. Benedict, "when you call me master, you give me pain. When you speak of me as your brother, and the brother of all those whom you represent, you pay me the most grateful compliment that I have ever received. It is impossible for me to regard myself as anything but the creature and the instrument of a loving Providence. It is by no power of my own, no skill of my own, no providence of my own, that I have been carried through the startling changes of my life. The power that has placed me where I am, is the power in which, during all my years of adversity, I firmly trusted. It was that power which brought me my friends—friends to whose good-will and efficient service I owe my wealth and my ability to make life profitable and pleasant to you. Fully believing this, I can in no way regard myself as my own, or indulge in pride and vain-glory. You are all my brothers and sisters, and the dear Father of us all has placed the power in my hands to do you good. In the patient and persistent execution of this stewardship lies the duty of my life. I thank you all for your good-will. I thank you all for this opportunity to meet you, and to say to you the words which have for five years been in my heart, waiting to be spoken. Come to me always with your troubles. Tell me always what I can do for you, to make your way easier. Help me to make this village a prosperous, virtuous, and happy one—a model for all its neighbors. And now I wish to take you all by the hand, in pledge of our mutual friendship and of our devotion to each other."

Mr. Benedict steps forward with Mrs. Dillingham, and both shake hands with Mr. Yates. One after another—some shyly, some confidently—the operatives come up and repeat the process, until all have pressed the proprietor's hand, and have received a pleasant greeting and a cordial word from his sister, of whom the girls are strangely afraid. There is a moment of awkward delay, as they start on their homeward way, and then they gather in a group upon the brow of the hill, and the evening air resounds with "three cheers" for Mr. Benedict. The hum of voices begins again, the tramp of a hundred feet passes down the hill, and our little party are left to themselves.

They do not linger long. The Snows take their leave. Mr. and Mrs. Yates retire, with a lingering "good-night," but the Balfours and the Fentons are guests of the house. They go in, and the lamps are lighted, while the "little feller—Paul B. by name"—is carried on his happy father's shoulder to his bed upstairs.

Finally, Jim comes down, having seen his pet asleep, and finds the company talking about Talbot. He and his pretty, worldly wife, finding themselves somewhat too intimately associated with the bad fame of Robert Belcher, had retired to a country-seat on the Hudson—a nest which they feathered well with the profits of the old connection.

And now, as they take leave of each other for the night, and shake hands in token of their good-will, and their satisfaction with the pleasures of the evening, Jim says: "Mr. Benedict, that was a good speech o' yourn. It struck me favorble an' s'prised me some considable. I'd no idee ye could spread so afore folks. I shouldn't wonder if ye was right about Proverdence. It seems kind o' queer that somebody or somethin' should be takin' keer o' you an' me, but I vow I don't see how it's all be'n did, if so be as nobody nor nothin' has took keer o' me, an' you too. It seems reasomble that somethin's be'n to work all the time that I hain't seed. The trouble with me is that I can't understand how a bein' as turns out worlds as if they was nothin' more nor snow-balls, would think o' stoppin' to pay 'tention to sech a feller as Jim Fenton."

"You are larger than a sparrow, Jim," says Mr. Benedict with a smile.

"That's so."

"Larger than a hair."

Jim puts up his hand, brushes down the stiff crop that crowns his head, and responds with a comical smile, "I don' know 'bout that."

Jim pauses as if about to make some further remark, thinks better of it, and then, putting his big arm around his little wife, leads her off, upstairs.

The lights of the great house go out one after another, the cataracts sing the inmates to sleep, the summer moon witches with the mist, the great, sweet heaven bends over the dreaming town, and there we leave our friends at rest, to take up the burden of their lives again upon the happy morrow, beyond our feeble following, but still under the loving eye and guiding hand to which we confidently and gratefully commit them.

THE END.

Holland, Josiah Gilbert

Sevenoaks

THE MUCKRAKERS

A series of American novels of Muckraking, Propaganda, and Social Protest

EDWARD BELLAMY
Equality
ARTHUR BULLARD
Comrade Yetta
CHARLES W. CHESNUTT
The Colonel's Dream
WINSTON CHURCHILL
Mr. Crewe's Career
JAMES FENIMORE COOPER
The Ways of the Hour
ERNEST H. CROSBY
Captain Jinks, Hero
REBECCA HARDING DAVIS
Waiting for the Verdict
IGNATIUS DONNELLY
The Golden Bottle
MARY EASTMAN
Aunt Phillis's Cabin; or, Southern Life as It Is
HAMLIN GARLAND
A Member of the Third House
ROBERT GRANT
The Orchid
SARAH J. HALE
Liberia: or Mr. Peyton's Experiments
ROBERT HERRICK
The Common Lot
RICHARD HILDRETH
The Slave; or Memoirs of Archy Moore
JOSIAH G. HOLLAND
Sevenoaks
JAMES M. HOPPER & FRED R. BECHDOLT
9009
FREDERIC C. HOWE
Confessions of a Monopolist
SYLVESTER JUDD
Margaret
REGINALD W. KAUFFMAN
The House of Bondage